An
Irish Country
Welcome

An
Irish Country
Welcome

PATRICK TAYLOR

A Tom Doherty Associates Book
New York

AN IRISH COUNTRY WELCOME

Copyright © 2020 by Ballybucklebo Stories Corp.

Maps by Elizabeth Danforth

A Forge Book
Published by Tom Doherty Associates
120 Broadway
New York, NY 10271

www.tor-forge.com

Forge® is a registered trademark of Macmillan Publishing Group, LLC.

The Library of Congress Cataloging-in-Publication Data
is available upon request.

ISBN 978-1-250-25730-7 (hardcover)
ISBN 978-1-250-25729-1 (ebook)

Our books may be purchased in bulk for promotional, educational, or business use. Please contact your local bookseller or the Macmillan Corporate and Premium Sales Department at 1-800-221-7945, extension 5442, or by email at MacmillanSpecialMarkets@macmillan.com.

First Edition: October 2020

Printed in the United States of America

10 9 8 7 6 5 4 3 2 1

To Dorothy

Acknowledgments

I would like to thank a large number of people, some of whom have worked with me from the beginning and without whose unstinting help and encouragement, I could not have written this series. They are:

In North America

Simon Hally, Tom Doherty, Paul Stevens, Kristin Sevick, Irene Gallo, Gregory Manchess, Patty Garcia, Alexis Saarela, Fleur Mathewson, Jamie Broadhurst, and Christina Macdonald, all of whom have contributed enormously to the literary and technical aspects of bringing this work from rough draft to bookshelf.

Natalia Aponte and Victoria Lea, my literary agents.

Don Kalancha and Joe Maier, who keep me right on contractual matters.

In the United Kingdom

Jessica and Rosie Buchman, my foreign rights agents.

To you all, Doctor Fingal Flahertie O'Reilly and I tender our most heartfelt gratitude and thanks.

AUTHOR'S NOTE

I find it hard to believe that I am sitting here typing the fifteenth author's note to accompany another novel in the Irish Country Doctor series.

As with its predecessors, some aspects of the work require explanation or validation. Real places and real people, both medical and nonmedical, will be identified and my personal involvement with many of them noted. Given that the action takes place between July 5, 1969 and late January 1970, actual events like the moon landing and the periodic outbreaks of sectarian violence in parts of Ulster must be mentioned but will not be dwelled upon in great detail. With regards to the violence, I have reported the historical facts and have not taken sides.

On one occasion in the nonpolitical part of the work I have, for dramatic purposes, bent the truth slightly, and I will note this instance in the coming paragraphs. Finally, I could not have written this work without the help of some of my friends, whom I will name and thank.

All of the following senior physicians and surgeons on the staff of the Royal Victoria Hospital in Belfast taught me: Doctor Minty Bereen, anaesthesia; Mister Eric Cowan, eye surgery; Sir Ian Fraser, surgery; Doctor D. A. D. Montgomery, endocrinology; and Mister Willoughby Wilson, general surgery. In July and August of 1963, Tom Baskett and I were part of a group of medical students "living in," that is to say resident and under practical instruction, at the Royal Maternity Hospital. We were the last group taught by Professor C. M. G. Macafee, who retired in August of that year.

Harith Lamki was two years my senior when I worked at the Ulster Hospital, Dundonald, for two years. He taught me a great deal, and he told me the story of Tippu Tib. Harith was a brilliant obstetrician and a man of deep compassion.

I'm afraid I stole your name, old friend Doctor Rahul Bannerjee (a pathologist with whom I worked in Winnipeg).

Doctor Virginia Apgar was the first woman to head a specialty division (anaesthesiology) at Columbia-Presbyterian Medical Center in New York. As an obstetric anesthesiologist, Apgar was able to document trends that could distinguish healthy infants from infants in trouble. This investigation led in 1953 to a standardized scoring system used to assess a newborn's health one minute after birth and subsequently in five-minute increments. The resulting system was referred to eponymously as the "Apgar score." This system is still in use.

Doctor Jamsie Bowman was a friend of my father's, our GP, and a keen wildfowler before he took up fly-fishing.

Mister Jack Kyle, 1926–2014, was arguably the best out-half to play rugby football for Ireland. He trained as a surgeon in the Royal Victoria and later worked in Africa.

Nonmedical people mentioned include Lieutenant-General Sir Ian Freeland, who was appointed general officer commanding British troops in Ulster on July 9, 1969 and was still in post when this book ends. Sir Edward Carson, 1854–1935, was a committed Unionist politician who bitterly opposed Home Rule for Ireland. In 1895, he defended the Marquess of Queensberry in a case of criminal libel brought by Oscar Wilde, which Queensberry won when Wilde withdrew the charge. Carson's bronze statue, with its right arm raised, stands with its back to the many-pillared, Greek classical-style portico of the Northern Ireland parliament buildings.

I will never forget Neil Armstrong stepping onto the lunar surface. The event was broadcast on BBC-TV from the Lime Grove Studios' special Apollo 11 set in London by science historian and broadcaster James Burke; Cliff Michelmore, BBC's regular current affairs presenter; and the astronomer Patrick Moore.

I know Bushmills and have stayed there recently but have not visited the Giant's Causeway for fifty years and was fortunate to have my hazy recollections confirmed, of which I'll share more later. While my fictitious village of Ballybucklebo serves as most of the background for this work, scenes set in or near Bangor, County Down—including Bangor Bay, Luchi's ice-cream shop, the Carnegie Library, Ballysallagh Reservoir, and the Crawfordsburn Inn—are all familiar. I grew up in Bangor from 1946 until 1964 and was a frequent visitor until I emigrated to Canada in 1970.

When O'Reilly goes wildfowling on the shores of Strangford Lough, his route would take him, in succession, through Greyabbey, past the Mount Stewart estate, through Kircubbin, into the townland of Lisbane (*Lios bán,* the white ring fort), and over the Salt-Water Brig (so called because at high tide the brig, or bridge, spans seawater) to an old church and churchyard that abutted Davy McMaster's farmhouse. I know this because as a young man I was a keen wildfowler and took the same route on as many Saturdays as possible in the season. Even the motorboat named *Grey Goose* is authentic. She belonged to a syndicate of four doctor friends, including my father and Jamsie Bowman, and served as their transport to the Long Island.

I remember Hawthornden Way, which runs past Campbell College. I attended that school from 1954 to 1958, and am able to describe ward 21, the neurosurgical ward in Quinn House at the Royal Victoria, because I was a houseman there for three months in 1965.

So much for accuracy. What is not authentic is that the marquis's great-grandfather did not found the Royal Ulster Yacht Club. It was the Marquis of Dufferin and Ava, on whose family and estate at Clandeboye Lord John MacNeill and his estate are loosely based.

I am deeply indebted to several people for their expert advice and wish to recognize all but two of them in alphabetical order. My friend of longest duration, Doctor Tom Baskett, obstetrician and gynaecologist, for his reading and correcting my obstetrical scenes. Incidentally, Tom is the coauthor of *Munro Kerr's Operative Obstetrics,* tenth and eleventh editions. Mister Tom Fanin, my senior at medical school and subsequently a skilled neurosurgeon in the Royal Victoria Hospital, for reading and correcting my description of the presentation, diagnosis, and surgical treatment of a case of a leaking aneurysm on the right middle cerebral artery. Doctor Rob Lannigan, an old friend who by chance happened to e-mail me from Bushmills en route to the Giant's Causeway, and who, after that visit, read and corrected my fifty-year-old description, to which I have alluded. Edward Lister R.N., of Travel Medicine Clinic of Rancho Mirage, California, returned my phone call and patiently explained to me what immunizations and medications would be required for passengers on a world cruise in 1969. Master builder Renée van Hullebush of Mountain Star Ventures, with his wife, Eva, guided my very nonexpert understanding to a credible scheme of how a crooked building material supplier might cheat an honest builder.

Last, and by no means least, I owe a very large debt to two remarkable women. Dorothy, my wife, as Ulster as I and with a steel-trap memory for details of the old place and who, heavily disguised as Kinky, creates the recipes.

Carolyn Bateman and I have worked together from almost the beginning of my fiction writing career in 1997. (My first publisher assigned her as my freelance editor.) She is an editor without equal who brings me back from the brink when I am writing myself into a corner, subtly suggests plot wrinkles when I'm stuck, and does not let me write plot holes. She even speaks pure Ulsterisms.

To everyone named in this section, I simply cannot thank you all enough.

And finally, some validation. I have striven for complete accuracy by consulting authoritative sources, including:

Books

Bardon, J., *A History of Ulster*. Blackstaff Press, Belfast 1992, pp. 665–677.

Baskett, T. F., *A History of Caesarean Birth*. Clinical Press 2017.

Clarke, R., *The Royal Victoria Hospital Belfast*. The Blackstaff Press, Belfast 1997.

Donald, I., *Practical Obstetric Problems*. Lloyd-Luke (medical books) Ltd., London 1964.

Chassar, Moir J., *Munro Kerr's Operative Obstetrics*. Seventh Edition. Balière, Tindall and Cox, London 1964.

INTERNET

1969: The North Erupts—History Ireland, for the Scarman Tribunal report.

CAIN (Conflict Archive on the Internet), CAIN: Violence and Civil Disturbances in Northern Ireland in 1969

The Cameron Report on Unrest in Northern Ireland, 1969

I hope this short note has served its purpose of explanation and validation and will add to your enjoyment of the work.

Patrick Taylor
Saltspring Island
British Columbia
Canada
July 2019

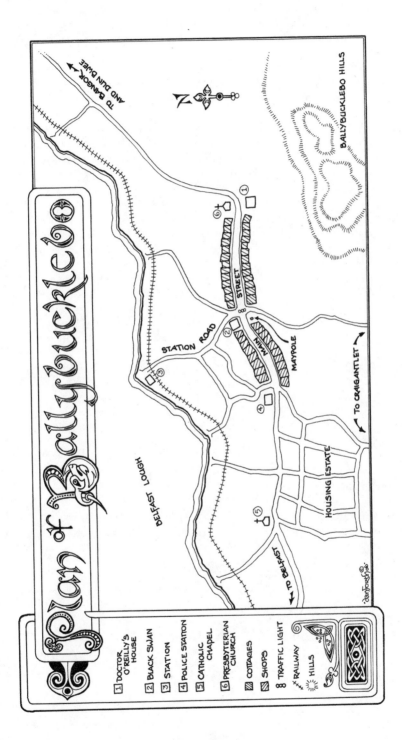

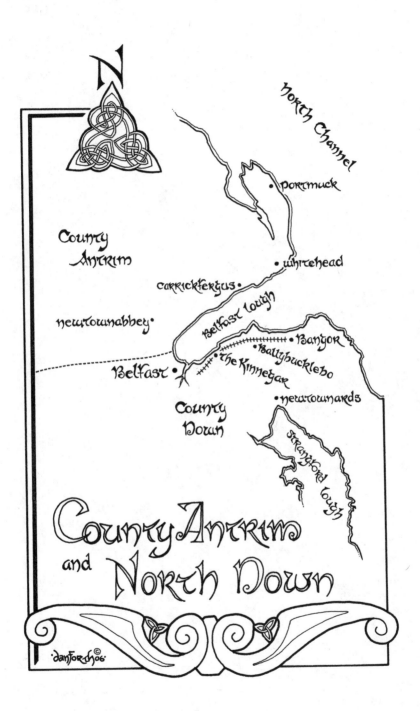

An
Irish Country
Welcome

1

Day and Night Love Sang

My heart at thy dear voice
Wakes with joy, like the flow'r
At the sun's bright returning!

Doctor Fingal Flahertie O'Reilly leaned back in his chair at the packed Ballybucklebo Bonnaughts Sporting Club hall. Not a sound could be heard but the soaring voice.

Flo Bishop, standing behind the microphone on the small stage, let her magical contralto caress the notes of Camille Saint-Saëns' "*Mon cœur s'ouvre à ta voix*" from the opera *Samson and Delilah*. The song was better known in English as "Softly Awakes My Heart." As she sang, her eyes were fixed on those of her husband, Bertie Bishop, who, after he had helped his wife onto the stage, joined O'Reilly's table. The man's eyes were overflowing with adoration, and O'Reilly clearly recalled how some months ago, when his brother, Lars, had helped Bertie draw up his will, Bertie had told the two men how he had fallen in love with the sixteen-year-old Flo McCaffrey at a *cèilidh* in a church hall many years ago.

O'Reilly let the notes flow over him and marvelled at the purity of sound coming from the throat of the rotund wife of the equally spherical Councillor Bertie Bishop. Bertie was one of the prime movers behind using the Ballybucklebo Bonnaughts Sporting Club on Saturday nights for social events like ballroom dancing, hops, and *cèilidhs*. Bringing the two already tolerant country communities closer together in Ballybucklebo seemed important given the recent outbreak of sectarian troubles, some violent, that had been going on across the six counties for more than a year. Tonight, Saturday, July 5, 1969, the Bonnaughts were hosting the first of what was hoped would be a regular series of talent contests.

Bertie's lips were moving, and O'Reilly knew the man was silently mouthing along.

Oh, bide here at my side!
Promise ne'er thou'lt depart!

O'Reilly glanced around the table, struck suddenly by the other love stories there. Kitty and he had celebrated their fourth wedding anniversary two days ago. She caught his eye and smiled. It would have been a longer getaway, but he had promised to attend here tonight.

Was it really thirty-eight years since a young Dublin medical student had fallen for a Nurse Kitty O'Hallorhan from Tallaght and in 1935 had left her to pursue his all-consuming interest in his work? She'd taken herself off to Spain during the Civil War to work in an orphanage and he'd lost track of her. Thanks to his partner, Doctor Barry Laverty, he and Kitty had met again, and the long-cherished embers of their love had burst into fresh flames. Barry sat across from him now, holding the hand of his wife, Sue. Five years ago, he'd been besotted with Patricia, a young engineering student who'd won a Cambridge scholarship, left Ulster, and broken Barry's heart. He'd been devastated, but some months later had fallen for Sue, paid court, and married her. Now they were expecting.

As winds o'er golden grain
Softly sigh roving by . . .

Next to Barry was his former classmate, the surgeon Mister Jack Mills, who sat close beside his fiancée, Doctor Helen Hewitt, although O'Reilly knew the engagement was still a secret. When would they make their plans public?

The party was completed by Lord John MacNeill, Marquis of Ballybucklebo, and his sister, Myrna. Both were widowed and O'Reilly wondered if they were thinking of their lost loves, perhaps moved, as he was, by the obvious bond between Bertie Bishop and Flo.

He returned his gaze to Flo, took a pull on his pint of Guinness, placed it on the table, and stuck his pipe back in his mouth. He thought of the aria's final words, but in the original French, which his father had insisted he and his brother Lars learn and which O'Reilly had polished with some French cruiser officers while serving in Alexandria on HMS *Warspite* during the war:

> Ah! respond to Love's caresses,
> Join in all my soul expresses!

Flo stood for a few seconds, then bowed as deeply as her considerable waist would allow.

Bertie was on his feet, hands ready to clap, but before the applause could begin, O'Reilly, with his basso voice, finished the aria with Sampson's reply:

> *"Dalila! Dalila! Je t'aime!"*

Bertie said with a smile, "That's my line, Doctor."

The room erupted. Not with its usual racket—say for a well-sung Irish song or neatly performed *sean-nos* hard-shoe dance—of whistles, foot stamping, and cries of, "You done good, you-girl-ye." No, tonight the audience responded with all the decorum that would be accorded a professional opera singer. Flo Bishop was given a standing ovation and the hand clapping was deafening.

O'Reilly looked over to the contest's judges, Father O'Toole and the Reverend Mister Robinson. From the way the men were grinning at each other, they were not going to have any difficulty deciding the winner, even if she was one of the event organisers. So far tonight a *cèilidh* band had played, Alan Hewitt had sung Irish songs, six girl dancers from the Dympna Kelly School of dance had skipped and jigged, and even O'Reilly himself had performed a rousing sea shanty—and there was only one more act to come.

The applause gradually died, replaced by the scraping of chair legs on the floor as people retook their seats and the dull hum of renewed conversations. A single voice that O'Reilly could not identify remarked above the murmuring, "—and Rod Laver beat John Newcombe in Melbourne in the men's tennis finals the day."

O'Reilly watched as Councillor Bertie Bishop helped his wife down, hugged her, and Ulster reticence be damned, planted a firm kiss on her lips before letting her accept the congratulations of some of the nearest members of the audience.

Her place onstage was taken by a carroty-haired buck-toothed young man. "All right, youse lot. Settle down. Settle down." He waved his right hand, palm down. "Crikey, Flo, but you done very good. Very good indeed. You was sticking out a mile." There was awe in his tone. "You have the voice of an angel, so you have."

Flo blushed and inclined her head.

More applause.

Since Bertie had made Donal a partner in the Bishop Building Company in May, willing the company to him when both Bishops died, the Bishops and the Donnellys were on Christian-name terms. Indeed, Bertie now treated Donal like the son he'd never had.

"I'll say that again," Donal said when a semblance of quiet had returned. "Voice of an angel."

"Aye, Mrs. Bishop has that," yelled Dapper Frew, Donal's best friend. "And you, you bollix, Donal Donnelly, you can't carry a tune in a bucket. I hope you're not planning to sing nothing."

Much laughter.

"Get on with what you're going til say. There's folks here with their tongues hanging out for a jar."

Donal Donnelly, carpenter by trade, architect of schemes for separating people like bookies and gullible English tourists from their money, was tonight's master of ceremonies. As was to be expected in a place like Ballybucklebo, there was much good-humoured ribbing between audience and MC. Donal cocked his head sideways, looked askance at his friend, and said, "Dapper? Away off and chase yourself, you buck eejit."

More laughter.

"But Dapper's right about one thing. Well, two things actually. It's true I couldn't sing in tune if my life depended on it, and with this crowd it might. And it is time for us to take a wee break before I introduce the last act. So, chat nicely among yourselves, stretch your legs, and youse all know where the bar is." Donal hopped down and the noise level rose.

O'Reilly joined in the general applause and as people began moving about the room, he called, "Bertie, bring Flo over here so we can congratulate her."

John MacNeill said, "Hear, hear."

As the couple approached, the men at the table stood as was proper when a lady joined the company.

O'Reilly pulled out his chair. "Have a pew, Flo."

Before sitting, Flo made a curtsey and said, "My lord. My lady."

O'Reilly and Bertie remained standing while the other men took their seats.

Above the background noise of voices Barry overheard Dapper Frew saying to Donal Donnelly, "Do you think them Yankees will get that there Apollo 11 up til the moon this month and a fellah out ontil the surface?"

"Nah," said Donal. "The moon's a quarter of a million miles away. They'll use special effects, like til make a film in Hollywood. It'll be the best con trick pulled ever."

Dapper laughed. "Takes one til know one."

O'Reilly was still chuckling as Barry said, "Hello, Bishops. Flo, you were amazing and I'm sure everybody wants to congratulate you, but first may I introduce you to my friend Mister Jack Mills? Jack, Mister and Mrs. Bishop."

Jack and Bertie shook hands.

Flo said, "Pleased til meet you, Mister Mills, although I'm sure we've met before. At Fingal and Kitty's wedding four years ago?"

O'Reilly laughed. "Of course they did, Barry. Jack here's an honourary member of the community."

John MacNeill said, "I must congratulate you, Mrs. Bishop, on a bravura performance."

Flo frowned. "Thank you, sir."

"My brother means your singing was outstandingly brilliant. I have had the privilege of hearing opera sung in three of the world's great opera houses, Covent Garden, La Scala, and the Met in New York, and I have never heard a contralto like yours. You are to be congratulated."

"Thank you, my lady. That's very kind of you."

"Not kind at all. Just the truth, Mrs. Bishop."

"You must be very proud of Flo, Bertie," Kitty said.

O'Reilly had never expected to see Bertie Bishop blush. But he did, and his eyes were damp. "I've always been proud of my Flo since she and I danced til 'My Lagan Love' the night we met. Flo's my Ballybucklebo love. Always has been. Always will be."

O'Reilly hid a smile behind his hand. He had no doubt that Bertie had always loved his wife, but it wasn't that long ago that the councillor's behaviour had not been that of the ideal husband. In the twenty-three years O'Reilly had known Bertie Bishop, the man had gone from unmitigated gobshite to rough-hewn gentleman. O'Reilly frowned when he thought of what it had taken to effect the sea change.

Sue said, "I think that is very sweet, Mister Bishop."

"Good for you, Bertie," O'Reilly said. "Flo, you were terrific."

"Thank youse all," Flo said. "Now, no more congratulations, please. I'll be getting a swelled head, so I will."

"Just one more, so," Kinky Auchinleck said.

O'Reilly looked in the direction of the distinctive County Cork accent and saw his friend and part-time housekeeper approaching.

"I'm here to offer you, from me and Archie, our most sincere congratulations and," she brought her left hand from behind her back, "a little something from both of us." She handed Flo a parcel. "I've heard you sing, Flo Bishop, so unless someone's bribed the judges—"

O'Reilly choked on his stout at that thought.

"—here's an extra prize. Some of my chocolate truffles, so. But don't open them now."

"Thanks, Kinky." Flo accepted the package. "My Bertie loves your sweets."

"And before you go, Kinky," O'Reilly said, "since you're here. There is one other thing to mention, and it'll not embarrass you Flo, but you and Bertie and your committee have done a great job organising tonight.

And Kinky, you and the ladies who catered have excelled yourselves. Our congratulations and sincere thanks."

"Hear, hear." John MacNeill bowed his head in acknowledgement.

Kinky made a little curtesy to his lordship. "I'll tell the other ladies, so, and I'll be off now."

O'Reilly watched her go. They had all worked like Trojans. He said to Bertie Bishop, "You'll all be glad of a rest when it's over."

Bertie smiled. "For the others perhaps, but there's no rest for the wicked, I'm afraid. You know what next Saturday is?"

John MacNeill nodded. "July the Twelfth. Marching season."

"Aye," said Bertie. "All over the wee north, aye, and in places in Canada and Scotland too, Loyalist Orange lodges will march to celebrate the Protestant Prince William of Orange's victories over the Catholic King James in the late 1600s. Near three hundred years ago and we're still crowing about it. Our lodge here thinks it's just a bit of *craic*. A day out and a few jars. I'm worshipful master so I've organised things til do, and I'm very glad til say the Ballybucklebo lodge will be walking in Comber so no risk of anyone taking offence here." He sighed. "If the rest of my loyal brethren could see the whole thing as fun, but there's them elsewhere as takes it all dead serious and uses it til annoy the Catholics. I just hope, seeing it's been quieting down for the last couple of months, that things don't get out of hand next week."

"But do you think that's possible?" Kitty asked. "I hope not. Do you think it might be wise to call off the marches this year?"

Bertie Bishop shook his head. "You being from the south—and I don't hold that against you. No harm to you but"—the Ulster peace offering before contradicting someone outright—"you'd be luckier asking the sun not til rise. I think—"

Bertie was drowned out by Donal Donnelly speaking into the microphone. "My lord, ladies, and the rest of youse, now it's time for the last performer—me."

Apart from fixing greyhound races, fabricating "genuine" splinters from Brian Boru's twelfth-century war club, and selling Irish two-shilling pieces as memorial medallions for the famous Irish racehorse Arkle, Donal had a richly deserved reputation as a comedian.

"And after I've done, our judges"—he indicated the two men of the cloth—"will announce the winner, but first I'll do my party piece."

Most folks in Ulster had an act, their party piece, ready to perform in public if called upon.

"Did youse hear about the crisis among gravediggers? It's true, you know. Honest. Ireland's going til ban all burials at sea. Every last one." Donal paused before continuing. "And you'll know about this, Mister Coffin." All eyes turned to the local undertaker, a lugubrious-looking man with the misfortune to have a rhinophyma, a blockage in the sebaceous glands that made the tip of his nose bulbous and red. "They're banning them because," another pause, "too many Irish gravediggers is getting drownded."

O'Reilly joined in the laughter that swept the room and was pleased to see that Mister Coffin was laughing too. It was going to take some time before Donal Donnelly could resume his act, and he clearly knew that when he had the crowd warmed up it was better to let them laugh themselves out before continuing.

Donal performed for five minutes before saying, "Right, youse'll need til use your imaginations for this one but picture a wee terrace house in the Liberties in Dublin."

That isn't difficult for me, O'Reilly thought. He'd begun his medical career in those slums in 1936 as an assistant to a Doctor Phelim Corrigan.

Donal's accent became the nasal one of a Dublin Northsider. "A fellah wit' his duncher held in his two hands says til the woman that answers the door, 'Mrs. Murphy, Guinness's brewery sent me, as your husband Paddy's best mate, to convey their deepest sympathy because,'" dramatic pause, "'Paddy fell into a vat of Guinness and,'" Donal sucked his breath in, "'he drownded.'"

Donal's voice went up two octaves to that of the new widow, in shock and hands wringing. "Lord thundering Jasus, and do you think did my Paddy suffer?"

"'Well no, Missus. We don't think so.'" Donal's pause was timed to perfection. "'Honest we don't.'" Another pause. "'He got out three times to take a leak.'"

A momentary silence, then the room erupted. Whistles. Gales of laughter. Applause.

When the room had returned to a semblance of quiet, Donal said in his usual Ulster tones, "And that's all from me, folks, but if our judges would—?"

Father Hugh O'Toole stood aside to let Mister Robinson the Presbyterian minister take precedence as they made their way to the stage, but it was the smiling priest's Cork brogue that came from the loudspeakers. "My lord, ladies, and gentlemen, it has been a labour of Hercules for my friend Mister Robinson and me to pick a winner, so. Every act in its own way was a gem, and all are to be heartily congratulated, but one stood above all. Mrs. Flo Bishop, will you please come up and accept your prize?"

Bertie Bishop was on his feet. He leaned over to O'Reilly and yelled in his ear, "I couldn't be more happy for her, Doctor. I love that woman and I still see her as being sixteen." He swallowed and hauled in a deep breath before yelling, "Well done, Flo."

She blew him a kiss.

The applause began to die down and all eyes, including those of O'Reilly's party, were on Flo Bishop, who accepted from a beaming Reverend Robinson a small silver cup shaped like an urn with handles on two sides.

"Thank you, sir, and first I want til congratulate all the other performers. Youse was all great." She peered at its base. "It says, 'Winner of the Ballybucklebo Bonnaughts First Talent Contest, July 5, 1969.' Thank youse all very much." There was a cracking in her voice and her eyes glistened. "Thank youse. It'll have a place of honour on our mantelpiece. I'll ask Bertie if I can move our stuffed cat onto a wee table to make room." She swallowed and bowed her head as the applause and laughter swelled again.

Bertie Bishop climbed up on the stage and helped her down as the applause died and conversations restarted.

"I remember," O'Reilly said, "when the idea of Saturday-night functions was first discussed. Bertie Bishop promised the Reverend Robinson that last orders would be taken at ten thirty with everybody out by eleven so the party wouldn't run over into the Sabbath or disturb the neighbours. The clock over the bar hatch says ten fifteen." He looked at his now-empty pint glass. "I'd go another pint. Anyone else?"

"Sorry, Fingal," John MacNeill said, "Myrna and I must be trotting along." They rose and goodnights were said.

Barry stood. "Sue and I should be heading for home too. Sue needs her rest now."

Because, O'Reilly thought, she was ten weeks pregnant. "Off you go," he said.

"Not for me, thanks," Helen Hewitt said, "but go ahead, Jack, if you want to."

"Pint please, Fingal."

"Kitty?"

She pointed to her half-finished gin and tonic. "I'm fine, love."

"Right." O'Reilly rose. "Two pints coming up." He started to make his way to the bar hatch, exchanging pleasantries as he passed occupied tables, bidding goodnights to those leaving. He had almost made it when Donal Donnelly tugged at O'Reilly's coat sleeve.

"Doc. Doc."

O'Reilly stopped in his tracks. "What's up, Donal?"

"Come quick. It's Dapper. He sat up straight, grabbed his head, and asked who had hit it with a hammer. Then he said he'd got a stiff neck, his head felt woozy, and he threw off."

2

My Head Is Bloody

Damn it, those symptoms sounded like something was wrong inside Dapper's skull. Possibly a bleed. O'Reilly turned and called over the hum of conversations and the noise of folks leaving, "Jack, something's up with Dapper. I need a hand." He saw heads turning, people frowning, and the hum of conversation increased.

O'Reilly quickened his pace. Jack would soon catch up. O'Reilly was already considering the possibilities as he marched to the back of the room. Confusion, the man's head feeling "woozy," and the sudden fierce headache and stiff neck worried O'Reilly. This could be a case to get to hospital as soon as possible.

Jack was at O'Reilly's shoulder when they arrived to find Dapper hunched, holding his head, and staring into space, his back to the table.

Connie Brown sat beside Dapper, holding his right arm. "Don't worry. You just took a wee turn, so you did. And here's Doctor O'Reilly for til take a gander at you. You'll be all right. Of course you will."

O'Reilly smiled at Connie and sat on Dapper's left side. "Not so hot, Dapper?"

"In soul I'm not, Doctor."

Jack slipped in to stand beside O'Reilly.

"Did you pass out?"

"Don't think so."

"He didn't, sir," Connie said.

"Good." O'Reilly was distracted for a moment and realised it was Bertie Bishop, come to see what was going on. "What's wrong with Dapper, Doctor? We've a blanket and a cushion in the van. Would you like them?"

"Please."

Bertie headed off, but others had begun to crowd round. O'Reilly tried to get on with his examination. "Dapper, what day is it?"

"Friday—I thuh—thuh—"

"Think?"

"Aye."

"Where are you?"

Dapper frowned. Looked around. "The Duck? But it's too full of pee—pee—"

"People?"

"That's right."

The man was disorientated in time and place and mildly dysphasic, unable to find words to express his thoughts. Intracranial bleeding caused those symptoms.

"Excuse me, Doctor." Alan Hewitt offered a glass of water. "Here y'are, sir."

He meant well but had interrupted O'Reilly's train of thought again. He shook his head. "No thanks, Alan." The man must have seen too many Westerns, where no matter the severity of the hero's wounds, water had miraculous curative powers.

"A wee taste of brandy then?"

O'Reilly shook his head. "Not yet."

Donal Donnelly arrived, pushed his way past the scrum of onlookers, and looked into O'Reilly's eyes.

O'Reilly put a finger to his lips and Donal nodded.

"Dapper. One at a time I want you to raise your arms and legs."

Connie released Dapper's right arm and up it went.

"Right leg," O'Reilly said.

Up it came.

"Left arm."

Dapper's face contorted as he tried to will his arm to move, but it hung limply at his side. Nor had he any success with his left leg. "Jasus, Doctor O'Reilly, don't say I've had a—a—stroke. Please."

The little crowd moved closer.

O'Reilly didn't recognise the woman who said with a sneer, "Likely he's just paralytic drunk."

"Right," O'Reilly said, "I want everybody to move back. I've a job to do. You're getting in the way. Let the dog see the rabbit, for God's sake." He noticed both Father O'Toole and Reverend Robinson with their eyes closed, heads bowed, and regretted his choice of words.

"Sorry, Doctor," said Ronald Fitzpatrick, and with both arms outstretched he shepherded most of the rubberneckers back several paces.

O'Reilly rose, stood beside Jack, and asked in a quiet voice, "Have I missed anything? I think he's had a subarachnoid bleed."

"I agree. No more we can do here. I'll phone for an ambulance and have a word with the duty neurosurgery registrar on ward 21 at the Royal Victoria. Tell him our findings and working diagnosis."

"I'll explain it all to Dapper while you're away."

"Right. I'm off."

O'Reilly turned to face the little crowd and raised his voice. "I know you're all worried and curious. But you know I can't breach doctor/patient confidentiality. All I can say is that our friend Dapper is quite ill and Mister Mills is sending for the ambulance."

There were muttered expressions of concern: "Och dear" and "The poor man" and "God bless him."

Flo Bishop arrived, carrying a grey wool blanket and a cushion. "Here y'are. Will he be all right, Doctor?"

"Thanks, Flo. I really hope so. All right now, everyone. Thank you for your concern. The drama's over. I suggest you all drink up and then go home." He took the blanket, draped it round Dapper's shoulders, and put the cushion between the man's back and his chair.

Dapper asked, "Doctor O'Reilly, I can't find wuh—wuh—"

"Words."

"And my left side doesn't work very well. My da had a stroke and he was no use til himself for six years. Couldn't speak at all. Then he died. For God's sake, Doctor O'Reilly, don't say I've had a stroke too. I'm on— I'm on—"

"You rest now, Dapper. Trying to talk will only upset you."

Dapper shook his head. "Only. I'm only twenty-six."

O'Reilly would have preferred to say nothing to Dapper, but he and Jack Mills were already clinically sure there was bleeding beneath the inner of the two membranes, the outer thick dura mater and inner thin arachnoid that sheathed the brain and contained the cerebrospinal fluid that cushioned and protected the brain. The current paresis and other symptoms might resolve with time, but at the moment that could not be predicted. He decided to be as gentle as possible while telling Dapper the truth. "You know I'm a country GP, Dapper. But Mister Mills here is a qualified specialist. He and I do believe you've had some bleeding inside your skull, but we can't be sure what it's from, where the damage is, or what can be done. An ambulance will be here soon and the doctors at the Royal will do everything in their power to help you."

Dapper's tears flowed.

O'Reilly looked away and saw small groups heading for the way out, all talking in whispers, all with sympathy in their eyes.

Mister Coffin, the undertaker, stood beside O'Reilly. "Excuse me, Doctor, but it'll take a while for an ambulance to come. I'd be very happy to run you up to the Royal, Dapper."

"Very kind of you," O'Reilly said, "but Dapper may need some of the equipment in an ambulance." And putting him in a hearse, even if in the passenger seat, would put the fear of God into an already scared man. And what it might do to any spectators didn't bear thinking about.

"Oh. I see. Good luck then, Dapper."

Donal Donnelly moved to stand protectively by his friend and pocketed the hanky he'd used to dry Dapper's tears.

Dapper took a deep breath. "I think I've had a stroke, Donal."

"Don't you say that, Dapper Frew. Has Doctor O'Reilly said so?"

"No."

"I haven't. Donal's right, Dapper, we mustn't despair. The hospital staff will do a more detailed examination. They may order special tests to find out exactly where the bleeding is. These days, brain surgeons can do operations to stop the bleeding and allow patients to make remarkable recoveries."

"Honest til God, sir?"

"Cross my heart." O'Reilly did just that.

Dapper managed a weak smile. "Thanks."

"And, oul' hand," said Donal. O'Reilly smiled at the affectionate term used only between the closest of friends. "You remember when I cracked my nut back in '65 falling off that there damn motorbike of Paddy Reagan after the Downpatrick races? The doctors at the Royal drilled a hole in my loaf, let the blood out, then opened my dome and stopped the bleeding."

O'Reilly marvelled at the Ulsterisms for "head."

Donal lowered his voice to a whisper. "The patient in the next bed told me Mister Greer, the surgeon, removed my whole brain and cleaned it before he put it back. Isn't that amazing?" Donal paused for effect.

O'Reilly had a great deal of difficulty keeping a straight face. Charlie Greer, one of his classmates at Trinity College Dublin, was a skilled neurosurgeon, but removing and then replacing the brain was quite beyond anyone's abilities.

"And look at me now. Good as new. You'll do rightly, ould hand." He touched Dapper's shoulder for reassurance. "I'm sure you will."

O'Reilly reckoned it would be unkind to explain that Donal had suffered from a very different kind of haemorrhage and that the patient talking of brain cleaning had been giving arch-schemer Donal's leg an almighty pull.

Jack Mills returned. "Ambulance is on its way and 21's ready for the patient. I reckon you'll not need me anymore so I'll go back to the table and keep Kitty and Helen company."

"Thanks for everything, Jack." O'Reilly returned to Dapper. "I don't think you'll need your brain cleaned, Dapper, and you'll know one of the staff there. Mrs. O'Reilly works on ward 21 so you'll see a friendly face on Monday. She'll be able to keep me posted about your progress."

"I'd like that."

O'Reilly inclined his head then spoke to Connie Brown. "Thank you for looking after Dapper, Connie, and if you and Lenny and Colin need to go home that will be fine. Donal and I'll stay with Dapper until the ambulance comes."

"Thank you, sir. We'll be running along then, and get you better soon, Dapper Frew. Take care of yourself. We'll be thinking about you." Connie rose and collected her family.

"Dapper," said Donal, "I'm just going to nip over and let Julie and Bertie and Flo know what's going on. Bertie's giving us a lift home."

O'Reilly made himself comfortable on a chair beside Dapper.

Neither spoke for some time as the level of conversation subsided and the hall gradually emptied. "See that there Donal Donnelly?" Dapper said. "See him? He's one sound—" Dapper's face screwed up as he searched for the word.

"He is that," O'Reilly said. "But don't try to talk, Dapper. You'll only tire yourself out. The ambulance'll be here soon."

"Thanks, Doctor O'Reilly." Dapper sighed and stared at his feet.

O'Reilly ached for the man. Here he was a bachelor of twenty-six, a well-respected estate agent building a successful career. There was no doubt about the bleeding into his brain; the question was would Charlie Greer be able to control the bleeding and give Dapper a reasonable chance for recovery?

"I know you're worried sick. I would be if it was me. It's the not knowing, wondering what's next that's the toughest for people to deal with."

Dapper nodded.

"I've been a doctor for thirty-three years, and this may surprise you, but not knowing on behalf of your patients is hard to deal with too."

Dapper sat back against his cushion and inclined his head.

"Some of my colleagues often say, 'Hope for the best but prepare for the worst.'"

Dapper frowned.

"I don't. How the hell do you prepare for the worst?"

Dapper managed a small, lopsided smile.

"So, I'll tell you how I keep sane. I say, 'Let's cross that bridge when we come to it,' and Dapper, you'll be coming to it very soon, you'll get some answers, and I promise you'll be in the best hands."

"Thank you, Doctor O'Reilly."

Donal returned and sat on the other side of his friend.

"This is a right oul' puh—puh—" Dapper frowned.

"Pickle," Donal said. "But sure, we've been through a brave few of those since the day we met." Donal nodded. "Pickle? It is that. Dapper and me goes back a long way, Doctor. I remember that day at MacNeill Elementary when two new boys joined my class in September. This fella was one of 'em and the other was a right dastard. At break out in the schoolyard he starts pushing me about. I was never big, and he kept calling me 'rusty crust' because of this." He pointed to his carrotty thatch. "Then up you comes Dapper."

"Don't like bullies."

"You stood between me and him. 'Leave you my friend alone or I'll give you your teeth til play with,' says you. Friend? I'd never met you in my puff."

"I near filled my pants that day," said Dapper.

"You remember then? The bully says, 'You and whose army?' He thought he was no goat's toe. You crouched like I'd seen boxers on the telly, leading with your left and with both fists clenched. Your man took an almighty swinging haymaker—and missed."

Dapper smiled. "Nothing like a straight right to the solar plexus to sicken someone's ha—ha—"

"Happiness. You take it easy, Dapper. I'm telling the story. You told me your daddy used til box and he was teaching you. Bloody lucky for me that day."

Donal looked at O'Reilly, who saw pleading in the younger man's eyes. "Dapper and me's been best friends ever since, haven't we? We've had a brave wheen of great *craic* together and pulled through a clatter of scrapes. I just hope til God you'll pull through this one. I really do."

O'Reilly looked up to see a uniformed man standing talking to Ronald Fitzpatrick, who had clearly been waiting at the door for the ambulance and was now pointing in O'Reilly's direction. The man left and returned shortly with the other ambulance attendant. They pushed a trolley-stretcher to where O'Reilly sat.

"How's about you, Doctor O'Reilly?"

O'Reilly recognised the man, but his usually encyclopaedic mind let him down when it came to the man's name. "I'm grand but my friend isn't so hot. You got here in jig time from the Royal. I thought you'd be at least forty minutes."

"Nah. We was called out til Cultra by a woman who said her husband was having a fit." He unbuckled the waist strap over the stretcher and let the buckle's halves hang down over its sides.

"We thought she meant he was having a fit like a convulsion. Fit, my arse. It was only a fit of temper."

He shook his head and bent to Dapper. "Can you stand up, Mister Frew? Me and my mate'll give you a hand." He took the blanket from Dapper's shoulders and together the attendants helped him onto the trolley. "Are you comfy there?"

"I'm rightly."

The attendant did up the strap's buckle. "Anyroad, we told the thran shite til behave himself or we'd call the Peelers. Get him lifted. He calmed down then. Right waste of our time." He smiled. "But it got us here quicker."

The two attendants took their places, one at each end of the trolley.

"So, we'll be off."

"Would you like me to come with you, Dapper?" Donal asked.

"Thanks but I'll be all—all—" Dapper expressed his exasperation by a grunt. "And how'd you get home at this hour?"

"Fair enough, but I'll come and see you. Good luck, Dapper," Donal said, and waved good-bye as his friend was wheeled away. He shook his head. "Doc, I'm dead worried about him. What're his chances of getting well mended?"

"Sorry, Donal, we'll get a better idea in a day or two, and I'll keep you posted. The hospital can only give details to the next of kin."

"He has none. His ma and da are dead and his one brother is in Australia."

"But I'm his doctor and Mrs. O'Reilly nurses there. We can find out how he's doing."

"Thanks, Doc." Donal picked up the cushion and blanket. "I'd best get these back til Bertie and get Julie and me away on home. Good oul'

Cissie Sloan's babysitting and she'll be sending out Constable Mulligan to find us if we're much later."

Together they walked through the almost deserted hall.

"I'm tied up tomorrow, Donal, but I'm free until noon on Monday. Would you like me to pick you up at eight and we'll take a run race up to the Royal? See Dapper. Have a word with Mister Greer?"

"I'd need til ask Bertie for time off, but I'd like that very much, sir. I'll ask him now and come and tell you."

"Right."

O'Reilly went to the table where Jack, Helen, and Kitty were sitting and, feeling a tad tired, plumped himself into a chair. "We'll head for home in a minute. I'd just like an update on what's going to happen to Dapper in the Royal, Jack. I'm a bit rusty when it comes to the treatment of subarachnoids."

"Well, they may have to do an immediate arteriogram to identify the damaged vessel and then operate at once, but I think he's only had a small leak."

"I hope you're right," O'Reilly said.

"If I am, he'll be observed for twenty-four hours then have a lumbar puncture, because by then one hundred percent of cases of subarachnoid bleeding will have xanthochromia, yellowish discolouration of the cerebrospinal fluid caused by the breakdown of the red blood cells."

"Go on."

"There's three possible causes of a subarachnoid: a clot in a blood vessel, usually due to atheroma often associated with high blood pressure. A rupture of an aneurysm. Or bleeding from an angioma, a congenital deformity of a blood vessel. Dapper's probably too young for the former. Only an arteriogram, an X-ray using a contrast medium to outline the intracerebral vessels, will tell for sure, and may help Mister Greer decide on a possible surgical avenue. It used to be that if it was a small aneurysm, the patient would be put on bed rest for ten days in the hope that a clot would form in the aneurysm and stop the bleeding. These days neurosurgeons tend to move more quickly and operate, but not for several days after the initial event."

"So, it's going to be wait and see time before we have any idea how well he's going to recover?" O'Reilly said.

"Excuse me, Doctors." Donal stood by the table. "Bertie says that's a grand idea, so it is. I'll be ready at eight. Thanks, Doctor O'Reilly. I'm off for home now." He raised his hands, the fingers all crossed, then turned for the door.

O'Reilly shrugged. "It's going to be hard on Donal, Kitty." And on me, he thought. "Waiting and wondering. Uncertainty is hard to take."

"Amen," Kitty said, and her voice was gentle. "But we'll all have to try to be patient because clearly only time will tell."

3

Walk in Newness of Life

The morning light coming in from the window warmed the room and brightened the colours of the dining table's centrepiece, a vase of scarlet snapdragons and pink and black tree mallows that Sue had picked only an hour before. Barry had deliberately seated his friends side by side facing the picture window at the far end of the lounge so they could enjoy the view of the sparkling waters of Belfast Lough, the Antrim Hills rising from the far shore to greet a clear blue sky above.

He did not approve of their tabby, Tigger, curled up on Sue's lap when people were eating, but if it made his wife happy? And she did look happy having Jack and Helen in the bungalow for breakfast this morning.

As he poured himself a second cup of tea, Helen said, "This marmalade's delicious. Is it yours, Sue?"

"Wish I could take credit for it, but it's Kinky's. She knows Barry got a real taste for it when he lived at Number One Main Street and I know Kinky's got a soft spot for our Barry." She turned to smile at him.

"I suppose she does. She was practically a mother to me when I lived there."

"Kinky always gives us half a dozen pots when she makes a batch." Sue put down her fork and her hand strayed to Tigger's head.

"Lucky you."

"Very lucky," Barry said, "and she made the soda farls and potato bread we had with our breakfast."

Jack had stayed overnight with the Lavertys, and Helen, now living at home with her father until she started her houseman's year, had joined them for breakfast. There was still a hint of the scent of frying drifting in from the kitchen.

Jack laughed. "I never knew you could cook anything except fried-egg sandwiches when we were students, Barry, but you turned that out like a pro."

"Me? Cook? Not really. Sue usually looks after that, but it doesn't take a Fanny Cradock to do a fry-up, and for the last couple of weeks certain smells—frying's one of them—can upset Sue."

"It's weird. I can usually still eat fried stuff but sometimes just the mention can set me—Oops, excuse me." She scooped up Tigger, deposited the cat on the floor, then, clapping a hand over her mouth, fled.

"Poor Sue," Barry said. "She's been having morning sickness for the last two weeks." He inclined his head to her plate. She'd left the rashers of bacon and two rings of black pudding, but had managed to eat the tomato, the soda farl, potato cake, and the eggs.

Helen started to rise.

"Please don't worry about her, Helen. Sue prefers to be left alone."

"You sure?"

"I'm sure."

Helen sat. "You men have it easy. Poor girl gets pregnant and before you know it she's getting dizzy, tired, sensitive to smells like Sue is now. She's probably in the loo throwing up."

"Even though I spent that six months at Waveney Hospital in Bally-mena doing ob/gyn," said Barry, "I never really understood how unpleasant some aspects of pregnancy could be. There's all those things you mentioned, Helen, and then there's backache and frequent peeing. They were so common, many of our teachers fobbed enquiries off with a patronising—" Jack joined in as Barry said with a complete lack of concern in his voice, "'Don't worry, my dear. You get that sometimes.' I'll certainly be more sympathetic to my pregnant patients in future."

"I should hope so," Helen said.

Sue came back.

"You all right, pet?"

"Fine." She smiled. "Sorry about that. I'm quite over it now."

"No need to apologise," Helen said. "It can't be much fun."

"Actually," Sue took her seat, "I really don't mind." She beamed at Barry. "It took us quite a while to get pregnant, so I couldn't be more delighted." She giggled. "I can hardly wait for it to show."

"By then you'll be halfway home." Barry took her hand. "And I'm sure you'll breeze through once this morning sickness settles down."

"And it will do," Helen said. "You told me you're ten and a bit weeks now so at most you should be okay in about five more weeks."

"I'll look forward to that, but I'll not let it get me down, and once my bump comes and I can feel the baby moving, Barry and I will start buying a cot, and a pram, nappies, decorating the nursery. I'm a country girl and that's the tradition. Superstitious nonsense if you ask me. I'm not worried." She smiled at Barry. "We picked out the room when we first saw the bungalow in '67 when the Millers lived here. It's the smaller of the two guest bedrooms."

"It'll be fun setting things up," Barry said. "And none of this 'pink for a little girl, blue for a boy' rubbish."

"Very sensible," Jack said. "With your luck, even if the odds are about fifty-fifty, Laverty, you'd probably still get it wrong and have to redecorate."

They all laughed.

"I was never much of a gambling man." Barry glanced out the back window. "It's a lovely day out there and Max needs his exercise. Who feels like taking a constitutional on the seawalk?"

"I'm all for working off last night's Guinness and this morning's brekky," said Jack. "Helen?"

"Just give me a few minutes to tidy myself up."

"I'll give you a hand with the dishes, Barry. You go and put your feet up in the lounge, Sue. Please."

"I will, Jack. Thanks."

Barry and Jack each took plates through to the kitchen, where Barry told the idiot Max, "Behave yourself." To Barry's surprise, their usually unruly springer spaniel retreated to a corner and sat.

"Hey, bye, your Max actually did what you told him. Mebbe this bodes well for fatherhood."

Barry laughed as he put the dishes in the sink, added detergent, and ran the taps. "That dog was trained, or should I say not trained, by my dear wife. Any of the animal's shortcomings are entirely her doing."

"I heard that," said Sue from the lounge.

Barry and Jack exchanged a smile and Jack stooped to give the dog a quick pat. "You're a grand old boy, so you are, Max. Don't listen to Barry." With that, Jack picked up a tray and went back to collect the rest of the breakfast things.

By the time he had rejoined Barry, he had rolled up his sleeves and was busy washing and putting the clean plates on the draining board.

Jack grabbed a tea towel and went to work. "You and Sue certainly sounded chuffed last night when you told us Sue was up the spout. Hey bye, I'm delighted for you both."

Barry put a saucer on the board. "We are too, and thanks, mate."

"It's a big step, starting a family. You feeling a bit nervous about being a daddy?"

"A bit. It's going to be all very new."

"You're right. No classes in daddyhood. You'll have to make it up as you go along."

"We can always ask our mums."

"True." Barry looked over at Jack and saw the fleeting look of sadness that passed over his face. Barry wondered if he was thinking of Helen's mother, dead now these past ten years of kidney disease. "Good luck anyway, mate," Jack said. "I wonder if we'll ever have a family."

"Why?"

Jack shrugged. "I'm twenty-nine now. Helen's twenty-five. She's one year as a houseman then four more to train as a nephrologist. She'll be thirty by then. Then like me, she'll have to wait for a consultant post." He picked up a plate, swiped it dry, and placed it on the counter. "She'll not want to lose her place in the queue to some junior by taking time off to have a baby. She's really worked her arse off to get where she is. I know Helen would be a terrific mother but all that's going to have to wait. She could be thirty-five or older when she has her first pregnancy. We were taught that makes her an 'elderly' primigravida."

Barry screwed up his face. "I never really liked that term, but it's true there's more potential for complications after that." Barry put the last teacup on the board and pulled the sink's plug. "I'd rather not think about possible complications. I want Sue's time to be as easy on her as possible, but I heard what you said, my friend. It is hard for women to juggle a career and have children."

Jack nodded. "There's an old Jewish saying, 'Thank God I was born a man.'" He dried the last cup. "I guess I've been thinking about this a lot these days."

"Thinking about what?" Barry dried his hands.

Jack's County Antrim accent thickened. "Complications. Career complications. It's going to be tricky for us both to get consultant posts at the same hospital or even in the same city."

"I don't see why. If you count the Ulster Hospital in Dundonald, that's five major hospitals in Belfast."

"I suppose, but I'll probably not be offered a post for another six or seven years. Surgery's a popular speciality. Lots of competition for those senior jobs. But what happens if one comes up, say, in Altnagelvin Hospital, Londonderry, while Helen's still training at the Royal in Belfast?"

"I hadn't thought of that." Barry frowned. "You're still thinking about overseas, aren't you?"

"I don't know, Barry. Mebbe."

"Some of our classmates who emigrated say that kind of thing's easier in places like Canada." He rolled his sleeves down and buttoned the cuffs. "But I'd hate to see you go. You know that. We've been friends since 1953."

Jack mock-punched Barry on the shoulder. "And we'll still be friends in another sixteen years. And your son or daughter will almost be ready to start borrowing the family car by then . . ."

Barry chuckled.

"Anyway, I'm sure it will all work out for us."

"You're right. One step at a time." Barry tilted his head to one side. "If Helen did fall pregnant—no contraceptive is without its failure rate, after all—she'd stop work anyway. Might solve your problem. Huh?"

"Ever heard of an American woman called Betty Friedan?"

Barry shook his head.

"Helen has. She says Friedan and now a lot more women who share her views are asking why should a woman have to give up her career to raise a family? I think it's a valid question."

"You mean she'd go on working after the baby's born?" Barry was puzzled. In rural Ulster, women had the babies and reared them while the husband provided for his family. Now, according to Jack, women wanted to change that. He frowned. He'd need to think about it, but already he could see a kernel of fairness in the idea. "I've not discussed it with Sue yet, but I'd assume she'd take her full maternity leave and then an unpaid leave of absence until the wee one, or ones, had started school."

Jack laughed. "Helen wouldn't. She'd take time off after the baby was born, but she's already told me that with two doctors working we can easily afford a daytime nanny." He adopted an American nasal twang, "In the immortal words of one Bob Dylan . . ." Jack sang a few lines from "The Times They Are A'Changin'."

Barry shook his head. "Indeed, they are. If that's what Helen wants? More power to her wheel. I hope you will have a family, though." And, he thought, that you'll not have to leave Ulster to find work together in a few years. "Just don't do what the British upper classes do with their children—put them up in the attic with the nanny and then send them off to distant boarding schools when they're eight."

Jack, bending his left elbow and draping his tea towel over his forearm, made a sweeping bow and said in his best upper-crust English accent, "The Doctors Mills will not just have a nanny. We'll have a butler too. Would sir care for a cup of Earl Grey tea?"

Barry laughed. "Stop acting the lig, Mills."

Jack returned to his normal County Antrim voice. "Don't you worry. If we have kids, we won't abandon them."

"I know you won't, and I know you and Helen will sort things out. But I'll say it again, I hope you'll be in Ulster forever."

"And as your senior partner is fond of remarking, 'I'll drink to that,' hey bye."

"To what?" Helen asked as she and Sue, dressed for the outdoors, came into the kitchen.

"It's just an expression," Jack said. "Barry and I were discussing his imminent daddyhood. He's like the fox who lost his tail and wants all other foxes to cut theirs off. Thinks we should start a family too, but I told him we're in no rush."

"Heavens," said Helen with a laugh. "We're not even married yet."

"And he hopes we'll stay in Ulster. I said I'd drink to that. Come on, Barry, let's get our jackets and we'll all go for that walk."

Barry inhaled the tang of the sea, heard the lapping of waves on the rocks below the coastal path and the mewing of gulls dancing overhead. The waters of the lough were rippled by the breeze, and yachts, their sails taut white triangles if they were heading into the wind, scudded over the waves. Most of the boats sailing downwind ran under ballooning, multihued spinnakers. He'd not mind being afloat himself. He held Sue's hand, which he squeezed. "It'll be fun teaching our offspring to sail."

Sue sighed. "Oh, yes, won't it?"

Jack and Helen were walking ahead, Jack holding Max's leash. They had to stop because the springer was exchanging sniffs with a British bulldog. Max and Winston were old friends who often met here.

Barry and Sue joined the group and stood to the side of the path.

"How are you, Billy? Haven't seen you for a while," Barry asked the middle-aged bus driver who Barry had seen last year suffering from psoriasis. The man politely lifted his duncher.

"Them lotions the skin specialists at the Royal give me done me good so I'm rightly, Doctor, but poor oul' Winston had a bad bout of the brownkitees and wasn't able til get his walk for three weeks, but the vet fixed him up."

"Bulldogs are susceptible to bronchitis," Barry said. "I'm glad he's better."

"Me too. And yourself and yours?"

"We're all grand."

"Dead on." Billy replaced his cap. "Come on, Winston. See you and Max again soon, sir." He strode off, with Winston rolling along on his bandy legs.

"You know, Barry, I'm a bit tired," Sue said, "and that picnic table up ahead's free. Could we sit down for a few minutes?"

They had been walking toward Helen's Bay for half an hour.

Barry turned to Jack and Helen, who were now coming up behind them hand in hand. "We're going to take a breather and sit at that table."

"Fair enough," Jack said.

Jack and Helen took the landward side, giving them a view over the lough.

Barry and Sue sat opposite and Max, after several commands and much pushing on his backside, eventually deigned to sit.

"You couldn't beat that view with a big stick," Jack said.

Barry half turned as Jack waved an all-encompassing arm from the head of the lough to his left past Cave Hill and the hills of Antrim, blue with heat haze, with the granite grim Norman motte and bailey Carrickfergus Castle at the foot of the hills. To the east the view continued on past Whitehead at the lough's mouth to the distant Scottish Mull of Galloway. "I'd not want to leave Ulster. I'd surely not and, Barry, never mind our work prospects, there's one other hurdle out of the way. Helen's dad has no objections to us getting married."

Barry turned to Helen. "He's a big man, your father. I remember him saying, 'Just because you and yours and me and mine worship the self-same God in different ways is no reason til hate each other. The Saviour preached, 'Love thy neighbour,' and he made it mean everyone, not just your own kind.'"

"He is a big man," said Helen. "And it must have been hard for him rearing me all by himself after my mother died. It's a great relief he's not going to cut us dead because we're going to be a 'mixed marriage.' I love him, and I love Jack."

He said in a plummy English accent, "And I'm quite fond of you too, old gel."

All four laughed so loudly that Max barked, and Barry had to pat the dog to calm him down.

"I just wish," Jack said, "my father was as open-minded as Helen's."

"Barry told me about your dad when he came home after the pair of you had dinner in that Chinese restaurant in Belfast. I don't quite understand why you've decided to keep it quiet, Jack. No ring."

"Helen had six months to go before she sat her finals. I—we both thought it better to have her concentrate on her exams and see what our families thought after she'd passed." He sighed. "I did raise the subject. Said I had a friend who wanted to marry a Catholic girl and he exploded. 'Damned civil rights groups,' he said."

"Like your Northern Ireland Civil Rights Association, Sue," Barry said, threading his fingers through hers.

"Went on about Ulster being for Protestant Ulstermen." Jack shook his head. "I wish he could have seen how both sides were getting on with each other last night."

"I'm afraid," Sue said, "there are a lot on both sides who feel like your dad. The Orange and Green are a blot on this little bit of Ireland."

"So, how are you going to break the news to him about your engagement?" Barry asked.

Jack sighed. "I'm going down to Cullybackey next Saturday for lunch. Tell him face-to-face. Hope he'll accept our engagement now it's a fait accompli. I know Mum will."

"I'll come with you, Jack," Helen said. "That might help."

Jack shook his head. "No, but thanks for the offer. I need to do this on my own. I'd rather you'd not be there if he blows up again, and I think he will."

Barry felt for his friend, and his eyes narrowed as two thoughts struck him. "Jack, would you like me to come with you?"

Jack frowned, hesitated, then shook his head. "I can't ask you to do that, bye."

"Sure you can. And it might help. I'm not a family member, so having me there might actually, out of good manners, make your dad moderate his response."

Jack looked down at the table, then over to Helen. "I don't know, Barry. The old man—" His voice trailed away as he took Helen's hand.

"Tell you what, Jack. We'll go together, and if you want to speak to him alone, I'll make myself scarce. But at least you'll have a friend there to back you up if it's unpleasant."

"Yes, okay. I'd appreciate that, Barry. It might help."

"And I'll drive. If things do turn nasty we don't want an upset man behind the wheel."

"Let's hope it doesn't come to that, but thanks, mate, that'd be grand."

"Never worry but, Jack, I wonder if maybe you should pick another day?"

"Why? What's wrong with the nineteenth of July?"

"Jack. Jack." Barry shook his head. "I don't know how you ever show up on the right day to operate. Even at school you could never keep dates right. Next Saturday'll be all Orange parades, anti-Catholic speeches, and drink taken. Next Saturday is the *Twelfth* of July."

4

Harmful to the Brain

O'Reilly had, as promised, collected Donal Donnelly from Dun Bwee at eight on Monday morning.

Wearing his Sunday-best two-piece worsted black suit and clutching a bottle of Lucozade, Donal followed O'Reilly past the outpatient department and the under-the-wards cafeteria and up the stairs to the main corridor of Belfast's Royal Victoria Hospital.

"Boys-a-boys," he said, stopping dead in his tracks, "but this is a quare nor busy place." He wrinkled his nose. "And I don't care much for the pong." O'Reilly was quite at home there with the smells of floor polish, antiseptics, and a faint tang of vomit, the bustle of medical students, doctors, uniformed nurses, physios, almoners, and porters pushing trolleys.

Donal clearly was not. "Reminds me too much of my time in here in 1965 with blood in my bonce. I didn't like it then and I don't like it now. Too many sick people." He sniffed the air the way O'Reilly had seen the man's greyhound Bluebird do when in the vicinity of one of the rabbits that wandered into Dun Bwee's garden. Donal turned and began walking back the way they'd come. "Mebbe I'll just wait in the car and you can tell me about Dapper after you've seen him and Mister Greer."

O'Reilly knew that quite a few country folk, with their strange superstitions like "don't get discharged on a Saturday for you're sure to be readmitted," didn't care for hospitals. He caught up with Donal, put a hand under his elbow, and propelled him around. "Don't tell me you've taken time off work and let me drive you up here so you can sit in the car? You want to see Dapper, don't you?"

"I do that. But, well, you told me last night when you phoned that you'd spoken to the ward nurse and he was okay."

"Yes, he is. But he'll be better for seeing you. And he's getting an important test this morning."

Donal nodded. Swallowed. "Right enough."

"Am I not with you?"

"You are, sir."

"And don't I know my way round here?"

"I'm sure you do that."

"Come on then."

Donal took a deep breath and straightened his narrow shoulders. "Lead on, Macduff."

To keep the man's spirits up and distract him from the busyness all around them, O'Reilly kept up a conversation until they passed wards 19 and 20, presided over by Sir Ian Fraser, one of the senior surgeons.

"We're out of the main hospital now," O'Reilly said as they entered a narrower passageway. "The place we're going to, Quinn House, was opened in 1953. It has seventy beds on two wards."

"And Dapper'll be on the same one I was on."

"That's right. It's the brain surgery unit and it has its own X-ray department and a dedicated operating theatre."

"Boys-a-boys, isn't modern medicine a wonderful thing?"

O'Reilly smiled. Now that they were out of the main hospital, Donal was looking a little more confident. "Much more so than when I started. Nobody then would have thought of putting up an octagonal unit with a corridor running through the place with four-bedded rooms on the outside of the corridor and single-bedded units on the inside. I hope Dapper has a single room."

"Me too."

They entered ward 21. O'Reilly knocked on the door of Sister's office and went in.

Donal snatched off his duncher and stood wide-eyed.

"Morning, Sister," O'Reilly said to the senior sister, neat in her starched white fall headdress and red dress under a white apron. "This is Donal Donnelly, a friend of Mister Frew's."

Donal stood to attention.

The woman nodded to both men. "Sister O'Reilly's briefed me, and I've spoken to Mister Greer. He says it's against the rules, but if your friend Mister Donnelly would like to have a short visit with Mister Frew"—she bent and with a perfectly straight face whispered in O'Reilly's ear—"bugger the rules."

"And I imagine those were his exact words, Sister?"

"They were."

Typical Charlie. Still the irreverent lad O'Reilly had met in 1931. He chuckled. "Grand."

"And Mister Greer's waiting for you in the ward office. You know your way, and I'll take Mister Donnelly to see his friend. He's two rooms along from here on the inside."

"Thanks."

"Dead on," Donal said. "Is he all right, Sister?"

"He's comfortable and he's resting. That's all I'm allowed to tell you." She smiled. "But I'm sure Doctor O'Reilly will explain once he has seen Mister Greer."

"Thank God for that. Doctor O'Reilly's very good at explaining, so he is, and we'll need that, for Dapper and me's dead ignorant about urology."

"Neurology, Donal."

"Aye. Right enough."

"I'll not be long with Mister Greer, but don't you be getting Dapper worked up."

"I'll not."

O'Reilly headed for the clinical room, a place where students might be taught, doctors would go to consult, and tea, coffee, and biscuits were always available. He let himself in. "Morning, Charlie. How are you?"

Charlie Greer, wearing a long white lab coat with two of the tools of his trade, a tuning fork and a patella hammer, sticking out of a pocket, sat at a plain wooden table surrounded by half a dozen upright chairs.

"Grand, Fingal. Tea or coffee?"

"Tea, please."

As Charlie went to a sideboard to pour, O'Reilly sat at the table and watched his friend of thirty-eight years. He reckoned Charlie was aging well. He still had shoulders like an ox and fingers like sausages. A potbelly had replaced the athlete's toned one—and given how often Alice Moloney, the village dressmaker, had to let out O'Reilly's own waistband, he would not criticise his friend. Charlie's shock of ginger hair, which once would have rivalled Donal Donnelly's ruddy thatch, was greying now and he was wearing spectacles. *Eyesight going—just like, damn it, I'm trying to ignore the fact that my hearing is.*

"Here you are." He handed O'Reilly a cup. "Have a pew. You want to know about your patient Mister James Frew?"

"Please. And thanks, pal, for putting him in a single room."

Charlie shrugged.

"I can't believe it was only Saturday night when Jack Mills—"

"Now there's a first-class young surgeon."

That pleased O'Reilly. "—helped me examine Dapper."

"Your diagnosis of a subarachnoid haemorrhage was top of the possibilities after a thorough examination here on Saturday night. We confirmed it an hour ago by my registrar finding xanthochromic cerebrospinal fluid after a lumbar puncture."

"I see." While it was always professionally satisfying to make the correct diagnosis, O'Reilly was more concerned for his patient. "So, what's next?"

"Apparently, he never lost consciousness, so I think it's fair to assume while there is blood in his skull, there has been no bleeding into the brain tissue. I'm even more confident now, because he is getting some return of function in his left side and his dysphasia has nearly disappeared."

"So, he's recovering?"

"Possibly. It's too early to tell. I think he's bled from a small aneurysm, probably on the right middle cerebral artery."

"Jack said you might do an angiogram next to be sure."

"Jack's right. One's scheduled for ten tomorrow morning, and if it shows what I think it will, I'll operate on Friday."

"So, we'll have something concrete to go on by tomorrow? Can you give me any idea what the chances are of recovery?"

Charlie shook his head. "Overall, about forty percent of subarachnoids don't recover—"

"You mean they die?"

"I do, but Frew's probably past the critical stage. I think his prospects are reasonably good, but I can't promise. Sorry. I hope I'll have a better idea if the surgery goes smoothly. There is a four percent operative mortality rate too."

O'Reilly sucked in his breath. While he usually felt it proper to keep patients informed, those figures could not be altered, and he saw no reason to scare Dapper or Donal. For once he'd keep statistics to himself.

"And you'll keep me posted about the angiogram?"

"I will or my registrar will." He glanced at his watch. "They keep me on the hop, and if I'm not in theatre in ten minutes a certain lovely Kitty O'Reilly, who is setting up for excision of what is probably a glioma, will geld me." He rose. "Finish your tea, go and see your patient, and have Kitty give Pixie a ring and let's have dinner together soon."

"I've a better idea. I'll need to talk to Kitty, but how about me rounding up Cromie and Button, and you two and your better halves come down to Ballybucklebo? Talk about old times in Dublin?"

"Sounds good."

"Thanks, on all counts, Charlie," O'Reilly said to the back of the lab coat of a man in a hurry.

O'Reilly smiled. Pixie and Button. His friends' wives had both attended Cheltenham Ladies' College, an exclusive school in England, an institution that mirrored the boys' public schools' tradition of handing out nicknames. He finished his tea and walked back along the corridor, stopping at Dapper's ward. The curtains were closed behind the glass windows that usually made it simple for nurses to keep an eye on their patients. He let himself in.

Donal bounced up from the chair he'd been sitting on at the head of Dapper's iron-framed bed. "You have the chair, Doctor."

"Not at all. Sit down." O'Reilly gently hitched his backside onto the blanket halfway along the bed where Dapper lay on his back with his head on a single pillow. He managed a tiny smile.

"How are you feeling, Dapper?"

"I'd rather not be here but I'm not too bad, sir. My headache cleared up and I'm not losing words much anymore. I've til lie flat like this for two hours. The doctor who stuck thon needle in my back said it's til stop me getting a headache. He said they were quite common after this test."

"That's true."

Donal fidgeted on his chair and O'Reilly watched the man's face going through its usual contortions, an event that usually indicated that Donal was wrestling with a decision. His features settled and he said, "Doctor O'Reilly, Dapper and me's busting til know. What did Mister Greer say?"

O'Reilly nodded. "He's sure, Dapper, you have had a little bleed inside your head. This morning's test proves it."

"I see. Little? How big's little? That doesn't sound good til me."

O'Reilly hesitated. Even if he knew the exact amount, there was no point in saying something like "about half a teaspoonful." It would be meaningless. "When folks have what Mister Greer is sure you have had, bleeding from a weak artery, many become unconscious. The ones that don't—and you didn't, I know because I was there—are the ones who get better quickest."

"That's good news, Dapper," Donal said. "Isn't it, Doc?"

"It is, and I'm here to try to explain what happens next."

"You said on Saturday, Doctor, that I might need an operation?" There was a tremor in his voice.

"I did. You're going to have a special X-ray tomorrow. The doctors will inject a dye to outline the blood vessels in your skull, and if it shows a weakness in the wall of one, Mister Greer will operate on Friday."

"My God." Dapper tried to sit up but fell back. His fists clenched.

"Lie down," O'Reilly said, shaking his head. "Eejit. You don't want to give yourself another headache, do you?"

Donal said, "Could Dapper give himself a percussion instead if he jerks his head like that?"

It took O'Reilly a moment before he said, "Concussion, Donal."

"Oh, right. Right. I knew that."

"No concussion. But it's better if he lies still."

"And I will. Sorry, sir. It's just I'm mortal feared of surgery, so I am.

And, well, I am getting better. I know that. Like I said, I've very little trouble finding words the day. That's got til be a good sign, isn't it?"

"It is."

"So, could they not wait and see for a wee while longer? My brain might just fix itself, like?"

"When I was a young doctor in Dublin, patients like you were treated for at least ten days and some did recover without an operation, but brain surgery was not very advanced then. Mister Greer is a very highly respected brain surgeon. I think we should take his advice."

Dapper looked as if he might argue, and then sighed. "All right. I'll bide, sir, but my stomach feels like it's got about a million butterflies in it, all flying and flopping round."

"I'll speak to the houseman. See about getting you some calming medicine."

"Thanks, Doc."

"I think it's wheeker, so I do," Donal said. "You've only four days til wait and then you'll get fixed up. And mind like I told you, I've had brain surgery and I come through it with flying colours and a clean brain."

"Clean brain? Take yourself off by the hand, Donal Donnelly, but thanks for trying til cheer me up." Dapper took a deep breath. "I'll bide quiet, but I wish it was over, so I do." He sighed. "Would you have any idea how long I'll be in for, sir?"

"It's usually a ten-day stay postop, and Friday's the eleventh. When all goes well, and I'm sure it will, you should be out by the twenty-first. That's a Monday."

"Can I go back til work then?"

O'Reilly shook his head. "I don't know. Probably not, but Mister Greer will give you a better idea by then."

"Good, for I'll have til let my office know when I'll likely be back. Sales are usually slow in July and August, but if I'll be out of action, another agent will have to pick up my work. I'll get sick leave money, but no commissions."

O'Reilly said, "I'd be pretty surprised if they haven't already heard you're in hospital. You know what Ballybucklebo's like."

"They know, all right. Joan Eakin, the wee secretary I used til date, come in til visit me yesterday all concerned about me. She'd seen Kinky at church on Sunday." He inhaled. "But they'll still need to know when til expect me back."

"Don't worry about that. I'll give them a ring when I get home and explain. And you come and see me when you're home. I'll give you a sick line so you can draw your benefits."

"Thanks, Doctor."

"Listen, oul' hand, never you worry about your work," said Donal. "Your job's til get better. I'll do all I can til help. I'll come and see you at every night's visiting hours. Bring you anything you need." Donal took and squeezed Dapper's hand. "Either Bertie'll borrow me his van or I'll get the train and buses."

"You're a sound man, Donal."

O'Reilly heard the catch in Dapper's voice. "There now, Donal is going to be here every evening, and Mister Greer will keep me advised. You're not out of the woods yet, Dapper, but things do look promising. But, Donal, you and I mustn't tire Dapper. He needs to rest."

"Thank you, Doctor O'Reilly." Dapper's frown vanished and his fists unclenched.

"I'll leave you to say good-bye to Dapper, Donal, but don't be too long." He let himself out into the corridor. The next few days would be critical for Dapper, but O'Reilly saw no reason to worry the two men any more than they already were. He was quite able to be concerned for them both.

5

Like Many of the Upper Class

"I reckon we'll time this to perfection," O'Reilly said to Barry in the Rover's passenger seat. O'Reilly wrenched the steering wheel of the big car to turn left off the Belfast to Bangor Road and onto the Crawfordsburn Road. As usual, he was probably driving just a bit too fast—he eased off on the accelerator. Luckily there were no cyclists in sight.

"I didn't think we'd make it with you up in Belfast, then running Donal to work and having to phone Dapper's office." Barry looked over at O'Reilly and smiled. O'Reilly liked that about the young man. He believed in punctuality. Young people these days didn't always.

"Better three hours too soon than a minute too late. We're in plenty of time."

"*Merry Wives of Windsor*," said Barry with satisfaction.

"Right you are, sir. We'll park at the Crawfordsburn Inn and give Kenny the run I thought he was going to have to miss. He loves the little glen there. We'll still be early for the young man, the trainee applicant George Irwin's sending down to us—what's his name."

"Doctor Sebastian Carson."

"That's the one. See if we want him for next clinical year's attachment to our practice as a trainee GP."

"Today's a bit of a scorcher, Fingal. Will Kenny be all right in the car while we're having lunch?"

"He'll not be in the car because—Holy thundering Mother of—" O'Reilly pulled the Rover to the side of the road and slammed on the brakes. "Bloody tractors. Look at that."

The shuddering halt hurled a protesting Barry against his seat belt and forced a yelp of surprise from Kenny in the backseat.

"Come on, Barry." O'Reilly piled out, slammed his door, ran round the car, clambered over a low dry stone wall, and charged ten yards up a sharply sloping grassy pasture to where the red Massey Harris tractor he'd just seen toppling over lay on its right side. The driver, a middle-aged, florid-faced man, was sprawled on his side, trying and failing to wriggle away. His left foot was on the tractor's seat, but his right foot was trapped under the steering wheel.

O'Reilly knelt at the man's head and raised his voice over the engine noise. "I'm Doctor O'Reilly"—Barry stood beside O'Reilly—"and this is Doctor Laverty. Where are you hurt?"

"I've split my lip and my ankle's stuck. I don't think it's broke but it's powerful sore, so it is, and I can't get it free."

"Right." O'Reilly looked at Barry. "Between the pair of us I reckon we can lift it just enough." He spoke to the driver. "When I yell, 'Now,' try to crawl away."

"Yes, sir."

O'Reilly stood. "Right, Barry. Trot round to the other side. I'll lift from under the steering wheel. I want you to pull on it. We only need to make about six inches." O'Reilly straddled the man's right leg, squatted, and grasped the lower part of the wheel.

Barry appeared on the opposite side of the tractor and took hold of the steering wheel's upper quarter. "Ready when you are."

"Okay," O'Reilly said. "On three. One, two, three." He hauled in a deep breath and put everything he had into flexing his forearms and extending his legs. O'Reilly's abdominal muscles tensed. He was aware of vessels throbbing in his temples and the strap muscles in his neck standing out. He heard a loud grunt coming from Barry and slowly, slowly the wheel began to rise. This had better work. Having to drop it on the ankle again didn't bear thinking about. O'Reilly clenched his teeth and heaved, felt the thing rise more, and judged there should be enough room. "Now." Dear God, he couldn't hold on much longer. He was aware of the farmer's leg inching out.

"I'm free."

"Let her go." O'Reilly felt the additional weight as Barry's contribution was removed, unclenched his hands, and hopped back as the steering wheel thudded onto the grass, missing his toes by inches. He exhaled and pulled in another lungful. His shirt was sticking to him and he used the back of his hand to wipe his brow. Barry had been right when he'd said today was a scorcher.

He was aware of Barry's return but rapidly turned to the patient, who was now sitting up, dabbing at his lip with a grubby hanky. "Aye," O'Reilly said after taking a quick glance, "you have split your lip and it's going to need stitches."

"Bugger it."

"Let's have a look at your hoof." O'Reilly, as gently as he could, removed the man's right Wellington boot and woollen sock. As he did, the farmer sucked in his breath and grunted. "Sorry if I hurt you." O'Reilly studied the ankle. He could see no deformity, the skin wasn't broken, but already the bruising had started. "Can you move it?"

The farmer flexed and extended his foot. "Aye, but it's dead sore."

"I'm sure it is. And I'm not going to hurt you more by poking it to make the point. My guess is you've only sprained it. Doctor Laverty?"

"I agree."

"So, Mister—?""

"Johnson, Desmond Johnson."

"Is that your farmhouse there?" O'Reilly pointed across a hedge about fifty yards away to a sturdy-looking grey two-storey house surrounded by outbuildings and facing what must be a farmyard. Two large elms formed a windbreak behind.

"Aye."

"And that's the gate into this field from the Crawfordsburn Road?" He nodded to a five-bar rusty iron gate ten yards from where the Rover sat. "Wide enough to get a car through?"

"Aye."

"Barry, nip off and bring the car, will you?"

Barry headed back the way he'd come.

"I'll be right back, Mister Johnson." O'Reilly stood, went to the tractor, bent, and turned off the ignition. It was a relief to be rid of the clattering.

"Are you the Doctor O'Reilly from Ballybucklebo?"

"I am."

"Jasus, sir, I don't know how til thank you and the young doctor." He looked at his hands. "Look at that. I'm all a-tremble."

"I'm not surprised. Shock. You know and I know how lucky you are. Every year farmers get crushed and killed when their tractor rolls over."

"Indeed I do, sir. And," he managed a smile, "I'm double lucky, so I am. How many farmers get rescued by two doctors? Thanks a million. You're not my doctor. Can I pay you something?"

"Don't be daft."

A small herd of white-faced, red-coated Hereford bullocks, beef cattle, had wandered over to see what was going on and O'Reilly could smell their breath. One tossed its head, bawled, and took off at the gallop followed by the rest as Barry drove up.

"I'll help you stand, Mister Johnson."

It took a bit of manoeuvring to get the man into the back of the car with Kenny.

As Barry drove to the farmhouse, O'Reilly half turned and said, "Have you a phone?"

"Och, aye."

"Good. I told you you're going to need stitches, so when we get you home, I'll call an ambulance to take you to Newtownards Hospital casualty. Then I'll call them, let them know why you're coming, and suggest they X-ray your ankle when you get there too. The ambulance men will splint your ankle. Make it less uncomfortable on the drive."

Barry parked outside the farmhouse's green front door.

"Just be a few minutes, Barry." O'Reilly helped the farmer, and in no time Desmond Johnson was sitting on a chair in his kitchen where his wife, having been reassured about her man's condition, was making a cup of tea.

"Not for me, thanks," he said. "Ordinarily I'd wait until the ambulance came but my partner and I are already going to be late for an appointment. I'll make my phone calls and be running on."

As O'Reilly climbed into the Rover, he sucked in his breath. "Oh boy, but my back didn't appreciate that heaving. I'm creaky. Must've pulled a muscle."

Barry, with mock sympathy in his voice, said, "'You're old, Father William, the young man said.'"

O'Reilly settled in his seat. He couldn't get cross with Barry. "*Alice's Adventures in Wonderland.* Chapter five—and my hair is definitely not turning to grey." He started the engine. "Time we were off."

"Has my guest, a Doctor Carson, arrived, Anne?" O'Reilly asked the receptionist at the inn's front desk.

"Sorry. Not yet, Doctor, but your table out in the back courtyard is ready." She smiled down at the big chocolate Lab sitting at O'Reilly's feet. "This must be Kenny. We don't normally allow dogs other than guide dogs indoors, but seeing it's yourself, just walk him through."

"Thanks, Anne, and when my guest arrives, please send him out."

"I'll bring him myself, Doctor."

"Thanks, Anne."

O'Reilly and Barry turned left along a wood-panelled corridor and right along another leading to the back courtyard.

A stranger leaving the gents' remarked, "Handsome-looking fellow, your dog."

"Thank you," O'Reilly said, but didn't linger to chat; his back ached and he wanted to sit down. They were late because of the tractor accident and the candidate wasn't here yet? First impressions are things you don't get a second chance to make. I hope the man has a reasonable explanation.

"I thought he was talking about you for a second, Fingal," Barry said.

"Less of your lip." But O'Reilly was smiling.

A waitress met them. "Nice to see youse again, Doctors." She showed them to a circular cast-iron table with four cushioned cast-iron chairs.

O'Reilly and Barry took their seats.

"Under."

Kenny's soft brown eyes looked at O'Reilly. The dog let his muzzle rest on the edge of the table.

"Un-der."

Kenny sighed, went under the table, and lay down.

Neil Diamond's 1969 hit came from speakers mounted on the white-washed back wall of the inn.

"I wonder," O'Reilly asked, "seeing we're the only ones out here, if it would be possible to turn off the speakers?" He detested piped music in public places.

"Certainly, Doctor O'Reilly."

"Thank you."

She put three menus on the table and said, "Can I get youse drinks?"

O'Reilly looked at Barry, who nodded. "Two pints, please."

"Coming up." She left.

O'Reilly looked under the table. "Sorry, Kenny. You've missed your walk and we're not in the Duck. No Smithwick's today either."

The big Lab sighed.

I swear to God he understands English, O'Reilly thought, and looked round. He was sitting with his back to the main building. The paved courtyard was flanked by three cottages. The largest was the honeymoon suite. Leafy sycamores at the far end of the yard towered above a small glen, from which came the tinkling of the burn running down to Belfast Lough. Overhead the sun beamed down. Barry'd been right. Kenny would have been baked in the car. Good thing O'Reilly had made the arrangements for him to be allowed out here.

The music was replaced by the twice-repeated notes of a song thrush.

Barry said, "I've always enjoyed thrushes. Much better than loud-speakers."

"I agree."

Barry picked up his menu. "So, Fingal, what do you know about this Sebastian Carson?" He frowned. "I don't think I know any Irish Sebastians."

"George Irwin usually sends me top-flight candidates. He says the man comes from a well-off family. Shipping, I believe. I think some of the highheejins look down on 'Paddy' and 'Mick,' and 'Francis Xavier' would definitely be a nonstarter. Some names definitely would not span the sectarian divide."

Barry chuckled.

"Sebastian qualified in 1968. He's finishing his houseman's year at Belfast City Hospital." O'Reilly looked at his watch. Twelve fifteen. "And apparently has no sense of punctuality."

"Here youse are." The waitress set two pints of Guinness on the table.

Anne, the receptionist, appeared. "Here's your guest, Doctor O'Reilly." She was accompanied by a fair-haired young man, five foot ten, O'Reilly guessed, pale grey eyes, clean-shaven. He wore a blazer with a crest featuring a lion rampant and the motto *Stet Fortunus Domus* on the pocket, and a navy blue background, narrow white-blue-white diagonally striped tie. O'Reilly did not recognise either.

"Thank you both," O'Reilly said.

Anne left. The waitress asked, "Can I get you a drink, sir?"

"It's why you're here."

O'Reilly flinched. The man sounded like a belted earl addressing a mere scullion.

"Bristol Cream sherry."

No "please"? O'Reilly thought. The waitress left.

O'Reilly said, "Doctor Carson?"

"Indeed." He thrust out a hand. "And you must be O'Reilly."

"I am." He accepted a limp handshake. "Have a pew." O'Reilly tried not to frown but thought, Although I don't take my title seriously, medical etiquette calls for its use when introductions are made, and a handshake is offered by the senior to the junior, not the other way round.

The man sat. "And you must be Laverty."

"We tend to be informal except in front of the customers," Barry said. "Barry's fine."

"Jolly good. I'm Sebastian." They shook.

"Your sherry, sir." The glass was set on the table.

No "thank you." "So," said O'Reilly, raising his glass, "cheers."

Barry and Sebastian toasted and drank.

O'Reilly gestured to the young man's jacket. "*Stet Fortunus Domus*. Let the fortune of the house stand?"

"Harrow. Went there after Garth House."

O'Reilly thought, Garth's a private preparatory school in Bangor. "I believe Harrow was one of the first seven original British public schools."

"Yes. We're rather proud of that, and of some of our old boys. Seven PMs, including Winnie—"

"Winnie?" Barry asked. O'Reilly knew his partner well enough to know that he was trying hard not to smile.

"Winston Churchill. One met him in 1962. Splendid man. Absolutely splendid. Was introduced to him."

That must mean Sebastian Carson had been head boy or captain of a sporting team. No lesser pupil would be accorded such an honour.

"Then we've had five foreign kings. Jawaharlal Nehru. Lord Byron. I could go on, you know, but I don't think so doing will help my cause in this interview." His smile was self-deprecating.

O'Reilly picked up his menu. "We'll start that in a few minutes, but I suggest we all have a look at the menu and order." His tummy rumbled. Fingal O'Reilly had already decided that he was going to enjoy scampi and chips just like the afternoon when he, brother Lars, and Bertie Bishop had met here to talk about Bertie's will. O'Reilly gave the other two more time, then asked, "Ready to order?"

"Please," Barry said.

"I've always enjoyed their fish-and-chips. I know it's a bit *infra dig,* but occasionally I do enjoy them."

O'Reilly signalled for the waitress and thought, Latin tags were still in use by some public schoolboys. *Infra Dignitatem* meant beneath one's dignity. Huh. Fish-and-chips were not beneath his or Barry's.

Orders were placed.

"Quick nonmedical question," O'Reilly said. "Carson. Was Sir Edward a family member?"

"As a matter of fact, he was. Great-great-uncle on the paternal side."

"Good Lord."

"We don't mention it often. He was a man of his time. Clearly of high principles. You'll both know he was a bitter opponent of Home Rule for Ireland. Signed the Ulster Covenant, which pledged to resist it, 'by all means necessary.'" Sebastian took a deep breath. "Here in Ulster we're paying for his legacy to this day."

"We are, but it's difficult to pick your ancestry. We'll not hold it against you."

"Indeed not," Barry said.

"There's one more thing you need to know about me now you know my lineage. I'll have no truck with sectarianism. I believe a doctor has no right, none whatsoever, to care about any patient's religion unless they require the attention of a priest or have doctrinal prohibitions like the Jehovah's Witnesses against blood transfusion. All patients have the right to the best care possible."

"That is right and proper," O'Reilly said. "I commend you." And he did. If young Carson had been an ardent Loyalist, he'd not be working in Ballybucklebo, that was for sure.

"Thank you."

"Right, Sebastian. Let's let that hare sit. Barry and I'd like to know your medical background."

"I went to Queen's—"

"In Belfast?"

Sebastian laughed. "No. No. No. Queen's College, Cambridge. Fine old spot. Three years basic sciences there, then three years clinical stuff."

Barry asked, "Which teaching hospital? Royal? Belfast City?"

"Um, no. Bart's, actually."

O'Reilly nodded. It was said that the graduates of Saint Bartholomew's Hospital, London, founded in 1123, always tacked the "actually" on as a mark of pride.

The waitress arrived and placed the plates before the diners. "Any drinks?"

"Barry?"

Barry shook his head.

"Sebastian?"

He finished his sherry. "Might one have a glass of Entre-Deux-Mers?"

"Certainly, sir."

"Mostly Sauvignon Blanc with a little Semillon and Muscadelle. Pleasantly dry."

O'Reilly indicated his pint. "Please." At least Sebastian hadn't made remarks like, "It's a cheeky little wine with very good legs and a fine nose." And what was wrong with a decent pint anyhow? He picked up his knife and fork. "I suggest we dig in," and fell to. Savouring his battered and deep-fried Dublin Bay prawns, he wondered about Sebastian Carson. At first sight O'Reilly had summed him up as a somewhat ill-mannered young man despite his education. There was no excuse for not apologising or offering an explanation for being late. He obviously came from a privileged background and didn't mind showing it. Attendance at some of the best preparatory and public schools, Cambridge—and Bart's? O'Reilly chewed on a chip, barely noticed the arrival of young Carson's wine and the pint and wondered if they were dealing with a pretentious upper-class snob or an insecure young man who was trying desperately to impress. O'Reilly speared another prawn.

Barry asked, "Why general practice, Sebastian?"

Sebastian's fork stopped halfway to his mouth. "In three years at a teaching hospital all you see are cases that need specialist attention. I'd like to see the other end of the spectrum, and I'd like to finish my training quickly, get good mentor reports, pass the exams of the Royal College of GPs and then an assistantship with a view to partnership. None of this four years as a junior, speciality Royal College exams, then waiting for a senior post. I've just about had enough of studying." He popped a piece of cod into his mouth, chewed and swallowed. "And there's another thing. Professor Irwin tells me you have four doctors who share night and weekend call and, assuming you'll take me, once you're satisfied that I can work unsupervised, it would become one in five." Sebastian frowned. "Most specialist trainees work very heavy on-call rotas. Even the consultants at Bart's, especially the surgical ones, were usually on call every other night. One rather hopes for time for a life of one's own as well as one's duties."

I see, O'Reilly thought. I'd not have survived in my early years here when I was single-handed if I'd believed that. Barry certainly didn't. And yet—since there now were Connor Nelson, Emer McCarthy, and Barry to share call, life had become more relaxed for them all. O'Reilly said, "Sebastian, those are nearly all reasons why you don't want to specialise.

I'd really like to hear what attracts you to general practice, particularly rural practice."

Another chip-laden fork stopped halfway to the young man's mouth. "I'm not entirely sure . . ." At least that was honest. ". . . but I've lived most of my life with boys and young men from my own kind of background. I know a bit about London and Belfast's working class. They're the bulk of patients in big-city teaching hospitals. I don't know how the rest of the world lives. I think I'd like to find out. My only experience of general practice is being seen by our own doctor in my own home once when I had measles as a boy and once when I had sinus trouble. I've never set foot in a surgery."

"I see," Barry said. "Neither had I when I came here in '64. Tell me, do you like people?"

"Pretty much. I'm told GPs get to know their patients better than the ones in hospital. I do rather think I'd like that." He smiled and ate the chip.

O'Reilly said, "It is very satisfying. You'd agree, Barry?"

"Absolutely."

Sebastian moved in his chair.

A short "woof" came from under the table.

Both of Sebastian's eyebrows shot up. "Good gracious," he said, bending to peer, "but there's a very large canine down here."

O'Reilly laughed. "Pay him no heed. That's my dog Kenny."

"Um, does he bite?"

"Kenny? He's as gentle as a lamb."

"I rather hope so. I didn't mean to kick him." He withdrew his legs.

"If you join us," Barry said with a smile, "you'll have to get used to Fingal's menagerie and mine. Both of us have a cat and a dog."

"I didn't. My only pet was a tortoise. I got him when I was seven. Called him Hector." Sebastian sighed. "They live for ages, but I had to let him go to a new home when I went to Harrow."

O'Reilly heard the slightest catch in the man's voice. Given his upbringing in the stiff-upper-lip school it was an interesting glimpse into him. O'Reilly said, "So let's see, you have a number of reasons for not specialising, you like people, not quite sure about dogs, you think you'd like to get to know your patients better, and you know nothing about GP work?"

"Yet—but I'm willing to learn."

"And you'd appreciate a fair bit of time off."

"Yes, actually. I would."

"I see." Fingal resisted the urge to ask why. "You don't see medicine as a kind of priesthood?"

"Good Lord, no. I think it is a very satisfying profession, but not to the exclusion of all else." He grinned. "And I'm single and twenty-four. I've not the remotest intention of being celibate. None whatsoever."

That remark hit O'Reilly's funny bone and he burst out laughing. "I'm not entirely sure that aspect of your private life is any concern of ours, but I will expect you to sleep in quarters in my house when you are on call. I assume you'll have somewhere to stay when you're not."

"I'll be living at home in Cherryvalley. It's only about a fifteen-minute run to Ballybucklebo."

Cherryvalley? One of Belfast's classiest suburbs. "And transportation?"

Sebastian smiled. "My Mini Cooper S is in the car park."

Sporty but not wildly expensive or ostentatious, O'Reilly thought.

"I'm living at home because Father died last year—"

That caught O'Reilly off guard. "My condolences," he said.

"Yes. Well. Thank you. A-a heart attack, you see. Very sudden. It was quite the shock."

"I'm sure it was." O'Reilly still remembered the death of his own father only six weeks after O'Reilly had graduated from Trinity. He said, "Thank you for answering our questions. Barry, anything else you'd like to ask?"

Barry cocked his head to one side. "Have you any hobbies?"

"Well, yes. As a matter of fact, I do. Fly-fishing . . ."

Interesting. Barry was a keen angler.

"And I used to like to sail in my summer holidays, but of course I've had to let that go for the last seven years. Hope to take it up again."

"I sail, and fish," Barry said. "Thank you for telling us."

"Well, jolly good." Sebastian looked at Barry quickly and then looked away.

O'Reilly noticed that Barry made no offer to take Sebastian fishing or sailing. "In that case, Sebastian, is there anything you'd like to ask us?"

"How soon will I hear if you'll take me?"

"Within a week," O'Reilly said. "Professor Irwin will contact you." The prof had set up that system to protect GP mentors who did not want to accept a certain learner. "Now, young man, your interview and our lunch are over. Would you care for dessert, coffee, another drink?"

Sebastian finished his wine. "I want to thank you for a fair and thoughtful interview. I would indeed relish another glass of wine," he glanced at his watch, "but I meant what I said about not regarding myself a priest. I'm meeting a most delectable young woman at the Grand Central Hotel on Royal Avenue for afternoon tea. Don't want to be late—"

But he was fine with being late for his interview, O'Reilly thought. He stifled a guffaw, leaned back in his chair—and was quickly reminded of his sore back.

"—and then we'll be seeing *Rosemary's Baby*." He winked at Barry. "I find the ladies tend to snuggle more closely during horror movies."

This time O'Reilly could not stifle a chuckle. Cheeky divil.

"Thank you both once again." He stood and reached for his wallet. "I'd like to pay for—"

"No, you won't," O'Reilly said. "My shout."

"Well, thank you again, Fingal." Sebastian offered a hand in turn to Fingal and Barry. "I shall await Professor Irwin's notification with intense anticipation."

After Sebastian had left, O'Reilly said, "Do you remember an article about Ulster by Alan Coren?"

"Didn't he become deputy editor of *Punch* this year?"

"Correct, and he wrote a satirical piece about the favourite occupation in our pubs."

"That of being hospitable to strangers—and making them the immediate topic of conversation the moment they'd left." Barry finished his pint. "So, what do you make of Doctor Sebastian Carson?"

O'Reilly waited. It was a naval custom at a court-martial to make the most junior officer speak first so he could not be influenced by his seniors' opinions. "You first."

"All right. I'm not sure. At first, I thought he was just a toffee-nosed snob, but then I thought, an upper-class background and coming from a first-class public school helps, but you need brains to be accepted at Cambridge. He's not afraid of authority. Initially, I wasn't impressed with his reasons for choosing GP and thought he sounded a bit work-shy. And yet—" Barry shrugged.

"And yet—Barry, we both enjoy our free time because of the bigger on-call rota."

"True, and I nearly bust when he said—" Barry cleared his throat. "Now, I know my upper-class accent isn't a patch on Jack Mills's, but I've give it a try, 'I've not the remotest intention of being celibate. None whatsoever.'"

O'Reilly laughed. "A sense of humour is critical in our work, and he has one."

"So, you'd accept him?"

"I'd like to sleep on it. I'm not sure how our patients would take to him." O'Reilly frowned. "I think he'd be a better fit in practice on London's Harley Street, home of the physicians to the very upper crust. I didn't like the way he spoke to the waitress when she asked if he'd like a drink, and if he condescends like that to some of our rough diamonds, we might start losing customers. And then there is the matter of his lateness. I won't tolerate that." He nodded to himself. "It's silly, but did you notice how he spoke of his tortoise?"

"I did. I think he still misses the creature. I wonder if he had many friends when he was little?"

O'Reilly nodded. "My thoughts exactly. All right, we'll both think on it. Under the crust there may be a decent chap, but I do worry about how he'd fit in in Ballybucklebo. I'll maybe drop in on George Irwin, see what he can tell me, but for now, I'll settle up and," he bent, "come out, you great lummox . . ."

Kenny emerged, shaking his head.

"We'll give the long-suffering hound his walk."

6

Who Knows If the Moon's a Balloon?

"There's the little devil." Charlie Greer pointed to a spot on the X-ray film that was slotted into the illuminated viewing box.

O'Reilly leant forward and saw what looked like a gnarled tree of a lighter colour than the black background. Its trunk, coming from the bottom of the angiogram, ran straight up, curved ninety degrees to the right, then left, then right again, narrowing all the while. Branches, all of lesser diameter, spread out upward like the ribs of a fan.

"See, after the second right bend, that bump inside the loop of the right middle cerebral artery?"

O'Reilly did. It jutted directly from the main vessel, had a body like a tiny hot-air balloon, and was attached to the vessel by a narrow neck.

"We'll soon sort that out." Charlie picked up a cloth face mask, put it on, and knotted the ties.

As O'Reilly pulled a white theatre shirt over his unruly dark mop, he thought how calm Charlie sounded, just as he had on Wednesday evening on the phone after confirming he and Pixie could join the O'Reillys and Cromies on Sunday for dinner. "Fingal, your patient Frew's improving, I'm pleased to say.

"The angiogram shows a middle cerebral aneurysm. I'll be operating on Friday. The ward sister will be asking his friend, Mister Donal Donnelly, to stop visiting until Saturday. We like to keep the patient as calm as possible for twenty-four hours preop."

Charlie had asked Fingal if he'd like to observe and he had said yes. And, still unsure about Sebastian Carson, O'Reilly had made an appointment to see Professor George Irwin after the surgery to find out more about the young doctor.

Now here he was on Friday morning, dressed in surgical whites, masked, wearing a white tube-gauze hat, and ready to accompany Charlie into the operating theatre to see exactly what was going to happen to Dapper.

Charlie was singing, "Hi ho, hi ho. It's off to work we go," as if he hadn't a care in the world, although he was going to be taking a man's life, quite literally, in his hands. More than 40 percent of such patients did not leave hospital alive. O'Reilly himself felt more than anxious. He knew that Dapper, if he survived, could in the short term suffer a stroke or epilepsy or brain damage. If Charlie were inaccurate, he could accidentally place the clip on a normal artery, causing more destruction. O'Reilly shuddered. He looked at Charlie's fingers and wondered how those fat digits could perform such delicate work, and he also noticed that the brain surgeon's hands had a noticeable tremor. Was the man quite as relaxed as he seemed?

"Your friend's already under anaesthetic, Fingal. Kitty and my registrar, Mister Wilson, will have started by shaving the area of the incision and painting it with antiseptic. Then they'll make scalp flaps over the place where I'm going to crack his nut." He pushed open the theatre doors.

That last remark may have sounded callous, but O'Reilly understood it was merely part of a surgeon's self-defence. He followed his friend into theatre. It had been four years since he'd last been in here, to observe Donal Donnelly's operation. Then he'd been concerned but not overly so. The mortality rate for Donal's type of surgery was less than 4 percent and Donal had, as expected, survived with no residual damage. He smiled. Donal's tendency to mix up certain words was something he'd had ever since Fingal had known him.

As an observer O'Reilly had no need to scrub up or wear a gown and gloves. His eyes narrowed as he approached the operation table. Nothing, it seemed, had changed physically in the theatre in four years. Same disinfectant smells, same brilliant overhead operating light flooding the table, patient, anaesthetist, and scrub sister (Kitty) in a brilliant circle of illumination. A circulating nurse who was not scrubbed and gowned waited near a trolley bearing sterile gowns and gloves.

Charlie began to scrub. "For those of you who don't know, this is my old classmate Doctor Fingal O'Reilly, who's come to observe us fix his patient. Fingal, this is our neurosurgical anaesthetist, Doctor 'Minty' Bereen, and my registrar, Mister John Wilson. Nurse Jean McKittrick, and I believe you know Mrs. O'Reilly."

"Just a little," O'Reilly said, and winked at her.

O'Reilly acknowledged the greetings but let his gaze linger on the grey-flecked-with-amber eyes of his wife, who stood with her instrument trolley to Dapper's left beside Mister Wilson. O'Reilly thought she looked perfectly relaxed, but then why not after more than twenty years as scrub sister?

The only sounds were the rhythmic pulsing of the anaesthetic machine's bellows as they breathed for Dapper, the running of water suddenly being cut off as Charlie finished scrubbing, and his "Thanks, Nurse," as he was helped into his sterile gown. As soon as he had gloved himself, he moved to the right side of the table. "Fingal, come and stand beside me."

O'Reilly did.

"Can you see?"

"Perfectly." Only the right front side of Dapper's skull was visible. It could be anybody under the green towels, but O'Reilly was very aware that it was a young estate agent who loved racing greyhounds, had an eye for pretty women, had given Donal Donnelly a roof over his head when the Donnellys' cottage had burned down, and who would have been terrified until the anesthetic made him unconscious.

Mister Wilson and Kitty had already opened the skull. He returned an instrument to Kitty, who dropped it on the floor where it bounced, clanging twice.

O'Reilly flinched and looked over to his wife. "Sorry," she said. "Nurse McKittrick, please pick it up and take it away." She sounded tense.

Charlie said, "Don't worry about it, Kitty. Accidents happen."

Kitty, with all her experience, making a mistake? Hard to believe. Although she had looked relaxed, perhaps the stress was affecting her. He had been trying for a couple of years to get her to slow down. She looked at O'Reilly, narrowed her eyes, and shook her head.

"Thank you, Nurse." Her tones were clipped. Kitty gave a set of forceps to John. "Sorry to hold up the procedure."

"Never worry. It was only for a couple of minutes and we're not in a race," Charlie said. "Anyway, Fingal, you see how John and Kitty have created a bone flap, wrapped it in a warm cloth, and laid it down on Dapper's cheek."

Fingal nodded.

Charlie said, "Go ahead, John. Open the dura."

Using the forceps, he lifted the membrane, then used scissors to incise it.

"Ordinarily I'd supervise John as he carried out the entire procedure, and he is a damn fine surgeon, but seeing the patient's your friend . . ."

"Thank you, Charlie. I appreciate that professional courtesy. And, so would my friend, Dapper. No offence intended, Mister Wilson."

"None taken, Doctor O'Reilly." Mister Wilson used a retractor to pull his part of the now-open dura aside. "Can you see that, Doctor?"

"Take a look, Fingal," Charlie said, and stepped back.

O'Reilly peered into the cavity at a piece of a living brain. Not any brain. Dapper's. In it lived his personality, his hopes, his prejudices, his beliefs, and his fears.

"That valley between those two pieces of grey matter," said Charlie, "is the sylvian fissure. If you look at the junction of the middle cerebral artery that runs up diagonally from left to right and the smaller vessel running down from the main trunk, you'll see the little devil I showed you on the X-ray. That's what's causing all of your patient's troubles."

Nestled between the main trunk and the descending branch was the aneurysm, exactly the shape he'd seen on the X-ray. A narrow neck and a balloon-shaped body.

"And," said Charlie, the laugh lines at the corners of his eyes suddenly evident, "a spring-loaded clip across the base of that neck stops any more blood getting into the aneurysm. It also stops it bursting or leaking through its thin wall. Yet it won't prevent blood flowing along the main vessel."

How could he smile? The next few minutes were critical. O'Reilly felt his breathing and his pulse rate speeding up.

"Sorry, Fingal, I need to get closer to make sure the aneurysm isn't held down by connective tissue and that placing the clip won't endanger any small arteries, called perforators."

O'Reilly stepped back.

"This is the tricky bit. If I'm not careful, I could burst the aneurysm."

Although not a religious man, O'Reilly mouthed, Please, God.

"It's free and there are no perforators. Come back and see."

O'Reilly moved forward.

"Clip."

Kitty handed Charlie an instrument with scissor grips at the near end. A spring-loaded steel clip was held open by jaws at the far end.

O'Reilly watched as Charlie slipped the jaws across the neck of the aneurysm—one in front, one behind. He squeezed the scissor grips, then opened them and withdrew the clip holder. "Got it."

O'Reilly exhaled the breath he'd not known he'd been holding.

"Syringe." Kitty gave Charlie a syringe.

"Just have to check the clip to be certain it's not nipping the main artery, then stick this needle into the dome of the aneurysm to be sure there's no blood flow into it." He paused. "Dry as a bone. Have a look."

O'Reilly peered in and saw the clip's bright jaws firmly in place. It would have been inappropriate to have cheered, but he felt like doing just that.

"Thank you, Minty, John, Kitty, and Jean. I'm going to pull my 'rank has its privileges' number. Fingal has another appointment and I'd like to have a cup of coffee with him, so close, please." He was already stripping off his gloves as he turned from the table and, followed by Fingal, headed for the door.

"Thank you, Charlie," O'Reilly started, pulling off his theatre whites. "Now what?"

"He'll stay in for ten days. There may be some residual effects and we'll be monitoring those closely. Minor epilepsy's quite common, but it usually goes away with time. His major preop difficulties were paresis in his left limbs. That's all gone and he's no longer dysphasic. I think he'll do fine." Charlie knotted his tie. "I had a patient with a history just like your patient's. He was an accounting student. Had epilepsy postop, which settled. He graduated top of his class. Twenty years later he became president of the accounting society."

Fully dressed, O'Reilly dragged a comb through his thatch. "I don't see Dapper becoming head of the estate agents' board. He's not the type to go in for committee meetings and intra-professional politics, but if he gets back to his old self, I'll be delighted—and so will Donal Donnelly. I'll let him know when I get home. Boy, am I glad that's over and you think things look promising. I hate to admit it, but I was pretty scared when you started to put on the clip."

Charlie shrugged. "I've been doing it for a lot of years. You have to get a bit hardened, but you do get used to it."

"Thanks anyway, old friend." O'Reilly grinned. "Now coffee. I've plenty of time before I see George Irwin."

"Fingal." Professor Irwin's silver hair was parted to the left, short sideburns coming halfway down beside his large ears. The man rose from behind a Formica-topped table that served as his desk. The tabletop was overflowing with books and manuscripts, an in-and-out tray, and a telephone. "How are you?"

"All the better for seeing you, George."

"Have a pew." George Irwin sat and O'Reilly followed suit on a small sofa with dark linen-covered cushions in front of the desk. "You said you wanted to talk to me about young Doctor Carson."

"That's right."

George Irwin frowned. "I'm a bit surprised. I've always tried to send you good prospects. What's the difficulty?"

"Good prospects? Connor Nelson and Emer McCarthy are both outstanding. It may sound petty, but our man Carson was fifteen minutes late for our interview over lunch."

George laughed. "I seem to remember so was I a couple of years ago when I asked you to come here and talk about your practice accepting trainees."

O'Reilly smiled. "True. But you apologised and explained why. He didn't, and he was patronising to a waitress. Very. That kind of thing will not go down well with our customers. Barry and I are pretty down-to-earth and so are they. Call a spade a spade. Less posh talking. The other thing was that he seemed to be more interested in time off than the nature of our work. Barry said afterward that he'd be willing to take Carson on but he also had similar reservations. I said I'd need to think about it, and when I heard two days ago I'd be coming up to the Royal I thought I'd seek your advice. I'm sorry to have left the poor fellah wondering, but, 'Buy in haste. Regret at leisure.'"

George steepled his fingers. "I must say I found him—um—cultured, I think would be the word. But you'd expect that given his background. A bit shy and tries to hide behind his upper-class façade."

Fingal nodded. "Might be, I suppose."

"You're not going to like this, Fingal, but could there be a bit of inverted snobbery here?"

O'Reilly sat back on the sofa. "On my part?" What George had just said could be true, and Fingal Flahertie O'Reilly was never a man who'd not face up to his own shortcomings. "You know, George, I don't like snobs, but perhaps I can go overboard a bit."

"Perhaps you can, Fingal. Let me tell you what I know about Sebastian Carson, and it's not a great deal. I have interviewed him. He tends to be a bit reticent about blowing his own trumpet, but he has an excellent record as a medical student. If you insist I can show you letters of reference from his dean at Cambridge and some senior consultants at Bart's."

"Not at all, George. I trust your judgement."

"Thank you. The chiefs of the four services he worked on at the City Hospital were all perfectly satisfied with his performance. In my opinion he is a well-qualified young man with an upper-class background that you might find grating."

O'Reilly cleared his throat and said, "Seems I may have misjudged the man."

"I think you might have, and remember you're not offering him a partnership. He'll be with you for only one year as a trainee."

"True."

O'Reilly considered his options. "I'll need to talk to Barry, tell him what you've told me, and if he agrees we'll take young Carson. I'll ring you as soon as I've spoken with Barry. We'll notify Connor and Emer on Monday if he agrees." O'Reilly rose and offered a hand. They shook. "Thanks, George. I'm sure Barry will agree. If he does we'll do our best with Sebastian, might even roughen up some of the smooth corners. Make a sow's ear out of a silk purse."

George laughed. "Of that I have no doubt whatsoever."

O'Reilly rose and offered a hand. They shook. "Thanks, George."

"Safe home, Fingal, and let me know as soon as you can. If you agree, I'll have him with you on August the first."

Fingal waited for a gap in the traffic and turned right onto the Grosvenor Road, remembering how he'd felt in the operating theatre this morning. It hadn't been the knee-weakening, hand-trembling, visceral fear he'd had to overcome during the war when his battleship HMS *Warspite* had been bombed or when, in the face of flames roaring near him and of live ammunition, he had amputated a sailor's hand. But it had been enough to make his pulse race wildly when Charlie had started examining the aneurysm—and O'Reilly an experienced doctor. The concern bordering on fear had been for his patient, Dapper Frew. Nor had O'Reilly often experienced such a sense of relief at Charlie's later optimistic prognosis. Since leaving the navy O'Reilly had rarely set foot in an operating theatre, and given the potential for serious long-term complications of Dapper's condition, he marvelled at how surgeons like Charlie could stand the stress. Come to that, how could theatre sisters like Kitty? She had been flustered after she'd dropped that guide. Was her job starting to tell on her?

O'Reilly turned left at the end of Grosvenor Road past the Fisherwick Assemblies building. For some time, the traffic was heavy, but after a left onto Victoria Street and a right at the Albert Clock to get him onto the Queen's Bridge over the river Lagan, his attention was caught by activity on the narrow streets of Ballymacarrett off the Newtownards Road. Union flags waved from every terrace house's first-floor windows, red, white, and blue bunting flying from each cross-street pair of lampposts.

He was about to leave the bridge but could make out an Orange Arch, a street-spanning plywood headboard supported on poles on either side of the road. He knew the slogans painted on it would be *Not an inch. No surrender. This we will maintain. Civil and religious liberty for all.* Men were dragging or carrying last-minute burdens of broken wooden pallets, crushed cardboard boxes, and smashed planks as others would be doing in many Loyalist enclaves all over Ulster. When lit tonight, the bonfires would rave and burn and try to singe the sky while, behaving like a bunch of hooligans, men, women, and children would dance in the flames' light, barely able to wait for the parades of tomorrow, July the Twelfth.

For the second time that day, Doctor Fingal O'Reilly was deeply concerned, and this time it was for the Ulster he loved.

7

A Formidable Opposition

Jack Mills rolled down the window on the passenger seat of Barry's Hillman Imp and took a deep breath. "Smells like the country," he said.

Barry inhaled air heavy with the scent of cut and drying hay.

"We'll be home in five minutes. Funny how I haven't lived here in sixteen years, since you and I started at Campbell College, and yet I still think of it as home." Jack looked out the window at rolling green fields. "I suppose I always will." He paused. "We've made good time."

And they had. The multilane M2 highway that had been opened three years ago had got them out of Belfast without having to go through the districts where local Orange lodges and their bands would be parading. But while they may have bypassed the marching, the stink of the previous night's bonfires as they passed the Shankill District had still hung in the air like methane gas over a swamp.

"Thank God there were no reports on the nine o'clock news of any trouble last night," said Barry. "I just hope the whole day passes without any violence."

"There'll be no ructions here," said Jack. "Cullybackey is nearly ninety percent Protestant. Let's pray it stays quiet everywhere else. With Dad being such a staunch Loyalist, I don't need him up on his high horse because things are going wrong in other parts of Ulster."

The two friends exchanged a glance. No words were spoken, but Barry knew the truth of what Jack had said. He indicated for a turn and swung onto the rutted lane leading to the Mills's dairy farm. He needed no direction. He'd been visiting here since he and Jack had become friends in 1953. He stopped at the gate and Jack hopped out, opened it so Barry could drive through, then closed it again and re-joined Barry.

"Just like old times, hey bye. You can take the bye out of the country, but you'll never stop him closing gates. I didn't do it once when I was a kid, and every last beast got out. Dad was livid. I ate my meals standing up for a few days after. Never again. Thanks, Barry, for coming. I hope it's going to help."

"Me too." Barry parked in front of the two-storey, redbrick, slate-roofed early Victorian building. A central front door, painted the colour of a chestnut, was flanked on each side by wide sash windows. He'd been coming to this house for fifteen years and he didn't like to think what Jack was going to do if his father refused to accept Helen as Jack's fian-cée. "We're here. Good luck, mate." Barry turned the engine off and got out into a clear sunny day. There was no difficulty recognising the place for what it was even if the herd of red-and-white Ayrshires had been out at pasture. Cow clap has its own nose-tingling smell. A series of clangs came from the byre at the back of the house. The clangs were accompa-nied by the strains of "The Boxer" sung by Simon and Garfunkel.

"That'll be Dad," Jack said. "Working on some piece of machinery. He keeps his transistor going for company." He laughed. "I think the old man's getting a bit deaf. That's why he keeps the volume up. Good thing he lives on a hundred acres. Let's go in and see Mum first."

Barry heard the relief in his friend's voice.

The front door opened. "Son. Barry. How are you both? Come on in."

Jack enfolded his pinafore-wearing mother in a hug. "I'm grand, Mum, and all the better for seeing you." He was a good head taller than Denise Mills but had her fair hair and blue eyes.

"And I'm very well thanks, Denise. Good to see you again." Barry followed mother and son along a spacious parquet-floored hall from which doors opened to the flanking dining room and lounge and into the red-tile-floored kitchen, which, with its attached scullery, occupied the ground floor of the rest of the house. A mullioned window with red-checked gingham curtains gave a view over the farmyard. He noticed four gutted brown trout on a plate beside the stovetop where fresh gar-den peas waited in one water-filled saucepan and shiny new potatoes still in their skins were being boiled in another. The fish would have been caught in the nearby River Maine, which harboured both trout and salmon. Jack's dad, Morris Mills, was a member of the Maine Angling Club and had often taken Barry to cast a fly on its more interesting runs. "Morris still fishing, I see?"

"Aye. He was out early this morning. Caught his limit. He was quare chuffed."

"Good for him," Barry said, and thought, Good for Jack. His dad should be in an expansive mood.

"I have the kettle on. Would anybody like a wee cup of tea? Morris said he had to fix one of the milking machines and he might be a wee bit late, hey. He knows we're going to eat about one."

"That would be great, Mum. Have a pew, Barry. Make yourself at home."

Barry sat at the kitchen table, opposite Jack. It was already set for lunch. The room was full of the scent of freshly baked bread. Four loaves covered by a tea towel were cooling on a rack. Six large cured hams, three strings of onions, and cloves of garlic hung from a beam overhead. A black cast-iron range bulked large against one wall and, being midsummer, was not lit.

"Here y'are, byes." Denise Mills's Antrim accent was clear as she set cups of tea in front of them. "Milk and sugar's on the table." She busied herself at the gas stove. "I'll get the trout under the grill now. Peas on a bit later." As she worked, she asked, "So, what have you been up to, the pair of you?"

Jack said, "They keep me pretty busy at work, but I got off last weekend. Spent it with Barry and Sue. On Saturday night I took Helen—" He hesitated.

Barry guessed his friend was waiting to see how his mother would react, but Denise Mills said nothing.

"—and the four of us went to a talent contest at the Sporting Club. Great *craic*. The local councillor's wife, Mrs. Bishop, won. She's a marvellous voice."

"Sounds like fun. And, Barry, how's that lovely Sue of yours?"

"She's glowing. We're not shouting it from the rooftops yet, but Sue's going to have our first in January."

Carrying her own cup, Jack's mother sat at the table. "Congratulations to you both. That's wonderful news."

"It is. Thank you. We're both very excited."

Denise Mills sipped and put her teacup down. "I'm sure your folks and Sue's are excited too."

"Mine certainly are. It'll be their first grandchild. Sue hasn't told hers yet. She's a bit superstitious."

Denise smiled. "Aye. Your Sue's from Broughshane. That's only half a dozen miles from here. Us country folk are"—she paused to consider her words—"we're cautious, but I'm sure she'll be fine, and they say a baby brings its own welcome." Her look at Jack was wistful.

He swallowed. Looked down. Pursed his lips. Looked up. Inhaled and said, "Mum, I'm glad Dad's not here yet. I've—I've, that is . . ."

"Asked Helen to marry you and she's said yes?"

Jack's mouth opened and he sat back in his chair. "How—how did you know?"

She chuckled. "You, my son, have had more girlfriends than a hedgehog has fleas. Until Helen Hewitt. It's nearly three years now. And I've seen the way you look at each other, bye."

"Sue and I are delighted," Barry said, "and so is Helen's dad."

She sighed. "Jack, you know fine well that we're Presbyterians and Helen's a Roman Catholic?" She paused.

Barry held his breath, waiting for what would come next.

"But I for one won't hold that against the pair of you. If Helen's dad approves, then so do I. God bless you and Helen both." She laughed. "And we'll be the only family in Cullybackey with two doctors in it, hey."

Jack rose, bent, and kissed the top of his mother's head. "Thanks, Mum. Thanks a million."

"We love you, Jack, and if Helen makes you happy—"

"She does, Mum. She really does."

"Then that makes me happy too." She stood and pecked his cheek. "Now," she said, rising, "time to turn the trout. I'll get the peas on in a couple of minutes, Jack. The clanging out there's stopped, so give Dad a shout out the scullery door. He's always in good form after lunch. I'll help you to break the news. He was happy after his stint on the river. Looking forward to seeing you and Barry. I think we can talk him round."

Barry heard the crackling sounds as she turned each of the fish to grill the other side. He knew he was grinning like a moon calf. It looked as if Jack were halfway home.

Jack opened the scullery door. "Dad. Lunch."

"Get Back" by the Beatles was cut off in mid-song.

Barry saw the scullery door open and Morris Mills strode into the kitchen. He must have left his boots at the door. No man would be popular if he trod cow clap into a house. "Jack. Barry." His voice was steady, but he had no smile on his square face.

"Dad."

"Morris."

He lifted off a tweed duncher to hang on a peg, revealing close-cut dark hair over brown eyes. His ruddy, lined cheeks were the trademarks of the Ulster farmer exposed for years to the elements. "Just need to wash my hands." He went to the sink and did so. "How's lunch coming along, Denise?"

"Ready in about three minutes."

"So, seeing it's Saturday and our son's home with his best friend, sherry for you, dear, and I'm sure you boys could face a beer. I've some bottles of Blue Bass. I'll have time to pour."

"Thank you," Barry said.

Jack nodded.

As Denise finished cooking lunch, Morris poured the drinks. He gave glasses of Bass to the lads, put her sherry at her place at the table, and sat at what would be his usual seat. He lifted his own glass and said, "Cheers."

The toast was returned.

Barry waited for the man to say something, but he refused to look at anything but his beer.

Denise said, "Did you get the machine fixed, dear?"

"Not quite."

Antrim men were not renowned for being loquacious, but Barry was starting to find Morris Mills's taciturnity unsettling. He had to stop himself from letting the doctor in him ask if something was wrong. Because he was afraid the answer would be: "Aye there is, bye. Very, very wrong."

Jack said, "You'd a good day on the river, Mum says."

"Aye."

Denise started to set steaming plates of grilled trout, new potatoes, and peas in front of both Barry and Jack. "Help yourself to butter, Barry. Jack, pass the salt and pepper over to Barry."

Barry busied himself splitting the new potatoes and putting dabs of butter between the halves while Denise served herself and her husband.

She said, "You were very good to catch four trout, dear. One each for us."

"And they're very tasty," Barry said, trying to keep the conversation going. "What did you take them on?"

"Dry fly. Royal Coachman." There was little enthusiasm in the man's voice.

Barry smiled. "I remember you showing me how to tie that one, and a humpy sedge, and a hopper orange."

"Aye. Orange." Morris Mills set down his knife and fork. "And bloody green. Orange and bloody green. I switched over to the one o'clock news. Half the province has gone mad. A bunch of Fenians started throwing bottles at an Orange parade in Belfast and now there's a full-blown riot the police can't control."

Barry realised he'd inadvertently used one word, "orange," that had caused what was wrong to explode from Jack's father, and now he was in full cry.

"Dungiven and Londonderry are at it. Same thing. Nationalists fighting with Loyalists. Cars burning. Houses on fire. It would break your bloody heart." He struck the tablecloth with his outstretched index finger to emphasize his points. "Can the bloody Romans not understand that Ulster is a part of the United Kingdom of Great Britain and Northern Ireland?"

Barry looked at Jack. The poor man's face had crumpled. Barry reckoned that his friend, who, like Barry himself, had been trained to hide his feelings, was close to tears. Any hope of Jack's father today accepting his son's engagement to Helen Hewitt was gone and, Barry wondered, would there be any chance ever of his doing so in the future?

"And if they don't like it," Morris made a fist this time and pounded the table, "there's America or Canada or the Republic of Ireland they can bloody well go to. I'd like to—"

The sound of a phone ringing in the hall stopped Morris. They all, as if in a trance, listened to it ringing. Denise got up slowly from her chair and began to walk to the hall. She passed behind Jack and as she did so, rested a hand lightly on his shoulder and then continued walking.

The phone stopped ringing and Denise's voice came from the hallway. "Jack, it's the hospital. You're needed back in Belfast."

8

We Are All on Our Last Cruise

"Can you not hear the phone, Fingal? I'll go." Kitty rose from the bog oak dining table where the wreckage of Sunday breakfast still remained at nine thirty.

"Sorry, Kitty." And he was, but not only for inconveniencing his wife. He understood his hearing was deteriorating, damn it, but he regretted it and was trying hard not to accept the onset of the aging process.

Kitty came back. "Councillor Bishop on the phone. He'd like to talk to you."

"Someone sick?" O'Reilly set his tea aside and put down the *Sunday Telegraph,* in which he had been reading its front-page story about the July the Twelfth's riots yesterday.

"No, it's a social matter, he says."

"All right." O'Reilly rose, left the dining room, and picked up the hall phone. "Yes, Bertie?"

"That you, Doctor?"

"It is. What can I do for you?"

"I know it's very short notice and all, but me and Flo was wondering if you and Mrs. O'Reilly would consider dropping in for a drink before lunch? It's not entirely social. We've a couple of quick medical questions to ask too, and you know I'm in the middle of a big contract. I can't seem to find time, over the next week or two, to sit in your surgery waiting room."

"Hang on." O'Reilly put his hand over the mouthpiece and yelled, "Bertie and Flo want us to come for a drink before our lunch."

"Fine by me. Kinky left all the stuff to heat up for tonight's dinner with our Trinity friends."

O'Reilly removed his muting hand and spoke into the mouthpiece. "Yes, we'd like that, Bertie. What time?"

"Twelve?"

"Great. See you then." O'Reilly heard the line go dead and replaced the receiver. He wondered what questions he might be asked, shrugged, and was about to rejoin Kitty when the phone rang again. "Hello. O'Reilly."

"Fingal. Charlie."

O'Reilly flinched. Was there bad news about Dapper?

"I'm just taking a break. I've been here all night. So's Cromie. It's bedlam."

O'Reilly frowned. What was going on?

"I'm calling to let you know we'll not be able to make it for dinner. It's all hands on deck. I'm sure you know about the rioting that started yesterday when Catholics began chucking bottles at an Orange parade coming from Peter's Hill. What you may not know is that Belfast's been going daft ever since. Houses and cars burned. You can smell the stink of smoke off the patients' clothes. People driven out of their homes. Skull fractures and brain damage—that's my end; broken bones—that's Cromie's. I saw young Jack Mills. He was sewing people up in the casualty waiting room. God alone knows when the fighting's going to stop. They're at it in Derry and Dungiven too."

Charlie's description brought home to O'Reilly with stark vividness what the printed word could only hint. "I've just been reading the paper but I'd no idea—" He paused. "Don't worry about tonight. Get some rest. Something to eat."

"We will, Fingal. Sorry again about letting you and Kitty down."

"Think nothing of it. We'll do it some other time."

"By the way, I had a look at your bloke Frew between cases. He's doing very well for forty-eight hours postop. If his friend wants to visit it should be fine. And I'll keep you posted anyway."

"Thanks, Charlie, and—"

"Hang on—"

Fingal waited.

"That was John Wilson. We've admitted a compound skull fracture. Gotta go."

The phone went dead. Fingal replaced the receiver. He shook his head.

He didn't need to imagine the unremitting stress his colleagues were under. He'd lived through the same thing after the second battle of Narvik in 1940 when HMS *Warspite* became hospital ship for most of the casualties, British and German. He still remembered a young German sailor with a bullet in his belly calling for his *mutti, mutti, du liebe Gott*—Mummy, for the love of God. And the remark of the sick-berth attendant who shortly after gave the man an anaesthetic. "I don't think much of the master race. 'Cepting they talk funny, they're not much different from us, are they, sir?"

Why the hell couldn't the local extremists feel the same way—for the love of God? He sighed. They'd buried the young German at sea on the seventh postop day. Surgery was never clear cut, but at least Dapper seemed to be doing well. O'Reilly decided that he and Kitty would pop in and let Donal know after they'd seen the Bishops.

"Come in, Doctor and Mrs. O'Reilly." Bertie Bishop led the way along a thickly carpeted hall where, behind oval glass frames, dried flowers adorned the walls along with a venerable aneroid barometer. Bertie's Orange sash, which usually hung on a coat stand, was noticeable by its absence. "I've just been going over some business with Donal. I've asked him to join us."

"Fine. I've some news for him. It'll save me a drive later."

They entered the spacious lounge/dining room with its view through a picture window out over an extensive lawn to the waters of Belfast Lough. A dining table in front of the window was covered in a red velvet cloth with gold tassels. A single brass flowerpot-holder squatted empty in the centre.

The carpet was fitted and bore a pattern of orange circles inside purple diamonds. Those were the colours of the Orange Order.

Flo's silver cup was front and centre on the mantel, as she'd promised the audience it would be. O'Reilly wondered where she'd put her stuffed cat.

Flo greeted them from an armchair at one end of a semicircle of seating arranged to face the fireplace. Donal rose from a straight-backed chair saying, "How's about youse, Doctor, Mrs. O'Reilly?"

"We're both fine, Donal," O'Reilly said. "And you're well?"

"Fit as a flea."

Before taking his seat, O'Reilly said, "We've known each other since 1946. You, Bertie Bishop, I must say, have mellowed considerably. Don't you think perhaps it's time we dropped the Doctor and Mrs.?" He offered a hand to Bertie. "It's Fingal and Kitty. Same to you, Donal."

Bertie accepted the shake. "Thank you very much, Doc—Fingal, that's very decent, but I think mebbe just in our homes, like. Ballybucklebo's a very traditional wee place. As our town's senior doctor, you've a position til uphold, so you have."

"Bertie's right," Donal said.

But from the bucktoothed grin on his face, O'Reilly could tell Donal was pleased to be included as an equal friend. O'Reilly understood. "If you both wish."

"My Bertie's right—" Flo hesitated before saying, "Fingal, and please sit down."

O'Reilly did, and noticed the stuffed cat sitting on a low table at his end of the sofa. By God, it was very lifelike. He'd nearly stroked it.

Bertie must have noticed. "That there's Snooks. I bought it for a bit of a gag for Flo on her birthday when we was on our holidays in Newcastle ten years ago."

"And we've had great *craic,*" Flo said, "when our guests try til pet her." She chuckled.

Bertie said, "Now, I asked youse round for a drink. Kitty?"

"It's early for gin. Would you have a glass of white wine?"

Flo rose. "We do. In the fridge, and I've a few nibblers in the kitchen. I'll fetch it and them through. Bertie, you see til Doc—'scuse me, see til Fingal." She left.

"Would you have a wee Jameson, Bertie?"

"Aye, certainly. And Donal?"

"Bottle of stout, please."

Bertie crossed to a sideboard and poured from a Waterford decanter into a cut-glass tumbler.

"Easy, Bertie," O'Reilly said. "That's plenty."

"Right. Flo always says I've a heavy hand with the hard stuff. I'll have a bottle of stout myself." He poured Guinness from two bottles into two tumblers, carried the drinks over, and gave O'Reilly his whiskey and Donal his Guinness.

Flo appeared, pushing a tea trolley. "Smith's potato crisps, chicken liver pâté on wheaten bread, mushroom puffs, sausage rolls, cheese straws, and them's all Kinky's recipes, except the crisps. Please help yourselves." She handed Kitty her wine, lifted a glass of what looked like C & C brown lemonade, and took her seat.

"Cheers," Bertie said, "and thank youse for coming."

The toast was returned.

"Our pleasure," Kitty said, "and, Flo, even though we've been here before, I'll say it again. You have a lovely home."

"Thank you."

"And it's all Flo's doing. Now I built it, sure isn't that my trade? But Flo furnished it."

O'Reilly heard the pride and the love in the man's voice. "Kitty's right, Flo, and you've every right to be proud of her, Bertie."

"Thanks, Fingal."

There was a comfortable silence in the room as they sipped their drinks together.

"So, Bertie, you said you had some medical questions for me?"

"Aye. Business before pleasure. Quite right. It was yesterday got me thinking about it. Our local Orange lodge and the Ballybucklebo Highlanders pipe band marched in Comber. We had great fun. Just a day out. The speeches didn't have no pope-bashing, just talk about fellowship and Ulster being part of the UK. There was a temperance lodge there, and as usual four or five of their members got stocious."

"Don't they always?" said Donal, who was pipe major of the Bally-bucklebo Highlanders. "It wouldn't be the Twelfth if a wheen of folks didn't get legless."

O'Reilly smiled and Kitty chuckled. She too must have found the thought funny, of a bunch of men pledged to abstaining from alcohol getting drunk. O'Reilly wondered where this was leading, but Bertie was a man who rarely beat about the bush.

"I thought nothing of it until I got home and switched on the nine o'clock news. Boys-a-boys, but what went on, and is still going on, with them there riots is desperate, so it is."

"I know," O'Reilly said. "I just hope it ends soon." He sipped his whiskey.

"I'm not so sure it will, and between the jigs and the reels of it—" Here we go. "—you mind when I made up my will with your brother, Fingal?"

"I do."

"And I said after Donal buys a quarter share of my company I'd use some of that money til take Flo on a world cruise."

Kitty said, "What a lovely idea. Lucky you, Flo."

"Lucky me too," said Donal. "Dead jammy. Here's me a partner. I still can't thank Bertie and Flo enough."

"But you are going to, just like I told you this morning," Bertie said with a grin.

O'Reilly wondered what that could mean, but presumably all would soon be revealed. He saw the looks Bertie and Flo exchanged. He sighed and remembered what it had been like to be sixteen and in love. Catching Kitty's eye, he half turned his head and stared into her eyes. God, she was a beautiful woman.

"I'm a very lucky woman," Flo said.

Kitty, still holding O'Reilly's gaze, nodded and mouthed, "Me too."

O'Reilly tingled.

Bertie said, "The cruise is going for til cost seven thousand, two hundred pounds."

More than O'Reilly made in three years. He whistled.

"But my Flo's stuck with me through thick and thin. Gave up her family for me, so she did. Nursed me when I was sick. You're worth every penny of it, pet, til me. Anyroad, there's no pockets in a shroud."

Flo stood up, crossed the room, and planted a smacker on Bertie's dome. "Thank you, sweetheart." She stood beside him with one hand on his shoulder.

He smiled. "Her and me's been planning it for a few months and we'd meant til go next year, but what's going on at the moment here made me think. I hope til God it does blow over."

"We all do," Kitty said, "but we Irish are cursed with long memories. Some of the enmity goes back two or three hundred years."

"Aye. You're right, Kitty. And I'm not so sure it will blow over, neither. Me and Flo talked it over and we'd like til move our cruise up til this September if we can. I know some folks might say we're deserting oul' Ulster in her time of troubles, but we're getting old and tired and, well, we need a change of scene. And so, we're going, so we are." He inclined his head to Donal. "And that's where Donal comes in. Our company has the contract for a new block of fifteen flats on that piece of wasteland near what used til be Maggie Houston's cottage before she married Sonny Houston and moved into his place. It's a big job and I feel comfortable leaving Donal to look after the start of the building until we get back."

"I'm dead honoured, so I am," Donal said, "and a wee bit nervous. It's a big understatement, so it is."

Flo said, "Undertaking, Donal."

"Aye. Right enough."

"And my Bertie has every confidence in you."

Donal smiled, but weakly.

"You'll do fine, son, I know it. And it'll only be for about three months. The cruise starts in Southampton on the fifteenth of September and lasts for one hundred and three days."

O'Reilly sipped his whiskey. "And forgive me, Bertie, but I'm not quite sure what the medical question is?"

"Sorry, Fingal. It's about getting vaccinations. The company's sent us a list of what we need. Things like yellow fever and typhoid. And we'll need malaria pills. I'd like til know if you could get them and give them to us." He rummaged in his inside jacket pocket and handed O'Reilly a small brochure.

O'Reilly scanned the document. They would require immunisation against yellow fever, diphtheria, tetanus, and polio as a single injection, as well as typhoid. They were also advised to bring a supply of the anti-malarial chloroquine. "I'll need to have a word with the prof of tropical medicine at Queen's, but I'm pretty sure I can get the injections and the pills." O'Reilly snaffled a mushroom puff. "And we've got ten weeks, so if I get moving tomorrow, we've enough time. There is one thing. The aftereffects of some of them can be unpleasant."

Bertie looked up at Flo. "I think we should risk it."

"All right, dear."

"And I think you should sit down."

Flo did.

O'Reilly's mushroom puff vanished, and he helped himself to a sausage roll and two cheese straws. When they were finished, he said, "Flo, if Kinky ever leaves me, would you come and cook for us? The puffs, and rolls, and straws are just as good as hers."

Flo blushed and grinned. "Away off and chase yourself, Fingal. Nobody can cook like Kinky, but thank you for saying it."

"Fingal O'Reilly, there are more interesting things to discuss than your tummy, even if he is right about your cooking, Flo. I'd like to know where you'll be going?"

"Tell them, dear."

"We'll be docking in"—Bertie adopted his address-the-council-meeting stance and ticked the places off with his right index finger on his left—"New York, Rio de Janeiro, Cape Town, Durban, Mombasa, Bombay, Bali, Hong Kong, Kobe, Yokohama, Honolulu, then through the Panama Canal and home."

"Gosh," Kitty said, "that's quite the trip."

"Aye," said Bertie, looking doleful but with a twinkle in his eye. "It is a world cruise. I don't know where the hell we'll go next for an encore. Maybe the moon. Thon Apollo 11 is set til be launched on Wednesday."

The appearance of a sense of humour in the usually practical Bertie Bishop caught O'Reilly off guard. He snorted a drop or two of whiskey down his nose, choked, grabbed a hanky, and blew. "Jasus, Bertie, go easy on the jokes. You're getting so sharp you'll cut yourself."

Flo grinned. "See my Bertie? It's true, you know. Still waters do run deep."

Kitty caught O'Reilly's eye, glanced at her empty glass, but made a tiny shake of her head.

He nodded and finished the last of his whiskey. "Bertie. Flo. Thank you both very much, but it's time Kitty and I were moving on. I'll get on with your immunisation stuff tomorrow."

Kitty said, "And before you go on your tour, Flo, perhaps you and Bertie would come to us for a pre-lunch drink?"

"That would be great, so it would."

Kitty stood. "And Donal, if you can get a sitter, perhaps you and Julie would join us?"

"My God. Us? Mrs. Kitty, we'd be rightly honoured, so we would."

O'Reilly rose. "We'll arrange it sometime later this month. Just for drinks and nibbles. We'll have a decent sendoff for you in early September, but there is one more thing today. We were going to pop in at Dun Bwee, Donal, because I was talking to Mister Greer this morning about Dapper."

"I was dead pleased when you phoned on Friday to tell me he'd come through the operation." Anxiety crept into Donal's next question. "He's not had a setback nor nothing like that, has he?"

O'Reilly shook his head. "Not at all. Mister Greer says Dapper's getting better every day, and if you want to visit it's fine."

"Wheeker." Donal grinned. "I couldn't be more pleased if I'd won the football pools. And Dapper, he give me the keys to his car so I can drive myself up to visit while he's in and collect him when he's discharged."

"Terrific." O'Reilly rose. "Thanks again, Bertie and Flo. Good luck when you take over the company for a while, Donal. Come on, Mrs. O'Reilly." He made a sweeping bow. "Your chariot awaits. We'll see ourselves out."

He followed her out of the bungalow and held open the Rover's door.

As she sat, her skirt rode up and he was treated to a view of a well-shaped leg from her stiletto heel almost to the top of her grey-nylon-covered thigh.

His breath caught in his throat. Was it having been in the company of the still-in-love-after-so-many-years Bishops? Was it the exchanged looks with Kitty just now in the Bishops' living room and the frisson he'd felt? He closed the door once she was in, waved to Flo on the front step, climbed into the Rover, and drove off.

He was sorry his friends weren't able to come this evening. Damn the sectarian violence in Ulster. He accelerated on the Bangor to Belfast Road, leaving a cyclist wobbling in his wake. But in a very short time, they would have Number One all to themselves. He'd forget the bad news for today. If he remembered correctly, there was a bottle of Catalonian Cava in the fridge. He reached across, squeezed her thigh, and heard her laugh.

He drove into the lane, put the car in the garage, and took her hand as they walked across the back garden.

Kenny was effusive in his greeting, but O'Reilly said, "Settle down. I'll take you out later."

Kenny sighed and retreated to his kennel.

Once in the kitchen he kissed Kitty. "I was thinking—"

She snuggled against him. "I know what you were thinking."

He laughed. "And you'd be absolutely right." He went to a cupboard and took out two champagne flutes.

Kitty's right eyebrow rose, and she smiled.

"But I did have something else in mind too."

"Oh?" The smile faded.

"It was what you said after Bertie told us about their world cruise. 'What a lovely idea,' you said. 'Lucky you, Flo.' That got me thinking. Actually, I've been thinking about it more since you dropped that guide in theatre on Friday—"

"What does that have to do with anything?" Her response was swift and defensive.

"Nothing really, pet. We've talked about this before—" He looked into her eyes and wondered if, after all, this was the best time to bring it up, but decided to plough on. "I believe it's about time you really thought about going part time."

She stepped back and cocked her head to one side, nodded, went to the fridge, and lifted out the bottle of Cava. She handed it to him. "I'm willing to concede it's something we should discuss—and not because of what happened in surgery. But, if you'd be kind enough to open this, I think it's something we might discuss later." Placing both hands at the back of his neck, she tilted his head down until their lips met. "Much later."

9

To Win or Lose It All

"At zero two fifty-six Greenwich Mean Time this morning, July 21, 1969, an historic date, Commander Neil Armstrong set foot on the lunar surface in the Sea of Tranquility." The BBC's technical advisor, James Burke, spoke from the Lime Grove Studios' Apollo 11 set in London. Beside him, seated, were Cliff Michelmore, the presenter, and astronomer Patrick Moore.

Burke was calm as he continued. "His first words, which we have received and will now let you hear, were—" The astronaut's transmitted words were distorted but audible. "That's one small step for man, one giant leap for mankind."

Barry and Sue sat motionless on the couch in their cottage watching the black-and-white images on their television. Tigger, their tabby, was curled up on Sue's lap, but Max, on this fine summer evening, was in his kennel in the back garden. They'd sat up late to watch.

"I never thought they'd do it," Barry said. "This is very exciting."

"Amazing."

Together they watched Armstrong move about on the lunar surface, collecting rock samples. Sue lifted Tigger and set the cat on the carpet. "All very interesting, but I gotta go."

Barry smiled at his wife's departing back. Urinary frequency was another of the less-pleasant aspects of pregnancy. He turned back to the TV.

Minutes later, lunar module pilot Edwin "Buzz" Aldrin Jr. joined Commander Armstrong. The pictures were grainy, but Barry had no difficulty making out the two astronauts in their bulky space suits. They were moving in two-footed kangaroo hops, puffs of lunar dust disturbed with each step.

"Barry." Sue's voice was tremulous.

He spun in his seat.

Sue stood in the doorway. Tears streamed down her cheeks. "Barry. I'm bleeding."

Barry was on his feet at once, moved to her, held her. Bloody hell. Could she be losing their baby? Not after all their waiting and hoping, and the final elation once they knew Sue had conceived. Damn it, no. Take a grip, Laverty. It could be other things too, not all as serious. Calm down. You're a doctor, so behave like one and comfort your wife.

"Come and sit down." He led her to the couch. He knew bleeding in pregnancy could be serious. "Try not to be scared, darling." It was twelve-and-a-half weeks since Sue's last period. Think, man.

"What's happening to me, Barry? Am I going to lose it?"

He sat beside her and took her hand in both of his. "It may be all right. About one in four women have a little bleeding early in pregnancy. It may not be anything serious." Which was not entirely true. Half of those who did, lost the pregnancy. But now was not the time to make Sue any more unhappy and scared than she already was.

Sue lifted her head. "Honestly?"

"Honestly."

Another sob. "Barry, we've tried so hard for this baby. I couldn't bear to lose it. Not now. We've only known for a couple of weeks and we were so happy."

I know, he thought. And I've grown from initial uncertainty about becoming a father to eager anticipation of having a family. Sue wasn't the only one worried sick. But for her sake he knew he mustn't show it. As a doctor he'd to decide what was the best thing to do medically and now he hadn't the slightest doubt what that was. He sat back, took Sue's face between his hands, and looked into her shining eyes. "Pet, I can't promise you it's going to be all right, but I'm sure the odds are in your favour. What colour was the blood?"

"Bright red."

So it was fresh.

"How much was there?"

"Lots. A big stain about the size of a soup plate on my knickers. I've changed them and put a pad on."

It was a well-known adage that a little blood goes a long way. Sue hadn't lost much.

"That's not a lot. Honestly. Any cramps?"

She shook her head.

"Good. Your womb isn't contracting."

"That is good, isn't it?"

He heard the pleading in her voice. "Yes. It is."

Her indrawing of breath was jerky. "So, what should we do? Call Doctor Harley?"

Barry shook his head. "I want you seen at once, and the Ulster Hospital where you had your laparoscopy is much closer. I'm taking you up there right now. Come on. We'll grab a towel for you to sit on in the car and get going." He helped her to her feet and glanced at the television.

History was being made but suddenly he couldn't care less about a man walking on the moon. Here, on Earth, an ordinary man and woman were trying to do a most natural thing, have a baby, and had run into what could be a serious snag.

The TV commentator was going on about when the command module would lift off the moon, but Barry was in a rush. He didn't even take time to switch off the TV.

Barry drove along the road leading uphill to the front of the Ulster Hospital in Dundonald. The sky was cloudless and the moon, which had been a waxing crescent, had set. The hospital ward blocks were dim, patients should be sleeping, but the emergency entrance and the sign saying EMERGENCY were well lit.

Little had been said on the fifteen-minute drive over the Ballybucklebo Hills. He'd asked Sue if she thought she was still bleeding and had been told she didn't think so.

He parked in the emergency spot outside the front doors. "Wait here.

I'll only be a minute. I'm going to get you a wheelchair." He trotted through the double front doors and went to the reception desk, where a young, blond, bespectacled woman asked, "Can I help you?"

"I'm Doctor Laverty. My wife may be threatening to abort." He used the proper medical term but knew he would never use it when speaking to Sue. She would feel guilty enough without thinking she was being accused of causing the loss. "She's in the car outside. I need a wheelchair."

"I'll get an orderly, sir. He'll bring your wife into casualty while you park your car in the visitors' lot." She picked up a phone, spoke into it, then replaced the receiver. "He's on his way. Go you back to your wife, sir. She'll be worried all alone, but a quick question first. Has she ever been a patient here before?"

Barry gave her the details of Sue's admission for the laparoscopy earlier in the year.

"I'll get her chart from medical records."

"Thank you, miss. Thank you very much." Barry hurried back to the car. "They're sending an orderly, Sue. I've to park the car once he's taken you inside, but I won't be long."

"Please don't be. I'm scared and I need you, Barry. I really do."

And Barry Laverty, trying to hide his desperate concern for his wife and unborn child, could find no words of comfort.

"Hello again, Doctor Laverty." The receptionist smiled. "First door on your left. I spoke to the casualty houseman and she said, you being a doctor and all, she'd just make sure your wife's not in shock and then send for the gynae senior registrar to come."

"Thank you." The last time he'd been in a casualty department was when he'd done a three-month stint as a houseman at the Royal Victoria in Belfast. Here, as it had been there, all was bustle and noise. Moans coming from a cubicle told of someone in pain. Two nurses hurried by pushing a stretcher-trolley bearing an older man wearing oxygen spectacles, an intravenous line in his left arm. In a small room, four patients sat waiting their turns to be seen. A student nurse stood beside one and held a kidney dish so he could throw up. The smell of acrid vomit was all-pervasive. This was a far cry from the relative tranquility of general practice. There was no sign of Sue in the waiting area. He hoped to God she had not been kept waiting long.

The sister there, sitting behind a low desk, asked, "May I help you, sir?"

Her voice startled him. "I'm, uh, that is, you have my wife, Mrs. Laverty."

"We do, Doctor Laverty. She's in there." Sister indicated curtains closed around a cubicle. "Doctor Lamki is on his way to see her."

Barry thanked her, headed to the cubicle, and pulled back the curtains. Sue, her copper plait coming undone, dressed in a blue hospital gown, lay on a stretcher-trolley, propped up on pillows. "I'm very glad to see you." She managed a small smile.

He stepped inside the cocoon of the cubicle and closed the curtains behind him. Seeing her smile seemed to make the bustle outside fade. "The young houseman took a quick look. She doesn't think I'm bleeding much. No fever. Pulse and blood pressure all normal. Perhaps it's not serious after all?"

He knew she was seeking reassurance.

"Probably not, pet." He dropped a kiss on her head, sat on a chair beside the head of her trolley, and took her warm hand in his. "We'll find out for sure soon enough. Doctor Harith Lamki's on his way." Barry, happy to keep the conversation away from Sue's condition, smiled. "I've met him several times. He's a good head and his reputation as a clinician is outstanding. He came here to train as an obstetrician and gynaecologist from what had been Zanzibar."

Sue nodded. "It united with Tanganyika in 1964 to become Tanzania."

"Tick VG in geography, Miss Nolan," he said, alluding to the letters a teacher would put on a piece of homework. Still the schoolmistress. "A couple of years ago I came up to Ulster to see a patient and ran into Harith. We went for coffee. I'd been reading this book, *African Bush Adventures* by J. A. Hunter, and was intrigued by the story of a famous Zanzibari ivory and slave trader, Tippu Tib. Naturally I asked Harith if he knew of him. He laughed. 'Yes,' he said, 'he was my great-great-grandfather.'"

"No." Sue's eyes widened.

The curtains parted and a big, dark-haired man with coffee-coloured skin let himself in. "I heard that. Yes. He was. His real name was Muhammad bin Hamad. His nickname was meant to imitate the sound of a musket being cocked." He nodded at Barry and said to Sue, "I'm Harith. May I call you Sue?" His voice was rich, deep, and unaccented.

"Please do."

"And, Barry. Good to see you again." He offered a hand, which Barry shook before Harith lifted Sue's chart from a clipboard hanging on the rail at the foot of the bed. "So, Sue. Please tell me what's happened."

Sue glanced at Barry, who nodded encouragement. "Barry and I have been trying to get pregnant for nearly two years. We were seeing Graham Harley, but all our tests were normal, then a bit more than two weeks ago Graham said my pregnancy test was positive. My last period was April twenty-fourth." She glanced at Barry. "We were so pleased." Her voice cracked when she said, "I started to bleed about half an hour ago, so Barry brought me straight here. I hope you can do something, Harith. I want this baby." Her voice rose in pitch. "Please."

Barry felt as if a vise were squeezing his heart.

Harith's tones were warm. Reassuring. "I'll try, but I need to know a bit more about you."

He took a very thorough history, made notes, then said, "It sounds as if you are having what we call a threatened miscarriage, but I have to exclude some other conditions, so I'd like to feel your tummy, then do a speculum examination." He rose and used a wall-mounted call button to summon a nurse. "Nurse will help me push the trolley, Sue. I know it's undignified, but I'll have to put you in the stirrups in the gynae examining room."

"That's all right."

A nurse appeared. "Hello, Mrs. Laverty." She bent and unlocked the trolley's wheel brakes. "Doctor Lamki and me's going til take you for a wee ride."

Barry did not want to intrude while Harith worked, so said, "I'll be here when you get back, Sue."

Harith and the nurse left, wheeling Sue.

Barry took a deep breath. He knew what Harith was looking for. Bleeding in early pregnancy could be associated with several conditions. The worst was an ectopic pregnancy, where the embryo implanted in a Fallopian tube, although Sue would have complained about pain. It was a potentially lethal condition, required surgical removal, and Sue would lose one Fallopian tube, reducing her chances of subsequent conception. Barry did not want to hear that diagnosis.

Inspecting her perineum and passing a speculum would allow Harith to see if the bleeding was from haemorrhoids or from a lesion like a cervical polyp and completely unrelated to the pregnancy. While both were unpleasant, neither put the pregnancy at risk.

If Sue's bleeding were coming through the cervix of her uterus it would be related to her pregnancy, and that was a cause for concern. Sometimes the gestational sac could be seen in the vagina. That was referred to as a complete abortion. Little more could be done but remove the sac. More often what doctors called the products of conception—early placenta, membranes, and the tiny foetus—might be stuck in the cervical canal. Barry dropped his elbows to his knees and put his head in his hands, suddenly feeling exhausted. That would be an incomplete but inevitable abortion. Once again, the pregnancy was doomed. Cervical dilation and uterine curettage were needed to remove the products, an impersonal term for hopes destroyed. Having to help Sue cope with the loss would not be easy. Barry too would be bitterly disappointed, but he knew he must be ready to support her with his love and compassion.

In most cases like Sue's, the cervix would be closed and only a trickle of blood escaping. That condition was known as threatened abortion, and the pregnancy was lost in only half those cases. But for all women, the waiting and uncertainty was very hard to bear. Barry pursed his lips. Inhaled. It wasn't going to be easy for him either. He heard footsteps approaching, and the curtains opened. Harith walked in.

Barry stood as the nurse parked Sue's trolley, bent down to lock the wheel brakes, then helped make Sue comfortable, and left.

"I'm pleased to tell you both that while I know it's very worrying and I do not mean to belittle things, Sue, you are having a threatened miscarriage and it is very probable that it will settle down and in about twenty-eight more weeks you'll be a mother. No one can promise you that, but we do know that at least seventy percent of women like you go on to have a perfectly healthy baby."

Sue said, "That means I'm more likely to continue than miscarry, doesn't it?"

Harith smiled. "Yes, it does. And I'm going to try to help you improve those odds. I'm going to admit you to the gynae ward, do some blood tests at once, and keep you on strict bedrest until the bleeding has stopped for seven days. I'm going to give you a sedative, phenobarbitone thirty milligrams twice a day. It will make you less anxious and may prevent your uterus from contracting. Your first dose will be ready as soon as you get to your room, and you'll be asleep in about twenty minutes."

"Thank you."

"Have you any questions for me?"

"Not just now, Harith," Sue said. "I'm sure I will have when I've collected myself, but I think now I'd like to rest." She swallowed and a tear trickled.

Barry stepped beside her and put a hand on her forehead, pushing a piece of coppery hair out of her eyes. "You and the baby are going to be all right. I just know it." He put force in his words even though he knew nobody could promise Sue that.

She clasped his hand and said, "Thank you, Barry. Thank you."

"If you'll excuse me," Harith said, "I'll go and get things arranged, and Barry, I'll keep in touch while Sue's in here."

"Thanks for everything," Barry said.

Harith smiled, shrugged, and left.

Barry bent and hugged Sue to him. He felt her tremble. "I love you, darling," he said, "and it will be all right. It will be."

Sue looked Barry in the eyes. "I hope so. I really do hope so. And I love you too."

Barry heard a discreet cough and turned to see the orderly who had brought Sue in from the car. He was accompanied by the nurse, who said, "We're going to take you to the ward now, Mrs. Laverty."

Barry straightened and stepped back from the trolley. "Try not to worry, pet. Do you want me to stay? I can take your clothes home and come right back with the things you'll need in the morning."

"Say goodnight to Mrs. Laverty now please, sir," the nurse said. "You can pick up her clothes when you come in the morning. It's late enough as it is, and we want Mrs. Laverty to get to sleep as soon as possible."

"I understand." Barry moved forward, dropped a kiss on Sue's forehead. "Sleep well, pet. The staff here will take good care of you. I'll see you in the morning."

"Thank you, Barry." She blew him a kiss as the trolley was wheeled away. "I'll see you in the morning."

Barry watched her go and his heart went with her. He could only hope she'd be among those lucky 70 percent for whom the bleeding stopped, and the cherished pregnancy continued. Tonight, he would try not to bedevil himself with his knowledge about how the rates of prematurity, stillbirth, neonatal death, and foetal malformations were higher in those women. And he wasn't going to tell Sue. By God, nothing would pry that information out of him. But he would know. He would know every single day of these next twenty-eight weeks.

10

Shutteth up His Bowel

Barry collapsed into a dining room chair at Number One and breathed a sigh of relief. The morning's round of home visits had been busier than usual. A farmer with painful thrombosed haemorrhoids had to be admitted to hospital and the process had been time-consuming. Then he'd had to drive to the other end of the townland to see an elderly woman with a chest complaint, which, unusually for summertime, had turned out to be pneumonia. She had also been admitted.

O'Reilly was taking the morning's surgery. Barry heard the senior man's booming voice as he conducted another patient from the waiting room to the surgery. "So, young Stanley here had a sore throat three weeks ago that Doctor Emer treated with penicillin?"

"Yes, sir. He got better but look at his wee face. Don't you think it's swollen up? And he's been shivering. I'm dead worried about him."

"Right, I'd better get a good look at him." The surgery door closed.

O'Reilly should be finished soon, and he had agreed to take emergency call this afternoon so Barry could nip over to Dundonald to see Sue.

Kinky appeared at the dining room door. For a large woman, she was light on her feet, and he had not heard her coming. She was bearing a plate like an offering. "I know you're in a rush to get to the hospital, Doctor Laverty, but you'll waste away if you don't eat, so. I've made a proper lunch for Doctor O'Reilly, but he may be some time, so here." She set a plate of ham sandwiches cut in triangles in front of him. "Eat up however little much is in it."

"Bless you, Kinky." Barry picked one up and took a large bite. The cold ham had been roasted to perfection and he suddenly realized how hungry he was. His solitary breakfast of cold cereal and toast this morning had been five hours ago. Good old Kinky. The hall phone began ringing and Kinky, giving him an encouraging look, headed for the hall.

Barry started to tuck in to his sandwich but was soon interrupted by O'Reilly. "Kinky's had a call from Linda Bradshaw. You delivered her wee boy, Tony, seven months ago. She's worried. Very worried. He's been vomiting, seems to be having abdominal pain, and is passing mucus and blood. Kinky interrupted my consultation to ask me what to do."

"I'll go."

"I would but I've to finish with Alma and Stanley Kearney—I think he's got acute glomerulonephritis—then I've got three more patients down there, so I'll be a while finishing surgery. I know you want to see Sue. I'll look after any other emergencies this afternoon, but go and see Linda first, please. She lives on the same street as Dapper Frew. Discharged on Monday. Give me a couple of minutes to write him a sick line. If you'd pop in and give it to him when you've finished with Linda, I'd be grateful."

"I'll wrap your sandwiches, Doctor Laverty," Kinky said. "You can get a quick bite before you go to Dundonald, so, without having to come back here." She grabbed his plate and trotted off.

The nutty fragrance of Kinky's wheaten bread disappeared with her and Barry sighed as he looked at his watch. There were some advantages to being a doctor, he thought. If he missed visiting hours, his professional status would still guarantee he saw Sue this afternoon.

***

Barry parked the Imp on the street outside a three-storey set of neat postwar semi-detached houses. Six identical pairs of dwellings, their white window frames bright in the sun, sat tall on either side of the short street that ran off Station Road behind the Duck. Each had a steeply pitched slate roof under which sheltered a dormer window. This redbrick one was surrounded by a well-trimmed privet hedge, the same boundary that separated each of the properties' adjoining front gardens. He'd been here before. This was a street popular with young professionals and not one but two estate agents. Dapper Frew's house was two semis up on the opposite side.

Barry got out, shut the car door, and headed across the footpath, through a wrought-iron gate, and across the flagstones of a path dividing a small but well-cut lawn.

Two raps with a brass knocker brought Linda Bradshaw to the door. He could hear a baby crying. "Thank God you're here, Doctor." Linda was twenty-six, married to an accountant. Her shoulder-length dark hair was untidy, and the deep brown eyes above her snub nose looked moist and troubled. "Poor wee Tony's in a state and I can't comfort him." She stepped aside. "Come on in."

Barry followed her into her lounge, where a pale-faced little boy lay restlessly in a spacious wheeled pram. His breathing was shallow, and he kicked and tumbled about. Barry knew these involuntary movements in babies were usually an attempt to get away from colicky pain. "So, tell me what happened, Linda."

She took a deep breath. "He was quite all right until about an hour ago, when he vomited. Twice. Then he filled his nappy, so I changed it. Then he started to howl and toss about. I just changed his nappy again there now just before I phoned. I kept it for you to see. I have it here." She lifted a cloth napkin and opened it.

Barry immediately noticed the lack of faeces but a mixture of mucus and blood, the characteristic "apple jelly" stool of the condition he already suspected from the other symptoms. "I just need to feel his tummy."

Tony had already kicked off his blanket. Barry lifted the little boy's nightdress and probed gently with his fingers, paying particular attention to the right side over where the ascending colon lay. As he expected, he found a small sausage-shaped swelling. The diagnosis was not in doubt. He replaced the clothing and pulled the blanket over the boy's body. The little lad was for the Royal Belfast Hospital for Sick Children.

"I'm afraid Tony has what is called an intussusception. I know that's a mouthful—"

"Sweet Jesus, it sounds awful." Her hand flew to her mouth. "Can you fix it?"

Barry shook his head. "Not me, but it certainly can be fixed. He'll need an operation. The bowel has somehow managed to slide up into itself, like a telescope. You know how the narrow bit slips into the wider bit?"

Linda nodded, her eyes wide and troubled.

"That's what's happened to Tony. It causes a blockage. The contents can't get moved along and it causes severe colic, the poor wee mite."

Linda picked up the child and pressed her lips to the top of his downy head. "An operation."

"Yes, but time is on our side. You said it started an hour ago."

"That's right."

"Which means we've got five hours. It seems that if the surgeons can get the bowel back to its normal self within six hours from the time of onset, the patients are fine."

"Honestly?"

"Honestly. Let me use your phone."

"In the hall."

It took only moments for Barry to get through to the children's hospital, be assured that an ambulance would be dispatched with all speed, and that the surgeon would be immediately available to confirm Barry's diagnosis and operate. He replaced the receiver and went back to where Linda was sitting in an armchair, holding little Tony and trying to comfort him.

"That's all set, Linda. The ambulance will be here as quickly as possible and take you and Tony to Belfast. I'll keep you company until it's here and I'll write a letter for you to give the doctors. Can you get hold of your husband? Let him know what's happening."

"I'll phone his office in Belfast."

"Let me hold Tony." Barry took the squirming little lad in his arms, stroked his back, made soft cooing noises while Tony whimpered and occasionally yelled. Barry'd always had sympathy for the parents of sick children. Now with the prospect of having his own family becoming a reality, he could really put himself in Linda's place and feel the kind of anguish she must be going through.

She came back into the room. "Richard says he'll drive there and meet me at the hospital. That way he can bring me home when the operation's over. Now, let me take Tony so you can write your letter, Doctor." She planted a kiss on Tony's forehead. "Hush. Hush. It won't be long, and the nice doctors will make you better, darling."

Barry stood on the footpath and watched the ambulance with Linda and Tony Bradshaw aboard drive off. The driver had his flashing lights and siren on. Good luck, little Tony.

Barry took some deep breaths and turned his face up toward the sun. He hated seeing people in pain, but especially small children. If he couldn't stop the pain, there was no way to tell them help was on the way. He headed out to the street and along the short distance to Dapper Frew's semi and through his small front garden.

The door of the house was already open and a smiling Dapper Frew, wearing carpet slippers, neatly creased trousers, and an open-necked shirt, stood in the doorway. He also sported a knitted brimless woollen hat. "How's about ye, Doctor?" He stood aside to let Barry enter. "First on your right, sir, and thanks for coming. I heard the ambulance and looked out and saw you through the lounge window heading this way. One of the Bradshaws?"

"Sorry, Dapper. Doctor-patient confidentiality."

"Aye. Right enough. Hope it's nothing too serious. Come on in."

Barry went through the door into a small lounge, well furnished with a modern three-piece lounge suite, some expensive-looking hard-backed chairs, and a table with narrow curved legs and a drop leaf on either side.

Dapper must have noticed Barry looking. "My folks were poor as church mice. That's why ever since I was wee I'd made up my mind to get a decent-paying job, and this one's been good to me. When I was starting out, my boss used to take me to estate sales. Taught me a bit about antiques. That there's a Pembroke table by Chippendale."

"It's very elegant."

"Surprising what you can find when you're asked to sell a house." He indicated a small footed bowl on the mantelpiece. "That's a sugar bowl, George the Third Irish silver." The piece was surrounded by get-well cards. Dapper pointed to a TV set in one corner. "I'm not much for the telly but you can be sure I'll be tuned in tomorrow when that there aircraft carrier, the USS *Hornet,* picks up Apollo 11 after they splash down in that wee capsule. Can you imagine, Doctor, hurtling through space crammed into something that looks like a giant badminton shuttlecock? It's daft, so it is."

Barry laughed. "You'd not get me up in one with two other blokes. I get a bit uncomfortable in a telephone box. I don't like small spaces."

"Now, Doctor, if you don't mind my saying, you look a bit done in. I'm sure you'd like to sit down." Dapper pointed at the settee, on which lay a rumpled tartan blanket and a copy of *Moby Dick,* spine up. "I never read much as a youngster but when I was about sixteen, I saw the film *A Christmas Carol* with Alastair Sim. I got the book out of the Carnegie library in Bangor. It was terrific so I read the *Pickwick Papers* next, and then all of Mister Dickens's novels. I've been reading ever since. Anyroad, that there's my seat," he said, "but please make yourself at home, Doctor."

Barry sat on an upholstered armchair close to the settee. "Now, Dapper, how—"

"Mind you, that there *Moby Dick*'s more a textbook on whales than a story, but it's got a great couple of opening lines." Dapper picked up the book. "Listen to this. 'Call me Ishmael. Some years ago—never mind how long precisely—having little or no money in my purse, and nothing particular to interest me on shore, I thought I would sail about a little and see the watery part of the world.'" Dapper shook his head. "'See the watery part of the world.' I like that. And thon Queequeg's a humdinger of a character. But look at me, blethering away. Sorry, Doc. Not used to being home alone all day. You was saying?"

Barry smiled. "You're missing your work and folks at the office, I'm sure."

"In soul I am, Doctor."

"Doctor O'Reilly filled me in on your case, Dapper," he said, "and he's sorry he can't come himself today, but he sends his best wishes. He knew I'd be passing your house, so—" Barry removed an envelope from his inside jacket pocket and gave it to Dapper. "Here's your sick line.

Doctor O'Reilly said it would save you a trip to the surgery. You should be able to go back to work on the eighteenth of August."

"That's great. Thanks, and no harm to Doctor O'Reilly, but I'm just as happy to see yourself, Doctor Laverty. Sure, after five years don't we all know and trust you?"

Barry smiled. That was one of the greatest perks of general practice. He felt warm inside. "Thanks, Dapper." He closed his bag. "So, you got home on Monday? Mister Greer said in his letter that your wound was healing well—"

Dapper whipped off his woolly hat. "See for yourself, sir. Joan Eakin at the office knit me this here hat. Said she didn't want me head getting cold. Even if it is July."

The skin incision, while still pink, was completely closed. There was no wound discharge. Any scalp swelling—and there always was some after open brain surgery, as Barry had learned when he'd been a houseman on ward 21 in 1965—had gone down. "It looks grand."

"Aye." Dapper replaced his woolly hat and grimaced. "I just look like a fellah whose scalping didn't go quite as expected. I'll be right glad when my hair grows back. Lucky I don't have long hair like one of them rock stars. Mine shouldn't take long. I'm going to be seeing Joan in a few days when I've got more of my strength back. I'll want to look my best."

Barry shook his head. "Your hair won't grow back as soon as that."

"Och, well, she's just coming here for tea and sure hasn't she seen me half-baldy-nut already? But I've always liked to look my best when I'm in company, so I'll have to bide."

The nickname "Dapper" suited this man. He had always dressed well, although in his work a male estate agent was expected to be a suit-tie-and-polished-shoes man. "It shouldn't take too long before you have your hair back, and Mister Greer said your arms and legs are all working properly now and you've no difficulty speaking. But you have had a few attacks of what he calls minor epilepsy."

"That's right." Dapper flexed and extended his left arm. "Good as new. No trouble with the words, but the nurses told me I had a few what they called absences. I'd stop in mid-sentence, close my eyes for a few seconds then open them and pick up the conversation exactly where I'd left off. But I'd no confusion and never went into coma. They said it's quite common after my kind of surgery. Mister Greer gave me some pills starting a week ago—"

"Troxidone three hundred milligrams."

"If you say so, sir. Three times a day, and I don't believe I've had any more wee turns. It's great I can go back to work in August, but Mister Greer said on account of the absences and the pills, I wasn't to drive until I'd seen him for my postoperative visit on August the twenty-second. Still, there's paperwork to be completed in the office."

"I'm sure you'll be fine, Dapper. Now, I must be off. I've to see a patient in Dundonald Hospital."

"Oh, aye. Would that be your wife, Doctor? We're all right sorry to hear she's poorly. Aggie Arbuthnot was in Dundonald visiting a friend last week and she heard your missus was a patient. When she got home, she told Cissie Sloan, and—" Dapper shrugged and held out his hands palms up.

Barry shook his head. Ballybucklebo. Trying to keep a secret here was like trying to keep Houdini in a straitjacket. "She's having some women's problem, but I hope she's on the mend."

"I hope so too. So, run you away on, sir."

"Thank you, Dapper. I appreciate that. But before I go, can I do anything else for you?"

"No thank you, sir."

"Don't hesitate to call if you need us."

"Thanks a lot, sir. I really do be grateful for your coming."

Barry rose and was about to leave when someone rang the front doorbell.

Dapper yelled, "Come on on in." Dapper's pencil moustache rose as he smiled. "That'll be Donal Donnelly."

Donal came into the room, stopping in the doorway when he saw Barry and snatching off his duncher. "Hello, Doctor Laverty. How's my oul' mate doing?"

"Hello, Donal. Dapper's getting much better." Barry would have left but Donal was still in the doorway and talking twenty to the dozen.

"Dead on," said Donal. He held out a brown-paper-wrapped parcel.

"These here roast beef sandwiches and slices of cherry cake Julie's put up for your lunch will strengthen you."

"Thanks, Donal, and thanks to Julie again. You two's been very good to me since I got home."

Barry tried to sidle by, but Donal seemed oblivious and stood his ground. "Sure, isn't that what friends are for? And speaking of friends, I've a wee favour to ask. Can I use your motor for some personal business? I want til look at a new building site."

"Of course you can, you great glipe. It'll be good practice for when I need you to chauffeur me around the odd time when I'm still not allowed to drive."

Donal smiled. "I'm your man."

Barry said, "Now, Donal, if you'd let me through—"

Dapper said, "Doctor Laverty's heading to Dundonald Hospital for to see Mrs. Laverty."

"Poor Mrs. Laverty. Julie heard your wife was in, and we both hope she gets better soon."

Barry smiled. "So do I, and I'll find out sooner, Donal, if you'd move and let me out."

"Aye, certainly." He stepped aside.

As Barry was leaving, he heard Donal say, "Sit where you are, oul' hand. I'll get the kettle on and we'll have a cup of tea."

11

Hope That Keeps up a Wife's Spirits

Barry sped over the Ballybucklebo Hills as his stomach grumbled its protest. Those few delicious bites of Kinky's ham sandwich had not been enough, and he pictured the rest of the sandwich sitting in the outside pocket of O'Reilly's game bag in the backseat of the car. He looked at his watch. He had time for a quick stop, and he knew the perfect spot.

A few miles farther down the road he turned down a rutted lane and parked beside Ballysallagh Reservoir. The local angling club kept the waters stocked with rainbow trout. He left the car and walked down to the rough-dressed granite blocks that formed the banks of the man-made lake where he sat, legs dangling over the water.

He opened the pocket to find the ham sandwiches wrapped in grease-proof paper. A second parcel held three pieces of Kinky's shortbread, and a small bottle of brown lemonade complemented his impromptu picnic. His mouth watered.

He tucked into a sandwich, savouring its smoky flavour and the air's piney scent coming from a small wood of conifers where wood pigeons made burbling coos. The calm waters of the lake, reflecting the cerulean of a cloudless sky above, were only disturbed by the passage of a family of mallard at the far end and the concentric rings which from time to time appeared as trout rose to swallow a floating insect.

No one was fishing today. Most of the anglers would be at work on a Wednesday so he had the place to himself. He listened to a rustling in the grass that suggested otherwise and, turning slowly, saw the black nose, long whiskers, pointed muzzle, ebony eyes, and tiny ears of an otter. It humped its way across the grass, clambered down the granite, and entered the water, swimming easily using its round tail for a rudder. The otter dived with a swirling of water.

Barry took a swig of lemonade and finished the sandwich, delighting in the warmth of the sun on his back, the utter peace of his surroundings. He hadn't been here since he was a young teen when his father, who knew a club member, had brought him and Jack Mills to the newly constructed reservoir to practice their fly-fishing casting. Almost fifteen years later, signs of construction had all but disappeared and the peaceful, man-made body of water had settled into its environment.

Perhaps one day he and Jack would bring their own children here to learn how to cast. He found a pebble and made an overhand toss into the calm water. He'd longed for Sue dreadfully since she'd been admitted in those very early hours of Monday morning. He had spent time with her, as promised, later that day. Fingal and Emer had been decent about letting Barry slip away. Sue'd slept well and there'd been no more bleeding, thank God. Nor had there been any by last night when, as soon as he'd finished his day's work, he'd nipped over to Dundonald. He hoped her condition was still improving today.

As soon as he'd eaten the last piece of shortbread and had had one more swallow of lemonade he'd make the short drive to the hospital. And when he'd kept her company he'd head back home, give the idiotic Max his walk, feed him and Tigger, and make himself a bit more to eat. He smiled. Max might be unruly and Tigger, like all cats, somewhat aloof, but they were company in the bungalow that simply wasn't the same without Sue's presence. He wondered what it would be like when there was—*when* not *if*, he said to himself firmly—when there was an addition to the family in January. That was something to look forward to. But for now, he had an idea for avoiding the empty house tonight.

And with that thought he put the bottle and wrappings back in the game bag, eased himself off the warm rock, and headed back to the car.

Barry let himself into Sue's room. "Hello, darling." He bent and kissed her. "How are you today?" She was sitting propped up on pillows, wearing a turquoise-shot-with-rose bed jacket over a pale blue cotton nightie. He noticed that her hair was in its usual single plait and her face showed some touches of makeup. Always a good sign that a woman was recovering.

She smiled. "Still no more bleeding. No cramps. The pills make me a bit dopey but that's all right."

"That's great news. I was hoping to be here sooner." Barry sat on the plain wooden chair at the bed's head.

"Your timing is perfect. Harith's coming to see me any minute. He's a lovely man, Barry, and you were right asking him to look after me for the rest of my pregnancy and delivery too, so I'll see him and not have to go to the regular antenatal clinic and see whichever doctor's available."

"He will look after you very well."

The door opened and Harith walked in. "Sue. And Barry. I'm glad you're here." He lifted her chart from its clipboard and scanned it. "I think you're nearly out of the woods, Sue, but to be safe we'll keep you in for a few more days. Your blood pressure's fine and I've got your lab work back. Your urine's clear. No sugar or protein. You're not anaemic, your blood group's O positive, and your Wasserman and Kahn tests are negative."

Barry smiled. "The last two are to detect syphilis."

Sue frowned. "Surely, Harith, you don't seriously believe that I might—"

"Whoa." He held up his hand. "It's purely routine for every pregnant woman."

"Harith's right. I know it offends a lot of people, but I've seen kids with congenital syphilis, Sue. Poor wee mites, no bridge to their noses, malformed teeth, runny noses. But if the disease is recognised in the mother and she's given penicillin for ten days, just ten days, before the sixteenth week of her pregnancy, she's cured. And the foetus is entirely protected. I remember reading in Professor Ian Donald's textbook: 'Any doctor who omits syphilis testing in pregnancy,'" Barry heard Harith's deep voice join his, "'is almost guilty of culpable negligence.' And I agree."

"So do I," said Harith.

Sue's frown faded. "I see. I understand. Sorry, Harith." She smiled.

Harith handed Barry a prescription. "I'll be starting you on iron tablets and folic acid pills today, Sue, and Barry, you can get that filled for when Sue comes home."

"Will do."

Sue cocked her head and turned to Harith. "If you're starting me on these vitamins you must be confident the baby's going to be all right?"

"I am. I won't promise, but Prof Donald in his chapter on antenatal care says the first antenatal session should be 'the earlier the better,' so it makes sense to get things going. Once I've let you go home, Sue, there are some restrictions. Plenty of sleep, about nine hours a night. Balanced diet. A rest after lunch at least for the next two or three weeks."

"Will I be able to start work in September?"

"I don't see why not."

"Thank you."

"No strenuous exercise though. No horse riding at all, and no sex until you're sixteen weeks—"

Barry let his face relax into a neutral expression as Sue's eyes searched his. He'd miss that, but if it was going to help keep their baby, so be it.

"—and that will be on August the sixteenth, when I've scheduled your next antenatal visit."

"I'll be here," Sue said.

Barry heard the confidence in her voice, and he must mirror that for her sake but there were some disadvantages to being medically qualified. He knew too much about the things that could go wrong, but he'd continue to keep that information to himself.

"All right," said Harith, putting Sue's chart back on the bed rail. "I'll be off. I'll see you tomorrow, Sue, and we're going to aim to get you home on Monday."

"Terrific," she said. "And thanks again."

Harith left.

"He really is a sweetheart," Sue said.

"You couldn't be in better hands, pet."

She laughed. "Sorry about the no sex until I'm sixteen weeks."

"I'll live. It's much more important that you and our baby keep well."

"I do love you, Barry Laverty."

"And I love you."

Sue yawned. "Oh dear. These barbiturates really make me drowsy. Would you be offended if I said I'd like to sleep for a while?"

"Not at all."

"And there's no need for you to sit watching me sleep. You run along but come and see me tomorrow."

"Of course. I'll pop up after work. I'm off now until nine tomorrow. I haven't seen hide nor hair of Jack Mills since we went down to Cullybackey on the twelfth. Now Harith's more confident about you, I'd like to get in touch with my old friend. See how he's getting on."

She yawned again. "Good idea. You do that. Give him my love."

"I'll give him a ring. See if we can get together this evening, but I'll keep you company until you've dropped off."

"That won't be long." She rolled on her side, and in a very short time her breathing slowed and she made little whiffling noises as she exhaled.

Barry rose. "Sleep well, pet. Sweet dreams." He silently left her room. Jack might just be free later, and the staff here would surely let Barry use the phone.

"I've a soft spot for the old Duck," Barry said, sitting opposite Jack at a corner table of the Black Swan Pub. "You could have come around to our place, but for once I'm happy enough to get out. The place feels empty without Sue." Barry managed a smile. "And I don't keep draught Guinness on tap. Thanks for making the drive out, Jack."

"My pleasure. It works out well. I've a late start tomorrow in surgery so I'm going to stay the night with Helen and her dad. She understands why you and I want to get together. She sends her love and hopes Sue will be fine. I'll see them later, and I for one am going to enjoy my pint with my old mate."

Barry sat back in his chair and looked around. Wednesdays were never busy. Colin Brown's father, Lenny, stood at the bar with his pal Gerry Shanks, both men nursing half-finished pints.

Bertie Bishop sat at a table with Donal Donnelly, deep in conversation.

Barry guessed it would be about the new flats. Otherwise the place was empty and there wasn't the usual ground swell of conversations or fug of tobacco smoke.

Willie Dunleavy, the pub's owner, came from behind the bar and set two pints on the tabletop. "Your pints, Doctors."

"Thanks, Willie." Barry paid. "Cheers." He lifted his straight glass and took his first mouthful, savouring the bittersweet Guinness.

Jack returned the toast. "To Sue, and you, my friend, and a healthy baby Laverty in twenty-eight more weeks. It sounds like things are settling down."

"That's right. It really was a very small bleed and hasn't recurred, I'm pleased to say, but it was a bit hairy at the beginning."

Jack leant over and touched his friend's hand. "Hey, bye, it seems a while since you confided in me that you and Sue were dealing with possible infertility—"

"On Saint Patrick's Day at the Schools' Cup final."

"And only a couple of weeks since you gave us the good news. I can imagine how you both must have felt when it looked like Sue might miscarry. I really do hope it all settles down."

"Thanks, pal." Barry looked at Jack. "You're a good friend, Mills." He took a pull on his pint. "And Helen's a lamb. How is she?"

Jack shrugged. Drank. "Looking forward to starting at the Royal in August. You know how we felt back then."

"Neither one of us had quite taken it in that we really had qualified after all those years."

"But we did." He stared into his pint.

Barry hesitated. He'd told Sue he wanted to find out how Jack was getting on, and by that he'd meant on Jack's home front, but perhaps he didn't want to talk about it?

Jack sighed and, taking hold of his pint glass, began to turn it slowly on the table. He kept his eyes on the glass. "Helen's excited about her houseman year, but both of us are at our wits' end about what to do about my dad. I let the hare sit for three days, and I know when he'll not be in the house. Dairy cows have very set routines, so I phoned Mum yesterday evening." He sighed again. Lifted the glass, took a pull, leaving another creamy ring on his now half-empty glass, and returned it to the table.

"And?"

"Not good. She says she's tried to talk to him twice about it. He just clams up. She says give him more time, but, och, Barry, hey bye, I just don't know. I don't think he'll ever come around."

Ulstermen could be stubborn when their minds were set, and Barry was inclined to agree, but he wanted to offer his best friend some comfort. "It may not be as bad as that, Jack. Your mum's right. Give him some more time."

Jack shook his head. "You saw what he was like. You were there when he blew up."

"Aye, I was." Barry had a vivid recollection of Morris Mills striking the table hard with his outstretched index finger to emphasize his points. "It's true. He was very angry, but even so, people can come around. Your father's a good man. He's a product of his time and the way he was reared, but he raised you. And you're open, accepting. You believe in equality."

Jack smiled. "I think I get that from Mum."

Barry finished his pint and noticed Jack's was practically finished. He caught Willie's eye and held up two fingers.

Willie nodded and started to pour.

"I think, Jack, a bit more patience. I'll come with you again if you like."

Jack smiled. "I appreciate that. Mebbe you're right. Mebbe a bit more time will let him cool down." Jack finished his pint and frowned. "But if there's much more sectarian violence, I think he might just dig in and never be moved."

Barry looked hard at his friend. "You might be right, and all I can offer is one of Fingal's adages: 'Let's cross that bridge when we come to it.' And hope it quietens down very soon."

12

To Begin with the Beginning

O'Reilly, sitting in the dining room of Number One Main, poured himself a second cup of tea and drummed his fingers on the tablecloth. Three weeks ago, he had secured Barry's agreement to take Sebastian Carson on as a trainee, let George Irwin know of their decision, and called the young man. He had sounded enthusiastic on the phone, agreeing to arrive at eight thirty today, Friday, August the first, for a quick briefing on how the practice ran and then start the surgery with O'Reilly at nine.

He looked at the Waterford crystal clock that sat on the sideboard. It was now quarter to nine. Damn it all. The young man had been late for his interview at the Crawfordsburn Inn and now he was late for his first day on the job. O'Reilly knew the tip of his own nose would be blanching, as it always did when he was angry. He took a deep breath and told himself to calm down. There was probably an explanation, but it better be good.

The front doorbell rang.

O'Reilly waited. The front door opened, and he heard plummy tones saying, "Ah. Yes, madam. I'm Doctor Carson. I believe Doctor O'Reilly is expecting me?"

"He is, so . . . and has been for some time. Come in, sir."

Kinky appeared in the dining room doorway. "A Doctor Carson to see you, Doctor O'Reilly." She gave one of her "strong enough to suck a shmall cat up a chimney" sniffs of disapproval.

O'Reilly rose. "Come in, Sebastian. You're l—"

"I'm most dreadfully sorry I'm late, Fingal. There was a bicycle accident on Hawthornden Way outside Campbell College. I had to help until the ambulance came. Poor chap had a broken arm. Held me up for half an hour. I'd actually planned to be here early."

O'Reilly bit back the rest of the word "late." "That was the right thing to do," he said. "Sit down. Cup of tea?" O'Reilly took his chair.

Sebastian, in tweed sports jacket, charcoal-grey flannels, a white shirt—and his old Harrovian tie—sat beside O'Reilly. "Jolly good. Milk and sugar, please."

O'Reilly poured, handed Sebastian the cup. "Help yourself. And try one of Kinky's scones and her raspberry jam. They make a change from toast and marmalade." O'Reilly passed over a plate of freshly baked buttermilk scones.

Sebastian spread butter and jam. Took a mouthful. "Quite delicious, but 'Kinky'? Um, I suppose that's a nickname. It has peculiarly risqué connotations these days."

O'Reilly chuckled. *"Honi soit qui mal y pense."*

"'Evil be to he who has evil thoughts.' Motto of the Order of the Garter. I was simply making an observation, you know."

"Mrs. Auchinleck, our part-time housekeeper, was once, in the '20s, married to a man called Paudeen Kincaid down in County Cork. She told me he'd nicknamed her 'Kinky' because he'd never heard of anything as kinky—the original meaning is odd—as her way of cooking *druishín*."

"Drish—?"

"Druishín. Blood pudding, a Cork specialty."

"Ah."

"Kinky fitted well with her married surname, too. She is a gem beyond price, and my first piece of advice to you, now you're here to work with us, is always keep on the right side of Kinky."

"Thank you. I shall endeavour to do that. I shall, in fact, address her as Mrs. Auchinleck until notified otherwise."

"Good. Other things you need to know. Surgery opens at nine every day except Saturday and Sunday. We try to get it finished by twelve."

"I noticed that on a brass plate beside your front door."

"Observant of you. I'll take you to the room we use when you've finished your tea and scone. Barry, whom you've met, Emer McCarthy, whom you'll meet later, and I take it in turns. Just as we each take turns

An Irish Country Welcome

to make home visits during the day and share emergency call from six at night to nine in the morning with Doctor Connor Nelson, whose practice is in The Kinnegar. After which we have the day off. One of us does one weekend in four."

"I rather like the sound of that."

O'Reilly pursed his lips. Told himself to give the lad some time. See how he performs with the patients. "At the start, you'll be working with me, and this morning we're in the surgery. Finished your tea, have you?"

"Yes. Do you think Kin—I mean Mrs. Auchinleck might give one the recipe for these scones?"

"You cook?"

"Oh. No. Me? Not at all. I'd give it to our cook, Mrs. O'Gara."

"I see. I'm sure Kinky would be happy to let you have the recipe." O'Reilly rose. "Now, come on. I'll show you the shop." O'Reilly crossed the hall and led Sebastian into the surgery. O'Reilly sat in his swivel chair in front of the open rolltop desk, its back standing against a green wall. Before Barry had joined him, the old desk would have been littered with piles of prescription pads and patients' records. The records were now stored alphabetically in a filing cabinet at one side of the desk and the desktop was tidy. "Have a pew."

Sebastian sat on one of two plain wooden chairs facing the desk.

"The surgery," O'Reilly said, raising a hand and sweeping it around. "All pretty basic." He pointed to an examining table with a neatly folded sheet on top and a set of folding screens jostling with an instrument cabinet against the left wall. A sphygmomanometer was fixed to the same wall. Above the blood pressure machine was an eye-testing chart. He noticed Sebastian pushing himself back up the chair, his brow wrinkled into a frown. O'Reilly chuckled.

"There's something rather peculiar about this chair."

O'Reilly had a quick flashback to a younger Barry Laverty saying much the same thing five years ago. "There is. I sawed an inch off the front legs. The one beside it's the same. Doesn't encourage the customers to stay too long."

"Good Lord." Sebastian's laugh was throaty. "I know what you mean.

Some folks can be a bit garrulous and I imagine you need to get them in and out quickly."

"Not the truly sick or upset ones, just the ones who come for a bit of *craic*. For that they should come to the Duck."

"The Duck?"

O'Reilly laughed. "All in good time. We will reveal all the mysteries of Ballybucklebo to you slowly." He indicated an upholstered armchair beside his desk. "Come and sit here."

"That's better," Sebastian said, settling himself into the new chair. He glanced across to the wall where O'Reilly's framed diploma hung. "So, you're a Trinity Dublin graduate, Fingal?"

"Class of 1936."

"And I happen to know you played rugby in the second row for Ireland back then too."

That took O'Reilly by surprise. "Are you interested in rugby? Do you play?"

"Used to. No time as a houseman."

O'Reilly was intrigued. "For Cambridge?"

"Well, um, yes, but one doesn't like to boast. I played inside centre."

O'Reilly leant forward. "Did you get a blue?"

Sebastian sighed.

O'Reilly couldn't decide whether he was genuinely shy about speaking of his accomplishments or simply feigning modesty.

"Yes. I was on the teams that beat Oxford in the Varsity Match in '62 and '63."

"Good for you." There was more to this young man than had been apparent at the interview. There was another sport hotly contested by the two universities. "Did you by any chance row?"

"Gosh. This is quite the inquisition, but if you must know, at number six for my college and for Cambridge against Oxford for three years: '62 to '64."

"I never miss watching the Grand National or the Boat Race when they're on the telly in April. Your lot won in '62 and '64."

"Well. Um. Yes, actually."

"I never did row. Well done, Sebastian. Now"—O'Reilly fished out his half-moon spectacles and put them on—"more about the way we work. The waiting room is down the hall next to the kitchen and it's first come first served, with any acute emergency taking precedence."

"That makes sense."

"I do try to." But O'Reilly was smiling. "We simply walk along the hall, look into the waiting room and ask, 'Who's next?' Bring them here, sort them out, and they leave by the front door. Stops them swapping symptoms or telling other patients what we've prescribed and suggesting it might work for them too. It still happens, but at least not here."

"Sounds practical."

"It's worked for me since 1946." He glanced at his watch. "Two minutes to nine." He rose. "I gave you some advice about Kinky earlier, now I'm going to give you some more. It was given to me when I was in my first year as a GP. A Doctor Phelim Corrigan in Dublin, my senior, said it was his first law of general practice. 'Never, never, never let the patient get the upper hand.'" O'Reilly had to wait until Sebastian had stopped laughing. "Now, come on. Let's get this show on the road. Oh, and you might be surprised by the decor in the waiting room."

O'Reilly headed there with Sebastian at his heels.

"The decor, Fingal?"

Both men stood at the doorway as Sebastian took in the wall of brightly coloured roses painted from floor to ceiling behind the row of chairs.

Sebastian appeared to be trying not to laugh. "Well, it's not the Sistine Chapel, but it makes a change from hospital green."

"It does that. Courtesy one Donal Donnelly, carpenter by trade. Morning, all," O'Reilly said. Only half of the chairs were taken. There was a chorus of, "Morning, Doctor O'Reilly."

He recognised Sonny Houston and Maggie Houston née MacCorkle. Maggie grinned. It was a formal occasion, because she was wearing her false teeth. Colin Brown, hand wrapped in a bloody towel, sat beside Mister Coffin, the undertaker. The publican Willie Dunleavy's daughter, Mary, sat in the corner reading a dog-eared copy of *Woman's Own*. He did not recognise the young woman seated two seats away from her.

Ballybucklebo had grown somewhat in the last year. He guessed she was a newcomer. It was early in the day. More folks would show up as the morning progressed.

"Good morning, all. Let me introduce you to Doctor Sebastian Carson. He is a graduate of Cambridge University and trained at Saint Bartholomew's Hospital in London. He just finished more training at our City Hospital and he'll be working here for a year."

"He's quare and young looking," said Maggie, "but if he's under your wing, sir, he'll do rightly, so he will."

There was an assenting muttering.

"Thank you. Right," said O'Reilly, "who's first?"

Colin Brown said, "I cut my hand, but it's only a wee cut and it's stopped bleeding. Mister and Mrs. Houston were here first. I can wait."

"Thank you, Colin," Maggie said. "Come on, Sonny." They rose and followed O'Reilly and Sebastian back to the surgery.

O'Reilly took the swivel chair as Sonny and Maggie sat on the wooden chairs.

"Doctor Carson, this is Mister and Mrs. Houston. Don't sit down yet, Doctor. You'll find their records," he pointed, "in that filing cabinet."

"Good morning, Mister and Mrs. Houston, just give me a minute to get your file and then tell me what I can do for you today?" Sebastian opened the filing cabinet, rifled through, removed the file, and sat again in the upholstered armchair beside the desk.

"What can you do, Doctor? You can't do nothing for me," Maggie said, "but Sonny says he can see nothing out of his left eye." She nudged her husband. "You tell them, you ould goat."

O'Reilly, who had known the Houstons since 1946 and knew Maggie's "ould goat" was simple affection, watched to see how Sebastian would respond. His eyes widened but he said nothing.

Sonny said, "I'm not getting any younger. Doctors O'Reilly and Laverty have me on pills for my mild heart failure—"

"Digitalis and a diuretic," O'Reilly added to speed up the consultation.

"Aye, and aspirin for these"—Sonny held out his hands to display how arthritis had gnarled his fingers—"but I'm here today because my eyesight's going in my left eye. If I close my right one I really can't see very much at all."

"I see. And for how long has this been going on?"

"Och, I'm not quite sure. Mebbe a year or more, but it's got worse in the last three months. It started by making things a bit blurred, I could see halos round streetlights, colours didn't seem so bright if I only used my left eye."

O'Reilly had made a diagnosis already from what were classical symptoms. He waited to see how Sebastian would proceed.

"And is this the first time you've mentioned it to a doctor?"

Maggie sighed. "He'd not be here today if I hadn't twisted his arm."

"Doctors are busy people," Sonny mumbled. "I don't like to take up their time."

"Goat." Maggie sniffed.

"Have you any other complaints, Mister Houston?"

Sonny shook his head.

"No headaches, dizzy spells, weakness?"

Good lad, O'Reilly thought. Some lesions inside the skull, a tumour or a bleeding aneurysm like the one from which Dapper Frew was making a remarkable recovery, could produce loss of vision in one eye. With those conditions, the loss of vision was usually much more rapid.

"Sonny wouldn't tell you even if he had, he's that nervous of you medical highheejins. But I can tell you he's not had any of those things. He can't hide nothing from me." The words sounded harsh but the look she gave her husband was not.

"I see. Well, jolly good then—I-I think. Let's have a look, shall we?" Sebastian said, and crouched in front of Sonny. "I'll tell Doctor O'Reilly what I'm finding as we go along and I'll explain to you both once I've finished."

O'Reilly thought, That's it, Sebastian.

"Go right ahead, sir," Sonny said.

"Right. Both eyes are of equal size, as are the pupils. I'm going to forego checking the eye movements because I believe the diagnosis is clear. And there are more patients in the waiting room."

That wasn't very tactful.

"The right pupil could be clearer but the left is white and opaque. Will you come and look, Doctor O'Reilly?" Sebastian stood.

O'Reilly stood, crouched, and said, "I agree."

"Mister Houston, you have cataracts. They are very common in old people."

Hmm, O'Reilly thought as he sat down again. He could have said something like "As we age."

"The lens in the eye is a protein like the white of an egg. You know what happens when you boil an egg?"

"Aye. It solidifies."

"And that's what has happened. The one in your right eye is very early, but the left one is what the eye specialists call 'ripe.' It can be fixed."

"See," Maggie said. "Didn't I say to come and see the doctor. It can be fixed, you buck eejit."

When Sonny spoke, there was a tremor in his voice. "Thank you, Doctor Carson, but will I have to go to hospital?"

O'Reilly remembered how Barry had treated Sonny's pernicious anaemia without submitting him to admission for a more detailed workup. Sonny Houston was deathly afraid of hospitals.

"I'm afraid so, Mister Houston; first the eye doctor's outpatient clinic to see the eye specialist, Mister Cowan, for a more thorough eye examination—"

"And sure won't I come with you?" Maggie patted the back of Sonny's hand.

He gulped in a deep breath.

"Then some time later, you will have to be admitted for the surgery, which is really quite simple, although the eye doctors do use a microscopical technique nowadays. The surgeon will remove the damaged lens and afterwards you'll be given spectacles with a strong convex left lens. It's a simple operation."

Perhaps simple if you're a doctor. Sonny Houston may hold a PhD, but O'Reilly knew he was terrified.

Sonny exhaled. His arthritic hands were trembling. "Very well. If I must, I must." He pushed himself back up his chair.

"Now," said Sebastian, retaking his seat and scribbling on Sonny's file, "I'll write the letter today and they'll send for you soon. Have you any more questions for me?"

"No. Thank you, Doctors. We musn't take up any more of your time." Sonny rose. "Come on, dear. We'll go home now."

O'Reilly said, "Try not to be scared, Sonny. Doctor Carson's right. It is pretty much a routine procedure. I promise."

Sonny nodded. "Thank you, Doctor O'Reilly." He and Maggie headed for the surgery door.

Sebastian preceded them and held the surgery door open. "Goodbye, Mister and Mrs. Houston." He closed the door.

O'Reilly said, "You got the diagnosis right, but do try to remember that no matter what the disease, it's affecting a human being, and human beings have feelings too."

"I thought I was extraordinarily polite."

"You were, but you're a young fellah. One day you'll be old and things will start to deteriorate." Like my bloody hearing. "You'll not like being told you're 'an old person.' You could have phrased that more gently."

"Um. I see." He pursed his lips and held his clenched fist against them.

"We'll say no more, and we have to keep moving. Seeing you're on your feet, be a good lad, nip out to the waiting room and bring the youngster with the cut hand in next. His name's Colin, by the way."

"Yes, Doctor O'Reilly."

As Sebastian disappeared, O'Reilly shook his head. The sudden return to formality, the "Doctor O'Reilly," had not been lost on him. For all his airs and graces, it seemed Sebastian Carson did not take criticism well. Not yet. But O'Reilly had a year to work with him, and that was going to change.

13

Around the Ancient Track Marched

"Now, you're sure you've got everything you need, Sue?"

Barry looked at his wife sitting in an armchair with her feet up on a circular pouffe, a rug over her knees and Tigger on her lap. She smiled at him.

"You're mollycoddling me, Barry. I've been home for five days, five days without any cramps or bleeding—"

"I am not mollycoddling you, just making sure you do what your doctor ordered. And he specifically said for you to rest after lunch." He bent and dropped a kiss on the top of her head. "I love you. I want this baby as much as you do. And if I remember our marriage lines, there was a bit about 'in sickness and in health.'"

Sue laughed. "I love you too, eejit, but I'm not sick. Having a baby is a natural part of life."

When everything goes smoothly, he thought as he tucked the rug more securely around her knees.

"Barry, I'm fine. It's August the first. I am in no danger of catching a chill." She picked up a book. "Now, you've left me a glass of water, tissues. Tigger is fast sleep, and I'm just getting into *A Small Town in Germany* by John le Carré, so off you trot. Knowing Fingal, he's probably still at his lunch, regaling his young colleagues with his encyclopedic knowledge of the world. I know you want to welcome this new Doctor Carson on his first day."

"I do. I'll go straight to Number One and straight home when I'm finished, so you'll know where to find me if you need me. Good thing no one called me last night and I'm off today." Barry pecked the top of her head again, smiled at Sue, began to leave, and then turned back. "Are you absolutely sure you have everything you need?"

"Actually . . ."

"Yes, anything, darling."

"Could you get me some vanilla ice cream from Luchi's in Bangor on your way home? They still make the best ice cream. I'd die for a dish."

Barry let himself in through the front door of Number One Main Street, crossed the hall, and turned right into the dining room. Sue had been right. Fingal, Sebastian Carson, and Emer McCarthy, last year's trainee and, as of today, assistant with a view to partnership, were seated at the big bog oak table. Fingal, as usual, was at its head, and today he was puffing on his briar. "Come in, Barry," he said. "Park yourself. Coffee?"

Barry sat beside Emer. "Please." He turned to Emer and Sebastian. "Afternoon, Emer. Welcome to the practice, Sebastian."

"Afternoon, Barry," Emer said.

Sebastian inclined his head.

As O'Reilly poured, Barry, who had grown used to the young woman long ago, still noticed her trim figure, cornflower-blue eyes, and shiny close-cut blond hair. She was wearing a knee-length sleeveless dress the colour of Kinky's wheaten bread and cream low-heeled lace-up shoes.

"Give that to Barry." O'Reilly handed the cup to Emer, who passed it over, saying, "How was your night, and how's Sue?"

"Both quiet. Sue's resting, but we've no cause for concern—now." He looked at Sebastian. "My wife, Sue, threatened to miscarry our first ten days ago, but it's settled down."

"I'm sorry to hear that," Sebastian said. "I do hope everything will turn out well. It does more often than not."

"Thank you." Barry hardly needed to be told that by a man who was just starting as a trainee. That extra time of obstetrics and gynaecology in Ballymena's Waveney Hospital had acquainted Barry with all the many things that could go wrong, and he still hadn't been able to shake the feeling of dread. He quickly changed the subject. "So, Sebastian, how did your first surgery here go?"

"Actually, some of it was not very different from the kind of stuff I saw at Bart's. Old chap—" He paused and looked at O'Reilly. "A gentleman called Sonny Houston came in with his wife Maggie. Man's got a cataract, so we've arranged for him to be seen at the Royal. Saw plenty of them at ophthalmic outpatients. Pretty straightforward stuff."

O'Reilly took a puff from his briar. "Sebastian's a good diagnostician." He looked the young man in the eye. "We need to help him a bit with his bedside manner, but I imagine a lot of Bart's graduates these days are more scientifically inclined."

Sebastian lowered his gaze.

"Some of our patients will take getting used to," Barry said. "Took me a while. Maggie MacCorkle, as she was then, was one of my first patients. She was complaining of headaches two inches above the crown of her head."

"Good Lord. A bit doolally tap, was she?" There was silence around the table.

Sebastian laughed, somewhat self-consciously, Barry thought. "I don't actually know what that means," said Sebastian. "But I like the sound of it."

"Doolally," O'Reilly said. "It's a corruption of Deolali, a British army transit camp in India where it was said you could go mad from boredom."

"Well, I never." Sebastian crossed his eyes. "Stark raving bonkers."

Emer giggled.

Barry smiled. "That's what I thought, but Maggie has all her marbles." He inclined his head to indicate O'Reilly. "The walking *Encyclopaedia Britannica* there sorted her out in jig time. Gave her some vitamin pills," he paused for effect, "to be taken exactly half an hour before the headache started—and the damn things worked."

Sebastian's eyes widened and he sat back in his chair. His laugh must have started at ankle level and its booming filled the dining room. "Crumbs," he finally managed. "I've never heard anything like it."

Barry chuckled. "And the rest of the morning?"

"A young woman, apparently her dad owns the local pub, has a skin rash that Fingal thinks is contact dermatitis due to washing-up fluid—"

"Mary Dunleavy. She has a feisty wee Chihuahua named Brian Boru who's fast friends with Kenny," Barry said.

"And a young man who seems to be accident prone had cut himself again. Chatted about his dog Murphy while I put in a couple of stitches—"

"Colin Brown," Emer said. "He wants to be a vet."

"Right. And a gentleman with an external haemorrhoid, the aptly named Mister Coffin—"

"The undertaker," Emer said. "The poor man has a large rhinophyma; his red nose does not suit his occupation. You must have noticed."

"Hard to miss."

"But he is a soft-hearted soul. Never married but dotes on his two nieces."

"Gosh, you two. I wasn't surprised when you, Fingal, seemed to know just about everybody except a young woman who moved here recently from Belfast. You've been here for years, but do all GPs get to know their patients quite so personally?"

O'Reilly let go a blast of tobacco smoke. "If they want to. I think it's the mark of a good country practitioner to become part of the community."

"I see," Sebastian said. "Thank you." He looked thoughtful. "I can see that for you folks who are full time here, but I'll be moving on when my time's up. I'll try to fit in, but I'm sure it'll take a while."

"That's true," Barry said, "and it's been worth it for me. I don't want to harp on about the sectarian rubbish that's been bubbling over in Ulster since last year and flared up again over the Twelfth. But I do want to tell you, Sebastian, about how those things work here."

"Anything that can help me do my job better."

"I think this will. You know that in 1941, the Luftwaffe blitzed Belfast over three days in Easter and then again in May."

"I do. My mother and father were living in Belfast." He paused. "As the expression goes, I wasn't even a twinkle in my father's eye then. But there was still bomb damage when I was a child and naturally, I asked them what caused it."

"I think," said Barry, "just about every kid of our generation asked the same questions. Almost a quarter of a million people fled that damage and made their way to towns and villages outside the city. Half of Belfast's houses had been damaged, and many people arrived with nothing more than the nightclothes they were wearing. Protestants took in Catholics and vice versa. There's been a spirit of cooperation and friendships in parts of rural Ulster ever since."

Sebastian nodded. "Including Ballybucklebo."

"Especially Ballybucklebo. Every year the kids from both communities put on a joint Christmas pageant. Father O'Toole and the Reverend Robinson are best friends and golf together. Sometimes it's hard to believe there are two sides here. A Protestant friend of mine's going to marry a Catholic girl and her dad has given them his unreserved blessing." It's a wretched shame Jack's own father hasn't, Barry thought. Still no progress on that front.

"And," said O'Reilly, "let me tell you about the man who is worshipful master of the local Orange lodge. He was pretty rigid in his thinking as recently as 1965, until he nearly died and had to rethink a lot about how he treated other people. Since then, he's got his membership to tone down their anti-Catholic stance. He was the prime mover this year in persuading the local sporting club to hold events on Saturday nights, like a recent talent contest, and open their licensed premises to nonmembers to foster cross-community friendship. Ballybucklebo may not be unique in Ulster but it sets a damn fine example."

"I just wish the rest of Ulster would behave like that," Barry said. "There could be trouble ahead in August."

"You mean when the Apprentice Boys of Derry march?" Sebastian asked.

"I do."

Emer frowned. "Can one of you Protestants explain to me about the Apprentice Boys. We all know about the Orangemen but hardly ever hear anything about this other group."

"Goes back to the Williamite wars," O'Reilly said. "The Catholic

King James II's forces tried to take Londonderry, a walled city, in December 1688. Before they could get in, thirteen boy apprentices slammed the gates. James's troops began a siege that wasn't lifted until six months later, when two ships broke a boom across the River Foyle. The end of the siege continued to be celebrated, and in 1814, the Apprentice Boys of Derry, a Protestant fraternal order, was founded."

"So, it's not just a Derry thing," Emer said.

O'Reilly shook his head. "There are branches worldwide. It has two parades in Derry every year. One is in December to celebrate the closing of the gates. The other, that Sebastian was talking about, is on the second Saturday in August, to celebrate the anniversary of the lifting of the siege. They'll march two weeks tomorrow."

"I see. And given we've just had all kinds of trouble after the Orange parades in July, I can see why there'd be concerns about more Protestant parades in Derry," said Emer.

O'Reilly said, "That's right. We can only hope mid-August passes quietly up there."

"I think," said Sebastian, "it is generally recognised that wise men do not go round waving red rags at bulls. But then I suppose linking wisdom with people who have a passionate belief in a cause might not be an altogether happy juxtaposition."

"You, brother," Barry said, "have said a mouthful, and sadly—I think you're right."

14

A Baby Brings Its Own Welcome

"I'm off," said Barry. "Got to buy some vanilla ice cream for Sue and get home."

"Give her my love," O'Reilly said.

O'Reilly watched as Sebastian's gaze followed Barry out of the room. He tried to interpret the look on the young man's face. If he had to guess, he'd say it was wistful.

"Um. So, what do we get up to this afternoon?"

"We wait," O'Reilly said, "until Emer comes back. We've got to have a doctor who can respond immediately to an emergency near the phone at all times, and it's particularly important when one of our patients is expecting. Rosie Redmond was due this week and it's now Friday. If Miss Hagerty, the district midwife, calls while Emer's still out I'll respond, and naturally I'll take you with me."

"I see." He sighed. "I'd rather hoped we'd be finished for the day."

O'Reilly shook his head. "Damn it, man, it's only two o'clock. We're here to provide service to our patients—and you're here to learn. Sebastian, I was a bit disappointed this morning with what I saw as your certain lack of empathy with Sonny, but I am willing to put it down to lack of experience in dealing with out-patients. In Bart's and the Belfast City Hospital you probably never saw anyone more than once at a clinic. General practice is different. We do get to know our patients. Some of them even become friends."

"I'm sorry. I will try harder."

"Good. But I don't understand your seeming to be work-shy. We simply do not keep bankers' hours in general practice."

Sebastian would not meet O'Reilly's gaze.

"Do you want to tell me why you want to be free on the afternoon of your very first day?"

"Um, well, I—I. Look here, Fingal, I've only just finished my house-man's year at Belfast City Hospital and, well, I suppose I'm ready for a spot of fun."

"A spot of fun?" O'Reilly mimicked Sebastian's upper-crust pronunciation. "A spot of fun? Well, you should have thought of that before you applied."

"Yes, I suppose I should have."

Sebastian continued to avoid O'Reilly's gaze, and the older doctor sighed. "All right. We'll let that hare sit for now, but I want you to know where you stand."

"I'll try to do better."

"I believe you. Now, let's shake on it."

Sebastian took O'Reilly's offered hand.

"We'll give this another try, shall we, Doctor Carson?"

Sebastian nodded. "I certainly—"

His words were interrupted by the telephone's harsh double ring.

"I'll answer it," O'Reilly said, rising. "Kinky's just popped out to look at new Hoovers. The old one's making the most God-awful racket." He went to the hall. "Hello. O'Reilly."

"Doctor, it's Miss Hagerty. It's Mrs. Redmond. Second pregnancy. Thirty-nine weeks and five days. Went into labour this morning. She's eight centimetres dilated and the head is engaged. Won't be long now."

"We're on our way." He replaced the receiver and bawled from the hall, "Come on, Sebastian. We've a delivery to do."

The Redmonds lived in a pebble-dashed farm labourer's cottage in the Ballybucklebo Hills. O'Reilly parked in the small front yard and both men piled out.

A border collie barked once then put its tail between its legs and crouched low to the ground, growling.

Sebastian hung back, staring at the dog.

"Come on, man. Shep's only doing his job protecting his family." O'Reilly bent. "Here, Shep."

The collie wriggled forward, and O'Reilly patted the dog's head. "Good dog. Now. Go home."

The dog, tail thrashing, crept into a kennel near the front door. "It'll take a while, but you'll get to know most of the farm dogs, and, more to the point, they'll get to know you."

"One can hardly wait," Sebastian said.

"It's all part of country practice." O'Reilly didn't bother to knock but opened the front door and strode into a kitchen with a tiled floor. "Miss Hagerty?"

A woman's voice came from along a hall. "In here, Doctor O'Reilly."

Pursued by Sebastian, O'Reilly strode along a narrow hall and into a bedroom, his nostrils instantly tickled by the acrid smell of amniotic fluid that always accompanied labour. "Afternoon, Miss Hagerty. Mrs. Redmond. This is Doctor Carson. He's our new trainee."

Miss Hagerty, a slim, middle-aged woman in a red rubber apron over her blue midwife's uniform, nodded briskly and turned her attention back to her patient.

Rosie Redmond's fair hair was damp and darkened by sweat. She lay on a red rubber sheet on top of newspapers on the bare mattress of her double bed. Her nightdress was pulled up. She forced a tight-lipped smile, then grunted and clasped her swollen belly.

"Pant, Rosie. Pant," said Miss Hagerty.

The patient opened her mouth and panted like an unfit athlete who'd just staggered to the end of a hundred-yard sprint. She stopped panting as the contraction passed.

"Will you listen to the foetal heart please, Doctor? The baby is lying longitudinally, right occipito-anterior, and the head is fully engaged." She handed him a Pinard stethoscope, an aluminium tube with a broad, round open end, a narrower neck, and a flat circular earpiece.

So, the baby's spine was in line with its mother's, the back of its head was turned slightly to the mother's right, and the widest part of the baby's head had passed the brim of the mother's pelvis. "Right." O'Reilly placed the broad open end on Rosie's swollen belly over the top of the baby's back, bent, and put his ear to the earpiece. Immediately he heard the rapid beat of the foetal heart. He stared at his watch as he counted. Thirty-six beats in fifteen seconds. "One hundred and forty-four per minute." Perfectly normal. "You and your baby are doing fine, Rosie. Won't be long now."

Rosie grunted and bit down on her lower lip.

O'Reilly left Miss Hagerty to encourage the patient to pant and turned to Sebastian. "I presume you did a few deliveries as a student?" O'Reilly could still recall his own experiences at Dublin's Rotunda Maternity Hospital. They were among his most vivid memories and satisfying moments from his student days.

"Twenty actually, but I'm a bit rusty. We don't do any midder in our houseman's year."

"Well, time for you to get going again."

Rosie's breathing had steadied.

"Come on then. Rosie, we'll be back in a jiffy. Doctor Carson's just going to wash his hands. I'll show him the way." O'Reilly had made several home visits here over the years.

When they returned, Rosie was panting again, and Miss Hagerty had opened a pack containing a sterile towel and rubber gloves.

When the panting stopped, Miss Hagerty rapidly palpated the woman's belly and listened to the foetal heart.

"I'll be here if you need me," O'Reilly said, "but now you'll get a taste of domiciliary midwifery. Dry your hands and put on your gloves."

Sebastian did as he was told.

"Head is fully descended, Doctors. Heart rate's one hundred and forty-four."

"Thank you," O'Reilly said.

Miss Hagerty had earlier set a pre-sterilised pack of the equipment that would be needed on top of the cleared dresser and opened it. She poured brown, strongly smelling disinfectant into a kidney dish.

Sebastian, with no prompting from O'Reilly, grasped a cotton swab in the jaws of some stainless-steel, sponge-holding forceps, dipped the swab in the brown solution, and explained, "I'm just going to wash you down below, Mrs. Redmond, put some towels on you, and examine you."

She didn't reply. She began panting again under Miss Hagerty's direction.

Sebastian waited for the contraction to pass and painted Rosie's nether regions. He spread one green towel over her pubic region and belly. "Can you lift your bottom a bit?"

She did and he tucked another green towel under, so most of it would be under the baby when it was delivered. "Now I'm going to examine you."

O'Reilly watched and listened.

"The cervix is fully dilated, and the occiput will be visible as I remove my fingers. I should be grateful, Miss Hagerty, if you might encourage Rosie to push with her next contractions. You're going to deliver your baby now, Rosie, so please part your legs and draw up your knees."

Sebastian moved to her left side.

Before he could do anything, O'Reilly saw the black circle of the baby's hair at the opening of the vagina.

"Sweet Jesus, it's coming," Rosie said.

Miss Hagerty helped her to a semi-sitting position and said, "Puuusssh."

O'Reilly watched as with his right hand Sebastian controlled the rate of descent of the baby's head. With the other hand, he eased the skin between the bottom of the vagina and her anus down and away from the pressure above them.

The contraction passed.

"Are you all right, Sebastian?"

"So far. It's a bit like riding a bicycle, you know. It all comes back to one when it has to."

O'Reilly smiled at that analogy and was impressed by the man's apparent sangfroid.

"Right, Rosie. Big puuush."

O'Reilly watched as under Sebastian's fingers the head advanced. He let it come until the widest part was clearly in the open. Then he allowed the head to extend. As it rotated, a wrinkled forehead appeared, damp and smeared with *vernix caseosa,* the white, greasy waterproofing that coats the skin of the baby in the uterus. A button nose came next, and in a rush a puckered little mouth, and a tiny pointed chin. Even before the shoulders were born, the baby gave its first, weak wail.

Sebastian used both hands to guide the slippery infant out of its mother and onto the green towel. "It's a boy, Rosie," he said. "He looks fine so far."

O'Reilly handed Sebastian another green towel to wrap the boy, who let a screech out of him like a banshee. "Grand set of lungs there, Rosie," O'Reilly said.

Sebastian set the boy on his mother's tummy, clamped and cut the umbilical cord, and gave the wee one to his mum, who was making cooing noises of delight. He put his hand on Rosie's tummy. "Uterus is firm and contracted. The cord's getting longer and there's some bleeding. Right, Rosie. One more big push." He gently pulled on the cord and as she pushed, the placenta was expelled.

O'Reilly had prepared the hypodermic. "Just a wee jag to make sure your womb stays contracted"—and gave ergometrine by intramuscular injection into her left thigh. "Now," he said, moving to the head of the bed. "Let's have a look at the chissler." Ten fingers, ten toes, intact palate and lips, no skull defects, no heart murmurs, although if there were heart defects, they may not show up until later, and no clicking of the hip joints when O'Reilly forced the wee one's legs open, so no congenital hip dislocation. "He's perfect." O'Reilly gave the baby back to his mother, where the little one contentedly latched onto her right nipple and began to suck.

"How are you getting on, Doctor Carson?"

"Splendidly. No skin tears. No bleeding. Placenta's intact. I'll just need to give Mrs. Redmond a bit of a wash."

"Don't you bother yourself about that, sir," Miss Hagerty said. "Tidying up's my job. You just take off your gloves and apron and go and wash your hands. And if you don't mind me saying, I've seen a lot of deliveries. You did that very well."

Sebastian blushed. "Um. Well, thank you, Miss Hagerty. I was well taught. And thank you, Doctor O'Reilly, for letting me go ahead." He looked at the mother and child. "You have a beautiful baby boy, Mrs. Redmond."

"Thank you, Doctor."

"Right," said O'Reilly, "we'll be off. Miss Hagerty will take care of things. And one of us will pop in in the next day or two to make sure the pair of you are doing well. If you are worried about anything, give us a call."

"I will, Doctor, and thanks again."

O'Reilly headed for the door. "Go wash your hands, Doctor Carson. I'll wait. But you did very well. I'm impressed."

Sebastian nodded and went into the bathroom. When he returned, O'Reilly said, "Right. We'll pop back to Number One and if Emer's there that'll be us finished for the day." He opened the front door and stood aside to let Sebastian out. "How'd you like to celebrate your first home delivery with a pint on me? We could nip over to the Duck." He opened the Rover's door, hopped in, and started the engine. The prospect of a pint to celebrate the new trainee's obvious obstetrical proficiency appealed mightily to O'Reilly.

Sebastian climbed in the other side and closed his door. As O'Reilly drove off humming to himself, Sebastian said, "That's a very generous offer, Fingal, but, honestly, if it's all right with you I'd rather head for home if you don't mind."

15

To Comfort All That Mourn

"This, Sebastian," said O'Reilly, driving slowly along a narrow street five days later, "is the council housing estate. Thrown up after the war as cheaply as possible." He braked as one of a group of boys in short pants kicking a football darted out into the middle of the road. "Eejit, boy," he shouted out the open window. "Watch where you're going, Sammy."

"Sorry, Doctor O'Reilly."

"It's always gloomy because it's in the shadow of the Ballybucklebo Hills. The rents are subsidised by the borough council so working folks can afford to live here. There's been a slowdown in the shipyards—we can't compete with South Korea's pool of cheap labour. So quite a few who are unemployed live here too."

Sebastian peered at the rows of gardenless terrace houses, all identical, all mean and cramped-looking. "It's not Cherryvalley, that's for sure, and the drizzle is hardly cheering. But I suppose there are worse places in the world to live."

O'Reilly had to brake again for a stray mongrel, which slunk off, tail between its legs. "There are. This is nowhere as bad as the Liberties in Dublin before the war, with the poorest of the poor crammed into tenements with no running water and only a few outdoor privies. I got my start in general practice there in the '30s before I came here to join old Doctor Flanagan." O'Reilly moved off and passed three more houses before he parked. "Come on. You'll not need your bag. The patient's not physically ill. He lost his wife, Anne, to lung cancer on June the fourth—exactly two months ago. I want to see how he's coping." O'Reilly knocked on the front door.

Guffer Galvin had aged in the months since Anne's death, and O'Reilly felt for the almost completely bald man who answered the door in a collarless shirt under a V-necked sleeveless pullover. "Doctor O'Reilly? What's up? I never sent for you."

"I know that, Guffer, but I was passing and thought I'd pop in and see how you are."

"That's dead decent of you, Doctor. Come in. And who's this young fella with you?"

"Guffer Galvin, this is our new trainee, Doctor Carson."

"Pleased til meet you, sir."

"How do you do, Mister Galvin?" Sebastian said.

Guffer led the way into his cramped lounge, where three ceramic mallard, garishly painted and decreasing in size, flew up at an angle on the whitewashed chimney breast. "Please sit down." He switched off the TV and sat on the sofa. "I only had it on for a bit of company."

O'Reilly and Sebastian took an armchair apiece. O'Reilly noticed some unwashed lunch plates on a table beside the sofa. They'd not have been left there for several hours while Anne was alive. "So," he asked, "how are you getting on?"

"Och." Guffer shrugged. "Anne's gone two months now. Our youngest, Seamus, went back to Palm Desert two weeks after the funeral, as you know, sir. He's a business to run, after all. And our older boy, Pat, he's back in Dublin. They both phone me and that helps, but—" He looked O'Reilly in the eye, sighed. "I miss Annie sore." A single tear glistened. "It's took me a while to accept she's gone. I'd think she was in the kitchen and call out to her. Silly of me."

"Nothing silly about it," O'Reilly said. "Grieving takes time."

"It certainly does," said Sebastian. "Perhaps your friends come to call?"

"Och aye. They've been great. And the minister, Mister Robinson, pops in often too." He looked from one man to the other. "And here's me forgetting my manners. Annie would have had me off to the kitchen by now to put the kettle on. Can I get the pair of youse a wee cup of tea in your hand?"

They had one more call to make and O'Reilly was torn between keeping

Guffer company for longer or getting to their next call. He noticed Sebastian taking a quick glance at his watch. At least he hadn't done it while Guffer was looking. The lad was learning. "Not today, thanks, Guffer. We've another patient to see, but I'll drop in on you again over the next few weeks, and if you really feel low and want to talk about it, give us a call and one of us'll come 'round."

"I will. Thanks, Doctor." He smiled. "It's great just til know you and the other doctors are there when we need you. Doctor Emer brought your Kenny round the other day for a bit of a visit. My Annie was daft about that dog, so she was. And she was very fond of Doctor Emer."

"We all are," O'Reilly said, rising, "and now we'd better be off. Take care of yourself, Guffer. We'll see ourselves out."

"Oh my, this is rather grand," Sebastian said as O'Reilly drove up the long, curved drive to Ballybucklebo House and parked near the front steps. The polite request for a home visit had come from John MacNeill after lunchtime. "Nothing urgent, Fingal," he'd said, "but would you mind calling in later today?"

"Lord of the manor's place," O'Reilly said. "Marquis of Ballybucklebo. He sounded fine on the phone. We shall see." He grabbed his bag. "Come on."

"I rather suspect that a peer of the realm can't be expected to sit in the waiting room with the hoi polloi," said Sebastian as they climbed the steps.

The butler/valet met them at the door. "Surgeon Commander and—?"

"Doctor Carson," O'Reilly said to his old *Warspite* shipmate, gunnery Chief Petty Officer Thompson.

"Please come in out of the rain. His lordship's waiting for you in the study. If you'll follow me, sir." Thompson led them along a parquet-floored, high-arched, cathedral-ceilinged hall where oils of earlier marquises and marchionesses hung. When O'Reilly had first brought Kitty here, she had remarked that one of the paintings had been done by Sir Joshua Reynolds in the mid-1700s.

Thompson held open a door. "Your doctors, my lord."

Lord John MacNeill, wearing a red velvet smoking jacket, sat on a black leather ottoman in front of a small fire. A family portrait of Lord MacNeill, his late wife, Laura, and their son, Sean, now a major in the Irish Guards, hung above the fireplace. "Fingal. Forgive me if I don't get up. I'm feeling a bit under the weather. Thank you for coming." He looked at Sebastian. "And young Carson. What a pleasant surprise. How are you?"

"Very well, thank you, sir. I'm a trainee with Doctor O'Reilly this year."

O'Reilly frowned. He had not realised Sebastian Carson was acquainted with his lordship.

John pointed to a couple of balloon-backed Victorian dining chairs. "Will you both please have a seat?"

"Thank you," O'Reilly said, and sat, as did Sebastian.

"I was very sorry to hear about your father. My condolences. I can't say I knew him well, but I do remember how proud he was when you won that scholarship at Harrow. I often saw him at various horse-racing events. He liked a bit of a flutter."

A sad look came into Sebastian's eyes. "Well, perhaps more than a bit of a flutter, sir." There was disdain in the young man's voice. "But thank you, your lordship."

What was this business about his late father's liking for a bit of a flutter?

"How's your mother?" John MacNeill asked.

"Trying to bear up, sir. It's hard on her."

John glanced at the family portrait. "I do understand."

So did O'Reilly, who had lost his first wife, Deirdre, in 1941 after only six months of marriage.

"Now, John," said O'Reilly, "what seems to be troubling you?"

He pointed to the lower part of his breastbone. "For the past several weeks I have been progressively more troubled by discomfort behind here. It's hard to describe, but it comes on suddenly and this morning it made me catch my breath. I thought I should ask you to take a look."

"I see." Typical marquis. Too polite to inconvenience his physician. Nothing urgent? Central chest pain in a sixty-plus man was always very worrying. O'Reilly immediately suspected angina pectoris, pain brought on by partially clogged coronary arteries, depriving the heart muscle of blood, and usually the precursor to a myocardial infarction. But it could be other things too. "Does anything in particular bring it on?" If John said exercise he was going straight to the Royal for an electrocardiogram and possible admission.

"Well, yes. When I lie down or if I bend over after a meal."

O'Reilly relaxed. He stood and said, "I'm just going to look under your eyelids and, if you don't mind, I'd like Doctor Carson to have a look too."

"Go right ahead."

O'Reilly crouched in front of John MacNeill. With a thumb beneath each lower lid he pulled them down to expose the conjunctiva, the transparent membrane that lines the eyelids and covers the front of the eyeball. That permitted him to see colour given by the blood vessels under the membrane. "Your opinion, please, Sebastian."

"Pretty pale."

"I agree." O'Reilly stood. "I'd just like to take your pulse and blood pressure." O'Reilly did, and reported, "Pulse regular, eighty-eight per minute. Blood pressure one hundred and forty over eighty. Not bad considering none of us are getting any younger." He took his seat. "Your opinion so far, please, Sebastian."

Sebastian swallowed, took a breath, then said, "When you said you had central chest pain, sir, I immediately thought you were having attacks of angina. Do you understand what that is?"

"I do. My own father suffered from it. I wasn't really worried that I might be on the way to having a heart attack like him, but I knew enough to seek your advice."

The more psychologically inclined physician might call that denial, O'Reilly thought.

"Um, even with you having a family history, one is fairly certain you're not. Your history of lying down and bending over after food is very typical of peptic oesophagitis, and the paleness under your eyelids suggests you may be a little anaemic, because the other effect of the condition is bleeding leading to anaemia." Inclining his head, he looked over at Fingal.

"I concur," O'Reilly said. "And your suggestions for treatment?"

"I'll, um, get to that in a moment after I've explained. You see, sir, your oesophagus—the tube or gullet from your mouth to your stomach—is not designed to withstand the effects of the acidic gastric juices. In some people, the juices do flow back from the stomach and cause ulceration, which hurts and may bleed. That is often associated with hiatus hernia, when the upper part of the stomach has made its way through the diaphragm, a big sheet of muscle that separates the chest cavity from the abdominal cavity."

"I see. Thank you for explaining, Doctor," John MacNeill said. "So, what's next?"

"For a start you should avoid stooping after food and try sleeping propped up on pillows. Eat small and frequent meals, avoid spicy and fatty foods, keep your coffee consumption down, and, if Doctor O'Reilly approves, I'm going to give you a prescription for some milk-alkali tablets, Prodexin, to be sucked between meals. That's to try to make you comfortable until we can get you an appointment to see Mister Willoughby Wilson, a surgeon at the Royal, who will order a special X-ray—a barium meal. He may also want to perform an oesophagoscopy, pop an illuminated tube into your gullet. He'll take a blood sample to determine if you are anaemic and prescribe accordingly. Doctor O'Reilly?"

"You're spot on. And don't think you've been shortchanged, John, because we didn't examine you. There will be no other physical findings of note. I do have a couple of other questions, though."

"Fire away."

"Do you have any difficulty in swallowing, and have you been losing weight?"

"No to both."

"Good." Those were the primary symptoms of carcinoma of the oesophagus, a disease with a grim prognosis regardless of how early it was diagnosed, and if he and Sebastian were wrong and had missed that diagnosis, it would show up on the X-ray. He saw no reason to add that burden of worry to his friend's concerns.

"Thank you both," said John MacNeill. "It's a relief to understand what's happening. Young Sebastian has explained things admirably. I imagine the hospital will contact me about my appointment and tests?"

"They will," said O'Reilly.

"Good. Now, would I by any chance be your last home visit this afternoon?"

"You would," said O'Reilly, who had deliberately made it so because he knew what would happen next.

"In that case, may I offer you a small libation?"

"Splendid," said O'Reilly. "Small Jameson."

"Sebastian?"

Sebastian sighed, glanced at his watch. "Dry sherry, please, your lordship."

The phone rang.

"Sorry, Doctors, but I must get this. Won't be a moment."

Sebastian leaned over and whispered to O'Reilly, "Fingal, I'd very much appreciate it if we don't stay too long. I don't mean to be impolite, but I have plans."

"What kind of plans? A spot of fun?"

"No. Not at all, just—" He paused. "—plans. Personal plans."

Just when he was getting ready to praise Sebastian Carson for his masterly explanation to John MacNeill of the findings, here he was trying to rush away again. What did the eejit boy mean by "personal plans" on a workday? Well, personal they may be, but if they affected his ability to do his job, then Fingal O'Reilly reserved the right to try to get to the bottom of the mystery.

16

Endure the Toothache

Barry watched as Kinky set O'Reilly's brace of grilled kippers on the table in front of him. "There does be your breakfast, sir. I'm sorry you overslept. Mrs. O'Reilly left for her work well before you got up." Kinky looked out the dining room window. "And it does be a fine Wednesday morning, so. Doctor Emer's already started the surgery."

O'Reilly growled and rubbed his left lower jaw.

Barry and Sebastian, both drinking tea, had come by Number One Main Street before nine. Barry had paperwork to catch up on and Sebastian would be making home visits with O'Reilly.

Barry noted the bags under his senior partner's eyes. "Not like you to be late for your breakfast, Fingal."

"Not like me to have a bloody toothache either. Didn't drop off until two this morning. Had to get up to find a couple of Panadol. At least they helped me sleep, but the damn thing's throbbing like bug—Sorry, Kinky."

"A man with a toothache can be forgiven for being a little bit grumpy, so. Would you like something easier to chew, like scrambled eggs?"

O'Reilly shook his head. "No, thank you. I'll just make do with tea." He pushed his plate away.

Kinky tutted but lifted the plate. "Very well, sir. I'll take them away." Her disdainful sniff was strong enough, as she herself might have said, "To draw the walls inward."

"Good gracious," said Sebastian. "I think someone's nose is out of joint."

O'Reilly glared at him. "Kinky Auchinleck has been my housekeeper since 1946. She is entirely within her rights to show her displeasure with me. And I know I'm short-tempered today. My tooth hurts, I'm concerned we're in for another bout of civil unrest, and I'm worried Kitty's in Belfast very near a district that could become violent if trouble breaks out in the city."

"Sue's very concerned—"

O'Reilly snapped, "No, Barry. No, I don't want to talk about it. I'll have to call Mister Drew, the dentist in Bangor, see if he can fit me in today. In the meantime, more Panadol to cut the pain. Excuse me. I've got some in the surgery. Emer won't mind me butting in." He rose and, still holding his jaw, left.

The two sipped their tea, the quiet descending as O'Reilly's heavy footsteps receded. Barry said to Sebastian, "I'm no dentist but it sounds like Fingal's got a dental abscess."

"I agree. Poor old chap."

O'Reilly reappeared. "The dentist's surgery should be open in a couple of minutes. Barry, I was going to take Sebastian with me to make home visits this morning, but could you do them, please?"

"I was planning to catch up on my paperwork—" Barry saw O'Reilly's nose tip start to blanch. "—but, of course, the government form-filling can wait. Who have we to see?"

"I haven't heard the phone ringing, so I don't think there's been any new calls, but there are follow-ups. I sent Stanley Kearney to the children's hospital three weeks ago with suspected acute glomerulonephritis. I'm happy to say I was wrong, but make sure he's doing well. Your patient, young Tony Bradshaw, was discharged after repair of his intussusception on July thirtieth, and it's only eleven days since you and I, Sebastian, saw the marquis. He has private health insurance and saw Mister Willoughby Wilson on Monday at the Musgrave and Clark Clinic. Nip over to Ballybucklebo House. Make sure he's all right, and then the pair of you pop back here to see if Kinky has any new calls."

O'Reilly was almost through the door by the time Barry said, "Will do, Fingal."

"Ow. Bugger this bloody tooth."

Barry smiled and finished his tea. "Come on, Sebastian." They headed for the hall.

O'Reilly was speaking into the phone as they passed. "One thirty? I'll be there. Thank you." He replaced the receiver. "Looks like I'll be a tooth short by this afternoon."

"The best of British luck, Fingal," Sebastian said. "I, for one, hate going to the dentist."

O'Reilly managed a smile. "You're not alone, but it can't be helped. At least the Panadol's starting to work. And speaking of work, off the pair of you trot. I'll be fine."

"Right," said Barry, heading out the door. "We'll see young Kearney first. He lives up on the estate. Tony Bradshaw next, and then the marquis. Save us backtracking."

As Barry drove off, Sebastian said, "Fingal's right to be worried about Mrs. O'Reilly. From what I heard on the nine o'clock news last night, the Apprentice Boys' march—and there were fifteen thousand of them marching—nearly passed off quietly, but then trouble started late in the day and things had got pretty much out of hand in the Bogside district of Londonderry by last night."

Barry sighed. "My wife Sue's been very active in the civil rights movement, NICRA, but she's been concerned it's being taken over by extreme nationalists who keep stirring the pot. I missed the news this morning. I hope to God the police are back in control."

He pulled over to the kerb in the housing estate. "We'll not solve Ulster's problems today. Come on, let's see to our first customer."

"Come in, Doctor Laverty." Alma Kearney, a fit-looking auburn-haired young woman, held her front door open.

"Thank you, Mrs. Kearney," Barry said, "and this is Doctor Carson."

"Pleased til meet you, sir."

"Doctor O'Reilly asked us to pop in to see how young Stanley's doing."

She laughed. "Well, I'm dead relieved, I'll tell you. Three weeks ago, your Doctor O'Reilly had my heart in my mouth. He said some kiddies who get a certain kind of sore throat Stanley had could develop kidney damage later. And that the only way the doctors could tell was by doing a blood test and daily urine tests, keeping him in hospital for bed rest and a special diet. He also said nearly all made a complete recovery. And thon Doctor O'Reilly, being a very honest man, said he could be wrong."

Barry glanced at Sebastian. The man's eyes had widened.

"Come on into the parlour." She led them into a small, neatly furnished room. "Please have a seat. Just a wee minute," she said, "I'll turn off the wireless." She shook her head. "Nothing but special reports of what's going on in the Bogside. Petrol bombs chucked at the Peelers. CS gas being fired back. Desperate, so it is."

"Not good," Barry said as he and Sebastian each took a chair.

"Anyroad, about Stanley." Alma perched on an olive-green sofa. "Praise be, they took blood, collected Stanley's pee for twenty-four hours, kept taking his pulse, temperature, and blood pressure." She inhaled deeply. "It near broke my heart leaving the wee fella there that night, but me and Harry, my husband, went up on Saturday afternoon and the nurse had a houseman talk til us." Her smile was radiant. "He said Stanley's urine was clear and he was passing lots, his blood test was normal, and so were his pulse and blood pressure. The senior doctors weren't sure what had ailed him and wanted to keep him in for a more few days." She laughed. "Come Thursday he was so well he'd started a pillow fight with another wee lad, and they said would we please take him home."

"I'm very glad it turned out for the best," Barry said. "Could we see him?"

"You can, but you'll have to go up til the hill at the top of the estate. Harry built Stanley a guider this year."

"A guider?" Sebastian sounded puzzled.

"Him and his mate, wee Rory Heather, has got one too. You'll understand when you see them, sir."

Sebastian frowned but said, "I'm sure I will. Thank you."

Barry chuckled. "Sounds to me as if he hardly needs a doctor."

She lowered her voice. "When Doctor O'Reilly said it might be Stanley's kidneys, I near took the rickets. We'd read about kidney transplants and hoped til God our wee lad wouldn't need one." She smiled. "He's well mended, so he is, but thanks for coming."

"Right," Barry said, rising. "We'll be off then. And if you need us, you know how to find us."

"It's only a wee walk til the hill. Just turn right and go about a hundred yards. You'll likely hear them before you see them."

Out in the fresh morning air, Barry and Sebastian walked up the way Alma Kearney had directed. "So, what did you learn there, Sebastian?"

"That doctors aren't infallible. I was a bit surprised Fingal had admitted up front he might be wrong."

"Fingal O'Reilly is a big man in more than one way."

"I'm beginning to see that. And I had it reinforced by Mrs. Kearney how that fear of the unknown is hard on people, in this case, parents worried sick over whether their son might need a transplant—"

From up ahead and around a corner came a high-pitched boy's voice. "Beat you that time, Rory. Come on back up the hill."

"Away off and chase yourself, Stanley. I'll knock your socks off next time."

Barry laughed. "Alma was right. That's them."

"The folks here speak a somewhat peculiar patois. I think I understood 'knock your socks off,' but what on earth does 'We near took the rickets' mean?"

Barry laughed. "It means we suffered a severe shock."

"Good gracious. I do have a lot to learn."

They turned the corner. At the crest of a shallow hill stood two boys, each pointing a little wheeled cart downhill.

One yelled, "One, two, three. Go!"

Each bent low, grasped his vehicle, started running, then leaped aboard, steering by means of a rope attached to the front ends.

Barry could hear the wheels on the tarmac and the excited screams of the two racers. It was a near-run thing, but Rory Heather was true to his word. His guider crossed a chalked finish line, close to where the two doctors stood, a good length before Stanley's. Rory gloated, "Nah-na-na-nah-nah."

But judging by Stanley's grin it was all good-natured. He climbed out of his cart and looked at Barry. "Hello, Doctor Laverty. How's about ye?"

"I'm grand. And how are you, Stanley? And by the way, this is Doctor Carson."

Stanley, a short boy of eleven, bowed his towhead in greeting. "Pleased til meet you, sir. I'm all better now, Doctor Laverty. My throat isn't sore, and I've got lots of energy, but thanks for asking. This here's Rory Heather."

"Rory," Barry said. "Good to meet you." He turned to Stanley. "We came to see how you are, and clearly you're fit as a flea. So, can we have a look at your guider?"

"Aye, certainly."

The low, four-wheeled cart consisted of a box where the driver sat between the two back wheels. A plank stuck out from the front of the box. Stanley pointed to a crosspiece at the other end of the plank, fitted with two more wheels. "See that there bolt in the middle of the crosspiece, attaching to the plank?"

Barry nodded.

"The front turns on it so you can steer the two front wheels by that there rope attached to the ends of the crosspiece."

"Ingenious," Sebastian said. "I'd have called the contraption a soap-box."

"You would, sir, being a toff and all, but toffs' kids don't ride on guiders."

Sebastian looked contrite. "I stand corrected." He smiled. "And like Doctor Laverty, I am delighted you are fully recovered."

"Nice to meet you, Rory. Now we'll be off. Have fun."

Barry watched as the boys turned and used the steering ropes to haul their guiders back uphill.

As Barry and Sebastian were getting into the Imp, Barry heard the racers' yells once more. "I didn't realise," said Sebastian, "rural general practice included consultations in the middle of guider races. I think that kind of thing's a lot of fun. And young Stanley was right about something else too."

"Oh?"

"I'd never seen a guider in my life, and I suppose I was a toff's kid."

He frowned. "One shall endeavour—no. I shall try not to come across as too toffy in future."

That, Barry thought, was definitely a step in the right direction. He glanced at his watch. "Hang about a minute." He turned on the car radio and found BBC Northern Ireland. A man's voice said, "—and reports have been coming in of disturbances in Dungannon, Armagh, Dungiven, and Newry. A police spokesman has said the officers are becoming overwhelmed." Barry clicked the radio off. "Bloody hell," he said, quite ignoring Sebastian. "Sue's going to have to quit NICRA. She's enough to worry about being pregnant without getting involved in sectarian politics."

"Quite."

As they turned onto the Bradshaws' street, Sebastian said, "Neat little neighbourhood." After Barry had parked, they walked together through the small front garden, where Linda Bradshaw, wearing leather gardening gloves, was pruning a small rosebush.

She turned from her task. "Doctor Laverty and—?"

"Our new associate, Doctor Carson."

"How do you do?" she said.

"How do you do?"

"We've come to see young Tony. How is he?"

"Asleep in his pram," she said, and pointed at a big Silver Cross four-wheeler with its navy-blue hood up, parked in the shade of the house. "I must say the staff at the children's hospital were wonderful when he was admitted. He was seen at once and they confirmed your diagnosis, Doctor Laverty. He was operated on two hours later and the surgical registrar came to see Richard and me when it was over. He told us they'd got it all sorted out and Tony was going to be fine."

"This is excellent news," Barry said. "Now, I'd like Doctor Carson to examine your son, Linda."

"Certainly." She stepped to the pram, followed by Sebastian, and lowered the hood.

"He's a very handsome little lad, with his dark hair and dark eyes."

Barry saw Linda smile.

"How old is young Tony?" Sebastian asked.

"Almost eight months."

"And what does he weigh?"

"Twenty-one pounds."

"Right in the middle of the range for a baby that age, fifteen and a half to twenty-three, splendid. Is he grasping things?"

"Only in the last week."

"And how does he get about?"

"He's been scooting and crawling for the last two weeks and he says things like 'da-da.'"

"He's certainly hitting his developmental milestones."

Linda smiled. "And that's good, isn't it?"

"Indeed, it is. Now I'd better take a look. Please pull back his blankets."

Linda removed her gloves and did so. "Oh, my, he's fast asleep."

"Let's try not to wake him. Can you pull up his nightie?"

"Of course."

Sebastian rubbed the bell of his stethoscope to warm it and plugged the earpieces into his ears.

Barry waited. So far Sebastian was doing things correctly and with consideration.

"Pulse rate one hundred beats per minute, respiratory rate thirty-six breaths per minute. Perfectly normal. There is a well-healed abdominal midline incision and"—he moved the bell of his stethoscope—"lots of borborygmi." He straightened up and removed the earpieces. "'Borborygmi' is a very cumbersome word, Mrs. Bradshaw, for tummy gurgles. Having them means there is no bowel obstruction." He smiled. "You have a perfectly healthy little boy, I am glad to say. You can wrap him up again."

The smile in Linda's deep brown eyes was that of a mother well contented.

Now that Sue was nearly fourteen weeks and no longer bleeding, her pregnancy seemingly progressing well, Barry was less worried about her. But as he noted the relief in Linda Bradshaw's expression, he knew he and Sue were at the beginning of a long journey as parents, with many potential trials ahead.

Tony muttered as his mother tucked him in but did not waken.

"Thank you both, Doctors. You for making the right diagnosis, Doctor Laverty, and you for being gentle and explaining things so well, Doctor Carson."

Barry saw the faintest flush suffuse Sebastian's cheeks. "Um. Well. Yes. Of course."

The man did have an endearing modesty and was even a bit shy, Barry decided. Fingal had earlier in the week discussed with Barry the young man's unfortunate tendency to want to get away early and his seeming lack of consideration for the feelings of the patients, but he had done a good job here today. "We're pleased it all turned out for the best. Tony had a rare condition. It affects about one in two thousand infants, and I'm happy to say the outlook for young Tony is excellent. And now, if you'll excuse us, Linda?"

"Of course, and thanks for coming." She raised the pram's hood and put on her gloves.

As Barry and Sebastian drove off in the Hillman, Barry said, "Well done, Sebastian. You explained things very well."

"Thank you, Barry. I wasn't taught to do that until Fingal showed me." Sebastian smiled. "I must say it does give one—you—a certain satisfaction when you sense the patient's, or in this case the mother's, relief when you've helped them understand."

"It does. I honestly think setting folks' minds at rest is just as important as making the correct diagnosis and giving the right treatment," Barry agreed.

He, and it seemed Sebastian, were content to carry on in silence until Barry had turned onto the drive to Ballybucklebo House. He parked outside the front door. "Here we are. Hop out."

Thompson greeted them. "Doctor Laverty. Doctor Carson. Please come in. His lordship will be pleased to see you." He guided them to the study. "My lord, your physicians."

The bespectacled and jacketless marquis sat at an open Chippendale slant-top desk. He turned from the papers he'd been studying. "Thank you, Thompson. Good morning, Doctor Laverty. Doctor Carson." He stood. "Just been doing some accounts. A rather wearisome business but needs must. Come, have a seat. Thompson, I think coffee would be in order."

"Coffee, sir?"

"Yes, Thompson, coffee."

"Er. Certainly, my lord." Thompson left, closing the door behind him.

The marquis led them to the fireplace, where he settled into the sofa, flanked by Barry and Sebastian in comfortably padded armchairs. "And to what do I owe this pleasure?"

"Doctor Carson and I were going to be in the neighbourhood, so Doctor O'Reilly asked us to drop in and see how you are, sir. He knew you'd seen Mister Wilson on Monday."

"Monday," John MacNeill said, "the day before all hell broke loose in Derry." He sighed. "Myrna and I are very concerned. I'm not going to like having her going to Queen's when term starts again in September. I can only hope matters are settled by then." He smiled. "But you didn't come here to hear my political concerns. It is most considerate of you, Doctors. I'm happy to tell you your dietary suggestions, Sebastian, have greatly alleviated my condition—"

Barry was not surprised by the marquis's use of Sebastian's Christian name. Fingal had explained to Barry last week that the marquis and Sebastian's family were acquainted.

"And Mister Wilson concurs with your opinion, but to be on the safe side has arranged for me to have that barium meal you mentioned, next Friday, so it seems everything's under control."

The study door opened.

"Ah. Thompson. Splendid."

Thompson set a silver tray on a nearby table, poured three cups, offering milk and sugar to the guests then the marquis. "I'll leave the pot, sir, if you promise—"

"Yes, yes, Thompson, I promise. Just one cup."

"Very good, sir." The butler straightened, turned on his heel, and left.

The marquis crossed his legs and adjusted the set of his sharply creased charcoal-gray trousers. "Thompson has taken your dietary suggestions to heart, Sebastian, and is trying to limit my coffee intake to one at eleven and another at eight. He's a good man." He sipped from his cup. "And he does make a fine cup of coffee. Now. Let's put my health behind us. How are you enjoying general practice, young Carson?"

"Very much, sir. I've two fine teachers."

"Indeed, you do."

Barry shrugged and wondered why the compliment embarrassed him a little. Was he becoming more like Fingal?

"And how's your mother?"

Sebastian sighed. "Probably as well as can be expected. I try to help out as best I can."

"Good lad, and are you looking after yourself?"

Barry sipped his coffee and listened.

"I don't have a great deal of spare time, sir."

Only working one night and one weekend in four? Barry's eyebrows rose. What the hell was occupying all that free time?

"You must have some relaxation, Sebastian. When you were younger you used to enjoy a day on our beat on the Bucklebo River. The trout are doing well this year. And you, Doctor Laverty. It's been quite a while since you've asked permission for a day on our water. Why don't the pair of you go out together when you both have the same day off?" He finished his coffee.

Sebastian looked at Barry, who was remembering the man's job interview when, not entirely warming to Sebastian, Barry had deliberately not suggested they go fishing together. Now he was willing to give the man a chance. "I'd like that very much, sir. Thank you. Sebastian?"

"Um. Well. Yes. Rather."

"Good. Good," said the marquis. "That's settled, then. I'll let the keeper know." He looked at the others' now-empty cups. "More coffee, anyone?"

Barry shook his head. "No, thank you, sir. We should be getting back."

"But of course."

Barry rose and put his cup and saucer on the tray. "Thank you for the coffee, my lord. We're pleased you're feeling better and are sure everything will be fine next week."

John MacNeill rose. "Yes, I'm sure it will. Let me show you out." And he escorted them to the door. "I'll expect you both on our water soon."

"Thank you, sir," Barry said, and climbed into the Imp. "Lord John MacNeill is the most gracious man I've ever met." He turned left onto the Bangor to Belfast Road and joined the traffic for the short drive to Number One. "You'll enjoy fishing on his lordship's water, Sebastian."

"Yes indeed. Most generous of the marquis to offer. I certainly had some good days there when I was home from school for the holidays."

Barry indicated for a left turn onto the road that led to the lane behind Number One.

Sebastian sighed. "I suppose if we're going in through the back garden, we'll have to brave the affections of Fingal's hound of the Baskervilles?"

"Kenny?" Barry said as the big chocolate Lab wandered over to them and licked Sebastian's hand. "He's a big softy. And," he opened the kitchen door, "don't call him that in front of Fingal. Particularly not today?"

"Why ever not?" Sebastian closed the door.

Barry smiled. "I only know of one thing more ferocious than a bear with a sore head. An O'Reilly with a sore tooth. I wonder how things will go for him with Mister Drew, the dentist."

17

Another Race Hath Been

O'Reilly, driving down to Bangor for his one-thirty appointment with Mister Drew, turned on the car radio, already tuned to pick up the BBC Northern Ireland one o'clock news.

"It seems there is no improvement in the trouble spots," said a woman's voice. "In Londonderry, where the police are trying desperately to keep the two sides apart, gangs of teenagers on the roof of the Rossville Street flats have been showering the RUC with homemade petrol bombs and rocks. The Nationalist MP, Bernadette Devlin, has been filmed breaking up paving stones to be used as ammunition while her fellow Nationalist John Hume has been urging the Catholic rioters to stop petrol bombing. He has been trying to arrange a truce between the rioters and the police. Rosemount Police Station is on fire."

She paused and O'Reilly shook his shaggy head. He took a deep breath and turned onto the Crawfordsburn Road.

The news reader was continuing, "Meanwhile in Belfast, both Catholics and Protestants are mobilizing and RUC forces are strained to their limits trying to keep the peace . . ."

He'd heard enough. He switched off the radio. The effects of the Panadol were lessening. He grimaced and stroked his lower jaw. Last thing he needed was a bloody toothache to worry about. He was more concerned about trouble on the Catholic Falls Road and, damn it all, wasn't the Royal Victoria Hospital right at the crossroads of the Falls Road and Grosvenor Road?

The Rover passed the hill where five weeks ago he and Barry had rescued a farmer, Desmond Johnson, from under an overturned tractor.

The cut in the man's lip would be healed by now. O'Reilly wondered how Johnson's right ankle was.

He passed through Crawfordsburn, past the Old Inn, and the tiny village of Carnalea, which always made him appreciate the beauty of the Irish language. The name came from the Irish Carnan Lao, meaning the Small Mound of the Calf.

In no time he was climbing Bangor's Dufferin Avenue with the railway station to his right. Left on Main Street, right on Hamilton Road and, glory be, he was able to find a parking spot not far from the grey, three-storey, cement-stucco terrace house where Mister Drew had his surgery.

O'Reilly walked along the pavement, up a short flight of steps, and in through the open front door of Mister Drew's house. A notice on the first door to his right said, *Patients, please take a seat in here. The dentist will be with you shortly.* O'Reilly managed a smile. Mister Norman Drew, like O'Reilly, practised from his home. The dentist had no receptionist. No dental nurse.

O'Reilly went into a deserted small room where half a dozen simple wooden chairs were arranged against pale green painted walls and took a seat. On the far wall, a framed print hung in which a small, redheaded boy with jug ears sat in a dentist's chair, hands gripping the armrests. He stared apprehensively at a dental drill. O'Reilly recognized it as the work of American artist Norman Rockwell. Hardly a comforting image.

A low table stood in the centre of the room. It carried some ancient magazines. *Women's Own, National Geographic,* as well as the recently founded *Ulster Tatler,* which featured stories about Ulster's upper crust.

Before O'Reilly could pick up a *National Geographic,* he heard footsteps in the hall and through the open door saw Mister Drew, a short, balding, bespectacled man in his late fifties, who wore a short-sleeved hip-length white coat over a blue-and-white vertically-striped shirt and grey flannel trousers. He'd opened his practice four years after O'Reilly had returned to Ballybucklebo following the war, and O'Reilly had been one of the first patients. He smiled in greeting. "Fingal," he said. "How are you?"

"I could be better, Norman. I've a raging toothache." He pointed at his lower left jaw.

"Sorry to hear that. You'd better come up and let me take a look." He headed off upstairs, followed by O'Reilly who, having noticed the empty waiting room, said, "Business a bit slow?"

"Not one bit, but I had a couple of cancellations today and I gave you the after-lunch appointment so you'd not have to wait."

"Decent of you." O'Reilly turned on the first landing and began climbing the second short flight of stairs.

"Did you hear the one o'clock news, Fingal?"

"I did. Not good."

"I think it's going to get worse. I've heard a rumour that the head of the RUC, Graham Shillington, is going to ask the Stormont Government to get Westminster to deploy British troops in Derry and Belfast." He went into the second-floor surgery and started to wash his hands.

O'Reilly followed. "I hope so. This rioting can't be allowed to go on." He paused in the doorway and thought of Kitty driving her little car along the Falls Road in another few hours and said a silent prayer. Then he entered the small room with all the enthusiasm of a heretic facing the torturers of the Spanish Inquisition.

A dental chair with a high headrest, padded leather arms, and a footrest stood in the centre of the room, facing a sash window. To the chair's left a foot-pedal-powered drill stood, all pulleys and thin wire cables. It was folded up, its drill bit quiet, but to his mind lurking like a coiled snake. It might be needed soon. O'Reilly had less than fond memories of its grating noise. A circular instrument tray was attached to the rising shaft of the drill and shining stainless-steel instruments were laid out on a green towel on the tray's top. A combined suction apparatus, water fountain, and spittoon stood closer to the chair than the drill. There was a pervasive smell of disinfectant and, O'Reilly imagined, of fear. Possibly his own.

The sound of the running tap was silenced.

"Hop up."

O'Reilly sighed and climbed into the chair.

Mister Drew tilted the chair back, so O'Reilly was semi-recumbent. He had a fine view out the window to the tall tan chimney pots and beyond the rooftops to Belfast Lough and the Hills of Antrim. What he wouldn't give to be tramping those hills with Kitty and Kenny at this moment. He thought of Kitty, undoubtedly in surgery. The pair of them should be outside, enjoying the sunshine and the fresh air.

"Point to where it hurts."

O'Reilly indicated the spot.

"Open wide." Mister Drew shone an overhead light into O'Reilly's mouth and put a small circular mirror between his left cheek and lower back teeth.

O'Reilly braced himself. The next step would be to tap the teeth in the vicinity and see which one hurt—a lot—but Mister Drew said, "All right. Your second lower bicuspid, or premolar, has a cavity as deep as the Marianas Trench and as black as old Nick's hatband." He removed the mirror. "If you've—"

"'—any tears to shed, prepare to shed them now.' Brutus in *Julius Caesar.* Jasus, Norman, you've been beating me to death with that line for nineteen years."

"Perhaps I'd better be getting some new material."

"Can you fill the tooth?"

"Sorry, Fingal. It'll have to go."

"Bugger it." O'Reilly blew out his breath through pursed lips. "Let's get it over with."

Mister Drew clipped a knee-length bib of white rubber to O'Reilly's shirt collar. "Open wide."

O'Reilly did. He stared through the window, trying to distract himself by ignoring the view and counting, over and over, the chimney pots opposite. The needle bit into the place at the back of his mouth where the upper and lower jaws hinged. There the inferior alveolar nerve, which supplies the teeth in the lower jaw, could be blocked with local anaesthetic.

"Just take a minute." Mister Drew began injecting Xylocaine.

O'Reilly's usually infallible memory failed him. He couldn't remember who had explained Einstein's theory of relativity by saying that five minutes with a beautiful woman passed in the blink of an eye, and five in the dentist's chair seemed an eternity. It was true.

Mister Drew removed the needle. "We'll give it a minute or two to work."

"Thank you."

Norman Drew was not a chatty man and O'Reilly was quite content to wait in silence until he felt tingling and numbness in his lower jaw, lips, and the left side of his tongue.

"Open."

O'Reilly did, and the dentist, by looking in his little mirror, used a metal probe to touch the gum beneath the tooth. "What do you feel?"

"Bit of pressure. Tingling. Nothing else."

"Right."

O'Reilly stared past the man and once more counted chimney pots.

He felt and resisted the pressure that was trying to pull his head upward, heard the crunch as the roots were torn free from the bone, and tasted the copperiness of blood.

Mister Drew held up his trophy. "That's better out than in."

O'Reilly had no difficulty identifying the twin crowns and roots of a bicuspid. He heard the *tink* of the tooth hitting the bottom of a stainless-steel kidney dish.

"Here." Mister Drew gave O'Reilly a paper cup of pink-coloured water. "Rinse and spit a few times."

O'Reilly did, noticing how bright red now tinged the ejected water.

Mister Drew put a cotton swab over the site of the extraction. "Bite down hard."

O'Reilly grunted but did as he was told.

"Have you plenty of Panadol, Fingal?"

O'Reilly nodded.

"You'll not feel any pain until the local wears off, but it's always better to head pain off before it starts, so take two as soon as you get home, then two every six hours until the pain's gone when the socket heals. Shouldn't take more than a few days. Rinse your mouth often with salt in warm water. Suck ice cubes. Soft and liquid diet for three days. Any heavy bleeding or severe pain, call me at once."

O'Reilly nodded.

"I'm sure you're glad that's over." Mister Drew smiled. "At least it's paid for by the National Health Service." He stood at the sink washing his instruments before setting them inside a water-filled metal box on a shelf beneath an electrical socket to which the autoclave was plugged. He switched it on. "Twenty minutes and they'll be ready for use again." He came back to stand beside the chair. "Let's have a look."

O'Reilly lifted out the bloodstained swab and opened up so the dentist could see.

"Dry as a bone. Good." He removed the rubber bib.

"Thanks, Norman," O'Reilly said. "Hardly felt a thing." He groaned when Mister Drew trotted out the old dentist's canard: "Neither did I."

O'Reilly got out of the chair. "I'll be off, and thanks again for fitting me in."

"Any time and come back in six months for your checkup and bring your lovely wife for hers."

"I will," said O'Reilly. He descended the stairs, opened the front door, and breathed in the fresh air, feeling the relief that it was all over. He didn't need Norman Drew mentioning his wife to remind him of his concern for Kitty. He'd be heartily glad to see her home and hoped it would be in time for their pre-dinner drink.

O'Reilly parked the car in the garage, letting himself into the back garden, where he was greeted politely by Kenny. The big chocolate Lab bounced out of his kennel and sat at O'Reilly's feet, tail sweeping the grass, gazing adoringly up into his master's face.

"Good boy," O'Reilly said. "I know what you're waiting for, but you're going to have to be patient. It's another eighteen days until the duck season opens, but we'll get a day or two down on Strangford as soon as it does." He patted the top of Kenny's head. "Come on. You can keep me company until Kitty gets home."

The Lab grinned and followed.

O'Reilly let them into the kitchen, where a meaty smell filled the room. Kenny looked at Kinky and immediately lay down in a corner.

"You've trained him well, Kinky."

"If he's going to be in my kitchen, sir, I can't be having him under my feet, so. And how do you be, you poor craythur?"

"Tooth's out."

"Well, better an empty house than a bad tenant. I do be making raspberry jellies, rice pudding, and this blancmange dessert, for I know that after having a tooth pulled, you'll be wanting soft foods, so."

"You really are a gem, Kinky. Thank you."

Kinky ignored the compliment. "Now you go upstairs and put your feet up. As I recall," she said, "you had no breakfast, Doctor. I'll bring you up a mug of my beef tea. It'll be only warm now. Not hot."

That would account for the meaty aroma. "Thanks, Kinky. Come on, Kenny." O'Reilly left the kitchen, headed for the surgery to pick up some more Panadol, and swallowed two. As he and Kenny came out, he met Emer McCarthy, who had come in through the front door. She was whistling a slip jig. "That's a cheerful tune."

She chuckled. "'Drops of Brandy.'"

"I remember you used to be a keen Irish dancer."

"Until a certain Eamon McCaffrey, the lad I'd been walking out with, decided to drop me." Her expression was wry, then softened. "Working here really helped me put all that behind me, Fingal."

"I'm glad of it. And I'm very glad you're part of the practice. What's it been, six weeks?"

"It has, and two weeks ago the same Eamon McCaffrey phoned me out of the blue. Said he'd made a terrible mistake, and would I consider giving him another chance."

"Did he now? And?"

"I'd dinner with him last week and I'm seeing him again this Saturday." She chuckled. "We're going Irish dancing."

O'Reilly smiled. "I wish you the best of luck." And he had reason to. He knew only too well how satisfying the rekindling of an old romance could be.

"Thanks, Fingal. But look here. Never mind me. How's your jaw?"

"One tooth short and still a bit numb."

She smiled. "That's not too bad."

"No, it's not, but I'm going up to the lounge. I'd appreciate a bit of peace and quiet. No Irish dancing with Kinky."

She chuckled. "Fine. I'm on call tonight, so I'll head off to the call quarters. You take care of that jaw."

They parted and O'Reilly led Kenny upstairs.

The big dog went to his usual place in front of the fireplace and O'Reilly to his chair.

Kinky arrived, carrying a mug. She set it on a mat on a table near O'Reilly. "Your beef tea, Doctor O'Reilly."

O'Reilly accepted the tea and took a long sip. "Thanks, Kinky."

"It does be my pleasure, sir. Now I must be getting back to my blancmange. It's about ready to simmer." Kinky left. O'Reilly glanced at Kenny, who was asleep and must be dreaming doggy dreams because his eyebrows twitched, his lips curled and uncurled, and the tip of his tail twitched.

"Emer's old boyfriend's come back. I'll be damned," O'Reilly said to himself, and took another long swallow of his beef tea. His lip and tongue still tingled. Emer's news had been cheerful, but the situation in Ulster was worrisome and he wished Kitty were safely home. O'Reilly yawned. Panadol was mildly soporific. And the beef tea was warm and soothing. He finished it and put the mug on the table. Perhaps it was due to the medication, or perhaps it was in sympathy with Kenny, but for whatever reason, O'Reilly felt his eyes drift closed.

"Wake up, sleeping beauty." A gentle voice. A kiss and a shake of his shoulder. "I'm home."

O'Reilly struggled to sit up and was vaguely aware of the little white cat jumping to the floor. "What? Uh?" He blinked, yawned, and rubbed his eyes. There was Kitty, looking a little tired but very beautiful. He had dreamed of her, he recalled, and now here she was.

"Must have nodded off. Welcome home, pet. How was your day? I've been worried about you."

"Let's talk about me later. How's your tooth?"

"Out. The local's worn off but I've taken Panadol, so there's just a bit of an ache starting."

"I'm glad it's over for you. Now I'm more than ready for my G and T. What'll you have?" She moved to the sideboard and began pouring her drink.

"I reckon whiskey might sting a bit, but there's a bottle of Bass."

"Right." Kitty levered off the cap, poured the beer, brought over both glasses, and sat in the vacant armchair. "My day? Long. I am being reminded daily," she said, kicking off her shoes, "that I'm not thirty anymore. It's tiring standing in theatre. Today we did an aneurysm like Dapper's. Almost three hours. Quick sandwich break and then a meningioma." She smiled. "Happily, it was benign." She lifted her glass. "Cheers." She sipped her drink.

O'Reilly returned the toast.

"And of course, all the ructions in Londonderry. The journalists are starting to call it 'The Battle of the Bogside.' The opinion of the senior staff in the Royal, based on news bulletins and some telephone conversations with colleagues in Altnagelvin Hospital in Derry, is that the RUC are losing the fight."

"I heard the one o'clock news. It didn't sound good."

Kitty shook her head. "It's not. Londonderry's not the only place affected. Catholics are demonstrating all over Belfast. Our casualty department's been very busy since late last night. Things are heating up on the Falls Road."

O'Reilly sighed. "I don't like to think of you so close. So far, no news of a Protestant backlash, but I fear it's inevitable."

"Precautions are being taken. I was stopped by two police checkpoints on the Grosvenor Road. The officers looked and sounded exhausted. I think there's more trouble to come." She took a swallow of her drink.

O'Reilly pursed his lips before asking, "Do you absolutely have to go to work tomorrow? You could be driving onto a battlefield."

Kitty sighed. "Charlie Greer has a full list. I will have to go."

"Bugger it."

"Don't be too worried, Fingal. I'm sure the checkpoints will still be there. If it's not safe, they'll not let me through or else they'll provide a police escort. I'm sure I'll be all right."

"Huh." O'Reilly scowled. "I don't like it. Reminds me too much of the war."

"Come on, old bear. Cheer up. Let's try not to worry about it tonight. There's something else I wanted to talk about."

He swallowed more beer. "Fine by me."

"You remember Consuela?"

"Of course. The little girl you met in San Blas in Tenerife in 1937 while you were nursing there." And with whose widowed father you had an affair? he thought. "We met her in Barcelona in '66. You still write to her, don't you?"

"I do. There was a letter from her for me in the afternoon post."

"And?"

"She has to be in London in mid-September and wonders about popping over to see us and whether we could show her some of the sights."

"I think that would be a wonderful idea—if the place has settled down." O'Reilly completely forgot about the dull ache in his jaw. "Let's hope so. Mid-September would be a good time."

"I'll take a couple of weeks off. You're always hinting I work too hard."

"Kind of you to call it hinting. I think I'm a bit more direct than that."

Kitty smiled. "I like it. It shows you care."

"I do, very much. I could use a break too. I thought she was a charming young woman when we met her in Barcelona at El Crajeco Loco. I'd love to see her again." Suddenly, he felt in a celebratory mood. Kitty was beginning to get the message about work. And when he thought of his wife's old romance, not a single spark of concern ignited in O'Reilly's heart. That hadn't been the case three years ago when he'd first learned about it. Now, despite the news from Derry and the dull throb in his jaw, he cheered. "Hooray."

O'Reilly's yell woke Kenny, who jumped to his feet and barked, occasioning her ladyship to stand, arch her back, and spit.

"It's all right, Kenny," O'Reilly said. "Settle down."

Kenny flopped back down in his place by the unlit fire and closed his eyes. The dog was right to get excited, but not as excited as he was. He took a great swallow and finished his Bass—and quite forgot to tell Kitty about Emer.

18

My Glory Was I Had Such Friends

"Come in, Bertie. Flo." O'Reilly held the front door to Number One open. "Donal and Julie are upstairs with Kitty, but I'd like you two to come into the surgery." He closed the door behind them and led the way. "About your immunisations. It seems you should get your yellow fever ten days before your trip, so we'll do that one in September, but the professor in Belfast says I can give you the others, the typhoid and the combined diphtheria-tetanus-polio, two weeks before you go or even earlier. I have them ready now, and your chloroquine tablets."

"Dead on," Bertie said. "Come on, Flo."

"Have a pew," O'Reilly said. "Who's first?"

"Me." Bertie shrugged off the jacket of his dark blue suit. "Into my shoulder? Which one?"

"Left, please."

Bertie loosened his tie, unbuttoned his top two shirt buttons, and pulled the sleeve down to expose his shoulder. O'Reilly dabbed a spot with a swab soaked in methylated spirits, pinched up a fold of skin and muscle, and rapidly gave two intramuscular injections, each punctuated by Bertie's sudden indrawing of breath. "All done."

"Thanks, Fingal." Bertie did up his buttons and adjusted his tie. "It's only a couple of wee stings, Flo. Nothing til worry about."

Flo swallowed. "I hate jags, but if I must, I must. You mind, Doctor, I fainted six years back when you give me penicillin?"

"I do. Please try not to today. I might suggest—"

Bertie interrupted, "Never worry your head, Flo. I'll catch you if you start to go."

She smiled her gratitude. She had a pale green cardigan draped over her shoulders and removed it. The matching dress beneath was sleeveless and revealed a meaty upper arm.

The injections were rapidly given. Flo re-draped her cardigan. "I'm glad that's over." She smiled. "And I didn't pass out."

"Now, before we join the others—" O'Reilly took a seat at the rolltop desk. "I must warn you that some folks can get a bit sore at the injection sites. Headaches, nausea, low fever, diarrhoea, bellyache—" He consulted a sheet on his desk. "Let's see, stuffy nose, joint pains, they can all occur."

Flo said, "Sounds ferocious, so it does."

"Probably all told only about ten percent of folks do get something. If any of them happen and you're worried, give us a call." He handed Bertie a paper bag. "That's your chloroquine. The ship's doctor will advise you about which countries you'll need anti-malarial protection in, but you each take one dose of chloroquine per week starting at least one week before travelling to the area where malaria transmission occurs, one dose per week while there, and for four consecutive weeks after leaving. I've written those instructions and put your certificates of immunization in the bag."

"Goodness," said Flo. "I feel like Doctor Livingstone, ready to explore darkest Africa." She was smiling, but O'Reilly sensed the smile was covering up some apprehension.

"Except the good doctor probably only had quinine to keep him safe from malaria," said Bertie. "We'll have something more potent than that, won't we, Fingal?"

"Indeed, you will. Chloroquine was discovered in 1934 but initially thought to be a little too potent."

"I don't like the sound of that," Flo said.

"No need to worry. During the war, the U.S. government sponsored clinical trials that proved conclusively it was superior to quinine and safe for use, and that's a good thing. Having malaria's not funny. U.S. civilian doctors have been using this against it since 1947."

"Fair enough," Bertie said. "A million thanks, Fingal."

O'Reilly shrugged. "Come on upstairs for drinks and nibbles."

"Nibbles?" Bertie rubbed his hands together and grinned. "Now you're talking. Come on, Flo."

Kitty and O'Reilly had earlier arranged six chairs in a semicircle facing one of the bow windows. A table, set in the bay, was arrayed with plates, forks, and napkins. Kinky had prepared her favourite party fare—smoked salmon on wheaten bread, sausage rolls, pickled herrings, and chicken liver pâté. Kitty had just finished making melba toast to accompany the pâté before the guests started to arrive.

As O'Reilly reached the open door to the lounge, he surveyed the pleasant scene before him. Lady Macbeth was curled up in front of the unlit fire. Donal and Julie sat beside Kitty, looking at the view past the steeple of the Presbyterian church, over roofs of houses and across the breadth of Belfast Lough to the hills of Antrim, lighter blue on this clear late-summer Saturday. When they heard O'Reilly and the Bishops coming in, all three heads turned to the door and Donal scrambled to his feet.

Kitty said, "Lovely to see you both."

Bertie and Flo greeted Kitty, Donal, and Julie as O'Reilly made his way to the drinks table. "What can I get you?"

Flo said, "Small sherry, please, and sit you down, Donal. It's just me."

Bertie asked for bottled beer.

Fingal gave his guests their glasses. "Now come and have a seat."

Kitty passed the Bishops plates, forks, and napkins. "Please help yourselves."

O'Reilly, needing no bidding, loaded a plate from the food on offer. He raised his Jameson. "Cheers. To friends."

Five voices returned the toast.

"You have a wonderful view from up here," said Julie.

"Thank you." Kitty smiled. "It is peaceful."

"Which, if youse don't mind me saying so," said Donal, "is more than you can say for the poor wee north. Have you been watching it on the telly, er, Fingal?"

Clearly Donal was still a bit uncomfortable with using O'Reilly's Christian name. He sighed. "Hasn't everybody?"

"What a relief," said Kitty quickly, "when the soldiers replaced the police on Thursday and, praise be, the people of the Bogside realized the troops were there to keep the peace and actually welcomed them and the fighting stopped."

"I grant you it's calmer," Bertie said. "But it's desperate, so it is. In Belfast, folks have died or been wounded so badly, they might not recover."

O'Reilly stole a glance at Kitty. She may have had some of them on her operating table.

"Lots of properties set on fire." Bertie took a sip of his beer. "That's why soldiers of the Queen's Regiment and the Royal Regiment of Wales got moved into Belfast."

"I hear things are quietening down a bit there," Donal said, "and that the troops are being welcomed there too as peacekeepers."

Kitty said, "That's promising. I hope it lasts."

"At least we've been lucky here in Ballybucklebo," Flo said. "None of that rubbish here. Nor likely to be, I'm happy to say."

"That's true," Bertie said. "And I'm sure our wee hooleys on Saturday nights at the club are helping. We're having a hop the night for the youngsters. Will you be there, Fingal and Kitty?"

Kitty laughed, glancing at O'Reilly's waistline. "I think our hopping days are over, Bertie."

"But we'll try to get to next Saturday's dance," O'Reilly said.

"It's the Belmont Swing College again," Julie said. "I like their music. Traditional New Orleans jazz." She smiled at Donal. "You'd not think it til look at your man there, but Donal can jive to beat Bannagher."

Donal smiled and shrugged.

"Speaking of things at the club," Bertie said, "reminds me. I seen the marquis about a job he'll have for you, Donal, and the company while me and Flo's away on our cruise. I'll tell you about it Monday. This here's no place for til be talking shop with all this grand food and the ladies present, and all."

"Fair enough, Bertie." Donal grimaced. "But I'll be up til my neck with building them there new flats."

O'Reilly asked, "How's that coming along, Donal?"

"Pretty well. Me and Bertie's got most of it ready to go. We'll start pouring the foundations next week and they'll be dry and ready for us till start on the building proper by late September, early October. With work for his lordship too, I'll be running around like a blue-arsed fly." He clapped his hand over his mouth, which had formed a soundless *O*. "I'm sorry, ladies, but I forget my manners when I'm a bit worried, like, and I am now. Some of the suppliers are real chancers. You have til watch them like a hawk or they'll try to give you short orders. Scam you, like." Donal glanced at Bertie to find the man glaring at him. "Sorry, Bertie. You just said we shouldn't be talking shop and here's me blethering on about the suppliers. Sorry."

O'Reilly smiled as the older man's look softened to one of pride.

"Aye, well, you're dedicated to the job. I like that. But don't worry about the suppliers. Who better to recognize a scam artist than you, Donal Donnelly?" Bertie chuckled, Donal looked uncomfortable, and both took hearty gulps of their beers.

Flo said, "You're forgiven for your slip of the tongue, Donal, and for talking shop. We're none of us shrinking violets here, are we?" Flo nodded to Kitty and Julie.

"I've been known to use some colourful language in my day," said Kitty.

"Aye, so have I," said Julie with a giggle.

"Don't I know it," said Donal.

"Now, Donal Donnelly. Don't you go telling on me."

Flo turned to Donal. "But I'm sorry to hear you're fretting. My Bertie says all the time how well you're doing the managing. Isn't that right, dear?"

Bertie nodded his affirmation. "I've no worries about you, Donal, and speaking of the marquis, he told me that the ould do-re-mi from the club functions is rolling in rightly. He reckons there'll be enough for us to send some kiddies to an interdenominational camp next summer."

Julie said, "Why, that's wonderful."

"Aye," Bertie said. "I do hope things'll stay quiet, but . . ." He shrugged. "And I know it may sound a bit disloyal to the rest of Ulster—but at least me and Flo's going til get a break from it on our cruise if any more trouble does start again."

Donal chuckled. "Lucky youse. Julie and me's not."

Bertie helped himself to another sausage roll. "I'll be here and available to help right up until we leave. Our cruise leaves Southampton on the evening of Monday the fifteenth of September. We'll be crossing on the Liverpool ferry on the Sunday before."

Flo said, "I know how much Bertie's looking forward to this. Me? I'm a wee bit nervous." She glanced down. "I've never been out of Ireland in my puff." She smiled at Bertie. "But I know you're bound and determined, love, so I'm sure it will be all right."

Wither thou goest, I will go, O'Reilly thought, and he'd been right earlier in the surgery. Flo was apprehensive. "I saw a lot of strange places during the war, Flo. I think you're going to find it all most interesting. Honestly."

"Thank you, Fingal."

"Of course you will," Bertie said, "and, Donal, don't you get worried. I'm still here for another month and I'll do everything I can to help as long as I'm here."

"And Donal's very happy about that, aren't you?" Julie said. She sipped her sherry.

"I'm very proud and grateful, and dead thankful, so I am."

O'Reilly, who had just tucked into some smoked salmon, heard the sincerity in the man's voice.

"Look at it this way, son. Me and Flo's no spring chickens. You're a young man at the beginning of what I hope will be a very successful career as a builder. Success means you've til work hard when you're young so when you start to get on a bit you can slow down. Like us."

O'Reilly smiled, caught Kitty's eye, held her gaze, and decided this was neither the time nor place to start nagging her about particulars on her plan to slow down. He looked at Bertie. "True on you, Councillor" was all he said. He took another pull on his whiskey and lifted a pickled herring onto his plate. "And when our friend Consuela comes over in September from Barcelona, Kitty and I are going to take two weeks off."

"Imagine that," said Flo. "You folks knowing someone from Barcelona. Who is she, Kitty?"

"A lovely young woman I met in a place called San Blas in Tenerife when she was a little girl during the Spanish Civil War. Fingal and I saw her in '66. She hopes to visit us next month."

"And Bertie and Flo, that reminds me," said O'Reilly. "Could you book the club for Saturday the thirteenth? When we were at your house in July, I promised you a proper sendoff. Where better to have it?"

Flo said, "That would be lovely. Thank you, Fingal. I'll get Kinky and Maggie Houston to cater, and I'm sure Alan Hewitt will look after the bar."

Bertie tucked his thumbs into his waistcoat. "I'll see to the booking."

O'Reilly held up his now-empty glass. "All this chitchat has given me a thirst. Who's for another, and let's hope this little part of Ireland has enough wit to still be settled down before you two leave, and stay that way."

19

Put a Duck on a Lake

"I'm awful sorry, sir—" A police constable in a dark green uniform stooped to speak through the Rover's open window. The officer had flagged O'Reilly down on the Portaferry side of Greyabbey where the road separated the waters of Strangford Lough from the walls of the Mount Stewart estate. "But may I ask what you're doing on this road at five of a Monday morning." He was one of two manning a checkpoint. This kind of thing had become more prevalent all over Ulster since the rioting in August. British soldiers now patrolled the streets to assist the police in maintaining law and order.

O'Reilly did not like the increased police and army presence one bit but understood the need for it. "Because, Officer, it is the first of September, the opening day of wildfowling season, and I am keeping a promise I made eighteen days ago to that great lummox of a Labrador in the backseat that we'd get a day on the lough down the stream at Lisbane. I'm here at five because opening day's a prime opportunity. The birds have been left in peace all summer and will be less wary, and as a bonus there's going to be a happy combination of dawn and an ebb tide shortly before six A.M."

"Right enough? Them's good conditions, all right." The officer shone his torch into the backseat where Kenny lay. "Handsome big fellah, and dawn flight's a good time. I don't want you til miss the tide. I like a shot myself once in a while, but I have til ask to see your firearm certificate, sir, and shooting licence."

"Bugger," O'Reilly muttered under his breath. He rummaged in the inside pocket of his waterproof jacket. "Here." He handed over a buff-coloured document certifying that he did own the weapon and that it had been properly registered. Enclosed in the certificate was the annual licence required to be able to shoot waterfowl. Taking game birds like pheasants and grouse, and hares, required possession of a different document.

"Doctor O'Reilly? Would you be related to Mister O'Reilly, the solicitor in Portaferry?"

"He's my brother. I'm having lunch with him later."

"He's a sound man. I'm sorry til have delayed you, sir." He handed back O'Reilly's documents. "Have a good day at the ducks." He saluted by touching the peak of his bus-conductor's-type cap with its harp cap badge.

O'Reilly tucked his papers back into his inside pocket.

The other officer lifted the red-and-white-striped pole.

O'Reilly drove on, sad that his Ulster had come to this but heartened by the thought that the authorities were taking steps to try to regain control. And things were much quieter now, with both sides accepting the military as peacekeepers. But how much longer would it last, this "honeymoon period," as Lieutenant-General Sir Ian Freeland, the commanding officer in Northern Ireland, called this truce between the troops and the local people and between the two factions? That was anyone's guess.

As O'Reilly passed through the village of Kircubbin, he could see that to the east the night's black velvet was softening to the greys of a gentleman's formal morning gloves. Never a patient driver and now running late, O'Reilly let the Rover 2000 have her head between the outskirts of Kirkubbin until, to the accompaniment of happy mutterings from Kenny in the back, the car was parked outside the churchyard in the townland of Lisbane.

O'Reilly let Kenny out. The big dog ran to the churchyard wall and promptly cocked a leg. O'Reilly took a leg-of-mutton leather gun case from the backseat, removed the barrels, stock, and fore-end, and put the case back in the car. With long-practiced ease, he joined the barrels to the stock and secured them by inserting the back of the fore-end into its place in the stock and clipped the rest under the twin barrels.

He took his game bag from the backseat, slung it over his right shoulder, and tucked the twelve-bore in the crook of his right arm. "Go over, Kenny."

The chocolate Lab, who had been sitting in front of a low stile in the church wall, now climbed over and waited for O'Reilly on the other side. The dog was well used to the way. This was his third season wildfowling with O'Reilly.

Kenny tucked in at his master's left heel, walked along a well-trodden footpath, past a leaning Celtic cross to one side and the small white-washed church to the other. Sunrise was still some time off, but there was sufficient light for him to be able to make his way.

Together they crossed a second stile onto springy turf at the near left edge of where the little stream had carved its path to the lough.

"Hey on out." Might as well let Kenny enjoy himself.

As the big dog, nose to ground, quartered the stream's bank, O'Reilly looked up to see the gentle hand of what promised to be a fine day soothing the stars to sleep. He was interrupted by a harsh whistled *cryc-cryc-cryc*, and the whirring of pinions as Kenny pushed up a brace of teal from a brackish pool. The little drake—as always—led, his chestnut head with its green crescent starting at the eye distinguishing him from the dark greyish brown pate of the duck.

The Lab turned and stared at his master with a look that said, "Have you forgotten? You're meant to shoot."

"Sorry, Kenny." And O'Reilly felt a lump in his throat as he remembered old Arthur Guinness, who used, on occasion, to look that way too.

They had come to the beginning of the mudflats through which the stream had made its course. Before the war, he and his brother, Lars, had built a rough stone hide at the edge of the stream near the low-tide mark. The ducks from time immemorial followed the stream when, at dawn, they flew out to sea from the fields inland. That site had always offered the best chance of a shot or two for the three hours after slack ebb and before the rising waters pushed O'Reilly off this part of the shore.

He pulled up his thigh waders to their full extent and called to Kenny. "Come." They strode together across the grey flats. O'Reilly's ribbed soles left inch-deep water-filled footprints to reflect the pink tinge now colouring the eastern horizon.

When they arrived at the hip-high, almost-complete circle of rocks that he and Lars had piled there with so much effort more than thirty years ago, O'Reilly leaned his gun against the rocks and hauled an ex-army waterproof gas cape from his game bag. It would provide a dry surface for Kenny to lie on and for O'Reilly to kneel. He laid the cape down and pointed to a sheltered corner of the hide.

Kenny obeyed, lay down, and put his muzzle on his front paws. But this was an alert dog. His nostrils never stopped twitching and his ears moved constantly.

O'Reilly set his game bag beside his gun and bent to gather armfuls of bladder wrack to use to raise the height of the rock rampart behind which he would crouch to wait for the morning flight. The weed was cold and numbed his fingers. The salty tang of the seaweed filled his nostrils.

The dawn sent shy pinks to the belly of a narrow bank of low clouds and, as the sun rose, deepened the red to a shade like the rouge on the cheeks of an aged courtesan.

"That should do," he said to Kenny and moved into the hide, taking several orange Eley-Kynoch cartridges from his game bag and putting all but two in his jacket pocket. Then he loaded and closed his shotgun, put on the safety catch, and leant the weapon muzzle up close at hand.

Kenny's head jerked up. He hunched forward.

O'Reilly crouched lower and stared along the line of Kenny's gaze. His right hand drew the shotgun close and he held it to him, right hand grasping the stock, left hand holding the fore-end, the barrels cold where his fingertips met metal.

He saw a flicker of movement inshore, an irregular mass darker against the low hills. As it came closer, straight at him, the mass separated into its component parts, five ducks in a loose *V* formation, necks outstretched, wings beating, coming closer, closer. O'Reilly stood, slipped off the safety catch, smacked the butt into his right shoulder, and sighted along the barrels with both eyes wide open.

The birds flared, clawed for height. Three wheeled to his left, two to

his right. He swung the muzzles so they passed over the body of the leading bird to his right. The bead sight moved ahead of the tip of the beak
and O'Reilly squeezed the front trigger, felt the jolt of the recoil against
his shoulder, heard the blast, and saw the duck's wings fold in death.
He lowered and broke the shotgun, catching a whiff of burnt smokeless
powder.

Labradors are line-of-sight retrievers. Kenny, now sitting bolt upright
and trembling with excitement, followed the arc of the bird's fall until
O'Reilly saw it land and heard the thump of it hitting the mud thirty
yards away. Kenny never took his eyes off his quarry.

"Hi lost."

As O'Reilly watched the big dog bound forward and gallop across the
now-glistening mud to lift the bird, he extracted the spent cartridge and
reloaded with one from his coat pocket. Snapping the breech shut, he
closed the safety catch and propped the gun against the wall.

Kenny trotted back to the hide, where he sat in front of O'Reilly and
offered his retrieve, which O'Reilly accepted. "Good dog. Good dog."

Kenny's tail thrashed with pride.

O'Reilly pointed to Kenny's spot and he went over and lay down.

O'Reilly examined the yellow bill, glossy bottle-green head, and white
ring separating the colours of the head from the purple-tinged brown
breast of a mallard drake. "You were a handsome chap," he said, and instead of the surge of excitement he usually felt after a well-executed shot,
O'Reilly was sad. He glanced over at a clearly happy dog and thought,
Kenny is just as happy retrieving sticks. Lars has stopped shooting and
works in wildfowl preservation. I've been thinking about it for a while.
Maybe it's time for me to do the same? His grin was wry. Undoubtedly
the ducks don't enjoy this as much as Kenny and me.

He tucked the bird into the game pocket of the bag, pulled out a
thermos, and poured coffee into the broad lid, which doubled as a cup.
O'Reilly sat facing inland toward the Ards Peninsula. The Saltwater Brig,
or bridge, so called because at flood tide it spanned seawater, was to his
left, the church and churchyard and Davy McMaster's farmhouse to his
right. He set his coffee nearby on the cape, fished out his already loaded
briar, lit up, retrieved his cup, and held it in both hands. The warmth

dissolved the numbness in his fingers, and the first sip was like nectar. He set the cup down again, found matches in his pocket, and lit up. The taste of the Erinmore Flake tobacco was soothing. The light was brighter and what had been vague shapes now stood out. Anchored off to his left, between the hide and the grassy bank, a grey-painted, thirty-foot clinker-built, double-ended open motorboat lay on its side on the mud. She was named *Grey Goose*. He knew that a syndicate of four doctors used her to get out to the Long Island, which they owned and used for wildfowling.

Inland, the incandescent sliver of the sun's upper limb crept above the horizon. Grian, the Irish sun goddess, had begun to leave her boudoir. The undersides of the little cloud bank heralded her triumphant progress with an ever-changing pattern of reds, yellows, and scarlets until she had cleared the land and bathed all around, including O'Reilly and Kenny, with her increasing brightness and warmth.

Kenny stiffened.

O'Reilly huddled against the wall and peered up. Six birds, webbed feet outstretched, bodies nearly vertical, wings beating into the air in front of them, slowed in flight and pitched into the stream with a series of splashes.

O'Reilly crouched lower. He knew by the sibilant whistling of the drakes that they were widgeon.

His earlier thoughts about putting away his shotgun returned. He remembered, three years ago, being on the Long Island with his friend and colleague, Doctor Jack Sinton. That day neither he nor Jack had fired at a flock of widgeon. O'Reilly had pleaded that he didn't like their fishy taste because they fed off eel grass.

Jack had replied that he hadn't taken a shot because he simply had a soft spot for the breed and went on to say that while he still loved a day at Strangford, "I just don't need to shoot everything in sight anymore."

Later that day, each man had taken a greylag goose. Old Arthur had made a storming retrieve of the bird that had fallen in the water. O'Reilly glanced at the faithful Kenny. "You've turned out to be a fine retriever, and a good friend, but there'll never be another Arthur Guinness, who's sleeping his long sleep in Lars's field. I miss you yet, you great lummox." And there was a lump in O'Reilly's throat.

He sighed and remembered how, as he'd taken the big bird from Arthur's mouth, O'Reilly had realized that shooting his first greylag goose that day had been the biggest thrill he'd ever had wildfowling. But he had recognized that although he'd experienced great excitement, the goose in its final moments would have been terrified, and he'd felt sad.

He peeped over the wall to where the widgeon, two drakes with buff pates and chestnut heads, and their four ducks, were paddling against the current. Let them be. Kenny and I are enjoying a beautiful day away from the sectarian idiocy, the need to run a medical practice, the everyday worries of life. He'd be content to sit here drinking his coffee and smoking his pipe. Later he'd take Kenny for a walk and let him retrieve the mallard a few times until it was time to drive to Portaferry. To O'Reilly, there was nowhere to equal the shores of Strangford Lough as a place to be at peace. Why spoil it for the birds?

20

He Turneth It Upside Down

Barry sat in the observer's chair, watching and listening. An errant beam of early-September sunlight through the surgery window warmed him, and he relaxed into the chair. There really wasn't much for him to do. Sebastian was clearly well versed in routine antenatal care and Barry wondered why it was necessary to supervise the man. Barry shrugged. His job was to supervise, and he'd do his job.

Sebastian seemed to have abandoned his habit of wearing his Old Harrovian tie, presumably understanding he'd not be seeing a school-mate here in rural Ulster. Instead he wore a plain green one, a Donegal tweed sports jacket, and a plain white shirt. Stethoscope in ears, he was in the middle of taking Mildred Anderson's blood pressure as part of a routine antenatal check-up. Mildred was twenty-three years old, carrying her second pregnancy. Barry knew her of old. A waitress in The Priory Inn in Holywood until two years ago, she had now elected to stay home with the couple's toddler son, Angus. Her husband, Ken, worked at Bangor station as a ticket collector for the Belfast and County Down Railway. Barry'd seen her for a fractured fibula four years ago. That had been the last time she'd played ladies' hockey.

Sebastian said, "Everything seems to be progressing as it should, Mildred. You haven't gained too much weight, your blood pressure is normal, your urine's clear."

And Barry, now that Sue had reached eighteen and a half weeks, hoped that Harith would be saying the same thing every time he saw her for the next twenty-one and a half weeks. Barry worried about her, but not as much as she had started to worry about herself. Once the great relief that she wasn't going to miscarry had subsided, Sue couldn't help question Barry about every little thing that was different. He shrugged. So be it. It was his job to reassure her.

Sebastian stuck his stethoscope in his jacket pocket. "There is one thing, but I don't think you need be unduly worried."

"Oh?"

Barry heard the apprehension.

"Your womb is where it should be for thirty-two weeks in a second pregnancy, and there's one baby lying straight up and down. But right now, its bottom is at the bottom of your tummy."

She frowned. "Oh. Is that what youse doctors call a breech, like?"

"It is but try not to worry. Babies wriggle about all over the place."

She laughed. "The way this one kicks you'd think I'd half the Linfield soccer team in there."

"And that's good. It'll almost certainly have got its head down where we'd like it to be by your next visit in two weeks. If not, we'll get you seen at Royal Maternity, where a specialist will try to turn it."

"How'd he do that?"

"He'll probably not need to. Only three percent of babies are breech at full term, but if he does try to correct the lie, it'll be by using the pressure of his hand on the baby through your tummy. It doesn't hurt and it won't hurt the wee one."

Mildred smiled. "Thank you, Doctor. That's a comfort."

She began doing up her blouse and letting it hang over her long denim skirt.

"Here's a lab requisition. I want you to get your blood test done at Bangor Hospital the day before you come to see us next. That'll be September fifteenth." Sebastian gave her the paper slip and helped her off the examining couch. "Doctor Laverty?"

"I agree. We'll see you in two weeks, Mildred."

"Thank you, Doctors."

Sebastian showed her out and came back.

"I'm feeling about as much use here as teats on a boar, Sebastian. You don't need any supervision for antenatal work," Barry said. "And once again, you set the patient's mind at rest very well. Good for you."

"Um. Well. Yes. Thanks." He sat at the desk, filled in Mildred's ante-natal record, looked up, and said, "By the by, Barry, seeing that patient reminded me, if you don't mind me asking, how's Sue coming on?"

"She's eighteen and a half weeks. Her morning sickness has stopped. She has a distinct bump now. No sign of foetal movement—yet, but that should happen very soon. Harith Lamki saw her last week and says all is progressing as it should."

"I'm delighted to hear it."

But since the threatened miscarriage, she was more anxious than his usual happy-to-be-pregnant patients. And that, of course, kept a concern for her just under Barry's surface. Perhaps when she started back at school in two days, her work, which she loved, would take her mind off it. There was no need to tell Sebastian that. Barry smiled. "Thanks for your concern." He got up from the chair beside the desk. "I'll go and get the next one." Barry walked to the waiting room, which was one-third empty. September was often not busy—it wasn't flu season or a time of infectious diseases for children. He smiled at Cissie Sloan, probably in to have her hypothyroidism checked, and Julie Donnelly with both twins in a double pram, from which came a low gurning. Probably one or both were teething.

"Who's next?" He recognized the florid face of a man who stood.

"Me, Doctor Laverty."

It was Desmond Johnson, the farmer Barry and O'Reilly had helped out from under a tractor eight weeks ago. Barry smiled and wondered why the man was here. "Hello, Mister Johnson. Come with me, please." He wasn't one of their patients and his farm was pretty much at the limits of the area the practice served.

"Hello, Doctor Laverty. The last time I saw you, I was in a bit of a pickle, so I was." He picked up a large brown-paper-wrapped parcel.

Barry nodded. "It was lucky Doctor O'Reilly and I were passing, and we were happy to help."

They went into the surgery and Barry closed the door. "Doctor Carson, this is Mister Johnson. Mister Johnson, Doctor Carson is training to be a GP. I'll get him to look after you, if that's all right."

"Fire away."

"Please have a seat." Sebastian indicated the patients' chairs.

The patient sat on one and set his parcel on the other. It immediately began to slide slowly off the seat. He frowned. "These chairs are a bit out of kilter, if you don't mind my saying."

Barry watched as the man tried to keep the parcel from sliding, and in the end, laid it on the floor. Barry said, "They're so old I think Doctor O'Reilly salvaged them from Noah's ark. We're going to replace them soon." When Fingal had arrived in 1946, right after being demobbed, the practice had been slow to build. But once word got around about the irascible but compassionate Doctor O'Reilly, his practice had been swamped, and he'd altered the chairs to ensure patients didn't stay long to chat. Getting patients in and out in a hurry was no longer a priority with three full-time doctors in the practice.

"Doctor Carson, Mister Johnson is not one of our patients, but back in July, Doctor O'Reilly and I were on our way to Crawfordsburn to—well, to interview you, Doctor Carson—and we saw Mister Johnson out in his field under his tractor and helped him out."

"And yet you were on time and, to my shame, I was late."

"Water under the bridge."

Johnson laughed. "So, it seems I've three doctors to thank for my rescue. I thought I was a goner until I saw these two gents striding up thon field."

"I can see your lip has healed. How's your ankle?"

"Doctor O'Reilly was right. It was only sprained. It's rightly now, so it is. But I'm not, and you and him was so decent I'd like for youse til take me and the missus on as your patients. Our doctor in Bangor retired last year and we haven't needed one until now." He offered Barry two buff cards. "I brung our cards."

"Give them to Doctor Carson, please."

Sebastian accepted the cards, went to the filing cabinet, and took out a new file.

"All the name and address business is on the cards," said Barry, "but you'll need to make a note of the National Insurance numbers."

Sebastian began writing and reading the numbers out loud. "HM seventy-nine fourteen sixty-five B and HM thirty-nine sixty-six twenty-three C."

"We haven't had a new patient since Doctor Carson came on board, so if you'll bear with us."

"'Course," said Mister Johnson, matter-of-factly. "I'm sure you'll want things all done right and proper."

Barry turned to Sebastian. "We fill in the forms after surgery and get them off to the Ministry of Health. Then once you've registered, Mister Johnson, the practice will receive an annual capitation fee from the ministry and we're then responsible for providing you and your wife and family with medical services at any time day or night as long as you remain on our list."

"Just me and the missus. Our son and daughter both live in London now." A stillness came over Mister Johnson's open face. "P'raps just as well what with all that's going on here. Anyway, I appreciate that, Doctor. Very much, and we'll try not til be a bother, but at the moment I'm feeling right peely-wally."

Sebastian asked, "Peely-wally? I don't think I've—"

Barry hid his smile. "It means under the weather. Brought over by the Lowland Scots farmers in the seventeenth century during the Plantation, the settlement of Ulster by Protestants to replace the native Catholic Irish."

"Aye, and we're suffering for it til this day," Mister Johnson said.

Barry nodded and waited while Sebastian collected the routine medical historical information, none of which was particularly dramatic.

"So, what exactly brings you to us today?"

"I'm just not at myself. I'm tetchy, I've the shakes." He held out his hand and Barry could see the tremor.

"I'm sweating, and I get the heart palpitations."

"And when did this start?"

"About four weeks ago, but it's getting worse, so it is."

Sebastian asked, "Have you noticed any muscle weakness?"

"Only in my right calf, but the doctors at Newtonards Hospital said that was til be expected after not using it til the sprain healed."

Sebastian nodded. "Are you swallowing a lot?"

"No, sir."

Barry had already begun to formulate a diagnosis and, judging by the last two questions, so had Sebastian.

"Right," said Sebastian, "time to take a look at you. Nip over to that couch. Jacket and shirt off. Loosen your pants waistband please and hop up on it."

In very short order Mister Johnson was ready and Sebastian was behind the curtain.

Barry heard him say, "I'm going to call out my findings to Doctor Laverty. Don't let any doctor talk scare you. I'll explain when I've finished, and you've got your clothes on again. Now I'm going to look at your eyes."

If those were the first organs Sebastian wanted to examine then his working diagnosis had to be the same as Barry's.

"They are not protruding, nor staring, nor are the pupils dilated. Look down, please. No lid lag."

A phenomenon where the upper lid lagged behind the globe and exposed the white of the eye. The absence of those eye signs, Barry thought, cast some doubt on his original working diagnosis, but Sebastian hadn't finished his examination yet.

"Look up, please."

"I can't look up far, Doctor."

"That's fine. Now I'm going to take your pulse and listen to your heart." Pause. "A hundred and ten and very forceful but no auricular fibrillation. Mister Johnson's skin is warm and a bit sweaty, his hair is silky. Mister Johnson, I'm going to examine your neck and I'd like Doctor Laverty to do so too."

"All right."

Barry rose and joined them. Sebastian had moved behind his patient, who was sitting up with his head bent forward. Both of Sebastian's hands were gently palpating the front of the neck. He nodded to himself, put his stethoscope in his ears, listened over the neck, nodded again, and said, "Swallow, please. Thank you." He turned. "Doctor Laverty?" And inclined his head to the patient.

"Sorry to do this to you a second time." Barry's fingertips immediately felt a swelling, which in part was beneath the strap muscles of the neck. The gland he was feeling, the thyroid, was enlarged, with scattered dense lumps. When Barry put his stethoscope over the organ, he heard a distinct continuous murmuring sound. A bruit. "Thank you. Please get dressed and come and join us."

Both doctors took their seats.

Sebastian said, "Thyrotoxicosis with a nodular goitre."

"Well done," said Barry. "I agree. Now you explain it to Mister Johnson, and what you propose to do." Funny coincidence, Barry thought, that Cissie Sloan, who suffered from a deficiency of thyroid hormones, should be in the waiting room.

Mister Johnson reappeared and took his seat. He looked expectantly at Sebastian.

"Sir, all of us have a gland in our necks called the thyroid. Its job is to produce a substance called thyroxine. Thyroxine's job is to go around in the bloodstream and talk to parts of your body. It's like a messenger from an officer ordering soldiers about."

Mister Johnson nodded. "I understand."

"Sometimes the officer sends too many orders and the soldiers work like slaves to obey, but the end result is that the patient—you—starts to notice differences. For example, a normal heart rate is somewhere between seventy-two and eighty-two. Yours is a hundred and ten."

Mister Johnson smiled. "So that's why I get the palpitations?"

"Exactly."

"Boys-a-boys."

"Too much thyroxine speeds up a lot of body functions. It's no wonder you sweat and feel too warm. But it can be fixed."

"Dead on. Can you fix it right now?"

Sebastian shook his head. "I'm sorry. We'll still need to do some laboratory tests, and we can't do them here. I'll have to send you to a specialist at the Royal Victoria. Professor Desmond Montgomery."

Mister Johnson smiled again. "Oh, aye. There's some good luck. Him and me's the same Christian name, so we do."

"Indeed, you do. He'll order some special tests. There are quite a few, but none of them hurt more than getting a blood test. Once he has the results, he'll see you again, explain what's going on, and pick a treatment for you."

Mister Johnson frowned. "You mean there's more than one treatment."

Sebastian nodded. "Most of the time it'll be one of three anti-thyroid drugs that slows down the production of thyroxine. A few research centres in English hospitals are testing—" He hesitated, and Barry knew Sebastian was deciding whether or not to say "radioactive"—"specially treated iodine, but it's not available in Belfast yet."

"I see."

"And sometimes removal of the gland is recommended."

"An operation, like?" He put a hand to his neck. "I don't much fancy getting my throat cut."

Sebastian smiled. "Generally, surgery is only called for with huge swellings, we call them goitres, ones behind the breastbone, or if the patient is experiencing a lot of what we call 'pressure symptoms' on their gullet or windpipe and have difficulty swallowing or breathing, and you're not, are you?"

Mister Johnson shook his head.

"Then I don't think there's much risk of you having to have an operation."

"Dead on."

And there wasn't in this case, unless the specialist had reason to suspect the presence of malignant changes in the thyroid gland. Sebastian had left that possibility out of his explanation and Barry applauded that.

"I'll get a letter off and they'll send you a letter back with an appointment time and date. I'm afraid there's not much us GPs can do to make life easier for you in the meantime, but I'll mark my request urgent."

"Thanks a million, Doc."

"Have you any questions for us?"

Mister Johnson rose. "No, sir, but I have this. I'm sorry I didn't know you was here, Doctor Carson, but this here's"—he gave the package to Barry—"a brace of geese to say thanks to you, sir, and Doctor O'Reilly for helping me out from under thon tractor."

"Thank you, Mister Johnson," Barry said, "on behalf of us both. That's very kind of you. Doctor O'Reilly's housekeeper is an excellent cook and so is my wife. They'll do your geese proud."

Desmond Johnson donned his flat cap and dipped his head in acknowledgment to the two men. "I'd best be off. Thanks, again, Doctors."

Barry watched Mister Johnson leave. "My compliments, Sebastian. Your diagnosis was spot on, in my opinion. A bit more teaching—it was more likely to be a nodular goitre because?"

"Because diffuse goitres are more common before age thirty-five and cardiac symptoms are not pronounced but eye signs are. Nodular ones occur after thirty-five and cardiac symptoms are prevalent, but eye signs are not."

"Good man." Barry grinned. "I also want to compliment you on your explanations."

Sebastian chuckled. "I learned not to say 'hormones' at Bart's when I told one woman that she would need hormone treatment. She screamed. You'd have thought I was suggesting hanging, drawing, and quartering. When I was a student there the oral contraceptive was being introduced. The papers were full of scare stories and 'hormone' became a word to conjure fear."

"I learned that lesson the hard way too. Particularly with country patients. I thought your not using the specific was kind." His voice became serious. "I also like the way you didn't mention the possibility of malignancy when you explained the indications for surgery. Well done."

"Better he blames me if it turns out to be the case—which is very unlikely—than put the fear of God, almost certainly unnecessarily, in the man for a couple of weeks."

"I agree," Barry said. "Now, while you're writing your referral letter, I'll take the geese to Kinky. Then I'll bring in the next customer." He hefted the parcel. The pair of geese were heavy and fleshy. They would make two wonderful meals. "There are some distinct advantages to rural practice."

"I'm beginning to see that. I could get to like it very easily."

As Barry trotted along the hall, he knew he was warming more to Sebastian Carson and realized they still hadn't taken the marquis up on his offer of a day's fishing. Trout season would be ending on September 30. Another season, wildfowling, was starting today, September the first. Those dates on the calendar heralded age-old seasonal changes all over Ireland. Fingal and Kenny were down on Strangford for opening day and Barry remembered how, back in 1964, he'd taken a girl called Patricia Spence down to Gransha Point for a picnic not far from Lisbane on Strangford Lough and it had rained. The girl was long gone and no longer missed. But Strangford remained. Timeless. Eternal. He wondered how Fingal and Kenny were getting on there?

21

No Man Is Born an Angler

Barry's car passed under some ancient elms on the rutted lane past Bally-bucklebo House. Their asymmetrical leaves looked dispirited and faded so late in the summer. Tree branches scraped the windows until, leaving the small wood behind, he entered a broad meadow. The lane crossed the field heading toward the banks of the Bucklebo River, where weeping willows wandered in a meandering line following the bends in the stream. When the lane petered out, Barry parked, grabbed his gear, took off his shoes, and tugged on a pair of Wellington boots. He slung his creel, shouldered his rod, and walked through the recently mown hay with its scent fragrant in his nostrils. At the bank of the river, the current, sunlight dappling its wavelets, flowed from left to right.

Behind him another car approached, turned—Sebastian's green Mini Cooper-S. When they had agreed to go fishing together five days ago and had sought the marquis's permission to do so on this Saturday afternoon, Sebastian had explained that it would suit him better to go straight to the river than meet Barry at the Lavertys' bungalow.

The Mini parked beside Barry's Imp, and to his surprise, Sebastian helped a woman out of the passenger's seat, opened the back door, and handed her what looked like a painter's easel. He dragged out a folding stool and then produced a fishing rod and creel. The pair walked across the meadow.

"Barry," he called, when they were close enough to be heard. "I'd like you to meet the mater, Mrs. Ruth Carson. Mother, Doctor Barry Laverty."

"How do you do, Mrs. Carson?" Barry was soon speaking to a woman whom he guessed to be in her early fifties. She was slim and blue-eyed with a fringe of auburn hair peeping out from under a green silk head-scarf.

"How do you do, Doctor Laverty?" She smiled and Barry saw regular white teeth and laugh lines at the corners of her eyes. "I hope you don't mind me tagging along."

"Not at all. It's a pleasure to meet you."

"Thank you. And you." Ruth Carson looked over at her son. "Dear Sebastian," she said. The fondness in her eyes made them sparkle like the sun glinting off the nearby river. "I'm having one of those days, I'm afraid. Since Sebastian's father died, there are times I just don't like to be alone. The shock, I suppose, so sudden. A heart attack, you see. I'm afraid I still haven't quite got my feet under me."

She stooped to pick a long wand of timothy grass that had escaped the mower and continued speaking, her eyes still on the ground. "My son kindly took me shopping this morning then out to lunch in Bangor at the Dufferin and Ava restaurant, and then invited me to join him this afternoon." She straightened and indicated her easel. "I'm a keen watercolourist. I can already envisage a lovely landscape here. I promise I won't get in your way."

"I'm sure you won't, Mrs. Carson." Barry glanced at Sebastian. He was busying himself with his mother's easel, the very acme of filial duty. Barry thought back to the interview at the inn and looked at Ruth Carson. Was she the reason her son needed time off? Perhaps Barry and Fingal had misjudged their young trainee.

"I'd rather prefer it if you'd call me Ruth. May I call you Barry?"

"Of course."

"Splendid. Now I shall be perfectly happy to set up my easel here while you boys trot off and annoy the fish. Do give me a hand, will you, Sebastian?"

While Sebastian got his mother settled, Barry realized that it wasn't only the influence of Harrow that had given Sebastian his upper-crust accent and speech patterns. His mother hadn't the slightest suggestion, as was prevalent among some top-drawer Ulsterfolk, of letting, in local parlance, the buttermilk show through the cream—when an otherwise perfect Oxbridge accent was marred by the sudden intrusion of Ulster tones or idiom.

"You're all set now, Mother," Sebastian said as Ruth Carson settled herself on her stool and opened her paint box.

"Indeed I am. Off you trot, boys. I believe in huntin', shootin', and fishin' circles the good-luck wish is 'tight lines.'"

"It is," Sebastian said, "and we'll not be far away. If you need me just shout. Come on, Barry. As I remember, there's a wide curve upstream. With a long ripple. There's usually a trout at the tail of the ripple." He started to walk, and Barry fell into step by his side.

Barry noticed Sebastian's Hardy split-cane rod and single-action reel. Trust him to have the Rolls-Royce of fishing tackle. Barry said, "On this side downstream of the ripple there's a still, deep pool shaded by a willow. Trout lurk there too. Do you want the ripple or the pool?"

"I'll take the pool and move slowly downstream so I can get close to Mother again."

Barry stopped. "Sebastian?"

He turned to face Barry. "Yes?"

"May I ask you a personal question?"

"Um. Well. Yes, actually."

"I've only known you for a month, but you strike me as a private person, and I don't want to overstep myself."

"Perfectly all right."

Barry inhaled, looked the man in the eye, and said, "Fingal and I have been a bit concerned about you needing a lot of time off. Getting away the minute work's done." He glanced downstream to where Mrs. Carson was holding up a paintbrush and squinting over it to establish perspective. "Something your mother just said about not liking to be alone made me wonder. Is it for her sake you're always rushing off?" He waited.

Sebastian stared at the toes of his Wellingtons before looking directly at Barry. "Yes." He swallowed. "I know I can trust you, Barry."

Barry nodded his encouragement.

"My father's death came as a terrible shock. I think the mater is finally coming around—at least I hope so. But she's been very needful and somewhat reliant on yours truly. There's more, but I'd rather not . . ."

"I understand. Say no more." Barry used his rod tip to point at the river. "I'll take leave of you here at the pool and hope the fishing will take your mind off things. Come on. I want to get a fly in the water."

Barry left his colleague, no, friend—that was closer to the right word now—setting up his rod and line and studying the pool.

Thirty yards farther on, Barry stopped a little upstream from the tail of the ripple, scrutinised it, and decided there was no evidence of any kind of insect hatch or rising trout. Nothing with which to match a specific fly. He reached in his creel, took out an aluminium fly box, selected a Williams Favourite, and replaced the box. The black-bodied fly, with its silver wire rib and black hen's hackle, often was effective in attracting the fish. He tied it to his fine nylon leader.

Right. Barry stripped a loop of line from the reel, bent his right elbow back, and quickly let the loose line be carried back. He made sure the rod tip was just past the vertical, then, as the line reached its full length, brought the rod tip rapidly forward. The latent energy built up by the weight of the line added extra push and let the fly drift onto the centre of the ripple at the full extent of the line. Borne swiftly downstream by the current line, the leader and fly arced downstream until the fly was brought to a halt. Any waiting trout would be presented with what looked like an appetising morsel that had drifted down to the fish.

No luck.

He retrieved and cast again.

Part of what he loved about fly-fishing was the near-perfect peace of the riverbank interrupted only by the tinkling sound of the water and today, on the Bucklebo River, the occasional bleat from a flock of black-faced ewes on the opposite bank.

He cast again. This kind of fishing, requiring as it did complete concentration, only gave him a split second to decide not to think about the state of Ulster, Sue's now uneventful and progressing pregnancy, and Sebastian's cryptic remark that "there's more but . . ." before he felt a tug and jigged the rod back to strike the hook deeply into the fish.

The rod tip arced down, and the reel screamed as the line ran out. He made sure the rod's tip was vertical to ensure the pressure on the line would keep the fish from throwing the hook.

The fish stopped running and Barry reeled in, but the trout wasn't ready to surrender yet. Barry felt the tension on the rod increase, stopped reeling, and let the line run out. In total, the brown trout made six runs before Barry netted it, dispatched it, admired its speckled scales, and put it in his creel.

He checked his fly to make sure it had sustained no damage and the fine nylon leader was intact. All was well.

Generally, one fish alone would occupy the tail of a ripple. Barry glanced downstream to where Sebastian, with a lovely fluid action, was working the pool. Barry decided to fish his way downstream. He took a few paces to his right and cast several times. No luck. A few more paces. Same actions. Same result.

His attention was caught by a splash from his right. Barry turned to see Sebastian's rod being held vertically, the upper section bent nearly double. A flash of silver reflected the sunlight as his fish hurled itself from the water before falling back on its side with a slap and splash. The rod tip sprang back and the bend in the rod flattened out. Sebastian had hooked the proverbial one that got away. Barry smiled, lengthened his stride, and decided to go and have a chat while Sebastian selected and attached another fly.

When Barry arrived, Sebastian looked up.

"That looked like a big one."

"About four pounds, I'd wager. Not that I'm a gambling man. Far from it." Sebastian frowned. "Anyway, he fell on the leader and snapped it." Sebastian smiled. "I saw you had a bit of luck."

Barry patted the creel. "He's in here."

Sebastian nodded. "Good for you, Barry." Sebastian leant his rod against his shoulder. "Before I start fishing again there's something I want to say."

Barry waited.

"I think I owe you and Fingal an apology."

Barry frowned. Was he going to hear what only half an hour ago Sebastian hadn't wanted to confess?

"When you both interviewed me, I told you my father had died last year. But I lied about what killed him." He took a deep breath. "Mother and I are dreadfully ashamed."

Barry waited.

"He hanged himself. Mother found him."

"My God." Barry took a step back and stifled the urge to ask why. "That's terrible. No wonder she's still upset."

"Quite." Sebastian stared into the distance before saying, "He had been a heavy gambler and had lost so much that most of the family's money is gone. The shock, the grief, and the shame nearly killed Mother."

"I'm so sorry."

"Thank you. Apart from the loss of my father—" He paused, and Barry saw a parade of emotions swiftly cross his face. "—it's not a complete disaster. He never mortgaged the house, thank God, so it's paid for, and there's just enough for Mother to get by on if she lives frugally, which she's learning to do. I give her most of what I earn, and it will get easier when I'm fully trained and can secure an assistantship with a better income."

Barry remembered Sebastian's answer to the question during his interview in July about why he had chosen GP. "I'd like to finish my training quickly." Was this the reason? It certainly seemed so.

"She told you there were times she didn't like to be alone, but until very recently that was pretty much all the time, dear old thing. So, she's desperately needed my emotional support too. Still, I think she's improving."

Barry moved closer and put a reassuring hand on Sebastian's shoulder. "I am so sorry. I do understand."

"Thank you. Thank you very much." He inhaled. "It's been hard not being completely honest. I don't think lying comes very naturally to me. Mother and I have been telling everyone he died of a heart attack and the police were very discreet." He took a deep breath and glanced over at his mother again. "I know you've both been aware of my wanting to get away the minute the work was done. One day, I led Fingal to believe I needed some fun after the gruelling workload of my houseman year, but mostly I've just been trying to cover up the reality of our situation. I once asked Kinky for a recipe I said I'd give to our cook, Mrs. O'Gara. I'm afraid Mrs. O is no longer with us." He shrugged. "I've been doing a lot of the cooking. Mother had never so much as boiled an egg before Father died. She feels we must try to keep up appearances and so I do my bit to try to help."

"You can count on me. I'd do the same. Sometimes secrets are necessary."

"I'd appreciate it if you don't indicate to Mother that you're in on the secret."

Barry decided that to say "confession is good for the soul" would be trite. "I'm flattered you would confide in me. You needn't worry about me letting anything slip in front of your mum."

"Thanks, Barry." Sebastian managed a weak smile. "You've no idea what a relief it is to have got that off my chest. You must have thought me such a prig at my interview. I really wanted the job and, well, I was nervous. And then all that rot about not having any intention of being celibate and running off for a date afterward. Complete fabrication. My social life has been nonexistent." Sebastian looked quickly at Barry and then away.

"I hope that changes now your mother's a little better. It's admirable how protective you are of her, but it's important to have some time to yourself. So apart from that free advice," he said with a smile, "is there any other way I can help?"

Sebastian shook his head once, then said, "I'd like you to explain to Fingal. I really want him to have a good impression of me. Will you do that?"

"Of course, unless you'd like to tell him yourself?"

"I'd rather not. Too embarrassing." He looked back to the water. "And I'd like it if we fished this pool together. I do find fly-fishing can be all-consuming. Takes one's mind off one's cares."

"It'll be my pleasure, Sebastian."

"Do you know, Laverty, you really are a brick." Sebastian offered his hand, which Barry shook, thinking that only an Old Harrovian would use terms that might have come straight out of a Frank Richards *Billy Bunter* novel.

Before the afternoon was out Barry had landed another brown trout and Sebastian two. By mutual agreement, they'd decided to pack it in and had walked together to where Ruth Carson sat admiring her work, a fine, subdued piece depicting the willows, river, and far bank populated by sheep beneath a cerulean sky where clouds like woolly celestial sheep roamed.

"Hello, boys. Have you had fun?"

"The whole thing was very relaxing," Sebastian said, "and we both took fish."

"I'm delighted," she said. "Trout for dinner tonight." She pointed to her frame-mounted paper. "And I've finished my painting. One of my better efforts, I think. This place agrees with me."

"It's lovely, Mrs. Carson—Ruth."

"Would you like to have it, Barry?"

"I couldn't possibly."

"Don't be silly. Our house is cluttered with the things. It's yours—for you and your wife."

"Thank you very much."

"Sebastian has told me you're expecting your first baby soon. Congratulations."

"We are, thank you. Sue will love the painting." He could already see the space in the Lavertys' living room where it would hang.

Two blackbirds fleeing from the elm wood both gave their alarm calls. The source of their annoyance appeared in the meadow—Lord John MacNeill, carrying a blackthorn walking stick and accompanied by his red setter, Finn MacCool.

Ruth started patting down her hair. Smoothing her dress. She muttered, "I'm not fit to meet a peer."

"Of course you are, Mother."

"Welllll, I suppose."

John MacNeill arrived. "Sit," and Finn MacCool obeyed. "Mrs. Carson." He lifted his paddy hat and smiled. "How lovely to see you."

She rose from her stool and made a small curtsey. "And you, my lord."

He replaced his hat. "Come, come, Ruth, our families have known each other for ages. It's John if we're among friends, and of course that applies equally to you, Sebastian, and you, Barry."

"Thank you, sir," Sebastian said.

Barry inclined his head.

"Now, tell me, how's my water?"

For a split second Barry thought the marquis was having urinary difficulties, then realised his mistake and had to stifle a laugh. Of course, he was referring to his beat on the Bucklebo River. "We've had a wonderful afternoon," Barry said. "Thank you again for allowing us to come."

"Anytime. Just ask." He looked at his watch. "The time's right and it's been ages since I've seen you, Ruth. How would the three of you like to come up to the house for a quick preprandial?"

"That would be delightful," Ruth Carson said.

"I saw your cars, so I'll walk on ahead, give you time to pack up. Let Thompson know you're coming." He bent to the easel. "I see you haven't lost your touch, Ruth. Right. Come on, Finn." And with no further ado, the Marquis of Ballybucklebo, militarily erect, strode off home with Finn MacCool at his heel.

Thompson ushered the guests into what was becoming to Barry a familiar room, the marquis's comfortable study. John MacNeill rose from an easy chair, welcomed his guests, and seated them in an arc of chairs facing his across a low circular coffee table. "Now," he said, walking to a sideboard, "what can I get you, Ruth?"

"Dry sherry, please?"

He started to pour and asked over his shoulder, "Boys?"

Sebastian emulated his mother.

Five years ago, Barry would have asked for the same, but now said, like Fingal, "Small neat Jameson, please, John." He'd never really developed a taste for sherry, no matter how dry.

The marquis handed each their drinks, returned to the sideboard, opened a door to reveal a small refrigerator, and poured himself a glass of milk. "Barry and Sebastian will understand, Ruth, but for your sake I'll tell you I had to consult my doctors last month for a little bit of chest trouble. Your son made a very astute diagnosis of nothing worse than simple gastric reflux—"

Barry saw Ruth glow.

"It was in early August and he referred me to a Mister Wilson. A subsequent barium X-ray confirmed the original diagnosis, I'm happy to say, but I'm afraid I'm not allowed much alcohol." He took his seat and drank, then wiped off his milk moustache with a white linen handkerchief.

Ruth said, "I'm very glad to hear it's nothing serious, John."

"Thank you. I'm relieved too." He smiled at her. "I must say, and if you don't mind my saying, Ruth, you are looking lovely. The country air clearly agrees with you."

"Thank you, sir," she said, inclining her head.

Barry wondered if he detected a tiny blush and thought, What a gracious man you are, Lord John MacNeill. Then he thought he saw something in the man's look, a look of interest that made him wonder about the long-a-widower peer. Barry decided he was no matchmaker and swallowed some whiskey, savouring its smoothness.

John said, "I'm afraid I owe you all an apology. It's Cook's day off so I cannot offer you any hors d'oeuvres." He chuckled. "In a pinch, Thompson and I can open a tin of baked beans—"

"That's perfectly all right, John," Ruth said. "It's delightful just being here. I haven't been out for a drink for ages." She sipped her sherry.

"Really?" John MacNeill looked thoughtful but did not comment. Turning to Barry, he asked, "So, Barry. How is your lovely wife?"

"She's back teaching, John, since Wednesday, and is very well, thank you."

"Excellent, and Sebastian, how are you enjoying working with Fingal O'Reilly? He can be a bit of a rough diamond sometimes, but don't let him fool you. Inside he's a marshmallow."

Sebastian said, "You could have fooled me—on both counts. He has always been straight with me, is a fine physician, and cares for and about his patients."

"An excellent physician indeed. And so are you, young Laverty."

"Thank you, John."

"And I know how easy it can be to feel a bit junior in a profession where seniority counts. I can still remember as a mere lieutenant being terrified of the major. Sebastian, don't be intimidated. I know you dislike blowing your own trumpet, but you already have a lot to be proud of."

Sebastian frowned. "Sir, please."

"No, Sebastian. Barry should hear it. Did you know Sebastian won an exhibition to Queen's University Belfast and also a bursary to Queen's College Cambridge? You chose Cambridge."

Barry whistled. Sebastian Carson was clearly a lot cleverer than the average young physician. "You never told us about that, Sebastian."

Sebastian smiled. "You never asked me."

"We—I'm very proud of him. His father was too. But my Sebastian's a modest boy."

And how, Barry thought, his respect for the young man increasing.

"And he takes very great care of his mother, since," she inhaled, "our loss."

"Yes. I do understand. And you both still have my deepest sympathy."

"Thank you."

"Tell me, Ruth, I was thinking about something you said a bit earlier. Have you begun to rejoin society?"

She looked down and shook her head.

"Would you think me very impertinent if I said I think it's time you did?"

She nodded. "I know you're right, John, but it's difficult."

He coughed. "I think if you would permit it, I might be able to offer some assistance."

"Oh?"

Barry detected some interest in her voice.

"Next Saturday the village is giving a going-away party for a local dignitary." As if to stiffen his reserve as he might have with a whiskey, John took a mouthful of milk and, ignoring the milk tide line on his upper lip, continued, "I would consider it a great honour if you would permit me to escort you there."

22

And Singing Still Dost Soar

"Ladies and gentlemen. Ladies and gentlemen. If I could have your detention—"

The volume of sound, which had been decreasing in the main hall of the Ballybucklebo Bonnaughts' clubhouse, was magnified by a huge outburst of laughter.

O'Reilly wondered sometimes if Donal's malapropisms weren't deliberate for the sake of getting a laugh. That one had certainly done the trick and lifted the mood in the room.

Donal waited for the laughter to subside. "All right. All right. What I want is your attention."

"You have it, eejit," the off-duty Constable Malcolm Mulligan called, "and don't be embarrassed, Donal. We all make mistakes and we all love you."

Several voices, including O'Reilly's, called, "Hear, hear."

"Thank youse all. And I need your attention so I can tell youse about this here party. Unlike the talent contest, I'm not MC and there's no structure. Youse all know Mister and Mrs. Bishop's going off on a world cruise the morra. We're here til wish them bon voyage, but my senior partner, Bertie, has a request. Feel free to drop by our table, but he doesn't want til make a speech, and he does not want any speeches made. He wants me to thank youse for coming out the night. He's dead pleased how everybody here in Ballybucklebo is like one big family and he's asked me til tell youse that the club is donating half the drinks profits to the summer camp for kiddies fund and Bertie's going to cough up the same amount."

That remark earned a solid round of applause and cries of, "Sound man." "Dead on." "Heart of corn."

"I'm nearly finished," Donal said. "There's no program, but if anyone wants til do a party piece, the mike will be on. That's all I have to say, but before I go let's wish Bertie and Flo a wonderful cruise and give them three cheers. Hip-hip . . ."

The thrice repeated "Hooray"s were deafening.

Donal came down from the stage and had his hand shaken by Bertie before he was able to take his seat.

O'Reilly noticed motion at the opposite end of the room. Lord John MacNeill was coming toward O'Reilly's table, and it wasn't his sister accompanying him as usual. The woman stopped, spoke to John MacNeill, and together they went to a long row of trestle tables covered in white linen tablecloths against the far wall where Kinky and Maggie Houston stood. The woman left something, and she and John approached O'Reilly's table. He studied the blue-eyed, middle-aged woman and thought, *My father, God rest him, would have described her as handsome.* As the couple progressed, men inclined their heads in mini bows, and any standing women curtsied, to be thanked by smiles from his lordship.

O'Reilly and Barry stood when they arrived.

"My friends," said the marquis, "may I present Mrs. Ruth Carson of Cherryvalley? Our families have known each other for years."

During the time it took for everyone else to be introduced, O'Reilly realized that he should not have been surprised. Earlier in the week over a pint in the Duck, Barry had briefed Fingal on how he had met Sebastian's mother and why Sebastian needed so much time off, his covering up of his father's suicide, his academic achievements, and how Mrs. Carson had yet to venture out socially since her loss. If this was her first real sociable venture, it was a baptism of fire. He looked around the crowded hall.

Bertie, Flo, Donal, and Julie sat at the next table. The other tables were all full, and indeed it was standing room only. Behind the bar hatch, Alan Hewitt was serving a short queue. Tobacco smoke blued the air and the level of noise was rising.

He hoped the crowd didn't scare Mrs. Carson away. But she looked relaxed and happy. Perhaps because the folks here were not part of her regular social set?

"And last, but not least, Mrs. Ruth Carson, may I present Doctor Fingal Flahertie O'Reilly?"

"How do you do, Doctor?"

"How do you do, Mrs. Carson?"

John MacNeill positioned her chair, helped her to be seated, accepted a warm look of gratitude, and pulled out his own. "I really do think," he said as he sat, "we are sufficiently far enough away from other tables that we can drop the titles."

"Thank you, John," O'Reilly said.

"And, Ruth, my dear. A drink?"

"Mrs. O'Reilly's drink looks very refreshing. Is that a gin and tonic?"

"It is, and please do call me Kitty. Barry mentioned the beautiful watercolour you gave him on Saturday. We have painting in common." The two women bent their heads toward each other and began talking.

John smiled at O'Reilly and nodded his head to the two women. "One G and T coming up. And can I get anyone else anything?"

Heads were shaken.

"Fingal, I have been most abstemious since it was suspected that I had reflux. But, tonight might I—?"

O'Reilly smiled. "Two pints. That's your limit."

"Thank you." And John MacNeill headed for the bar hatch.

A voice arose above the hubbub, asking, "Did any of youse see pictures on the telly of that there August music festival on the Isle of Wight?"

"I did," a woman answered, "with Bob Dylan and Jane Fonda, and all. He sang 'Tambourine Man' and—"

A roar of laughter from elsewhere drowned out the rest of her sentence.

Ruth and Kitty looked up from their conversation at the sound of the laughter and O'Reilly took the opportunity to say, "You must be very proud of Sebastian, Ruth. We are getting to know him much better. I know you'll agree, Barry, Sebastian's very well trained and has the makings of a first-class GP. We're enjoying having him."

"Thank you, Fingal. And he's enjoying being with you. I'm so sorry I've taken up a great deal of his time until recently."

"He didn't go into details," Barry said, "but he explained that you have been upset, for which we are sorry, so we don't hold it against him."

Tactful, O'Reilly thought. Of course, Ruth didn't want anyone to know the true facts. It must have taken a great deal of spunk for Sebastian to have confessed to Barry. O'Reilly could admire both the young man's support of his mother and his later honesty. Fingal had told Kitty, because he told her everything. He'd had no need to ask her to keep it confidential.

Ruth smiled. "Thank you both. I'm afraid I've played havoc with his social life, but tonight, because I'm here, he is seeing a young woman."

O'Reilly smiled, remembering Sebastian's remark that "I've not the remotest intention of being celibate." He glanced over to Bertie's table, where a short queue of well-wishers had formed. Ronald Fitzpatrick and Alice Fitzpatrick, née Moloney, were at its head. O'Reilly wondered how married life was suiting them.

He got his chance to find out when Ronald and Alice stopped beside Fingal, who automatically rose.

"Please do sit down, Doctor," Alice said, but O'Reilly remained standing. "Ronald. Alice. Great to see you both. That dress really suits you, Alice. A beautiful colour. What would you call that?"

She smiled. "Thank you. I believe Ronald called this cerise, the colour of cherries. Even though I am a dressmaker, Ronald chooses all my clothes for me now. He has a wonderful fashion sense."

Ronald's Adam's apple bobbed. "It's my pleasure. A beautiful woman like you should be well dressed."

"You really are a sweetie of a husband," said Alice.

O'Reilly watched as the two beamed at each other. He was delighted for them. He looked over at Barry and Sue, wishing they looked as happy as the Fitzpatricks. Barry had shared with him the strain that Sue's early miscarriage scare was having on the two of them. Although she looked as lovely as ever, O'Reilly could see the telltale signs of Sue's anxiety—the smudges under the eyes, her gaze darting to and fro, her hands playing with the end of her plait.

"We'll be trotting off," Ronald said. "We won't interrupt Kitty's conversation with the marquis's guest, so please give her our regards."

"I'll tell her," said O'Reilly as the couple, Ronald's arm round Alice's waist, moved off.

"Excuse me—"

O'Reilly looked up to see Sonny Houston standing beside the table, holding Maggie's hand. She had her dentures in and two purple freesias in her hatband.

Sonny wore a black patch over his left eye. "We went over to wish Bertie and Flo bon voyage and—" He smiled at Ruth, who was a stranger to him. "—we don't mean to intrude, but I just wanted to pop over and tell my doctors that I had my operation last week. It was easier than I had expected, and Mister Cowan says he's very pleased. I've to wear this patch to rest my eye until I'm told to get my new glasses. So, thanks again, and please thank Doctor Carson."

"I will," O'Reilly said. "I'm glad it turned out well."

A voice from the other side of the hall called out, "Hey, Sonny, you look like a pirate. Where's your parrot? Get yourself over here and tell us why you're done up like that."

Sonny waved and they took their leave.

"Ruth, that was Sonny Houston and his wife, Maggie," said Barry. "Sebastian diagnosed Sonny's cataract. I'm not sure Sebastian can learn much more medicine from Fingal and me. He is a fine diagnostician and our patients do like him."

"Hearing that gentleman say thanks was most gratifying, and your praise even more so." She turned from O'Reilly and looked up as John MacNeill set a G & T on the table in front of her.

"Thank you, John."

And, clutching a pint of Guinness, he took his seat beside her.

He raised his glass. "To friends and good company."

Glasses were lifted and everyone drank.

"Ah," he said with a grin. "Mother's milk." He turned to Ruth. "I hope my friends have been keeping you entertained, Ruth."

"They have indeed. Thank you all." She smiled at him.

"It really is a pleasure to meet you, Ruth," Kitty said. "And I hope we'll be seeing more of you. I'm sure Sebastian, like all of our previous trainees, will end up becoming one of the practice family." She glanced at Fingal. "We'd like to include you, his mother, as an honorary member. Have you and your son round for dinner."

Ruth inclined her head. "That is most gracious."

O'Reilly smiled. Letting Kitty in on the secret of Mrs. Carson's social withdrawal was paying a dividend. He overheard, "Did you see that yesterday, Donal, the powers that be released the Cameron Report about the recent civil unrest?"

"Aye, Bertie, but I've no idea what's in it."

"Nor me." Their conversation moved on.

A bloody good thing, O'Reilly thought. The unrest was the main topic of conversation these days, and the report was causing quite a stir, but tonight was a party. He didn't think any of his group had heard the exchange, but to be on the safe side, he changed the subject. "Right. Ruth. You and John have just started, but who'd like another gargle?" He took the order. "Come on, Barry. Give me a hand to carry them back."

As he stood, O'Reilly noticed the queue at Bertie's table had not shortened. Gerry and Mairead Shanks were its head now, followed by Dougie George, Ballybucklebo's bellicose barber, then Dapper Frew with a full head of hair, his surgery scar no longer apparent.

O'Reilly made his way across the noisy room, stopping occasionally to greet friends and neighbours at tables or standing and chatting, until he arrived at where Alan Hewitt, acting as barman, stood behind the bar hatch.

Snatches of conversation rose above the general murmuring. O'Reilly recognised Lenny Brown's voice: "I see your man Rod Laver won the U.S. tennis open five days ago," and Mister Coffin's reply, "That's four Grand Slams this year—Melbourne, Paris, and at Wimbledon too."

"He's no dozer, thon boy."

"True on you, Lenny."

O'Reilly arrived at the hatch. "Evening, Alan."

"Evening, Doc."

"Two pints, a gin and tonic, and a brown lemonade, please."

"Coming up."

Barry arrived. "Evening, Alan."

"Hello, Doctor Laverty. While the drinks is being poured could I have a word with youse both?"

"Of course."

"You know, Doctor Laverty, that Mister Mills is dead opposed to his son marrying my Helen, and I've got no problem in sharing that news with you, Doctor O'Reilly. And hasn't he gotten worse since that Bog-side nonsense?"

Barry sighed. "I know, and yes, he has. I had a drink with Jack the week after the riots. He'd been very upset, and I'd no useful suggestions to make. And I discussed my concerns with Doctor O'Reilly."

"Well, I've had a notion." He paused. "Mebbe I'm crazy, and it's good to have you here too, Doctor O'Reilly. You'll tell me straight, won't you, if you think it'll make matters worse?" He paused again.

"Go on, man. We'll be honest with you," O'Reilly said.

"Well, do you think Jack could finagle an invite for the four of you—him and Helen, and you Doctor Laverty and your Mrs.—for lunch in Cullybackey?"

"I'm sure he could get us invited. Jack and I've visited back and forth since we were at Campbell College together, but I don't see how Sue and I could help. But I'm not so sure taking Helen would help either."

"By all accounts, he's a stubborn man," said O'Reilly, frowning.

"I know, and I don't expect you and Mrs. Laverty to convince him otherwise, but we all know the laws of Ulster hospitality. They'd not turn Helen, a friend of Jack's, away even if she's not been down there for a while."

Barry looked down to the floor. "No, they wouldn't. But I think she'd get a frosty—but polite—reception."

"Aye. I know. And it'll get worse with what I have in mind. I intend to go with Helen. Wait until she's inside. I want you til be closest til the door, Doctor Laverty, and let me in when I knock."

O'Reilly saw the man's eyes mist. "So, you're hoping to talk him round?"

"Doctor, I love my wee girl. I don't really approve of mixed marriages either, but her happiness is all I want. And all her mother would have wanted too, God rest her soul. Maybe there's a chance I could get him to see that if I can bend, then mebbe so can he?"

O'Reilly offered his hand. "You, Alan Hewitt, are a gallant gentleman. I honestly think it's worth a try, and I wish you well."

"And I'll do all I can do to help," Barry said.

Alan dashed the back of his hand across his eyes. "Thanks a million, to youse both."

He turned his back, clearly wishing to hide his embarrassment, then turned back and pushed full glasses across the counter. "Now here's your drinks."

O'Reilly paid.

"And, Gerry, I know you're next in line, but I'll just be a wee minute. I've things til do in the back."

"Take your time, oul' hand," said Gerry Shanks. "I'll wait my turn."

O'Reilly and Barry looked at each other and shook their heads. The din was too loud for any lengthy discussion now. O'Reilly planned to alter course on the way back. He'd seen Archie and Kinky Auchinleck, and Sonny and Maggie Houston sitting at a table near the buffet. Poor Jack and Helen. A real-life Montague and Capulet, he thought, and wished them and Alan well, but given the age-old antipathy could neither be sanguine nor offer Barry any comfort.

"Sue's thirsty, so I'd better take this lemonade back to her."

"How's she doing, Barry?"

"Glad to be back working, and trying to be cheerful, but she's getting a bit desperate to feel the baby's first kick, wanting that confirmation that all's well. I've tried to reassure her it was quite normal in a first pregnancy not to have felt the baby move by twenty weeks, but she says some women start feeling the baby earlier and she will not be reassured." Barry looked over at their table.

"You're doing your best. You can do no more."

"Thanks, Fingal. I'd better—"

"I understand. Go on with you." He watched as Barry headed back to the table and continued on to see Kinky.

"Good evening to the table," O'Reilly said.

His greeting was returned.

"All the catering under control?" Kinky smiled. "I think the English would say everything is A1 at Lloyd's. And do you know, Doctor dear, Doctor Carson's mother dropped by the trestle table on her way in with his lordship and brought a plate of meringues, introduced herself, said her son had a sweet tooth and these were his favourite, and that she wanted to contribute something to the evening. She's quite grand, so?" Kinky sniffed, rose, pulled back a corner of the cloth that covered the food, and pointed to a gold-edged china plate bearing the meringues. She leaned across the table to whisper to O'Reilly. "I shouldn't say, but the marquis's first wife, Lady Laura, never would have come to a hooley like this in the Bonnaughts' clubhouse. And if she had, she wouldn't have brought meringues for the dessert table, so."

O'Reilly studied Kinky, trying to decide whether she approved or disapproved of the late Marchioness of Ballybucklebo. "Well, I'll be damned. That was kind of her. Enjoy yourselves, ladies," he said. "I'll get these drinks to my table."

He returned, and as he set the drinks down, Donal's voice boomed from the loudspeaker. "My lord, ladies, and gentlemen." He waited for the noise to settle. "We'll be opening the buffet soon—"

"About time. My belly thinks my throat's cut."

Laughter.

"Sounds more like you're half-cut, so houl' your wheest. I've an important announcement til make. Many of youse will remember the song our guest of honour, Flo Bishop, sang at our talent contest. Well, she has agreed to give us another."

Rather than cheering, there was a respectful silence.

"So, Mrs. Bishop, if you'd kindly—"

Bertie helped Flo up.

Every eye, O'Reilly's included, was fixed on her.

She said into the mike, "Bertie and me's off on a sea cruise and this here song is also about the sea and ships." She took a deep breath and began,

Blow the wind southerly, southerly, southerly,
Blow the wind south o'er the bonny blue sea;

Blow the wind southerly, southerly, southerly,
Blow bonnie breeze, my lover to me.

O'Reilly remembered Bertie once boasting that Flo's rendition of that song would give Kathleen Ferrier's 1949 version a run for its money. He was right. He closed his eyes and sat back, letting the music flow over him. He thought, even if politically matters in Ulster could be better, there were moments of complete tranquility to be relished. He savoured this one.

Flo concluded,

As lightly it comes o'er the deep rolling sea?
But sweeter and dearer by far when 'tis bringing,
The barque of my true love in safety to me.

And at that point she gazed fondly at a clearly enraptured Bertie.

Silence. Then one pair of hands clapping was soon followed by a thunderous round of applause.

When at last the applause faded raggedly away, Flo spoke. "Thank youse all very much. And like my Bertie said, thank youse all for coming out." She bowed, left the stage, and was replaced by Donal. "Amazing Flo. Amazing."

Truly, O'Reilly thought.

Donal continued, "The buffet is now opened, and you will see a number on your table. When you go up, please hold it up so the next table in sequence will know it's their turn next. But before we start to dig in, gentlemen, please." He pointed to where Father Hugh O'Toole, and the Reverend and Mrs. Robinson sat.

Both men of the cloth came up onstage.

Everyone bowed their heads.

The Reverend Robinson began, "Oh Lord, bless this food and this companionship—"

Father Hugh continued in his Cork brogue, "In a spirit of brotherly love regardless of persuasion, so. In the name of Jesus Christ our Lord . . ."

Both men and the crowd said, "Amen."

As the clergymen left the stage, the buzz of conversation grew.

Bertie stood, held up his number one, and led his table to the food.

O'Reilly, feeling the volcanic rumbling of hunger in his tummy, got ready to attack the buffet tables, but before he could stand, Sue clapped her hands to her belly and grunted. Her smile was radiant when she said to Barry, "Our baby kicked me. It kicked me," she inhaled, "and it's just done it again."

Barry reached over to cover his wife's hands with his. "And again," he said, and laughed. The happiness and relief on both their faces lightened O'Reilly's own heart.

"There must be something about this place," said Barry. "When we were here in July during the talent contest, we told you all that we were expecting."

She beamed, still holding her tummy. "And another one." She giggled. "And where better to get kicked than in a football clubhouse?"

O'Reilly said, "If it's a boy, one day he might grow up to be another Jack Kyle."

"Not if I can help it. Nasty rough game," said Sue with a wink.

O'Reilly chuckled, thought about how protective all mothers were, and watched as Barry bent his head over Sue's belly to listen, pretending he had a stethoscope, making the whole table laugh. The young couple had become close to being the son and daughter the O'Reillys had never had, and he hoped this wee one would become one of the O'Reilly family too.

He grinned. "Before we go to eat, lift a glass with me and toast to the next generation. May they be beautiful, wise, and healthy—and live in an Ireland at peace."

23

I Have Had My Labour for My Travail

Barry heard the telephone in the hall. All four doctors were enjoying a cup of tea before Emer took the surgery and O'Reilly made home visits.

The single *ting* of the receiver being replaced was followed by the appearance of Kinky.

"That," she said with no sense of urgency in her voice from long years of practice, "did be Ken Anderson. He asked for a doctor to come quick. He thinks Mildred may be in labour, so."

Barry rose. "Thanks, Kinky. Come on, Sebastian. Give me a hand with the maternity bags. Fingal, the pair of us saw her two weeks ago, so she'd be thirty-four weeks today. She was meant to be coming in for an antenatal checkup. I was just going to brief you, Emer. She might still have a breech presentation. We'd better get moving."

O'Reilly put down his pipe. "Premature breech? If she's in labour, get onto the flying squad at once."

"Will do."

"So," Sebastian said as Barry steered the Imp out of Number One Main's back lane and onto the Belfast to Bangor Road, "what do you reckon?"

"I hope to God it's false labour. Prematurity's bad enough. We've got time for a little teaching—do you know the neonatal survival rates?"

"Depends on the birth weight. Under two pounds, it's one in thirty. At three pounds, one in three, and at four pounds, three out of four. But that's in uncomplicated deliveries. If hers is still a breech, the odds are not nearly so good because of the risks during the delivery."

"Correct." Barry had no difficulty making a left turn from the main

Belfast to Bangor Road onto the country byway that led to the six-house terrace of cottages where the Andersons lived. Although the railway had, in 1952, sold up what had once been subsidized housing for its workers, everyone still called them "the railway cottages."

"Home is no place for a couple of GPs to be conducting the delivery of a premature breech. We'll leave our maternity bags in the car until we're sure she's in labour and delivery is imminent." He parked in front of a neat redbrick, two-storey, slate-roofed house. The railway track was one hundred yards away and Barry smelled the diesel as the single motorized car, known to the locals as "the covered wagon," rattled by on its way to Bangor. He grabbed his doctor's bag.

Ken Anderson answered the door. He was a big, heavyset man. "Thank God youse've come. And dead quick too. Come on on in. She's in our bedroom." He led the way up a narrow staircase, calling, "We're coming up, dear." He pushed a cream-painted door open. "In thonder. I'll wait downstairs with wee Angus."

Barry led Sebastian into a small, neat room where Mildred lay propped up on pillows in a double bed. The eiderdown and blanket had been turned back and she was only covered by a sheet. She tried to smile, but instead clenched her teeth and held her stomach with both hands.

Barry fervently hoped she was only having Braxton Hicks contractions, named after the English doctor who first described them in 1872. All pregnant women experienced them, and certainly Sue, now in her twenty-second week, had had a few. They did not presage imminent delivery.

"Sorry about that," she said, and did manage a smile.

"I'm asking Doctor Carson to help you, Mildred."

"Dead on. You was real nice til me last time, sir."

Sebastian nodded, looked embarrassed, and finally asked, "Um, can you tell me what's been happening this morning?"

She nodded. "Och, I've been getting the odd twinge for a month or two now. I paid no heed, but about five o'clock this morning I got a real humdinger. Woke me up, so it did." She pursed her lips. "I didn't want til panic. Sure, hadn't I had a few like that the last time I was up the spout that meant nothing and, anyroad, youse doctors need your sleep."

Barry saw Sebastian smile.

"They kept coming about every twenty minutes until about sixish, but since then they've been coming every ten or less. I reckoned this was the real McCoy so a couple of hours later I asked Ken to send for you—" She inhaled deeply, bit her lower lip, and grabbed her tummy.

Barry didn't like the sound of that. He glanced at his watch to gauge the timing of the next pain.

"And then he phoned the stationmaster to get the day off so he could stay home and look after wee Angus."

"He did the right thing," Barry said, although he often wished that country patients weren't quite so considerate of their doctors. If she'd called at six, she'd be safely at the Royal by now.

"Yes, he did," Sebastian said, and when the pain had passed continued, "Have your waters broken?"

"Not at all."

"Good. Now, I'd like to examine your tummy." He folded back the sheet to be level with her pubic hair. "Just like last time I'm going to tell Doctor Laverty what I find."

"Fair enough."

"Uterus proper size, singleton, longitudinal lie, back on the left, and I'm pretty sure the breech is engaged. That means it's dropped into your pelvis, Mildred."

Not good, Barry thought. He handed Sebastian a Pinard foetal stethoscope.

After fifteen seconds, Sebastian said, "One hundred and forty-four."

The baby was not in any distress—yet.

"I'd like to wash my hands, please."

"I'm sorry, Doctor. The privy's outside. These here cottages was built in 1865. Ask Kenneth to get you a towel from the hot press and use the sink in the kitchen."

Sebastian left.

"Did you understand what Doctor Carson said?"

"Aye. Well enough. There's still only one babby, and it's got its bottom in my pelvis. If I am in labour, it's very early—six weeks early—and it's still a breech." She sighed and little tears slipped down her cheeks. Barry, and to hell with his not having a chaperone, put his arm round her shoulders and said in a soft voice, "Don't worry. It's going to be all right." And it might, but inside he was none too sanguine.

She did not reply.

Sebastian reappeared, took a pair of rubber gloves from Barry's bag, and pulled them on.

"Oooooh." Mildred's teeth showed over her lower lip.

It had been only six minutes since the start of the last contraction. Barry had taken Mildred's hand in his right. As the contraction waxed and waned so did the pressure on Barry's fingers. At its peak, Barry had pulled out a linen hanky and wiped the sweat off her brow. When this one, lasting almost two minutes, had passed, Sebastian said, "Mildred, can you pull the sheet down a bit, bend up your knees, and part your legs?"

After his examination, Sebastian stripped off his gloves and pulled up the sheet. "The cervix is about seven centimetres dilated."

Barry, despite his disappointment, kept an expressionless face. Labour was already well advanced. Widening and thinning of the neck of the womb were sure signs.

"The membranes are still intact. The breech is engaged and has descended deeply into the pelvis and I'm pretty sure it's a frank breech."

That at least was a promising sign. Of the three types of breech presentation, frank was the least difficult to deliver and associated with the fewest complications. In a complete breech, the baby was in a cross-legged position, in "footling," one leg or both legs would be flexed, below the breech. With a frank breech, at least both legs were extended and the feet above the head. But if labour started four hours ago, this baby was coming quickly.

"Oh my God, that's desperate, so it is." Mildred's tears still flowed but were interrupted by another contraction.

Sebastian said, "Do you have a telephone, Mildred?"

She sniffed. "No, but Joyce Devlin, next door on our left, she does."

"I'll go," Barry said, "We need to get you to Royal Maternity as soon as we can." He left Sebastian explaining how a specially equipped ambulance and staff would be dispatched at once and should be here in about thirty minutes.

As Barry headed next door he remembered being taught about "the flying squad," probably named for a special unit of the London police formed in 1919. The Belfast obstetric one was still operating in 1969 because a full 20 percent of deliveries still took place in patients' homes. While the aim was to get the patient to the hospital, the team was able to, if necessary, carry out any obstetrical procedure short of Caesarian section. As he knocked on the door, he sighed. The flying squad could surely handle Mildred's premature breech.

While Sebastian and Ken were arranging a hospital bag for Mildred and bringing her down to the living/dining room, ready for immediate transport if that were to be possible, Barry held young Angus against his chest, very aware of the little lad's clean baby smell, a combination of warm milk and talcum powder. Jogging him up and down in an effort to stop the wee one crying wasn't working. Barry's "Rock-a-bye Baby," sung off-key, had not been a great success either. It struck Barry forcibly how little he knew about the care of small children and he was again reminded that when it came to having children, anything could go wrong.

"Well, Master Anderson, I think I'd better hurry up and learn about babies," he said. Even as he said it, he could feel an uncomfortable shiver walk up his spine. He wasn't superstitious, was he? And yet even alluding to a happy outcome for Sue's pregnancy felt like tempting Providence somehow. Finding a rattle on the table beside him, he shook it tentatively at Angus. The baby cried all the harder.

"Oh, aye, he's afeared of thon thing. I don't know why we still have it," said Ken Anderson as he came into the room, looking harried and exhausted. Until Sue's pregnancy Barry'd never fully understood the emotional toll pregnancy could take on expectant mothers—and fathers. He certainly was beginning to.

Mildred was supported by Sebastian and Ken. They soon had her teed up on the sofa under a tartan rug.

Angus set up a steady chant of, "Want Mammy. Want Mammy," and with his little fists he pounded Barry's chest.

"Here, I'll take him," Ken said, and stretched out his arms.

"Want Mammy."

Ken carried the little boy over to Mildred, who cuddled her son for a few minutes before grimacing and handing him back.

"I'll take him upstairs. Doctor Carson's explained what's going til happen. Angus's too young til understand, and if the hospital doctors have til deliver Mildred here it's going til get crowded."

The *nee-naw* sounds of an approaching ambulance drew close then stopped.

"I'll go," Sebastian said, returning soon after, accompanied by some of the flying squad team.

The leader, Doctor Bill Howard, had been at Campbell College with Barry and Jack Mills. "Hello, Barry." Bill had been no stickler for formality. "Sebastian explained about the space in here. I've left the gas-passer and midwife back in the ambulance until we see if we're going to need them."

"That makes sense. Sebastian's looking after Mrs. Anderson. He'll fill you in." He turned to Mildred. "Mildred, this is Doctor Howard and—"

"Michael Doak, final-year medical student," a dark-haired man in a short white jacket said, "from Royal Maternity."

She nodded at them. "Pleased til meet youse."

It took a very short time for Sebastian to give the necessary clinical details.

"Thank you."

"Mike, nip out and ask Joan to bring in a sterile glove pack. Is your kitchen that way?"

Mildred nodded.

Bill disappeared and came back holding his hands in front of his face, water dripping from his elbows. The navy-blue-uniformed midwife held open a sterile pack from which Bill removed a green towel, dried his hands, and put on rubber gloves.

He reported his findings. "I can just see the buttocks, so delivery is imminent. We'll not be taking you and your baby to the Royal Maternity until it's over."

"Oh my God."

"It's all right, Mildred," Barry said. "Doctor Howard is the specialist you'd have been seeing at the hospital. Instead he's come to you, and Doctor Carson and I'll be here too."

"I can't tell the state of the cervix because I can't get my fingers past the breech. But bums, particularly premature ones, are narrower than the head, and can slip through a partially dilated cervix. Unless we can wait until the anterior buttock is born, it's hard to be certain about the cervix."

Barry wondered why Bill was explaining all this within earshot of an already worried woman.

"You may feel like pushing, dear," Bill said. "Do not, I repeat, do not, until we're ready."

"I won't, Doctor."

Barry heard a tremor in Mildred's voice.

Dear? Do not? Barry shook his head. "Try not to" would have been kinder. During his trial experience of obstetrics in the Waveney Hospital a few years ago he had noted a certain lack of humanity creeping into his work. He had thought it came from rarely seeing patients more than a few times, and it was one of the reasons he had returned to GP work.

"Joan. Michael. You both know what we need to do. Joan, why don't you bring in the rubber sheet and a bucket first."

Barry wondered where Bill intended to conduct the delivery. Certainly not on the couch.

He went to the dining table. "Solid oak. Ideal. Barry. Sebastian. Give me a hand."

Together they cleared it, putting items on kitchen shelves.

Joan came back, carrying a red rubber sheet and a stainless-steel bucket.

Bill spread the sheet on the tabletop and tucked the end into the bucket, which was placed at the end of the table.

Joan arranged two cushions at the head end of the table.

"Now," said Bill, "Michael and I are going to help you up on the table, Mildred."

"Here"—Barry pulled over a low pouffe—"use that as a step."

Between them, Bill and Michael helped Mildred up.

"Oh God. My waters has just broke."

Barry's nose was assailed by the smell of amniotic fluid and he heard splashing in the bucket.

While this was going on the midwife and anaesthetist had brought in the squad's instrument bags. He had returned to the ambulance and she had been setting out the instruments on green sterile towels on convenient surfaces. She hung the strap of a rubber apron round Bill's neck and tied the waist ties behind his back.

"I'm ready to deliver your wee one, and the first thing I'm going to do is freeze your behind, so we'll have to move you down the table."

Barry inhaled and told himself not to worry. He'd just told Mildred that Bill was a specialist, and perhaps Barry could try to make up for the man's cold, purely technical approach. He said, "The freezing really helps, Mildred, and it's just two tiny jags."

"I know," she said. "I had that there block with my first one too."

Once that was done, and Barry knew Mildred was as comfortable as possible, he was going to have a front-row seat at the delivery of a premature breech.

24

The Nearest-Run Thing You Ever Saw

"Bring your bottom to the end of the table."

"Yes, Doctor." With the midwife's help, Mildred inched her way down the length of her dining room table.

"Barry. Mike. Give Mildred a hip to rest her feet on. They may not be stirrups, but they'll do in a pinch." Bill stood between them and loaded a syringe with a long needle from a rubber-capped bottle of Xylocaine held by Joan. "I'm putting in a pudendal block," he said as he guided the needle past the baby to the right side of the patient's vagina. "The pudendal nerve runs just past the ischial spine near the knobby bit of your backside that you sit on. There's one side done. Now the other."

As he worked, Mildred had another contraction.

Barry hoped its pain would distract her from the sting of the injection needle.

"Nearly set. Sebastian. Nip out and ask Doctor Bannerjee to join us. I don't think we're going to need a general anaesthetic, but better to be safe."

A minute later, a barely accented voice called from the hall, "Looks a bit crowded in there. Doctor Carson and I, and the portable machine, will wait in the hall until you need us."

Bill called out, "Thanks, Rahul." He turned to the midwife. "Will you stand to Mildred's right, Joan, encourage her to push with contractions when I ask you to, and once the buttocks are born, keep one hand on the fundus to exert pressure there to try to stop the arms extending." For the student's benefit, Bill said, "If the arms do extend past the head, they increase the difficulty of effecting a simple delivery."

Joan took her place. "Contraction starting. Try not to push yet, Mildred. Pant. Pant."

Barry, his nose still filled with smell of amniotic fluid, heard her huffing and puffing.

"Keep it up, Mildred," said Joan. "You're doing fine."

Bill, standing between the patient's legs, moved to her left. "Barry, can you see the baby's anterior buttock?"

Barry leant forward. "There's a little buttock and the left edge of the natal cleft clearly visible. So, even if Mildred doesn't push, the uterine contraction will still move the wee one on?"

"Correct. Now, dear, your next contraction is the start of the time to push."

That "dear" again. Thank the Lord Harith Lamki was looking after Sue. He was a man who did not patronize his patients.

Every time Mildred had a contraction, she pushed down with her foot on Barry's hip, and presumably Michael's. Barry could see her grimace. Every time, Joan, one hand on the uterine fundus, encouraged Mildred with "Hold your breath and puuuush. Puuush. You're doing great." And every time Mildred ran out of breath, she exhaled explosively and dragged in deep lungsful of air.

Barry heard the repeated words of encouragement, the strangled grunts, and occasional cries of the patient. The left buttock was born. Now it was the turn of the right one. Barry watched its gradual progress, a combination of coming farther and farther out while ascending toward the maternal pubis.

"Episiotomy with the next contraction," Bill said. "It'll straighten the birth canal and lessen the pressures on a softer than usual head."

All right, so Michael had to be instructed, but Barry had seen Mildred's eyes widen, how she clapped a hand to her mouth, tensed up. Enough. He said to her, "Doctor Howard is right, and that's why he's doing this to protect your wee one. All preemies' heads are a little"—in fact at thirty-four weeks a lot, but why distress her?—"softer than babies born at term."

He saw her relax a little. "Thanks, Doctor Laverty."

He could barely hear her but said sotto voce to Bill, "For God's sake lower your voice, Bill. You're scaring her to death."

Bill shook his head and blew his breath through semi-closed lips. "Puuush."

Barry flinched as the scissors cut through the perineum. There was little bleeding, but he could detect blood's coppery smell. God, how he hoped Sue would not have to endure that.

"You're doing very well, Mildred," Barry said. "Won't be long now."

The baby's right buttock appeared in its entirety. There was only a scant amount of vernix caseosa, the sebaceous white substance that coats every newborn's skin, because the glands that produce it were immature.

Bill continued to teach his student, but in fairness he did lower his voice. "Michael, now we have to be patient and do nothing until we can see the umbilicus."

At least as Sue was the wife of a colleague, she'd have no students in attendance.

One more push and buttocks, thighs, and umbilicus appeared. Bill first pulled down one leg then the other, as well as a loop of umbilical cord. The baby's legs flopped down between the mother's buttocks. Its lower back faced up to the ceiling.

Barry saw, as was usual in breech deliveries of boys, that the scrotum was swollen. He said, "You're having a boy," but she did not reply because the next contraction was starting.

The shoulder blades appeared, and Bill reached into the birth canal under the baby. "Praise be," he said, "the arms have not extended past the head. Good work, Joan. They're folded across the chest and I can flip them out so there's no risk that they'll interfere with the delivery of the head."

Bill turned toward the hall. "Rahul, we won't need a general, but in about three minutes I'd like you to give her some intravenous Pentothal. Sebastian, come in too. I'll need you then to suck out the baby's naso-pharynx."

Joan, now freed from trying to prevent the baby extending its arms inside Mildred's womb, left her patient's side and returned with the suction device. The three-inch cylindrical plastic bottle had two narrow tubes at opposite sides of the top. One stretched from close to the bottom of the bottle out through the lid and ended in a red rubber tip. That was the baby's end. The rubber was kinder than plastic to babies' tissues. The other tube barely entered the bottle, so that when Sebastian put its far end in his mouth to suck, he was in no danger of inhaling anything. "Here you are," she said before returning to her place.

Even though Bill had looked disbelieving when he'd been asked to lower his voice, he spoke now so only Barry and Michael could hear. "I mustn't rush, but as the head enters the pelvis, it will nip the cord and cut off the baby's blood and hence oxygen supply. We've four minutes to get the baby able to breathe for itself. Barry, start clock-watching."

Barry shot his cuff to expose his Timex watch and took note of the time.

"Right. We'll wait for one more contraction and the baby's hanging weight will get the head into and most of the way through the pelvis."

Barry could picture this, and although he knew it would not happen, he had a horrid mental image of the smaller head slipping through and the baby landing in the bucket positioned at the end of the table. He told himself not to be silly.

As if reading Barry's mind, Bill held his hands cupped beneath the baby's bottom. He said, "We'll know when that's happened when I can see the hairs on the nape of the neck. Rahul, please give her the Pentothal as soon as the next contraction's over."

"Right," said the anaesthetist. "She'll be awake again five to ten minutes after I've given the drug."

Barry said, "Mildred, Doctor Bannerjee's going to put you to sleep for about five minutes very soon. It's another way of making the delivery easier on your wee one."

She nodded and managed a weak smile.

Amazing, Barry thought, how maternal instinct means that for a mother no sacrifice is too great on behalf of her baby. He wondered about paternal instinct, if there was such a thing, and in particular how it might—or might not—affect him.

"Thanks, Rahul," Bill said, still speaking softly, "and for your information, Michael, premature babies' heads are very fragile, and I want a completely controlled delivery of this one's. An involuntary push would make it pop out in what we call a 'champagne cork' delivery. God knows what damage the compression and sudden decompression might do. That's why she's getting the Pentothal." He raised his voice for the patient's benefit. "And the plus is with the head blocking the cord, no drugs can enter the chissler's circulation."

That was kind. Ever since the thalidomide crisis of the late '50s linking maternal ingestion of the drug with foetal deformities, pregnant women were terrified of taking any medication.

Barry asked, "Did you hear that, Mildred?"

"Only the last bit, but I'm glad to hear it and—oh-oh—"

"Puush. Puuush."

Barry was tiring and braced himself to withstand the pressure of Mildred's foot by leaning on the edge of the table.

The minute the contraction ended, Doctor Bannerjee said, "A little jag," followed shortly after by, "Now, please count backward from one hundred."

"One hundred, ninety-nine . . ." She stopped counting by ninety-one.

"She's out."

"Thanks, Rahul."

To Barry's delight, he saw the hairs on the nape of the baby's neck. It seemed like the longest three minutes of his life since the end of the last contraction, but now Bill could complete the delivery of the head.

And the four-minute clock was running.

Bill used his right hand to grasp the baby by his ankles and exerted gentle outward and upward traction that did not allow the baby's body to pass the horizontal. Allowing the arms to dangle, he brought more of the head into view. Meanwhile, his left hand controlled its descent.

One minute. Barry willed the uterus to contract.

Two minutes. Come on. Come on.

Three minutes.

"Right, Sebastian, suction. I can see the mouth."

Yes. Yes. The tightness in Barry's chest began to ease.

"It's like Paddy's market in here with all of us," Sebastian said as he knelt, put the tube in the baby's mouth, and started to suck the end of his tube.

Barry, for a second, was irritated by Sebastian's flippancy, but in fairness the man had been out in the hall, quite detached from the drama.

"Now," Bill said, "we've all the time in the world. Finished sucking, Sebastian?"

Before Sebastian could reply, the little boy gave vent to his annoyance at being removed from a warm, dark womb to a world of noise and coldness. His yelling was harsh and frequent, even though his head was still to be delivered.

"Finished? It would certainly seem so."

Barry realized his laughter was more from the relief of tension than at any great wittiness by Sebastian, and more to the point, the louder the boy cried, the more he would open up his lungs with each inhalation. He was surprised that Mildred didn't immediately awake from her drug-induced sleep to respond to his cries.

"Then, Sebastian, please take over holding the ankles. Do not allow the body to begin to become any more vertical. That would put the neck vessels at risk, Michael, and I'm going to need both hands to put on forceps. They'll make delivery of the head more controllable and will also protect it from pressure." He lifted one shiny half of a set of forceps and slipped the concave blade between the side of Mildred's pelvis and the baby's head, repeated that on the opposite side, and locked the handles. "Joan, let me know when a contraction is starting."

Bill wasn't using the forceps to tug the baby out, as was their usual function. Instead, by exerting pressure against what was being expelled, he ensured the slow and controlled delivery of the head. Two contractions later the little boy was completely out, attached to his mother by only the umbilical cord.

Sebastian continued to hold the tiny baby aloft until the cord had stopped pulsating and Bill had clamped and cut it. The maternal end lengthened, accompanied by a small gush of blood.

Joan said, "The uterus has shrunk and is very firm."

"Thanks, Joan. See to the baby now, please."

Sebastian handed the boy to Joan, who immediately wrapped him in a blanket.

Barry knew the uterine shrinking was an indication that the placenta had separated from the uterine wall. As Mildred had not woken up yet, she could not help by pushing, so Bill used his left hand above the pubic symphysis to ensure that the uterus remained in place and pulled on the cord with his right. In seconds, the placenta, looking like a small slab of raw calf's liver, lay on the rubber sheet.

Bill quickly inspected it. "It's all there."

Good, Barry thought. If bits of the placenta remained inside the uterus, they would prevent Mildred's uterus from remaining properly contracted. It was that contraction which effectively shut down the maternal blood vessels supplying the placental site. If that failed, severe postpartum haemorrhage would ensue.

Bill asked, "How's your patient, Rahul?"

"She's awake and knows where she is."

"Thanks. Now, I've some sewing to do, so, Sebastian, please relieve Barry as a foot support while I sew up the episiotomy."

Barry and Sebastian changed places. The stiff back that Barry had ignored during the birth sent him a reminder and he grunted.

"Now, Barry, there's a syringe on a shelf behind me filled with ergometrine."

The drug provoked strong uterine contraction and, as a further safeguard against haemorrhage, it was undoubtedly important. But was no one going to tell Mildred she had a baby boy? The ergometrine could wait. Barry called to Mildred, "Your lovely wee boy's here. I've only got a quick look at him, but he's got all his fingers and toes. I've just to give you a jag and then I'll come and tell you all about him."

"I'm very glad til hear that he's got all his bits and pieces. And another wee lad? That's great, Ken'll be tickled pink. Me? I don't care as long as they're healthy." And he heard her chuckling. Now it was time for that ergometrine. Barry picked up the syringe.

"Please give intramuscularly."

Barry shook his head. "You may be a specialist and me only a GP, Bill. We've been friends since school, so as a friend"—and Barry smiled as he spoke softly—"don't try to teach your granny to suck eggs."

Bill had the courtesy to laugh. "Fair enough. I know I can be a bit thoughtless, but you do know the pressure I've been under since we got started here."

Barry nodded and said, "Wee jag in your leg, Mildred."

"Right."

Barry gave the injection.

"After you've had a word with Mum, nip off and let the father know. He'll have to wait to see his son until the little lad's in the incubator."

"Will do." Barry went and half-sat on the edge of the table. "So, Mummy, how are you feeling?" He took her pulse.

"I'm main glad til be rid of them pains, so I am. It says in Genesis, 'In sorrow thou shalt bring forth children.' I think it must have been a man wrote that. I was never unhappy, but it hurts like blazes. Good thing you can't really remember pain."

She wasn't the first recently delivered patient to tell him that. He was sure it would be the same for Sue, but he did not envy her labour, even though the profession had quite effective means of pain relief.

She looked him in the eye. "Never mind me. What about the wee lad? I know I had til be put out, but I missed his first cries. I'll never forget his big brother's."

"Number two was announcing himself to the world in no uncertain terms even before he was all the way out. Doctor Howard did a great job. Breeches are tricky, but it was a very smooth delivery. I'm sure your wee lad came through it perfectly. As soon as the midwife has him cleaned up, she'll let you see him."

"I can hardly wait." She looked down. "And I want til thank you, Doctor Laverty. The wee midwife was very good at helping me, but you brung me comfort. Thank you, sir."

"And I've brought you something else," Joan said. "If you could help Mildred sit up, Doctor?"

"Here you are, Mother," said Joan. "He's perfect."

The boy was completely swaddled in a blanket and wore a white roll of tube-gauze, knotted at one end as a hat, to help prevent heat loss.

Mildred, eyes glistening, held out her arms and cuddled her sleeping son and made crooning noises in her throat. "You're beautiful, my little son. And you're going to grow up into a big strong boy. You are. Just look at his wee rosebud mouth."

Joan smiled. "I know you'd like to keep him a bit longer, but I'm sorry. I have to get him into the incubator in the ambulance at once so we can keep him warm and supplied with oxygen too. When I've seen to him and left him with Doctor Bannerjee, who'll examine him more thoroughly, I'll come back, and I'll get you ready to go with your son."

Mildred handed her boy back. Her gaze never left him as Joan walked away. "Mammy's coming soon, son. Soon."

Barry smiled. "He is beautiful." He patted Mildred's shoulder. "Now I'll leave you in peace and pop up and tell Ken. I'll keep in touch with the hospital while you're there, see how the pair of you are getting on. And we'll be here for you both when you get home."

"Thanks again, sir. For everything."

Barry turned to where Bill was finishing sewing up the episiotomy.

Mildred's legs were still supported by Sebastian and Michael.

Bill snipped a stitch. "I heard that, Barry, and I know you of old. I have your home phone number. I'll give you a call in the next day or two and let you know what's happening."

"Thanks, Bill. I'd appreciate that."

"Go on with you." He carried on with his work. "And Daddy can have a wee peek at his new offspring, but only a wee peek. Preemies are very prone to infections."

"I'll tell Ken."

Barry walked away. He felt at peace. The happiness spread by a new mother was infectious. He looked forward to the birth of his first in January as he headed upstairs to where Ken was sitting on a wooden chair in what must be Angus's bedroom. Angus was fast asleep in his cot.

Ken leapt to his feet. His eyes were wide. "Well? Well? I heard the bairn's cries."

Barry smiled. "Mildred's fine and you've a lovely wee boy." Who, Barry thought, has made it through a difficult delivery, but who is not out of the woods—yet. This was not the time for that discussion.

Ken's eyes sparkled. "Another wee boy? He'll be a pal for Angus. Can I see him?"

"Just for a minute. He is premature, you know."

"Aye. Right enough."

"He's in an incubator in the ambulance. Run on down. I'll keep an eye to Angus."

Ken glanced at his sleeping son and whispered, "You've got a wee brother, Angus Anderson." Ken thrust out his hand and Barry shook it. "Thanks, Doc," he said, and left.

Barry sat in Ken's chair and took some deep breaths. Thank the Lord for the flying squad. He and Sebastian could not have managed on their own, and what could have been a disastrous situation had been turned into a semi-triumph by the skill of fellow professionals. And it had been decent of Bill to say he'd keep Barry posted. While there were many wonderful aspects of rural general practice, not being able to follow more complicated cases was frustrating.

He shifted in his chair, rubbed his sore back, and thought of his tumult of feelings during the delivery—from concern, to outright fear as Bill had begun, to relief when the neck hairs had appeared, to a feeling of triumph at hearing the wee one's first cry. And if that was how he had felt as a trained physician, how was Sue going to feel during her own labour? And, he thought, how will I feel? A little shudder shook Barry. He had to be brave for her and stop letting her sense how he couldn't help worry for her. Because if a little knowledge was a dangerous thing, a lot of knowledge could be terrifying.

25

Launched His Frail Boat on the Rough Sea

"Oh, shut up, Max." Barry looked up from where he sat in an armchair reading Mario Puzo's *The Godfather*. "Bloody dog," but he smiled as he said it. By some sixth sense, the springer always detected Sue's approach well before Barry heard her car.

Max charged through to the kitchen, thrashing his tail and panting.

Tigger, the stray tabby Barry and Sue had rescued from a winter gale, looked up from where she had been sleeping in front of the unlit fire, first at Max and then at Barry. She yawned, arched her back, and licked her backside to show that she had little time for excitable dogs.

Barry smiled. Tigger knew felines were the superior species.

He heard the kitchen door open and Max's barking rise in crescendo until Sue said, "Come on, silly. Settle down." He preceded her by backing into the living/dining room, tail going so hard his behind swung from side to side.

Barry stood, wanting to hug and kiss his wife, but she made a beeline for the dining room table and unloaded her armful of exercise books. "Welcome home," he said. "How was your day?"

She shrugged, came to him, and kissed him firmly. "Hectic. My class is still settling in. But I'll live. I do so enjoy teaching and being with the children." She sat on the settee and patted the seat beside her. "Not long until we'll have one of our own."

Barry joined her.

"What time did you get up?"

"Eleven. Sebastian and I had to go out at two to see a six-year-old with mumps. Only child. Mum and Dad at panic stations. Not all country patients are considerate of their doctor's sleep. Poor little thing hadn't been immunized." That was not going to happen to young Laverty.

"Poor wee button," she said. "I didn't hear you two go or come back, or the phone ring, for that matter."

"Nine years of being on call. I hear that first ring and I'm out of bed like a racehorse out of the starting gate. More to be sure I don't wake you than any hair-trigger emergency."

"I appreciate that. You had an exciting day yesterday. Breech delivery in the morning. Mumps in the wee hours today."

He shrugged. "It's my job, but now with the expanded rota, it's great we all get the day off after twenty-four-hour call. Sebastian had gone home by the time I got up." He laid his hand on her tummy. "It's a good thing we've got three bedrooms. One for us, one for the nursery, when the bump arrives, and one for Sebastian when he's paired with me for emergency call." He felt movement under his hand. "Active little divil." Barry couldn't help but wonder where the head was, and immediately told himself to stop worrying. It could be anywhere, and that question did not need to be answered for another twelve weeks.

She smiled. "It's a funny feeling when our baby kicks, but this seems to be a pleasant part of pregnancy. My morning sickness is long gone and the backache some new mums have warned me about hasn't started yet." She shook her head. "Seven months ago, I never thought this would happen and you know I could get pretty low. Now I couldn't be happier."

"This is the time pregnant women are supposed to glow. You do, and you are beautiful."

She kissed him. "Flatterer. Now tell me, what did you get up to today?"

He paused. Feeling the baby kick had made Barry wonder about Mildred Anderson's wee one. Barry had hoped for a call from Bill today, but so far nothing.

He looked out the window. "It's been a lovely day, blowy but sunny. I made myself combined brekky and lunch at twelve. Did a bit of gardening. Dapper Frew was wrong when I was buying the place. He told me nothing grows this close to the sea but nasturtiums and snapdragons. But your hydrangea bushes have come on a treat."

"And you've weeded round them. They look wonderful."

"And there was still some time for a good read." He pointed to the table.

"I'm glad. You work too hard."

He shrugged. "Speaking of working hard, looks like you've got lots of marking tonight."

"Essays. Can you guess the subject?"

"What I did on my summer holidays?"

She chuckled. "Spot on. Tick VG."

Barry laughed and said in a high-pitched, childlike voice, "Thank you, Mrs. Laverty."

"And I'd better get at them."

"Aaaw. But you don't usually do them until after dinner. How'd you like to hop in the Imp, take Max for a run on Bangor beach. I know your food cravings have stopped, but now I've got them." He laughed. "We could pick up some ice cream from Luchi's for dessert. I got quite a taste for it when you simply had to have it."

Sue looked over at the pile of essays and shrugged. "They can wait, can't they? Dinner's in the fridge. There's lots of the seafood casserole I made last night. Give me a minute to put on slacks and walking shoes, grab Max's leash and I, as they say in Belfast, I'm your woman."

He heard her giggle receding. He'd never seen her so happy, and his heart swelled.

Barry had been lucky. He'd found a parking place on Queen's Parade. The seafront street started at the bottom of Main Street and its junction with Bridge Street and ended at the junction of Grey's Hill and Marine Gardens. At the far end of the path through the gardens, Barry could see the outdoor seawater swimming pool, Pickie Pool, with its latticed, thirty-metre diving tower. Dad had bought Barry a season's ticket for the pool when he was sixteen. He'd only managed to go off the fifteen-metre platform, but he'd met a stunningly beautiful, ebony-eyed girl who, as much as he loved Sue, still had a wee corner of his heart.

Sue got out and Barry clipped the leash on Max's collar, and, keeping it short, took Sue's hand in his other. Together the three crossed the street and walked along the pavement to a shallow ramp that led down to the sand. To their left was the tall granite-block seawall that fronted Queen's Parade. At right angles to it, the Bridge Street seawall was pierced by an arch closed off by an iron railing to keep children out and still allow the stream running from the lakes of Ward Park to flow under the town.

The beach here was interrupted by one of Bangor's three piers, South Pier. Barry looked at its bulk. In April 1914, a ship called the *Mountjoy* had docked there and unloaded arms to equip the Ulster Volunteer Force in case Protestant armed resistance to home rule became necessary. There had been other landings at Larne and Donaghadee. He was glad things seemed to have settled down in Ulster for the time being, and hoped it stayed that way.

The wind was tossing Sue's copper plait around and she smoothed away a lock of hair that had escaped. "See something? A seal?"

He shook his head. "Just history." He wouldn't share what he was thinking. It would darken the mood of their walk, and the day was too sunny and his wife too happy and lovely for that. He squeezed her hand. "Come on." He strode off along the beach in the direction of Pickie Pool, named for the small fish that had inhabited rock pools before the swimming baths had been built. Once the three had passed the seaward end of the South Pier, few other people and no dogs were braving the elements today. Here there was no protection from the stiff northeaster and the nearest shelter was Scotland.

The sea, at half tide, was running high with whitecapped combers roaring up the shelving sand and bursting with loud crashes. Spume flew inland and drops from time to time wetted Barry's cheeks. He could taste salt.

"I don't believe it," Sue said, pointing. "He must be nuts. Paddling a kayak in that sea."

The paddler had turned the little craft's bows directly along the track of one enormous wave and, keeping her exactly at ninety degrees to the crest, hurtled toward the beach. The red-hulled, white-decked, canvas-and-lath kayak projected over the wave's crest. Barry could see she was flat-bottomed.

"I've seen films of surfing in Hawaii and California," said Sue. "He must be getting the same thrill, and I think he'll be all right when he grounds. That bottom will slide over the damp sand. I miss kayaking, but I certainly wouldn't go out in one in seas like this."

Sue had learned to kayak from a certain Monsieur Hamou, a colleague she'd met as an exchange student in Marseille three years ago. He squeezed her hand. "I was jealous as hell, you know."

Sue turned to look at him, knowing exactly what he was referring to. "Silly. You'd no cause to be, you know. Jean-Claude was a perfect gentleman and it was all strictly business." She gave him a mischievous grin. "Well, almost."

"Now you tell me," he said, laughing.

She looked seaward. "Now watch."

Coming in now at breakneck speed, the wave broke. The kayaker gave a great roar of triumph. The water became progressively shallower until, as Sue had predicted, the kayak was high and dry on wet sand. The young man waved cheerfully at Barry and Sue, hopped out, spun the kayak on its axis, pushed it out to sea again, and with one hand on each side of the coaming, hopped into the cockpit and paddled furiously out to the waves.

"That looked like a lot of fun," she said. "I want to see if he does that again, because when he makes his turn, he'd better not spend too long beam on to the sea. Flat-bottoms are easy to tip."

Barry let go of her hand and, actions matching his words, said with his mouth to Sue's ear, "And pretty round ones are easy to pinch."

Her laughter pealed. "What made you think of that?"

"Remembering drying you off after your heroic rescue of my friend Andy and every towel stroke getting closer to your lace-edged, peach nylon knickers."

She laughed again and kissed him long and hard. "Fancy you remembering that."

"How could I forget?"

"I do love you, Barry Laverty, and I think I must be the happiest mother-to-be in all of Ireland."

Barry looked at her and just caught a glimpse of the kayaker running in again. "I'm delighted you're happy, pet."

"I am, very. Let's finish Max's walk, get the ice cream, and get home."

They set off hand in hand and, out of curiosity, Barry looked back. To his disappointment, the kayak was grounded upside down and the soaked kayaker was wading ashore.

Barry was starting the scene where Michael Corleone had been released from military service and returned home when he heard Sue say, "Good Lord. Listen to this." With Tigger curled up on her lap, she was sitting at the dining room table, marking the essays. "This eleven-year-old, Francis Wallace is his name, has relatives in England. They live in a place called Chester-le-Street on the banks of the River Wear. He was out for a walk—now listen, 'I saw a funny-looking shape drifting downstream. Then something floated out in front that looked like a man's tie. Then'—they shouldn't start sentences with then—'I saw a hand. Holy Moses, was it a dead body?'"

"That's a bit morbid. Some kid's been told too many ghost stories."

"Crikey. No. He hasn't. There's a clipping from the local paper stapled to the back page, and—here, I'll quote an excerpt, 'Young Francis Wallace gave evidence of his discovery and report to the police concisely in a steady voice and was complimented by the coroner.' How on earth am I going to mark—"

The telephone in the hall rang.

Barry rose. "I'll see to it." He went into the hall, closed the door behind him, and lifted the receiver. "Hello. Laverty."

"Barry. Bill Howard. How are you? Sorry I haven't called sooner, but by the time I'd finished last night it was too late to call, and today's been hectic. I promised I'd let you know how Baby Anderson, to be called Robert, is doing."

"I understand, but thanks for phoning now. How are Mum and baby?" Barry braced himself to hear bad news.

"Hang on." Barry could hear muffled voices in the background and thought about young Robert's survival prospects. They were good, but there were any number of nonlethal complications to which preemies were at risk. Barry had picked up some information during his time in the Waveney, but his knowledge of neonatal medicine was still sketchy.

"I'm back. Sorry about that, Barry. Mildred's fine and Ken's been to visit today. Only fathers are allowed to see preemies—they're prone to infection, as you know. Robert's not showing any signs of that yet, and the paediatrician can't find signs of any nervous disorder, so we can pretty well rule out birth trauma."

"Good. That's great news."

"Everything was happening so fast yesterday Joan hadn't time to tell you the Apgar scores were both six."

Barry nodded to himself. "That's about as good as we could have hoped for."

"It is. There's no sign of respiratory distress syndrome—yet—but we're keeping the nipper on humidified oxygen at a concentration of thirty percent, and warm, of course."

Barry's sigh was one of relief. If the lungs didn't function properly, the mortality rate was about 30 percent, and higher oxygen concentrations in babies under five pounds could cause blindness. "This is sounding better and better."

"Perhaps one snag, but the paediatricians are on top of it. Kernicterus."

"I'm not very up on that condition."

"Because their livers are immature, preemies have difficulty processing bilirubin, the end product to the normal breakdown of haemoglobin. If serum bilirubin levels rise, they cause jaundice—"

"Like some kinds of jaundice in adults?"

"Exactly, but in preemies, the bilirubin also causes brain damage, unfortunately. That leads to mental deficiency or death."

"Oh-oh. I do not like the sound of that."

"It's really not as bad as it seems. Kernicterus because of prematurity doesn't usually occur until the third or fourth day of life. Looking on the bright side, and given all the good aspects of Robert's progress, he probably won't develop it. But they're measuring the serum bilirubin levels daily and if they do get too high, they can exchange the baby's blood with donated blood with normal levels."

"So, you're saying Robert's chances are good?"

"I'm not saying it. It's what the paediatricians think, and they're the experts."

"Thanks for letting me know, Bill. I've been worried about them," and by extension about Sue.

"That's the big difference between us. Your patients almost become like friends, and when something serious comes along, you can ship them off to folks like me and we only see them briefly."

"Too true, so thanks again for keeping me posted."

"And I'll be in touch on the kernicterus front too." He paused. "Seeing you yesterday reminded me about the good times you and Jack and I had at Campbell. Any chance the three of us could get together for a jar? It's been ages since I've been out that way. Perhaps we could meet in Ballybucklebo?"

"Sure. Ask Jack, and when you pick a day, I'll make sure I'm free too. Jack's girlfriend is living-in in the Royal's housemen's quarters but her dad's here and is happy to put Jack up. And we've a bed for you here. Keep you safe from the Peelers. Don't want you getting snagged for being over the limit."

"Good idea. Thanks, Barry. I'm off." The line went dead.

Barry replaced the receiver and clenched his teeth. The news about young Robert was good, he told himself, yet there was still that one unknown, and Barry couldn't change the habit of a lifetime. He was worried about the little lad, but he'd not let his concerns show. He had not seen Sue as happy for months. He went back into the living room.

Sue, still marking, looked up. "Well?"

He smiled. "It was Bill Howard, who delivered yesterday's breech, giving me an update. Everything's fine."

"Huh," she said, "it took him a brave while to pass on a simple message. Are you sure?"

The lie rolled off his tongue with almost no effort. "He's a school classmate of Jack's and mine. We had a bit of *craic* about the old days, and he wants the three of us to get together soon for a drink. I'd like us to give him a bed. Jack can stay with Helen's dad."

She smiled. "Of course, we'll put Bill up."

Barry sat, then reached down to stroke one of Max's long, soft ears. "How's the marking going?"

"Nearly done. A lot of 'It was a lovely summer and I had a lovely time doing lots of lovely things.' I don't think most of this class have a trip to Stockholm in their futures."

"Stockholm?"

"To collect a Nobel Prize for Literature. Except possibly the author of 'How I Found a Corpse.' He has a very good storytelling style. I gave him an A plus."

Barry rose, bent, and dropped a kiss on her head.

"I wish you'd been my teacher."

"I'd like to be tonight," she said. "I was remembering getting a bit hot and bothered in my lacy, peach-coloured nylon knickers, and you know Harith says it's all right for us to make love now." She stood, put her arms around him, and kissed him long and hard. "Come on," she said in a husky voice, taking his hand and heading for their bedroom. "Let's see if I can give out another A plus."

26

And There We Saw the Giants

The sun was high and the sky blue in the village of Bushmills near the north coast of County Antrim. O'Reilly waited for the bill for a late lunch that he, Kitty, and their guest, Consuela Rivera y Navarro, had enjoyed on the stone forecourt of the Bushmills Inn. The two-storey whitewashed building to his right was covered with a dense Virginia creeper, its leaves now deep Merlot red, stretching from roof to ground. This part of the building met at a right angle with a squat, whitewashed replica of an Irish round tower with one latticed window and a conical slate roof.

The waiter appeared and O'Reilly paid.

"Thank you, sir."

"Right, girls," he said, standing and starting the walk to the car park. "It's only about a ten-minute drive to one of the wonders of the world. I promise you, Consuela, it'll take the light from your eyes."

Consuela Rivera y Navarro seemed younger than her thirty-five years, with her long dark hair hanging to the small of her back, ebony eyes that were slightly slanted above high cheekbones, and full lips. She frowned. "Please? What does this mean?" Her English was slightly accented.

Kitty shook her head. "Come on, Fingal. Consuela's English is a damn sight better than your Spanish. The old bear means a sight that will impress you very much."

"I see. Thank you, Tia Kitty."

As a very little girl, Consuela had called Kitty her "*tia*," or auntie. She was the only mother Consuela had ever known. She'd been two when her own mother had been killed during the shelling of Madrid in November 1936 during the Spanish Civil War. Kitty, while she was working as a nurse in an orphanage in San Blas, Tenerife, had met Consuela's father and had fallen in love.

"Already you have done that. Giving me the front seat so I could drink in those views along the Antrim Coast Road. I have some wonderful pictures to remind me. The sea views, they are majestic. Would that be the right word?"

"It is," Kitty said. "*Majestuoso*."

"It's been a wonderful two days since I arrived from Barcelona. And your Mrs. Kinky, so charming. Yesterday morning she asked for a recipe for paella, but I don't know if you can get cuttlefish in Ireland."

"Hmmm. Neither do I," said O'Reilly.

"You don't?" Kitty said with a mischievous grin. "Fingal does not know something. I'll put the date in my diary."

O'Reilly smiled. Kitty had been in a great mood since last Friday, when they had started a two-week holiday. She should take more time off.

Consuela chuckled. "Always you two tease each other and, Fingal, you make me laugh. When I asked you, what means 'Bally'? You have so many towns that start with that name. Tell me again, please."

"'Bally' means a townland, a village and surrounding country, but it can also be a polite way of saying 'bloody.' That lets us use the names of four real places to say, 'If you weren't so Ballymena with your Ballymoney you could have a Ballycastle for your Ballyholme.'"

Consuela's laugh was rich and throaty. "Thank you." She shook her head. "So, Fingal, what is the next treat?"

"The Giant's Causeway."

Kitty feigned amazement. "The Giant's Causeway? Good Lord. I was sure you were going to say the Bushmills Whiskey Distillery."

"No," he said, "although it does have the distinction of being the first-ever licensed distillery in the world. King James I issued one in 1601. I believe they make some very good whiskeys, but I'm not sure it would be of great interest to you ladies."

Kitty smiled. "You surprise me." She took his hand. "Not about the date. Knowing you, you probably know the colour of ink on the paper. Thank you for being considerate. We don't want to tire Consuela out."

"Oh, I am not tired. And I am very fit," she said. "Our daughter Josélita is a very keen tennis player. Her heroine is Maria Bueno. Already at twelve, Josélita wants to win Grand Slams too. She beats me regularly. She will have to rely on her father to play her while I am away. She will probably beat José too."

All three stopped at the Rover 2000.

"Thank you, Tia Kitty, thank you, Fingal. You are showing me this country which I have wanted to see since I was a little girl, when Tia Kitty first told me stories about her beautiful Emerald Isle."

The narrow road ran through small fields, some enclosed by dry stone walls. Stubble left from the harvest, golden in the sun, kept company with the pastures of green that gave Ireland one of her nicknames.

O'Reilly pointed to Consuela's right. "That dark green island shaped like a fat wishbone is Rathlin. On a clear day like today you can see clouds of sea birds, eider ducks and gannets, over the island. Some of the same geologic formations that you'll see here are there too. Way in the distance in the heat haze is the Mull of Kintyre at the mouth of the River Clyde in Scotland. The island of Ailsa Craig is thirty miles from here, in the middle of the river." He changed to a lower gear to descend a series of hairpin bends built to enable cars to get down a high, steep, grass-covered escarpment. "The causeway was formed after a sheet of lava ran over the cliffs. In some places it's ninety-two feet thick."

"Lava?" Consuela looked around. "Ireland has volcanoes?"

"Oh, yes," said Kitty. "Many. But they're all extinct now. Not like your Mount Tiede in Tenerife."

"It is close to San Blas, Fingal. Papá remembered when Mount Tiede erupted. He was just a little boy then."

Kitty leaned forward from the backseat and laid a hand on Consuela's shoulder. "Fingal and I were so sorry for your loss, but very pleased that your letter brought us together again three years ago." The three were quiet for a long moment before O'Reilly spoke again.

"These are like no lava formations you've ever seen, I'll reckon. There are about forty thousand columns forming the causeway, making perfect stepping-stones. The same basalt formations are at Fingal's Cave in the Scottish Hebrides. But these have to be seen to be believed. And that's just what we're going to do. Here we are." He parked in a circular parking lot near some construction vehicles and a pile of granite stones.

O'Reilly and his passengers got out.

"There was a once-in-a-lifetime storm last year that washed away part of the causeway. It is being properly protected with these great granite blocks as rock armour."

"Please. Rock armour?"

"They're laid at the water's edge to protect the causeway from further damage by the waves."

"I've heard the sea is never calm here," said Kitty. "Just look at the line of white water smashing on the rocks below." She pointed at the shoreline and then out to sea. "And that's the North Atlantic. Waves that start forming off America or Greenland have a long way in which to build up their strength."

Consuela leaned back into the car and brought out her camera. "I must take some more pictures to show to Josélita and José."

A rough path led them to the way down to the causeway.

Even from above, O'Reilly could hear the sound of the waves smashing on the peninsula and the rocky shores of the two convex beaches, one on either side of the causeway proper. The Atlantic, although blue in the shallower water inshore, gradually became darker the farther he looked. The smell of the ocean filled his nostrils, but no spray was thrown up to where he stood.

He looked up to see a pair of large glossy black birds with wedge-shaped tails and single "finger" feathers at their wingtips soaring on the updraft from the escarpment. Ravens. If it were May, the waters would have been filled with fulmars, a tube-nosed seabird that returned to this area to breed each year. But now those pelagic birds would be living far out at sea.

O'Reilly and the two women arrived at the edge of the lava columns.

Consuela clapped her hands together and stopped dead. "*Dios mio.*

I did not know what you mean by columns, Fingal, but now I see. *Increíble.*" She handed him her camera. "Please, will you take Kitty and me in the foreground?"

O'Reilly did, and returned her camera. "They say the place was drawn to the public's attention by the bishop of Derry, who visited here in 1692. This is the Little Causeway. The columns are interlocking and it's easy to walk on them. From here to the end of this peninsula, where the causeway disappears into the ocean, is about half a mile, and we'll take our time. It's not difficult to twist an ankle." As he looked down, he reckoned there were about thirty other people ahead, some going, some returning.

"I'll go first," Kitty said. "You'll be closer to Fingal, Consuela, and he's a very good tour guide."

O'Reilly pointed down. "Do you see, Consuela, how most of the black basalt columns are six-sided? But not all on this stretch. They can range from four to eight. The next bit, the Middle Causeway, has the best stretch of interlocking hexagonal ones."

She nodded but did not turn her head because, like O'Reilly himself, she was concentrating on where she was stepping. As they picked their way along, the pattern underfoot took on the marvellous geometrical symmetry he had described.

Gradually, the columns were stepping down ahead. Those to their left ended in a shallow plateau that made a beach where two little boys and a man, presumably their dad, were examining a lump of lava. It was a large hollow cylinder bent at ninety degrees in the middle with one side lying on the pillars and the other sticking vertically up. "Look left. There's the Giant's Boot."

Kitty's voice came back. "Glad I don't have to wash his socks."

O'Reilly chuckled. "We're getting there. Kitty, start angling to your right. You can see tall columns that almost stretch in a row to the end of the peninsula fringing the right shore. I want Consuela to get a good look."

"Right." Kitty set a diagonal course. As they passed a low, reddish, weathered column, O'Reilly said, "That's a giant's eye. They're all over the place."

Now on the Grand Causeway, where the going, still downhill, was harder, no one spoke, and they steadily neared the forty-foot columns. O'Reilly made a quick calculation. He was more than six feet tall. They were nearly six and a half times his height, and to fully appreciate their dimensions he had to hold his head back and stare up.

Kitty and Consuela were both gazing up.

"Give me your camera." O'Reilly captured the shot, the small people in the foreground giving perspective to the towering black columns. "Those are the pipes of the Giant's Organ. I find it most impressive. It ends about one hundred yards from the sea." He sat on one column with his back leaning on an organ pipe and put his feet on the next column below. "I think a short rest might be in order." From behind the pipes, he could hear men shouting, and the crash of rock on rock. The rock armouring was going on apace.

And all the while the Atlantic combers noisily threatened the basalt shore with breaking and entering and filled the air with spray.

Consuela, from where she sat between O'Reilly and Kitty, said, "You Irish are great storytellers. There must be many legends about your causeway."

"Indeed, there are," said O'Reilly. "All concern a giant called Finn MacCool, who must have been a quarrellsome so-and-so. One has it he was engaged in a running battle with a Welsh giant. One day he ran out of stepping-stones. He was so enraged he pulled up a huge sod—"

"Please. Sod?"

"Grass with the earth beneath attached."

"I see."

"And hurled it at his enemy. It fell short into the sea. Today that sod is the Isle of Man, and it is said that the crater it left is Lough Neagh."

Consuela chuckled. "I like that story."

"As children we were taught that story, and the Lord knows how many generations before us have passed it on. If you draw the outline of the isle and hold it over a picture of the lough, the outline is not such a good fit." Kitty laughed. "But some people still believe it."

"That's true," O'Reilly said, "and I'm with Mark Twain. 'Never let the truth get in the way of a good story.' And remember what I am going to tell you are legends going back to Celtic times. If you take them literally, I'll be happy to introduce you both to the faeries at the bottom of our garden when we get home."

"I think Arthur Guinness chased them away years ago," Kitty said.

O'Reilly hesitated. Poor old Arthur. Och well.

He said, "I've always liked that story of the lough and the island, but I'm fonder of one of the two concerning the Scottish giant Bennandonner—it means 'mountain of thunder'—who challenged Finn to a fight. You remember I told you about there being basalt columns in Scotland as well. They're on the island of Staffa, just across the sea. According to one legend, Finn hopped over to Scotland and beat Bennandonner. That's easy enough to believe—assuming you accept giants. The other one is much more subtle and shows how Finn's wife, Oonagh, outsmarted the Scotsman."

"Women usually do, dear old bear," Kitty said with a smile and a stuck-out tongue tip for Fingal. "At least the ancient Irish took us women seriously. One of the reasons Pope Adrian IV, the only ever English pope, gave Ireland to the Norman Henry II in 1155 was to reform the Irish Catholic Church. Not only was His Holiness unhappy that Irish monks shaved their tonsures from side to side at the front instead of circular ones like all other monks but, perish the thought, the church in Ireland ordained women priests."

"This would never be allowed in my country." Consuela looked out toward Scotland. "And still you have religious troubles to this day, I know," she said. "We see reports on our television. Ireland is not alone. In Spain in this century, many Catalans have been trying to separate since 1922, and many Basques are constantly agitating for independence. It is so sad. José and I, we do not agree, we feel we are stronger together, but people," she sighed, "they wish to have their own countries rather than work together." She smiled at Fingal. "But I am having a lovely day and I do not want us to be sad. Please, Fingal, tell us the other story."

O'Reilly was silent for a moment, struck by the not-quite parallels between the two countries. Here in Ulster one side wanted to unite with the rest of Ireland. The other wanted to remain separate and stay united with the UK. "Right, well, it seems that Oonagh got word that Bennandonner was on his way across the causeway. Now make no mistake, Finn MacCool was no coward, but Oonagh hated bloodshed. She persuaded Finn to let her disguise him as a baby, put him in a cradle, and gave him a great stone to pretend to chew on."

Consuela's eyes were sparkling. Laugh lines ran from the corners of her eyes and mouth.

"Bennandonner arrives looking for Finn, and Oonagh tells him to lower his voice. He was going to disturb Finn's baby.

"'Holy thundering Jas—' sorry ladies—says the Scot to himself. 'If MacCool has sired a child of that size, how big is this Finn himself? I'm not waiting to find out!' And off he runs, ripping up the causeway as he goes so Finn can't give chase." He smiled at Consuela, who was clapping her hands in obvious delight.

"Oh, that is a wonderful story," she said. "I like how Oonagh stopped the fight."

"Aye," Kitty said. "'Blessèd are the peacemakers—' We could use a few here in Ulster."

O'Reilly rose and changed the subject. "Come on, Consuela, I want us to get to the very end, then we'll go back to the car. I'll take us home by a shorter way and we'll be at the Culloden in time for dinner. I'm going to have Scottish salmon." He smacked his lips.

"I like the sound of that, Fingal. Thank you."

Together they set off, and soon reached the end of the peninsula.

"Now," said O'Reilly, "you can tell your friends you've seen the famous Giant's Causeway. I hope you've enjoyed it."

"Very much, and before we go . . ." She waved her hand so she could take a photo of Fingal with his arm round Kitty's waist and the causeway in the background.

O'Reilly laughed. "We're glad you enjoyed it, and that makes you one up on the renowned Doctor Samuel Johnson. His chronicler, Boswell, quotes him as saying about the Causeway, 'Worth seeing; but not worth going to see.'"

"What?" Consuela came close to stamping her foot on a hexagonal stone. Her face flushed. She took a deep breath. "You and Kitty have shown me one of the world's most beautiful coastal roads and a thing of beauty that you said, Fingal, 'Would take the sight, no, the light from my eyes.' It has. And as for your Doctor Johnson, to borrow a phrase I overheard yesterday when Kitty took me shopping in Belfast—" Her look was angelic but her words vitriol, "His head was full of hobby-horse shite."

O'Reilly laughed so hard he missed his next step up and grazed both palms in breaking his fall.

27

Make Haste Slowly

O'Reilly ushered Kitty and Consuela into the hall of the Royal Ulster Yacht Club. The building, erected between 1897 and '99, was richly Edwardian inside and contained a treasure trove of yachting memorabilia. O'Reilly had always had a particular fascination with the tiller from Lord Cantelupe's yacht *Urania,* which in 1890 had been wrecked on the rocky shore nearby. Although the crew had been saved, the gale had hurled the young viscount onto the rocks and his body had been found by a fisherman a month later. A reminder of the deadly power of nature.

"This is very grand," Consuela said, looking around the hall, half-panelled in dark oak, a large fireplace filling most of the left wall. "I am a little nervous about meeting a real marquis. In Spain a *marqués* is second only to a *duque,* and both must be addressed as 'The Most Excellent.' How shall I speak to your lord, please, Fingal?"

O'Reilly smiled. "A duke outranks a marquis here too, but among friends Lord John MacNeill is very informal. No need for you to curtsey, but don't offer to shake his hand. That is his prerogative. Call him 'my lord' or 'sir' unless he gives you permission not to."

"You'll like him," Kitty said. She smiled. "He's a charming man and we're all very fond of him." Kitty moved closer to Consuela and lowered her voice. "He's bringing Mrs. Ruth Carson, the mother of Sebastian, our trainee."

"Ah," Consuela said. "A romance, perhaps?"

"Ladies, you're missing the architectural splendours of the Royal Ulster Yacht Club." Fingal pointed to a staircase to their right. "Have a closer look at that, Consuela."

She moved over, scrutinized it, and returned. "The side panel is covered in carved ships and flowers. And very beautiful."

"Isn't it?" He led them through the lounge, where more half-panelled walls, their upper sections decorated with photographs of famous yachts and yachtsmen, rose to a white embossed ceiling. Members and their guests stood at the bar or sat at tables. The hum of conversation was pleasantly low, the tobacco smoke minimal, and its smell mingled with that of old seasoned leather.

Now in the dining room, O'Reilly excused himself while Kitty and Consuela carried on to where the marquis was standing, waiting to greet them at a window table. O'Reilly wanted to stop and exchange pleasantries with a friend and colleague. "How are you, Jamesie? Haven't seen you for a while. You're well?" Doctor Jamsie Bowman, who practiced in Bangor, was one of a four-doctor syndicate who owned the Long Island on Strangford Lough.

"Well? Och, aye, and it has been a while. I think last year on the island?"

"In October."

"Would you like to come down for a shoot someday this season?"

"Thank you, but no. I've hung up my gun."

"Have you now. Good for you. I'm thinking about packing it up too." He grimaced. "Too bloody cold down there at four A.M. when you get to our age."

O'Reilly laughed. "Maybe you and your missus will come over to Ballybucklebo some evening?"

"Love to."

"I'll be in touch, but I'd better join my party now." O'Reilly walked across the dining room where wooden tables sparkling with silver and crystal on white napery, and flanked by plain hard-backed, leather-cushioned chairs, were arranged in parallel rows. Not many were taken, and the reason was obvious to anyone looking out the window. People tended to stay at home on such a miserable day.

As he approached their table, set at right angles to and abutting the sill of a wide window, the wind-driven squalls rattled the sashes and rain ran down the glass.

John had seated the party with Consuela and Kitty opposite each other and closest to the view. Ruth Carson sat beside Consuela. John MacNeill stood at the head of the table and inclined his head to the vacant seat between him and Kitty.

O'Reilly shook John MacNeill's hand. "Hello, John."

"Fingal. Good to see you, and I'm charmed to meet your Spanish guest. I've made sure she and Kitty have the best views, despite the weather."

They both sat.

Fingal's own prospect of the turbulent lough was nothing to complain about. This side was clear, but the far-off Antrim Hills were hidden behind rain squalls. "Heaven help the sailors on days like this."

John nodded. "The bigger keelboats have a race scheduled, and the race committee has agreed to let them start. The winds are force five gusting up to twenty-one knots from the southeast and not expected to freshen. It'll be a tough sail, but they should be all right."

"I think, John—" Consuela said, looking out the window.

So, titles had already been dispensed with.

"—the sailors must be *loco*—crazy."

He laughed. "You may be right, but you've got a front-row seat for the craziness. Do you see down below, that long, whitewashed building with the convex roof? On the rocks at the very edge of the water?"

She nodded.

"We call that the Battery, because there's a room on the seaward side that holds a miniature cannon pointing out to sea, and—"

"Excuse me, my lord. I don't mean to interrupt, but here are the drinks you ordered for you and the lady, the menus, and would the rest of your party care to order some refreshment?"

"Thank you, Brian."

Orders were taken.

"I'll be back with your drinks and to take your meal orders, sir. Today the chef particularly recommends his fisherman's pie. All the ingredients came in fresh this morning."

As Brian withdrew, O'Reilly heard the *bang* of the miniature cannon that fired blank twelve-bore cartridges.

"That," said John, "is the ten-minute warning. You can see the boats off to the right."

O'Reilly turned in his chair. Ten dark-hulled Glen-class yachts, white sails taut, heeling alarmingly, were jockeying for position downwind of the start line between the Battery and a wave-tossed white motorboat, a quarter of a mile offshore.

"They'll get another gun in five minutes, and five minutes after that a final gun will signal the start. Then they'll have to cross the start line, round an upwind mark, sail to the downwind mark, then back to the start line to finish." He looked up. "Ah. Here are your drinks."

The drinks were served, orders given, and a toast drunk. O'Reilly was particularly looking forward to his pie.

"Do you sail, Fingal?" Ruth asked.

He shook his shaggy head. "Not really, but when I was on *Warspite*—"

"Please, what is a *Warspite*?"

"A British battleship I served on during the war. Tom Laverty, Barry's father, was a shipmate. He taught me to sail in one of the boats called whalers that we carried. I understand the principles enough to know I'd not like to be out there today."

A gust rattled the panes, immediately followed by the bark of the little cannon, and through the rain O'Reilly could see serried ranks of white horses advancing from left to right shedding spume as galloping horses shed sweat. He was quite happy to sit back, sip his pint, and listen to the conversation. He was glad John had invited Consuela. She'd be off home tomorrow, but he and Kitty still had a week's holiday to look forward to. He glanced at her, seeing how the little bags that had been under her eyes last week had vanished, how relaxed she looked talking to her Spanish friend. He wished she looked like that every day, relaxed and well rested. She should slow down. God knows, he had been at her about it for two years now. He'd not mentioned it since he'd tried to get her to agree back in July. The time had never been right.

He looked at John MacNeill, who seemed enraptured by Ruth Carson. The man's gaze never left her face even though his remark was addressed to O'Reilly. "Ruth and I went to see *Bullitt* at the Tonic Cinema on Wednesday."

She smiled at him. "I thought Steve McQueen was very handsome, and that car chase. The cars bouncing up and down on San Francisco's hilly streets. To use Consuela's word—*loco*." She took a sip of her sherry. "But very exhilarating." She addressed O'Reilly but looked at John. "Fingal, John is doing me so much good taking me out of myself. We're both at a time in our lives when we should be enjoying our leisure, and he's certainly helping me with that. You really are a dear man, John MacNeill." She reached across and squeezed his hand.

"Thank you." He kept her hand in his.

Quite a show of public affection for two upper-crust people of over sixty, O'Reilly thought. Fair play to them both. He wished them well.

Consuela, who had been chatting to Kitty, said, "I'm always interested in the history of things, John. Tell me a bit about this royal club? 'Royal,' meaning?"

"Excuse me, sir." Brian reappeared and set down everyone's starters. "And would anyone care for another drink?"

There were no takers, but John MacNeill said, "As everybody's having a fish main course, I think a couple of bottles of the Chablis Premier Cru—and yes, Fingal, my reflux seems to have gone away—would suit, unless anyone disagrees?"

No demurral.

"Certainly, my lord. There are some chilled." He left.

"Now, Consuela, you asked about the club."

O'Reilly tucked into his melon balls with ginger, kept one eye on the heeling yachts smashing through the waves, and listened.

"In 1866, my great-grandfather and a group of well-off gentlemen decided to reactivate the old Ulster Yacht Club, which had been founded in 1806. He became commodore and in 1870, presumably because of his connections from his previous employment as undersecretary of state for India, he was able to obtain a royal warrant—permission from Queen Victoria to add the title 'Royal' to the club's name."

"I understand. I think before the Civil War we had something similar when organisations could, with permission, use the title 'Real.'"

"Exactly the same. Here in Bangor, our title was to become very important in 1898 because—"

The simultaneous crash of the starting cannon and the arrival of Brian and a fellow waiter to clear the first course interrupted John's brief history. All eyes stared out the window.

O'Reilly leaned back to see past Kitty.

Kitty said, "You understand these things, Fingal. All of the yachts seem to have very small sails and they're leaning over quite far."

"The wind's coming down the lough and they have to sail up it into the wind. To do that, they have to sail at an angle to it. The sails are trimmed to get the best from the wind, but that exerts a tremendous pressure on the rig, which if uncontrolled could capsize the boat. So, the skippers reduce it by flying smaller headsails called storm-jibs and making the main sails smaller by partially lowering them and tying the loose canvas to the boom. It's called shortening sail or reefing."

"Look at them. They look like they're about to fall over."

O'Reilly watched as the pack thinned out. Two boats, bows cleaving the waves and throwing up sheets of water, were already well ahead of the other eight. The leaders heeled to starboard and their crews huddled along the port rail to add their weight to counterbalance the wind's pressure. He watched as yellow oilskin–clad figures ducked to avoid the flying spray. O'Reilly shivered. Bloody cold out there.

"Excuse me, sir." Brian set a plate of steaming fisherman's pie in front of O'Reilly then showed the label of a chilled bottle to John, who nodded. Brian uncorked the wine and poured some to be tasted.

"Excellent."

All glasses were filled.

"Fingal, join me please." John raised his. "To the ladies."

"To the ladies." O'Reilly drank with his left hand and used his right to give Kitty's thigh a squeeze. He savoured the warmth under his hand and the crisp cold wine in his mouth. He noticed how John and Ruth exchanged fond looks. O'Reilly's smile was vast. So was Kitty's. One more squeeze. Damn it, he enjoyed his wife's company and would have a lot more of it—if she'd slow down. He tucked into his main course, tasting a piece of halibut. Lovely.

John had taken a few mouthfuls, then said, "To finish my story, Consuela, a rich tea merchant who had been knighted, Sir Thomas Lipton, was a keen sailor. He wanted to mount a British challenge for a very prestigious trophy, the America's Cup."

"I have heard of this. My husband, José, is a keen sailor."

"So is Barry Laverty," Kitty said. "Next time you come to visit, bring José, and I'm sure Barry, who's a member of Ballyholme Yacht Club, will take him out."

"Good club. A lot of their members are members here too, but back in the 1890s, there was a lot of snobbery attached to who would be admitted to 'royal' clubs."

"Excuse me. Snobbery?"

"Sorry, Consuela. Upper-class people looking down on those beneath them in rank." He smiled at Ruth. "There's not as much of that today."

As my brother, Lars, found out, O'Reilly thought, when he had an affair with John's sister, Lady Myrna. In the end it hadn't been the class thing that had broken them apart but simply two people with different ways of looking at life. He bit down. Gosh, that morsel of Dublin Bay prawn was really tasty. Another mouthful of Chablis complemented it perfectly.

"Sir Thomas applied to join the Royal Yacht Squadron at Cowes because only members of royal yacht clubs could mount a challenge. But he was rejected because, despite his knighthood, he was merely 'in trade,' as the expression went, and not a proper gentleman."

"I believe," said O'Reilly, finishing his last mouthful, "that Kaiser Wilhelm, a keen sailor, referred to Sir Thomas as 'the boating grocer.'"

"Well," Kitty said, "we taught that nasty little man with his ridiculous moustache his manners in 1918."

While everyone laughed, O'Reilly thought, But at what cost?

Consuela frowned and nodded. "In Spain we still have people who consider anybody below their rank of *hidalgo* very inferior."

"Well, here at the Royal Ulster, they took Sir Thomas in as an equal and a skilled sailor," John said. "And a good thing, too. Between 1898 and 1930 Sir Thomas, a most persistent man, mounted five unsuccessful challenges, all in elegant yachts called *Shamrock*. There are photos and paintings of them, and of Sir Thomas, all over the place. I'll take you round to look at them after lunch."

"I would appreciate that, John. I also admire persistence, but I believe there comes always a time to concede."

"Very good point, Consuela," said O'Reilly as Brian started delivering orange and chocolate soufflés.

Kitty said, "I see some of the racers have rounded the first mark."

O'Reilly peered out the window through the lashing rain. She was right, and the first four boats were altering their rigs. He watched storm-jibs come down and be replaced by regular ones. As reefs were shaken out, mainsails were hoisted to mastheads. All that took a lot of crew team-work. He chuckled. At least the effort would warm them up a bit. Now with the wind on their sterns and sails set on to either side, the hulls had stopped heeling but were pitched and tossed as the waves passed under the keels. He hoped the crews had strong stomachs.

Brian said, "Would anyone care for coffee? A liqueur?"

John looked around. "Bit early in the day for liqueurs, perhaps, but I think we'll take coffee in the lounge later. You can smoke your pipe, Fingal."

"Thank you, John."

Consuela stood. "I should like to thank you, and I wish to be formal, Lord Ballybucklebo, for a wonderful meal and a most instructive explanation of your club. And Fingal and Tía Kitty for a wonderful holiday, which I wish could last longer, but I must return to my husband and daughter. Thank you." She sat.

"It's been lovely having you," said Kitty, "and don't be sad when good things are over. Fingal and I have to get back to work soon too."

"Good Lord," said Ruth Carson. "I hope you don't mind me asking, Kitty, but are you still working full time? I don't mean to intrude, but I think you heard what I said earlier about being at a time in our lives when we should be enjoying our leisure."

O'Reilly's eyes widened.

Kitty frowned. "I—well, I've always worked full time." She sounded puzzled. "I enjoy my work."

Fingal decided to say nothing.

"But do you really have to?"

Kitty looked down to the table, then up. "Have to?" She glanced at Fingal, who cocked his head to one side as an unspoken "I'd rather you didn't."

"Well, no. Not really, I suppose. No, in fact. I don't."

Ruth took a deep breath. "I was married for thirty-five years. I was looking forward to spending a lot more time with my late husband. There were all kinds of things we wanted to do. I don't want to be morbid and spoil a lovely afternoon, but I feel compelled to say this, Kitty. None of us know how long we have. You and Fingal are still quite young. I have to say," she looked from one to the other, "make the most of however long you have left. Please."

Far from spoiling O'Reilly's afternoon, Ruth had made it. He looked over to a thoughtful Kitty just as Consuela reached out her hands to her across the table. "You know, Tia Kitty, Fingal, that I lost my father three years ago. Perhaps it's not my place, being much younger, but I agree with Señora Carson."

John said, "And I think it's a lovely thing for you both to suggest." He looked over at Kitty and raised his hands in supplication. "Kitty, my dear, this is not a conspiracy. Fingal and Ruth and I are not trying to get you to retire, I assure you. I had no inkling Ruth was going to say anything like this, and I applaud you, my dear."

O'Reilly kept his counsel until Kitty finally said, "I'm touched. Truly I am. Thank you both. Fingal has been asking me to slow down for some time now and I've kept putting him off. But this last week has been a lesson, a lovely lesson, and we've still a week to go." She took a deep breath and Fingal felt her hand reach for his under the table. "As soon as I'm back to work, I will ask Matron about the possibility of a part-time job next hospital year, I promise, Fingal."

Fingal's heart soared. "Thank you, Kitty. Thank you." He tightened his grip on her hand. "And I'll try to slow down too."

"We shall hold you both to that," said John. "What are friends for, after all?" Something out on the lough grabbed his attention. "Good Lord. Look at that."

All eyes stared out to sea.

As best as Fingal could determine, one of the lagging skippers, in what must have been an ill-advised attempt to catch up, had tried to hoist his spinnaker, the great, multicoloured balloon of a sail that under kinder conditions was a terrific adjunct to sailing downwind. Today the wind was too much. The mast and sails had collapsed in a tangle of snapped rigging and torn sailcloth. It would be panic stations on board trying to rid the vessel of all the wreckage. Already the club rescue launch, always on standby for races, would be on its way to tow them in. He hoped the crew would be all right.

Consuela's earlier words came back to O'Reilly. "I admire persistence." Any skipper who tried to fly a spinnaker today was persistent, all right, but, like Consuela had said, there comes a time to concede. For racing yachtsmen, who must protect themselves and their craft, conceding had been forced upon them and he was sorry for it. For a certain beautiful nursing sister who had persisted a bit too long and for whom the concession had been voluntary, Fingal O'Reilly's big heart swelled.

28

Fight like Devils

Barry sat at a table in the Duck, nursing a pint. The tide mark was less than an inch down. Five days after Bill Howard had suggested it, Barry, not without protest from Sue, was waiting for Bill and Jack Mills. Mid-pregnancy was beginning to take its toll and she was now experiencing both urinary frequency and the promised backache. Barry could tell she was trying to be stoic about the physical symptoms but emotionally she was on edge. "Do you really have to go out?" had been her petulant question as he'd picked up the car keys from the hall table.

"Come on, Sue," he said. "I'll not be gone long. It'll be a reunion for me and Jack with Bill Howard." He'd kissed her. "And you usually do your marking on Saturday evenings if we're not going out."

"I do, don't I?" She'd managed a small smile. "Off you trot. I didn't mean to be snarky." She put a hand on her tummy and patted it. "This little one is playing with my hormones." She'd kissed him back. "But don't be too late."

"I'll not." He glanced over at the exercise books on the dining room table, accompanied by a pot of tea and Sue's favourite Belleek mug, the delicate white porcelain stamped with a raised design of shamrocks. "What's the subject tonight?"

"Geography. They've each drawn a map of one of the six counties, complete with topographical details and historical sites. I've had a quick look and, you know, I think we have some budding cartographers and surveyors in there." She looked fondly at the pile and waved her hand at him. "Now, off you go. I've got to crack on with these. Enjoy your pints."

The noise in the Duck interrupted his reverie. He glanced at his watch.

As usual, his lifelong habit of punctuality meant he had ten minutes to spare before his friends arrived.

He looked around through the haze of tobacco smoke. The Saturday-night crowd was here in force. He didn't get to the Duck as often as he had when he'd been single and living at Number One. The regular suspects were all in attendance: Gerry Shanks, Lenny Brown, and Alan Hewitt at one table, Constable Mulligan and Mister Coffin at another. Most tables were taken, and ten men lined the bar, some standing, others sitting on barstools.

He overheard Lenny say to Gerry, "I see Independent TV in the U.K. made its first broadcast in colour earlier this month."

"Modern science is a wonderful thing." Gerry laughed. "Fat lot of good it does me with a wee black-and-white set with rabbit ears for an aerial and—"

The general level of sound drowned out the rest.

He noticed a new face. A young man in his early twenties. His lank red hair reached his collar. He was dressed in a shirt, jeans, and guttees and hoisted himself onto a barstool with an empty one beside him. Barry had not seen him in here nor in the townland. Must be a newcomer.

Desmond Johnson, the farmer with a nodular goiter, was standing at the bar chatting with the barber, Dougie George. Desmond caught Barry's eye, pointed at his own chest then at Barry, who smiled and nodded. Leaving his drink on the bar, the farmer approached. He touched the peak of his duncher. "Evening, Doc. It'll only take a wee minute and please forgive me for asking you til be professional on your night off, but can I tell you what's happened? It might save you time in the surgery?"

"Of course, you can, Desmond, and by the way that goose roasted and with sage-and-onion stuffing was delicious. Thank you."

"Dead on. Glad you enjoyed it. Anyroad, I seen Doctor Montgomery on September the first, had all my tests, and seen him again a week later. He put me on, and it's a powerful mouthful, propyl thiouracil—did I say that right?"

"You did. We got a letter the next day about your medication and information that they would keep you under follow-up until they were satisfied you were stabilized on treatment. They're the experts. We don't have the lab facilities, but I'm pleased you're keeping me up to date in person."

"My pleasure. And I think it's starting to work. I'm not as tetchy and I'm not getting no palpitations no more."

"Good."

"Would you say thank you til Doctor Carson, sir?"

"I will, of course. He'll be pleased." And relieved, as am I, Barry thought. His memory of the visit to the surgery now jogged, he reckoned they'd been right to decide the risk of malignancy was low.

"So, I'll be off, sir, and thanks for your time."

"Don't worry your head. I'm glad you're getting better. When is Doctor Montgomery seeing you again?"

"October the sixth. He expects to get youse a final report then."

"One of us might pop in if we're near your place after we get the report."

"Great, sir." Desmond left and Barry took a pull on his pint.

The batwing doors opened and Donal Donnelly, accompanied by Dapper Frew, came in. Barry thought Donal Donnelly looked concerned and as they passed Barry's table, Donal took the next one but Dapper stopped. "Would you do me a wee favour, Doctor Laverty?"

"If I can."

"I saw Mister Greer yesterday. That's ten weeks since my operation. He give me a clean bill of health. Would you please tell Doctor O'Reilly?"

"Of course. That's great news, Dapper."

"Aye, it is. I'm feeling like a new man, so I am." Dapper laughed. "I'm tempted to think maybe Donal was onto something when he said the doc cleaned his brain for him while he was in there."

"Mister Greer's an excellent surgeon. If brain cleaning is what's needed, he's your man." Barry had spoken with a straight face and for a few seconds Dapper looked at him quizzically and then burst into laughter.

"Thanks a million, Doc, and thank Doctor O'Reilly for me too." Dapper headed for the bar to get drinks.

The batwing doors opened, and a dark-haired young man came in. Another stranger. He made his way to the empty barstool. In one of those lulls in the general conversation, Barry clearly heard him ask, "Is this here taken?" and the redhead answered, "Help yourself."

Barry lost interest, but during the same lull heard Dapper Frew. "So, you think you're getting short-changed by one of your suppliers, Donal?"

"I'm near sure, but I can't be certain. The divil. He must think I'm as thick as two short planks and—"

A great bellow of laughter came from the back of the room. The hum of general conversation swelled, drowning out the rest of Donal's words, and Barry realized Jack and Bill were standing by the table. Both were grinning.

Greetings were exchanged and Jack said, "My shout, Bill."

"Pint of Harp, please."

"Right." Jack left and returned, saying, "Willie will bring them over. So, Barry, how's Sue?"

"Physically she's fine. Twenty-one weeks and two days. Emotionally, she's a little on edge. I wish I could help her to stop worrying." The rest of that thought he kept to himself—that it was hard to help someone stop worrying when you were concerned yourself.

"I didn't know you were an expectant dad," Bill said. "Congratulations. Your wife is halfway there. As you well know, pregnancy can be a disturbing business. But the happiness can balance that out."

"It is. She's becoming a little irritable, but I'm hoping that phase will soon pass."

Willie arrived with a pint of golden Harp lager and a black-bodied, white-topped pint of stout, both products of the Guinness brewery.

"Barry's Sue is beautiful and sweet and as sharp as a tack. How she ever ended up with a bollix like you, Laverty, we'll never know." The three of them laughed. "To Sue Laverty. May she be delivered of a fine, healthy baby right on time." Jack raised his glass and all three drank.

Bill said, "I'd like to say something about work first, get it out of the way. Knowing Barry and how you get concerned about your patients, I'm sorry to tell you that we start worrying about kernicterus if a newborn's serum bilirubin gets to fifteen milligrams percent and regard levels of more than twenty milligrams as an absolute indication for exchange transfusion. Baby Anderson had one yesterday."

Barry nodded. Poor wee mite. He hated not being able to follow his patients closely, but it couldn't be helped.

"On the bright side, there's still no sign of respiratory distress and we've been able to maintain the oxygen down to below a level that can cause blindness in preemies, and young Robert is gaining weight at a satisfactory rate. All in all, the paediatricians are optimistic that his outlook is good."

"Thank you." A relieved Barry took a deep pull on his Guinness. He wondered how Mildred was coping but knew that that was information he couldn't get from Bill. The man was a medical doctor, and a busy one at that, not a psychologist.

Jack said, "Those last weeks must be very anxious-making for the mums-to-be."

"It's no raging hell for dads-to-be either," Barry said with a laugh. "But I reckon Sue and I will survive." He wanted to get on to a different subject. Bill Howard had not come here to talk shop. "Did you get to the School's Cup rugby final on Saint Patrick's Day, Bill?"

"Yes. To our collective shame as Old Campbellians, Bangor Grammar School beat us six to three."

"We were both there," Barry said, remembering the shock when Jack had said he and Helen were leaving Ulster as soon as Helen was qualified. It was something Barry feared might yet arise if a solution couldn't be found to Morris Mills's unforgiving opposition to his son's marriage to a Catholic.

A barstool crashed to the floor.

Barry whipped round to see what was going on. Conversation stopped as if a switch had been thrown. Every head turned to see the two unknown young men glowering at each other. The redhead crouched, fists clenched, eyes locked on those of his opponent.

The dark-haired one, who had not put up his guard, said, "Look, I don't want no fight. I was only pulling your leg. I'm sorry."

"You think calling me a Fenian git is funny?"

The men glared at each other.

Barry flinched. The expression could be said in jest between two best friends like Alan Hewitt and Lenny Brown. But Fenian, the name for Finn MacCool's followers and used later by a group dedicated to Irish independence, The Fenian Brotherhood, had become a derogatory name used by Loyalists. "Git," from "begotten," implied out of wedlock: Catholic bastard. Calling a stranger a Fenian git was either supremely stupid or a deliberate provocation. This could get ugly. He stole a quick glance as Constable Malcolm Mulligan slowly got to his feet.

The dark-haired man took a step forward, hand extended. "Look, I've told you I'm sorry. The name's David Dempsey. Let me buy you a pint."

The redhead, still crouched, fists raised and clenched, took a pace forward. "You buy me a pint? You're looking to have your teeth to play with."

There was a slight slurring of his words, but it did not seem that Redhead was drunk. Unless he'd had one or two before he'd come in, he'd only had time for a pint.

Dempsey, who must have accepted the situation, took a deep breath and took up a boxer's stance, preparing to defend himself.

The men flanking them at the bar moved back.

Barry, who had seen spontaneous barnyard cockfights, saw the same thing here. Fluffing up to look bigger. Vocal challenge. And both men were sweating. He could smell the odour.

Willie Dunleavy, from behind the semi-protection of his bar, called, "You two. Settle down. None of that in my bar. None of that sectarian rubbish, and no fighting."

Barry saw many heads nodding in agreement.

Redhead ignored Willie.

Constable Mulligan moved closer to the pair. "Everybody stay back. We don't need any hurt heroes."

Good man, Barry thought.

The police officer's voice was calm. "Listen. Listen, you two. I'm an off-duty constable. I've seen the whole thing. That was a bloody stupid thing to call him, Mister Dempsey, but it's not a criminal offence. And you," he addressed the other man, "so far, you've only disturbed the peace. Now put your fists down. Calm down and I'll turn a blind eye, but if you throw one punch and he fights back, he's acting in self-defence and I've a roomful of witnesses."

There was a low murmur of assent.

"And I'll do you for disturbing the peace, assault and battery, GBH"—policeman slang for "grievous bodily harm," Barry knew—"and resisting arrest."

Redhead did not turn away from his opponent. His voice sounded a little less angry, but he said, "You and whose army? Them Brit sojers with their Saracen armoured cars and Belgian FN rifles?"

Malcolm Mulligan kept his voice low. Steady. "No, son. I'm a simple Peeler doing his job." He held out his hands, palms up. "I've no weapons."

Barry held his breath as Malcolm edged toward the more belligerent of the two. He could see that David Dempsey, while keeping his guard up, was not so stiff. So aggressive.

Redhead drew back his right fist, but before he could launch the punch, the policeman uncoiled like a striking cobra, grabbed the man's wrist, and jammed his arm up behind his back.

He tried to struggle—once. Whimpered, "Ah, Jasus. Stop it. You're hurting me."

Barry exhaled.

Malcolm produced a set of stainless-steel handcuffs. "Doctor Mills. You're nearest. I'll hold him. Can you put those on his wrists?" He gave a now-standing Jack the cuffs, then grabbed the man's other wrist and held both of his arms fully extended behind his back.

Jack slipped on the cuffs and clicked them shut.

The dark-haired man lowered his guard and began to tremble.

Wonderful stuff, adrenaline, Barry thought, and moved to his side. "I'm a doctor. Come and sit down." He led him to an empty chair. "Willie. Glass of water, please. You'll be all right. Take a few deep breaths." Barry got the man seated, sat close by, and took his pulse, not so much to make any inferences but simply to give the man the reassurance of human physical contact. Barry was able to see what happened next.

Malcolm sat Redhead in a vacant chair. He spat and screamed, "Bloody Protestant police brutality." Alan Hewitt leant over and said into the lad's ear, "Be a good boy. Calm down. Answer the officer's questions or we'll pull your lungs out through your nostrils. We *will not* tolerate sectarian violence in Ballybucklebo—and half of us here, like me, are Catholics."

The prisoner hung his head and mumbled, "I'm sorry. I've had a few."

Alan said, "Louder."

"I'd a row with the missus. I had a few before I come in. I'm sorry."

"Good."

Malcolm said, "Right. On your feet. We're going to the station. I'll not be pressing charges."

Because, Barry thought, given the volatility in Ulster, doing so, if it became public knowledge, might well add fuel to the fire.

"But you're too worked up and a bit full to be let loose. You can calm down and sleep it off in a cell overnight. Come on. It's not a long walk."

As the pair moved toward the door, Willie Dunleavy called, "See you? See you? You are barred for life. Never, never ever set foot in here again."

The prisoner made no comment.

Willie came around the bar and gave Barry a glass of water, then righted the tumbled stool. "I don't allow any sectarian rubbish in here. Folks get along. You, David Dempsey, you made a bloody stupid mistake, and I don't know what you were thinking, but you apologized—twice, so I'm not barring you if you promise to think twice next time you open your bake. We treat each other respectfully in my bar; Protestants, Catholics, no difference. Got it?"

"Yes, sir."

"Good. So, when you've collected yourself, finish up your pint. It'll have gone a bit flat, so I'll top it for you, and then get away on home." He offered the man his hand.

As they shook, the man said, "Thank you. I've only been here a week. Not exactly a brilliant beginning." He turned to Barry. "And thank you too, Doctor. I'm all right now, so I'll do as I'm bid."

"Good." Barry rejoined his table.

The buzz of conversation was above its usual level as, Barry surmised, what had just transpired was dissected, pulled apart, and analysed.

"Gosh," said Bill, "are things always as exciting in here?"

Barry shook his head. "I've only been coming here since '64, but to my knowledge there's never been a fight in the Duck. I must say Constable Mulligan did a splendid job, and his approach to the red-haired fellow was very diplomatic." He shook his head. "I wish, I really wish, that all these centuries of hatred would simply go away." He took a drink.

"We all do," Bill said quietly. The three were silent for a moment and then Bill stood. "If you'll excuse me, I need to shed a tear for old Ireland."

Jack pointed the way to the toilet.

As Bill left, Jack said, "You know Alan wanted me to arrange for Helen and me, and you and Sue, to be invited for lunch in Cullybackey with my folks?"

"I do."

"They're going to ask you down for next Saturday. Can you?"

"You're damn right. It may take some persuading to get Sue to come. She's emotional right now and she may be concerned about what will happen, but she knows how important this is. We'll be there."

"Great." He rose. "I'll just go over and let Alan know." Jack crossed the room.

Barry watched him stop and bend to say something. Alan rose and accompanied Jack back.

Alan, who remained standing, said, "Hello, Doctor. I'm delighted Jack's got the lunch set up. Me and Jack and Helen will come down together."

"And Sue and I will too and get there first. I know what you want me to do."

"Dead on. We can't thank you both enough for your support." He managed a weak smile. "And I think I've some more ammunition to help Helen and Jack."

Barry was intrigued but could see Bill heading back and didn't want to discuss it in front of him. "In a nutshell?"

"The Cameron Report."

Barry frowned. "The one released last week?"

Alan nodded. "I suggest you get a copy and read it. See you in Cullybackey next Saturday."

29

Are Beautiful Through Love

"Wake up, pet. We're here." Barry parked in the farmyard outside the two-storey, redbrick Victorian building and turned off the windscreen wipers, glad to be rid of their incessant rhythm, which had persisted all the way from Ballybucklebo to Cullybackey and had lulled Sue into a semi-sleep. "I'll go first. Stay where you are until they come to the door." He turned up his raincoat collar and pulled his duncher down before getting out and turning his shoulder into the wind of a late-September downpour. At once he inhaled attar of cow clap and wrinkled his nose.

The Mills's border collie stuck its nose out of its kennel, barked once, and retreated inside. Sensible dog.

The door was opened by Jack's father, Morris Mills, his close-cut dark hair damp. "Barry, come in out of thon, hey bye, and bring Sue. I got soaked just coming from the barn."

Barry beckoned to her and, shoulders hunched, transparent plastic rain hood glistening, she trotted from the car and in through the door.

Barry followed.

As Morris helped Sue off with her coat and hood, Barry saw Jack's car pull up alongside the Imp. Jack helped Helen out and hurried with her to the door. Alan Hewitt was hardly visible behind the car's rain-streaked windows.

Barry and Sue had picked up Alan in Ballybucklebo and transferred him en route to Jack and Helen's car at a well-known local landmark, the Tudor-style gateway to Shane's Castle Estate in Randalstown, ten miles from Cullybackey. Alan's earnest instructions to Barry were still clear in his mind: "I'll stay in Jack's car until you're well settled in, then

I'll knock. You be ready to answer it, Barry, so once I'm inside I'll be hard to turn away."

Barry brought himself back to the present, and the second his friends were in the spacious, parquet-floored hall he shut the front door.

"Hello, Dad," said Jack with cheerful humour in his voice. "Shocking day out there. Even the ducks are walking." He nodded to Helen. "You remember Helen Hewitt?"

"Hello, son. Doctor Hewitt," he said, inclining his head. "It's been a wee while since Jack brought you down after you graduated in June."

Barry heard no warmth in the man's voice and noted the formal use of her title. No smile. But at least he hadn't refused to see her. Barry recalled how Jack had phoned his mum when he knew his father would be out of the house to arrange the invitations. "Dairy cows have very set routines," he'd said. Denise Mills must have told her husband Jack was bringing Helen and, while he may have objected deep inside, he'd clearly acceded to the request. Could the man be softening?

Helen smiled. "I'm sorry about that, Mister Mills. Both Jack and I have been very busy, but it's lovely to see you again."

Since last Morris Mills had seen Helen Hewitt, the Twelfth of July riots had happened, and the Battle of the Bogside. Surely these events had intensified the man's dislike of Roman Catholics. Barry tried to study Morris surreptitiously but couldn't decide what he might be thinking or feeling. At least he was maintaining a civil façade.

"And how's Mrs. Mills?"

"She's in the kitchen getting lunch ready. She's fine. Looking forward to seeing our son."

Inwardly Barry flinched.

Morris avoided looking Helen in the eye. "If everyone's got their gear hung up, let's go through." He led the way along the corridor from which doors opened to the flanking dining room on the left and lounge to the right.

Barry and Sue followed Jack and Helen, Barry whispering to Sue as they walked, "Frosty, but polite, and he didn't cut Helen dead." At least, as Alan had predicted, the Ulster rules of hospitality were working in Helen's favour, and the presence of Barry and Sue inhibited any unpleasantness in front of them.

"I wonder," Sue whispered back, "when Alan will appear?"

The group entered the red-tile-floored kitchen that occupied the rest of the ground floor of the house.

Denise Mills turned from the stove. "Hello, everybody. Just be a minute but these chickens need basting. Morris, get everyone a seat, please." She opened the Aga range's oven door, releasing a small cloud of steam and the smell of roasting chicken.

Soon the little party was seated around the kitchen table, which sat beneath a mullioned window with red-checked gingham curtains giving a view over the farmyard. The panes rattled as the wind drove the rain against the glass. Barry positioned himself nearest to the corridor that led to the front door.

"Ladies, would you care for a pre-dinner drink?"

"Not for me," Sue said, patting her now-obvious twenty-two-week-plus tummy, "but a glass of water would be nice."

Morris had soon poured drinks for everybody and Denise had joined the group. "If you don't mind me asking, Sue, is everything going well?"

"Mind? Not at all. We had a bit of a wobbly at the start, but it settled down. I saw my doctor a week ago and he says everything's going very well." She smiled.

"Lucky you." Denise inclined her head to Jack. "When I was carrying that great lump there, I didn't stop throwing up until I was twenty-two weeks."

"Come on, Mum. You'll be showing pictures of me naked in the bath next."

"Don't be silly. All mothers talk about their children and you will too, Sue. You'll see." She sipped her wine. "And tell me, Helen, how are you enjoying being a doctor?"

Barry had noticed how Denise was keeping the conversation on neutral subjects and Morris was keeping mum, looking down at the tabletop and not at anyone else.

"I love it, Mrs. Mills, but it keeps me pretty busy. I don't see as much of Jack as I'd like to."

Barry glanced at Morris, afraid there might be a growled rebuttal to that, something like "And a bloody good thing too." But the man's face was completely impassive when he said, "Whatever else I might feel, Doctor Hewitt—"

Oh-oh, Barry thought.

"I have the most sincere admiration that you, or indeed anyone from a wee place like Ballybucklebo or Cullybackey, could get into medical school, never mind win a gold medal too."

Barry looked at Jack, who sat opposite. He was frowning, but it faded to a small smile.

He must be realising how big a concession that was, coming from a man with rigid views on Catholicism. Might there be hope of a reconciliation after all?

"Thank you very much, Mister Mills."

"I try to be fair and look at the facts."

Sue said, "That's very generous of you, Mister Mills. The whole village is proud of Helen, and her father was fit to burst with pride. She's all he has."

"I remember how we felt when Jack graduated and again when you qualified as a surgeon, son."

Jack, who Barry knew was an inherently modest man, shrugged. "Well, I—"

Barry was on his feet by the second knock on the front door. "I'm closest. I'll see who it is."

Mister Mills said, "Thanks, Barry, and don't keep them hanging about on the doorstep in this weather."

Barry closed the kitchen door behind him, tore down the hall, opened the front door to Alan Hewitt, and closed it behind him.

Off came Alan's coat and cap. "How's it going?" he said.

"Hard to say, but Mister Mills has been gracious to Helen, if distant and cold." He bit down on his lower lip. "He said something a minute ago that you might be able to use. 'I try to be fair and look at the facts.' Sue and I have read the Cameron Report. I think you're right. You might be able to use it to argue your case." He clapped Alan on the shoulder. "We're all there to give you all the support you need."

"Thanks."

"How do you feel?"

Alan's smile was wry. "Like Daniel."

"Daniel?"

"Aye. Before King Darius stuck him in thon lions' den. Absolutely on eggs."

Barry forced a smile. "Aye, but Daniel got out in the morning. Come on."

As they headed for the kitchen, Alan muttered, "For Helen and Jack's sake—here's hoping."

Barry opened the kitchen door and ushered Alan in.

All heads turned. Morris Mills's chair scraped across the tiles as he rose, a puzzled look on his face. He extended a right hand to welcome the stranger.

Barry said, "Mister and Mrs. Mills, may I introduce Mister Alan Hewitt, Helen's father, from Ballybucklebo."

Denise Mills began to smile but Barry, who was holding his breath, recognized she was trying to maintain the fiction that she was surprised. She controlled herself.

Morris withdrew his welcoming hand. His shoulders stiffened. His breathing quickened. The colour rose in his already ruddy, lined cheeks. "Mister Hewitt, I'll not say welcome to this house and we both know why—"

Alan nodded.

"—but I have no doubt you have come on important business." He glanced from Jack to Helen and back before looking Alan in the eye. "I will not ask you to leave. I'll get you a chair—"

Barry exhaled. His shoulders relaxed.

A chair was brought to the table and set beside Morris's own.

"I will ask you to be seated, bye."

Alan crossed the floor and sat. Barry noted his pallor.

"And I will ask you to state your business."

"Morris. Where are your manners? Please ask Mister Hewitt if he'd like a drink."

Morris's nostrils flared, but he asked formally, "Can I get you a drink?"

"I'd like a beer, please."

"I'll get it," Denise said.

"Now, Mister Hewitt?"

"Mister Mills, I'd prefer to keep this informal. I'd be pleased if you'd call me Alan."

Morris Mills frowned, rocked in his chair, pursed his lips.

Barry waited. In Ulster, the use of someone's Christian name was a privilege granted between close friends. Respect was also shown by use of titles like Mister and Mrs.

"Surnames."

"Surnames it is then, Mills. You asked me why I'm here. Because I love my daughter very much and I am concerned for her happiness."

"Go on." Morris leant closer to Alan.

"I'd noticed how close she and your son've been for three years, so back in April I took him aside and asked him why didn't he ask her to marry him, even if they were of different faiths?"

Barry saw Jack and Helen exchange fond looks.

Morris sat back, his eyes wide. "Never mind religion. What is your business? I want a straight answer."

A look of irritation and dislike crossed Alan's face. "That's all you'll get from me, Mills." He started to rise.

"I'm sorry. Sit where you are. I didn't mean it like that. I can see where this is going." His eyes narrowed and his gaze went to Helen and to Jack before he shook his head and looked back at Alan. "There were clues I should have picked up on sooner. I'm a bit tense."

"You're not alone." Alan lowered himself into his chair.

"So, never mind religion. Are you an Irish Nationalist?"

"Are you a Loyalist?"

"Would you shed blood for your cause?" Morris barked back.

"Would you?"

Silence.

"Mills, when the majority of people living on this wee island agree to unite, I'll be delighted, but not one drop, not one, would I shed to try to make that happen."

Mills nodded. "And I'm a proud British subject and I intend to remain one, but I'd only fight in self-defence of me and mine."

"So, we are of one mind about violence."

"I hate it."

"Now, I've a question. There's been a deal of it this year. Three major outbreaks. Who started them all?"

Morris hung his head.

Again, the man's earlier words, "I try to be fair and look at the facts," came back to Barry.

"Excuse me." Denise Mills rose quietly and went to her stove.

Ignoring her, Alan asked, "Have you read the Cameron Report? I have. It came out two weeks ago."

Morris Mills nodded. "I have. It was . . ." He paused, choosing his words, it seemed, with care. ". . . disturbing reading." He glanced round the table. "Does everyone know what we're talking about?"

Sue spoke up. "Mister Mills, I was with the Northern Ireland Civil Rights Association from the beginning. We're a mix of Protestants and Catholics trying to put an end to discrimination against Roman Catholics. We had no Republican or Loyalist agenda. We wanted equality and fairness. I've read the report from cover to cover on the causes of violence since the fifth of October last year. It confirms everything we'd been fighting against. It is a very damning document, stating that the root cause of the violence was organised discrimination by the other community against Roman Catholics abetted by the Ulster Special Constabulary, the B-Specials, a partisan paramilitary force."

Morris clasped his right hand with his left and looked down. His voice was low. "I know, lass. I know. And I'm not sure it's fair to tar all Protestants with the same brush. Discrimination in jobs and housing has always been accepted by people like me as being in the normal way of things, and that was wrong. But the recent violence? That's due to a group of extreme Loyalists who fear being a minority in a United Ireland. Frightened people do incredibly stupid things."

No one spoke. Sue leaned forward and then leaned back again as if deciding not to comment. The sound of a clock ticking, a pot boiling on the Aga, a beast lowing outside intensified the silence around the table.

"I've lived here in Cullybackey all my life. It's a Protestant town. Our family has always been Loyalists. Part of my rearing was to hate the pope and all of his flock. And for no logical reason except my side have been doing it for generations." He grimaced. "Hating Catholics is still being preached from some pulpits: 'From thieves and popery, and wooden shoes, good Lord deliver us.'"

Alan Hewitt spoke quietly, as if only to the man in the chair beside him. "'Love thy neighbour' goes right back to the book of Leviticus, and Christ called that the 'Greatest Commandment.'"

"You're right—Alan," Morris said, "and don't anybody think this is some kind of Road to Damascus experience for me." He looked from Jack to Helen. "Ever since Jack told me that cock-and-bull story about a 'friend' who wanted to marry a Catholic lass and I lost my temper, I've been trying to come to terms with who you were really talking about, and it didn't take me long to puzzle that out. I felt like Spencer Tracy in *Guess Who's Coming to Dinner.*" He turned to Alan Hewitt. "How do you feel about your daughter wanting to marry a Protestant, and the son of a Loyalist at that?"

Alan shrugged. "I love Helen. I don't like mixed marriages either, but her happiness is all I want. It's all her late mother would have wanted. I've already given my blessing."

"And it's what I want," Denise Mills said.

Morris shook his head. "Already? Already, Hewitt, you've given your blessing?" He turned on Jack. "Are you two already engaged? Without talking to your mother and me? How dare you, Jack Mills."

Barry had been delighted by the way matters had been progressing but now felt a lump in his throat and swallowed. Hard.

Denise Mills was trembling as she spoke. "Please, Morris. You've just talked about when you lost your temper. Jack has talked to me. We both wanted you to calm down a bit before he spoke with you about it again. All his life, Jack's always obeyed us. How do you think he's been feeling?"

"How do I think—?" Morris Mills buried his head in his hands, raised it, shook it, and stared at his son. "I don't imagine it's been easy for you, Jack. I really don't." He looked Alan Hewitt right in the eye. "And you disapprove—like me—but you've given them your blessing?"

Alan nodded.

"You're a man with a big heart, Alan Hewitt—"

Jack interrupted. "I'm sorry, Dad. I really am, but Helen and I . . ." He took Helen's hand.

Barry tensed. The only sound now was the gentle bubbling of spuds boiling on the range top.

"Before you go any farther, son, I want to finish. Those months of puzzling, and then these last couple of weeks after learning the facts in that report about how wrong us Loyalist have been. Well, they've changed me, and they've changed my mind. If you and Helen are in love . . ."

"We are, Mister Mills," Helen said.

"And if you two are determined to get married . . . I heard you there now, Denise; you've been working on me for months to see sense."

"I have, you stubborn oul' eejit."

"Then you have our blessing, son, and Doctor Helen Hewitt, welcome to the Mills family. And Hewitt—it's Morris from now on."

Helen was weeping through her smile.

"It's Alan. You called me a 'man with a big heart'—Morris. Well, you sir, you are a man with an open mind. On behalf of us Hewitts"—he offered his hand, which Morris Mills shook—"thank you."

Jack said, "Thank you, Alan, for having the courage to enter the lions' den today. And we'll never be able to thank you enough, Dad and Mum, for being open to what Alan had to say." His voice cracked. "Now there's something I'd like to do in front of my two families and my best friends." He fumbled in his jacket pocket, produced a small, velvet-covered box, took out what Barry knew was a round-cut solitaire-diamond ring. "You accepted my proposal back on New Year's Eve, and now with your blessing, Alan, and yours, Dad and Mum . . ." He slid the ring on Helen's third left finger. "I love you, Helen Hewitt, and here is the outward sign that in the not-too-distant future, my love, we will be man and wife."

30

The End Is to Build Well

"Good Lord," said Sebastian as O'Reilly parked the Rover at the corner of a large cleared building site. "I thought dropping in on Mister Johnson to let him know we'd got his final report from Doctor Montgomery was our last home visit today."

O'Reilly laughed. "And I thought we'd got long past your urgent need to get home to your mum now she's spending time with John MacNeill and seems to be getting her feet under her."

"Actually, I am exceedingly happy about that." Sebastian smiled. "And touché about my wanting to gallop off before, but not anymore. Well, I'm more likely to want to get away to see a certain blond physiotherapist."

O'Reilly glanced at Sebastian as the two men began walking toward the building in progress. The lad looked well. He'd lost that slightly harried expression and there was some colour in his cheeks. As a physician, O'Reilly approved.

Sebastian was surveying the buzz of activity before them. "I must say I do enjoy home visits a lot more than the typical hospital outpatient clinic routine, get 'em in and out as quickly as possible. But I didn't think GPs practised industrial medicine on building sites too."

"We don't. I'm merely here to satisfy my innate curiosity. I don't think you've met Bertie Bishop, senior partner of Bishop's Building Company?"

Sebastian shook his head. "I've yet to have that pleasure."

"But you have met Donal Donnelly?"

"Red hair? Buck teeth? In the Duck a couple of weeks back when Barry and I popped in for an after-work pint?"

"That's him. He's Bertie's junior partner. Bertie and his wife are off on a world cruise." O'Reilly pointed ahead to where concrete foundations lay in straight lines, bricklayers were building walls, a forklift truck juddered maniacally around the site, and tools and building materials were stockpiled. "This is going to be a three-storey block of fifteen flats. It's a big job and Bertie has said he's comfortable leaving Donal to look after the project. I know for a fact Donal's a wee bit nervous about the responsibility. It's the first big job where he's in charge. I'd like to see how he's managing."

Sebastian tilted his head to one side. "Fingal, you, and I've noticed Barry too, you don't only see to the illnesses of your—damn it, if you were a man of the cloth I'd say your flock—you take an interest in every aspect of the lives of people here, don't you?"

O'Reilly, who for many years had cultivated the façade of being a gruff old ogre, got ready to bluster but changed his mind. "When I came back here after the war and opened my practice, I had no intention of doing anything of the kind, but"—he held his forearms wide, hands palms-up—"the bloody place grows on you. I've had, and am still having, a wonderful time. If work is doing something for money when you'd much rather be doing anything else, I've not done a day's work since 1946—except when it comes to filling in bureaucratic forms."

Sebastian looked thoughtful. "I think you, Fingal O'Reilly, are a very lucky man, I really do." He sighed. "I've known since before I took the traineeship here that there'd be no prospects of a permanent position, but . . ." He pursed his lips. "But I do wish that wasn't the case."

O'Reilly looked at Sebastian, nodded, and took the remark under advisement. "You'll find your place, young man. You're a fine doctor. Now, I would be a luckier man if it wasn't drizzling," he said as he opened his door, "but that's Ulster in early October for you." He pulled his paddy hat down, his raincoat collar up, got out, and closed the door.

The apartment block at this point was white concrete foundations, a rectangle longer on its front and rear aspects, and closed at each end. The inner space was divided up the middle by a single strip of concrete, and by four solid slabs of concrete running across the structure from front to back, dividing it into ten boxes of equal size. Three groups of two men were laying bricks on these foundations, supports for the weight-bearing walls.

The flats might just look like concrete boxes at this point, but one thing was for sure, their front windows were going to give uninterrupted views over the sea-walk, past the glistening rocky shore, and across Belfast Lough to the Antrim Hills. Today that view was blurred and featureless, dark grey beneath the lighter, drizzle-filled sky above and the leaden waters beneath. Glaucous gulls swooped and squabbled over the shore.

"Cluttered places, these sites," O'Reilly said to Sebastian. "But I see the drive from the road under the railway bridge is complete right up to the front of the foundations." Half a dozen men were busy there while a motorised cement mixer puttered away nearby.

O'Reilly stopped to examine a heap of discarded and broken bricks lying beside wooden pallets stacked with more bricks. O'Reilly assumed in any load there might be a few unsatisfactory ones. Next to them were bags of cement and a heap of sand.

As he spoke, a loaded flatbed lorry with FINLAY BUILDERS' SUPPLIERS,-BELFAST painted across the side of the cab drove in and parked near the stack of pallets.

The driver got out. A big middle-aged man, two days' stubble on his chin, a turn in his left eye, brushed past O'Reilly, audibly muttering, "Get you to hell out of my way. This is a building site, not a country club."

O'Reilly arched an eyebrow at Sebastian and stepped back and back again to avoid a rapidly approaching yellow forklift. With a great roaring of engines and stink of diesel fumes, the vehicle began unloading a new pile of brick-laden pallets.

"What a charming chap," Sebastian observed. "From a purely medical point of view, I wonder what caused his squint?"

"I suspect he was dropped on his head when he was a baby." O'Reilly was unused to being ordered about and didn't care for it one bit. "Didn't do anything for his manners, either."

A heavyset young man in a cement-stained yellow oilskin jacket with the hood up approached, pushing an empty wheelbarrow. "Hello, Doctor O'Reilly. Grand soft day, so it is." The Ulster euphemism for "Damn this rain."

"It is that, Tommy." Tommy Gillespie had been a labourer for Bishop's Building for eight years. O'Reilly had treated him on several occasions for the cuts and bruises that were occupational hazards of his job. "This is Doctor Carson."

"Pleased til meet you, sir."

Sebastian said, "Likewise."

"Donal about the place?"

Tommy shook his head. "Nah. We're finishing a job for the marquis too, and Donal had til nip over and supervise something, but he'll not be long. The tea's on, and if youse don't mind getting a bit wet out in the rain, a cup in your hand would warm youse til he gets here."

"Fine by me," O'Reilly said. It was easing a bit. More like Scotch mist than rain now.

"Talk til Dusty Miller, our head brickie."

O'Reilly had known Dusty Miller for years. He was Bertie's senior skilled bricklayer.

"He'll get the teaboy til see youse right. I'll be back when I've loaded this barrow." He started to stack bricks from the first pile of pallets.

Together O'Reilly and Sebastian walked over to where two men were shovelling sand and cement powder into the mouth of the mixer. The engine's clattering made conversation difficult. The mixer was a strange metal contraption with a bottom like the lower half of a pear that continued into a narrowing open cylinder at the top. A hand wheel at one side was turned and the entire mixing compartment was tilted to let the semi-liquid cement flow into a wheelbarrow.

"Where's Dusty?" O'Reilly shouted.

One of the men, now running water into the mixer from a hose attached to a standpipe, pointed ahead to the nearest pair building a wall.

"Thank you." O'Reilly walked with Sebastian to where a man in his late fifties, duncher pulled down over thinning grey hair and wearing damp moleskin trousers and a blue shirt under a sleeveless leather waistcoat, was showing a teenager how to lay a course of bricks.

O'Reilly, not wishing to interrupt, watched.

"Now, lad, we're halfway along a new course," the older man said. "Look at the already laid top course of bricks and tell me their names."

"For starters, all them lower bricks is lying in cement-based mortar, called the bed, on their longest and widest part—also called the bed."

"Right."

"That narrow one there, a grey-blue colour, is the header. It's the narrowest part of the brick that's sticking out. Next til it is the longest part, a sort of orangey colour. It's the stretcher, and next to it is another header. With the different colours repeating in groups of three we'll get a pretty-looking yoke when the wall's finished."

"Good lad. Now, put some mortar on your trowel and cover half the next uncovered lower stretcher, a header, and half the next stretcher."

The youngster did.

"Set this brick on the mortar so its three-eighths of an inch from the ones underneath." He gave the boy a folding ruler. When the apprentice was satisfied, Dusty laid a spirit level on the brick and studied the bubble. "Dead on," he said. "You're a quick learner."

"Thanks. I should get you to talk to me ma."

"Next time I see her, I'll do just that. Now, see that mortar running vertically up between the header and the stretcher? It's called?"

"The perpend, and it must always be above the centre of the stretcher below to give the wall maximum strength."

"And what's the whole wall built that way called?"

"A Flemish Bond. It's strong as a horse and used in weight-bearing walls."

"Good. Good lad."

Dusty must have become aware of O'Reilly's presence. The brickie turned slowly, and a broad grin split his crumpled face. "How's about ye, Doc? I never heard you coming, so I didn't. This here's Jackie Wilson, my 'prentice who I'm learning the trade."

"How are you, Jackie?

"Rightly, Doc."

"Last time I saw your boss, here, he wasn't too well."

"Had to have my gallbladder out. Five years ago. Never better since."

"And this is Doctor Carson."

Everyone inclined their heads.

"Here y'are, Dusty." Tommy Gillespie parked a wheelbarrow full of bricks. He pulled a ballpoint pen from behind one ear and handed Dusty a sheet of paper. "Here's the invoice. I know Donal give you the right to sign for things."

Dusty, using a brick to lean on, dashed off his signature. "Here."

"I'm off til help to load the empty pallets onto the lorry."

"Thanks, Tommy."

O'Reilly said, "Tommy thought we might get a cup of tea while we were waiting for Donal."

"I'd not mind one myself, and I'm sure Jackie would too. We just need to put on a few more bricks. Won't take long." They bent to their work.

O'Reilly heard a new engine noise and turned to see a van bearing the slogan BISHOP'S BUILDING pull onto the site. The van came to a stop at the front of the foundations and Donal, his carotty hair sticking out from under his cap, strode over to where O'Reilly stood.

"Afternoon, Donal," O'Reilly said. "Doctor Carson and I were driving by and thought we'd drop in and see how things were coming on."

"Good to see youse both, Docs." He lifted his cap, scratched his thatch. "Just about finished at Ballybucklebo House and getting a fair start here. The foundations is poured and set, water's connected to the mains, and the sewage is installed to be hooked up to the building when we're ready. The building inspector's passed them, and the drive and foundations. My crew of brickies is getting a good start on putting up the weight-bearing walls and—"

"Thundering Jasus. Not again."

O'Reilly turned to see Dusty Miller holding a brick on his left hand and striking it with the sharp edge of his trowel. The side of the brick crumbled into a small heap of chunks and red dust.

Donal frowned. "What's up, Dusty?"

"Mister Donnelly."

O'Reilly noted that now, as a partner in the company and Dusty's boss, Donal was being treated with due respect.

"I think that there Finlay's trying til pull a fast one, so I do. We've used two loads with only the occasional duff brick. We always get the odd bad one in a load. But since we've been using the third delivery, there's far too many in it that're not up til snuff." He pulled out the invoice. "And I'm sorry, but I wasn't thinking and signed for the fourth load that's just come in."

"You could hardly check every brick before you did, but if you're worried about the third load we'd better take a keek now at it, and at load four."

"Sorry, boss."

O'Reilly thought Donal might get angry with Dusty, the usual response of a new boss unsure of himself and wanting to shift the blame. But he just shrugged. "Can't be helped. It's my job to decide when to run the occasional spot check. We can't examine every bloody brick when a load come in." He shrugged. "I wasn't here, anyroad." He crossed his arms in front of his chest, frowned, pursed his lips. "Come on, we'll check the new load. Have a word with Finlay. We've never used him before but seeing this is the biggest job the company's ever handled, Bertie needed to use a Belfast firm. It's not one of the huge ones, but for some reason Bertie wanted to use Finlay's. He liked the idea of it being owner-run."

"You'd better get a move on," O'Reilly said, pointing to the man himself, who was leaning against the cab of his lorry, lighting a cigarette. "Your forklift operator seems to have only a few more pallets to unload."

As they all walked across, Dusty shook his head. "I know, Mister Donnelly, that you worked out exactly how many loads we're going to need. I think Finlay's playing the oldest game in the book. Deliver a couple of good loads, then start filling up later orders with second-rate bricks disguised with a couple of layers of good bricks on top. We should take a good gander at one of the later pallets."

They arrived as the forklift driver laid another pallet on a growing pile.

Donal said to the driver, "We want to work on this one. Start another pile over there, please."

"Right, sir."

O'Reilly and Sebastian watched Dusty and Donal determine that the upper and outer three layers of bricks were in very good order.

Finlay wandered over, his cigarette stuck to his upper lip. "Hello, Donal. I've delivered your load on time, so I have."

No "Mister," O'Reilly noticed. Probably thinks Donal Donnelly is just the foreman.

Finlay bent and picked up one of the first examined from the new batch. "Good-looking brick."

"One of the few," Donal said.

"What are you on about?" Finlay stiffened.

"Look." Donal inclined his head to a pile of broken bricks that had been taken as random samples from deeper layers. "This is the second load with far too many useless bricks."

Finlay shrugged, smiled. "Sorry about that, but look, you ordered so many loads. I'm delivering that many loads. We have a contract Mister Bishop signed and made a down payment on."

"Bertie Bishop left me in charge. I'm his partner."

"You? A partner?" Finlay laughed. "I don't believe it."

Donal lowered his voice and said calmly, "I am, and Bishop's Building didn't pay for you to bring useless bricks."

Finlay's tone was sibilant. "I did not deliver any. For God's sake."

"Look at that from load four. There certainly are, and there were in load three too."

Finlay sneered. "It can happen. I haven't the time to check every load. And more to the point, you signed for the delivery of the first three loads, Donal. Dusty signed for this one, so they're all accepted and as good as paid for. So, like it or not, it's your problem now, not mine. I just order them from the brickworks and bring them round. You're stuck with the duff bricks, not me. And if I was you, son, I'd get a couple of replacement loads right now. Once I've delivered what I've already contracted for with the brickworks, they're going til up the cost per pallet. You just see if they don't."

O'Reilly watched Donal's expressions change. Surprise. Anger. Cunning. "I think you're a chancer, Finlay. I'll think about ordering two new ones when I see what number five looks like." He looked at the now-empty lorry. "Your work's done for today, so take yourself off by the hand. I'll be in touch when we need another delivery. And, see you? You make sure them bricks is perfect next time."

Finlay made a mock bow, unstuck his smoke, dropped the butt, and ground it out with his heel. "I'll be seeing you," he said, "and I don't take instructions from blown-up labourers neither."

Donal watched as the man climbed into his truck and drove off with a spray of gravel. "Far too many poorly fired bricks inside this load, and already, Dusty, you're getting too many in load three. Like I told him to his face, Finlay's a chancer. Reckons I'm too young to be a boss so thinks he can put one over on me."

O'Reilly laughed, "One over on you, Donal? I've known you all your life. I suspect by the time you've finished with Finlay you'll have sold him the deeds to the Queen's Bridge."

Everyone except Sebastian, the newcomer, laughed. Donal's reputation as a great trickster was a solid part of Ballybucklebo folklore.

"Mebbe so, but to be serious, I don't like til think how those bad bricks would creep if we used them."

"Creep, Mister Donnelly?" Sebastian looked down at the bricks.

"Sure, the stress of weight-bearing can produce little cracks in bad bricks that join up into bigger cracks. That's called creep. Sometimes the whole building falls down."

"Crikey," said Sebastian. "That would be a catastrophe."

"This place is going to be home for fifteen families. There'll be kiddies living in here." Donal clapped Dusty on the shoulder. "You done very good, Dusty. Thank you."

To O'Reilly's surprise, Donal did not start worrying out loud about what he was going to do. Instead his face went through a series of contortions that always signified he was wrestling with a problem. His face calmed. "What I have til do is work out a way to make sure we get our money back on these two loads, check how many more duff pallets are in load four, and get our money back on them too."

Donal Donnelly bent, picked up a crumbling brick, and hurled it to the ground, where it disintegrated more.

"I want all the pallets of duff bricks replaced. I want that ignorant bollix, Finlay, to pay to dispose of all the rubbishy ones. I need til con the blurt into refunding the cost and into replacing them for free so this nonsense about the price going up at the brickworks doesn't matter. And I'll have til be certain there'll be no more shenanigans from Mister Finlay fulfilling the rest of our order." Donal looked at O'Reilly, who saw the fires of hell in the man's eyes. "This is going to be a strong, safe building, Doctor. I'm going til fix Finlay, and with your help, maybe some advice from your brother Lars the solicitor, and a bit of playacting by Dapper, I think we can pull it off."

31

Harvest Is Truly Plenteous

"Amen." O'Reilly and Kitty added their voices to those of the crowd and of Father O'Toole and Reverend Robinson, who had finished blessing the opening of the 1969 Harvest Festival in the main hall of the Bonnaughts' sports club.

Only three days ago, the two men of the cloth, as well as John MacNeill and himself, had met in the marquis's study at Ballybucklebo House.

The meeting had been short and to the point as they charted a way to do what little they could at a local level to counteract a new outbreak of sectarian violence in the wake of the release of the Hunt Report on Northern Ireland policing.

"So, we're agreed," the marquis had said, "that as a country community we want to do something."

Three heads nodded.

Father O'Toole crossed his legs and rearranged the skirts of his black cassock. "This report quoted in here—" He pointed to a copy of the *Belfast Telegraph* that lay on the coffee table around which the men sat. "—is the result of only a few weeks of intense work. And it has arrived at conclusions that have been asked for, and heartily welcomed, by my community. Disarm the Royal Ulster Constabulary and relieve them of any peacekeeping responsibilities. Disband the B-Specials and replace them with a new reserve force. And recruit more, particularly Roman Catholic, officers into the RUC."

The marquis leaned back in his chair. "A pity those conclusions weren't welcomed by some Protestants. There has been almost continuous rioting in Belfast by them since. One policeman shot dead, and for the first time the soldiers have had permission to return fire if fired upon."

"Two rioters dead," muttered O'Reilly. "But it's been quiet for more than twenty-four hours, and our prime minister has said he holds out hopes of lasting peace."

"And that," said Mister Robinson, "is something Father O'Toole and I want to continue to foster here. Lasting peace. The local churches will, of course, have their usual harvest thanksgiving services, but it was Father Hugh who thought we should also have a celebration open to all. We'd like to use the Bonnaughts' hall as soon as possible."

"I cannot see any difficulties," said the marquis. "I'll make some phone calls, set up a working party, cancel Saturday's dance, and make sure the Harvest Festival happens."

And now, three days later, O'Reilly was looking across their table in the hall to a smiling marquis, his arm protectively around the back of a chair occupied by Ruth Carson.

"Your attention, please. Your attention, please." Donal Donnelly was at the microphone.

Conversations had barely begun since the blessing, so the packed room rapidly fell silent except for the occasional childish interruptions and parental shushings. This afternoon was one for families.

"Right. First, thanks to you, Father, and to Your Reverence and to youse all for coming out to celebrate a great harvest in a spirit of friendship and tolerance." He waved his arm round a hall decorated with sheaves of ripe yellow whiskery-headed barley, bowls of sweet red eating apples, and sour green Bramley cooking apples. Huge vases of Michaelmas daisies sat on every table. "Thank youse, Bonnaughts, for letting us run this event here." He bowed to John MacNeill and applauded him. "Now, I'm going til tell youse what's planned. For starters, as this is usually a religious event, the bar will be closed, and no strong drink will be sold—"

There was a subdued muttering.

"But"—he pointed at a low white-tablecloth-covered table upon which stood ranks of small glasses and many bottles—"we have five contestants in the dandelion wine competition."

A less subdued muttering and one loud, "Whoopee."

"Entry fee is two shillings per taster. Alan Hewitt will take yer money. The prize will be a gift from Lord MacNeill as well as half the tasting fees, so let's have lots of tasters . . ."

"Dead on."

"Bottles of the same wine will be on sale for those of youse with your tongues hanging out. If you'll talk to Mary Dunleavy behind that other table, and—sit down, Mister Coffin. You'll not die of thirst while I'm still speaking."

Waves of good-natured laughter.

"And she'll have soft drinks for the kiddies."

A high-pitched voice yelled, "Wanna Coca-Cola. Wanna Coca-Cola."

Donal continued, "There will be the same kinds of competitions for best plum cake"—all eyes turned to Kinky, whose plum cakes were famous—"and for the biggest vegetable marrow, and last but not least, Sonny and Maggie Houston, great dog lovers as you know, and Colin Brown, who's going til be the first vet til come from Ballybucklebo, will judge the best-dressed dog or puppy competition." He paused, then continued, "Victoria sandwich cakes, Madeira cakes, pickles and chutney, strawberry jam have been donated and all of these items will also be for sale, so they will."

More applause.

"And we've donkey rides outside—"

As if to punctuate the remark, one let go a deafening bray.

Donal pulled himself up and stood on his mock dignity. "As I was trying to say when I was so rudely interrupted, all the money made today will be given to the Ballybucklebo Bonnaughts' fund for sending children to the cross-community summer camp next year."

The earlier bursts of applause had been a little subdued. This one raised the roof.

Donal left the stage and rejoined Julie, little Tori, and the twins in their pram, as well as Dapper Frew and a young blond woman.

"Barry, any idea who that is with Dapper?"

Barry looked over. "When Sebastian and I visited him postop in August he was wearing a knitted hat. Said a Joan Eakin from his office had knitted it and that she was coming to his house later. You know, I'll bet that's her."

"Thanks." That was August and here it was mid-October. Two months? Not like Dapper's usual form with young women. Good for him. No question his recovery was complete. O'Reilly smiled. "I'm going to taste the wines, and I'll bring a bottle or two back. How many glasses will I need?"

Sue, now in her twenty-seventh week, shook her head. "No thanks, Fingal."

"For Ruth and me, please."

"And two for Kitty and me. That's five." He rose. "Come on, John, Barry. Come taste some dandelion wine with me. All in a good cause."

The three men began to cross the room, where the noise level was steadily rising in the now tobacco-hazed air.

Sonny and Maggie—she with a huge purple dahlia in her hatband, he with a matching one in his lapel—were sitting with Archie and Kinky.

John MacNeill said, "Good afternoon, all. Mrs. Auchinleck, Mrs. Houston. Will you be competing today?"

Kinky said, "Yes, sir. I've my plum cake in, so. And I've donated pickled beetroot, tomato chutney, a Victoria sandwich cake, and strawberry jam."

Maggie giggled. "I've a plum cake in too"—she put her hand on Kinky's—"but it's Kinky's recipe."

"Good luck to you both." John MacNeill had to step back to let a little boy rush past, being chased by Tori Donnelly. High-pitched childish laughter and a baby's cries rose above the hum of conversation.

Barry made it to the wine-tasting table before Fingal, with John MacNeill bringing up the rear. A young, dark-haired man was smiling and chatting with Alan Hewitt.

O'Reilly saw Barry half turn his head to eavesdrop and wondered what that was all about.

Barry paid, and collected three cards. He turned and gave one each to Fingal and John. "My treat."

"I'm buying the wine for the table, "O'Reilly said. "And some lemonade for Sue."

In very short order Barry, then O'Reilly had completed their tasting, returned their ballots to Alan, and O'Reilly had bought two bottles of wine and a glass of lemonade from Mary. "You seemed to be very interested in that dark-haired young man immediately ahead of you, Barry? I don't recognize him."

Barry nodded. "I was in the Duck last month. The lad's a newcomer, a Protestant. He said something very foolish to a Catholic fellow in the pub and it almost ended in a fight, but Malcolm Mulligan intervened before anyone got hurt. Alan was there, and now, a month later, Alan and this Dempsey fellow are chatting away like a pair of old friends. If there's a bit of goodwill, the gap can be bridged."

O'Reilly nodded. "That Alan's one sound man."

"I know. I do know."

"Time to rejoin the ladies," John said with a grin. "I inherited a substantial cellar from my father, full of vintage Bordeaux and clarets. I've never had dandelion wine before. It's rather good."

O'Reilly sang softly as they crossed the room,

> Dandelion wine will make you remember
> The first days of spring in the middle of December
> Dandelion wine. Dandelion wine.

"When I was fourteen and my uncle Hedley was teaching me about wildfowling, he took me along to look at a gundog he fancied. While he and the owner were appraising the dog, the woman of the house gave me a glass of her dandelion wine. When the men came back, I was legless. Uncle Hedley and the dog's owner and I went straight to the car. 'Be kind to him, sir,' says your man. 'Herself only lets me drink that wine—so I secretly fortify it with vodka.'"

Barry laughed so much he nearly dropped the glasses he was carrying.

"You're in good form," Sue said when they arrived back at the table. "Thanks." She accepted her lemonade.

Fingal poured, raised his glass, and said, "Cheers to this table."

Donal, back onstage, took the mike. "My lord, ladies, and gentlemen, your attention. We have our first winner. At fifty-six pounds twelve ounces and grown from giant-marrow seed, Mister Desmond Johnson's entry is declared the winner, beating the nearest competitor by eight ounces. Will you come up here and bring the beauty with you, please?"

The farmer passed his prize squash up to Donal, climbed up himself, and cradled it across his body. O'Reilly reckoned the green-and-yellow-ridged squash was about three feet long.

The applause was as big as the vegetable.

A blushing Desmond accepted his prize and said into the mike, "Thank you all very much."

Between him and Donal, they maneuvered the monster off the stage. "Now, if you please, I'd like the competitors for best-dressed dog to come forward and the judges to come up here with me."

Sonny and Maggie Houston and Colin Brown joined Donal.

Four dogs and their handlers waited their turns.

O'Reilly could not stifle a guffaw when Mary Dunleavy's Chihuahua, Brian Boru, tried to mount Donal Donnelly's greyhound, Bluebird. The last time that had happened the offspring had been the oddest-looking creatures, which, naturally, Donal had conned people into believing were a rare Australian breed of quokka herding dogs and had sold them for a substantial profit.

Mary lifted Brian Boru, set him on the stage, and followed him up. The little dog with great bulging brown eyes wore a wide-brimmed sombrero held on by a tie under his chin, a black Pancho Villa moustache drooping over his muzzle, and a red, blue, and green serape draped across his narrow shoulders.

As Mary paraded Brian in front of the judges, Donal announced, "Mary Dunleavy and Brian Boru."

Next up, with her mum, Julie, hovering in the background, was little Tori Donnelly leading Bluebird, Donal's racing greyhound, in a white frilly chiffon tutu around her rear end, a sparkly paste tiara on her head, and satin ballet slippers with bows on her hind feet.

Both groups had been widely applauded.

"The next competitor is Billy Singleton and his British bulldog, Winston."

A middle-aged man led a snuffling liver-and-white, bandy-legged bulldog wearing a London bobby's helmet with a huge silver star on its front, a dark blue tunic with silver buttons in the middle, and a small black truncheon on one side.

As more applause bounced around the hall, the dog responded with a gruff bark.

"And, finally, Mrs. Fitzpatrick and her Pekinese Fu Manchu."

"Good Lord," said Kitty to O'Reilly, "I didn't know Ronald and Alice had a dog."

"More to the point, Alice is a dressmaker and, boy, what a costume."

The pug-faced, hairy little dog wore a conical blue hat with an attached pigtail and a magnificently embroidered long overcoat with baggy sleeves covering its forelegs and long skirts, split so his bushy tail stuck through.

"That's a mandarin's outfit," Ruth Carson said.

"I'm certainly glad I'm not judging," John MacNeill said as the applause died down and Alice and Fu Manchu hopped off the stage.

Donal turned to the judges. "Have you picked the winner?"

Sonny, Maggie, and Colin all nodded.

Colin Brown, smart in a two-piece dark suit, Bangor Grammar School tie, and highly polished black shoes, stepped forward. "We have, Mister Donnelly."

All attention was fixed on Colin.

"We congratulate all the competitors. Every costume is outstanding."

"Hear, hear" from someone in the crowd.

"The prize is a giant bag of Bonios. And as we were so impressed with every competitor, we have decided not to award a first place but to divide the prize between all four. There's plenty of Bonios for everyone. Well, the dogs, anyways. If you'll please take your canines to the committee room." He pointed to a door.

The applause was deafening, and the judges had left the stage by the time it had subsided.

"That leaves only the dandelion wine and the plum cake prizes to be awarded," Donal said, "so those of youse still wanting to taste either, I'd ask you to get a move on. The rest of youse—talk nicely among yourselves." He left the stage and rejoined his group, spoke to Dapper, and came over to O'Reilly's table. "My lord, and everyone else, good after-noon. I don't mean til intrude, but Doctor O'Reilly, could Dapper and me maybe have a wee short word outside?"

"Of course. Excuse me. I'll be back." O'Reilly ignored questioning looks, rose, and followed Donal and Dapper. Outside the air was cool, but the sun shone down on children enjoying donkey rides on the rugby pitch.

"Sorry til drag you out here, but this is private, like."

"Fair enough, and by the way, you're running a good show, Donal."

"Thanks, Fingal, and Dapper and me's all set to run a better one on Monday and we'd like you to be there on the building site at three when Finlay makes his next delivery."

Dapper said, "That's right, sir. Thanks a million for talking to your brother and telling Donal about that there Weights and Measures Act. Donal and me has it all worked out, we just need someone with a posi-tion in the village there as a witness."

O'Reilly grinned. "I know. Lars told me. I'll be there."

"Dead on," Donal said. "That's all we need to know. Go you on back and join your friends. I'll be in soon to start giving out the last prizes."

O'Reilly retook his seat and waited for Kitty and Ruth Carson to fin-ish their conversation. "Sorry about that," he said to Kitty. "The boys need my help with something on Monday."

"You're forgiven," Kitty said. "We all know there's no rest for the wicked."

"Speaking of rest," Ruth said, "I haven't seen you, Kitty, since we had dinner together at the yacht club with your delightful Spanish friend. I'm incurably curious. Did you have a chat with your matron? I hope you don't mind me asking."

"Mind? Not at all." Kitty laughed. "I did, and Fingal and Barry and Sue all know. When the next hospital year starts, in August 1970, I will be going part time."

"Wonderful. I congratulate you."

"And your next job, Ruth, is to try to persuade old Hippocrates here"—she nudged O'Reilly—"to slow down too."

Everyone laughed.

Before O'Reilly could reply, Donal spoke into the mike. "My lord, ladies, and gentlemen, it now falls to me to announce the winner of the dandelion wine contest." He waited for quiet. "Bottle number five is a clear winner. Will the maker of number five please come forward?"

John MacNeill smiled. "I picked that one."

"Me too," said O'Reilly.

Barry shook his head. "Number three."

To increasing applause, Archie Auchinleck was making his way to the stage. He climbed up.

"Here y'are, Archie. A cheque and a very special bottle of claret presented by Lord MacNeill."

Archie accepted and, leaning forward to the mike, announced, "Thank you all, and thank you, my lord."

John MacNeill lowered his head.

"And finally," Donal said, "it's time to announce the winner of the plum cake contest—and all the tasters had to work very hard"—until recently, the most appropriate adjective for Maggie Houston's version—"because we had eleven entrants. Now, if this was the Oscars, like, I'd be given an envelope and youse would all hold your breath while I opened it, read the card inside, and announced, and the best picture award goes to . . ."

"It was *Oliver* last year, and you're making this presentation as long as the Oscar ceremonies, Donal. Who the heck won?" Gerry Shanks was getting impatient.

"Whoever baked cake number seven."

O'Reilly glanced at Kinky's table, confidently expecting to see her rise, but instead a grinning but tearful Maggie was struggling to her feet. She planted a kiss on the top of Kinky's head and walked, head erect, to the stage. "I'm too old to climb up on that stage, Donal."

Donal, grinning hugely, handed her prize down to her. "Congratulations, Mrs. Houston. Very well done."

The room erupted, people stood, whistled, yelled, and clapped, O'Reilly among them.

Eventually it was quiet enough for her to speak. Her voice was shaky but loud enough to hear with the microphone Donal had passed down.

"I don't know what to say. Thank you, Donal. Thank you, tasters who voted for my cake. But it's not really my cake." She pointed at Kinky. "Stand up, Kinky."

Kinky stood, grinning from ear to ear.

She's the most generous woman I've ever met, O'Reilly thought.

"It's Kinky's recipe. She stood over me and taught me how to make it. Thank you, Kinky. Thank you." She handed the mike back up to Donal.

Cissie Sloan was on her feet. She yelled, "I was a contestant too. And Kinky gave me her recipe, and I'll bet she gave it to the other eight entrants too. Put up your hands if she did."

O'Reilly counted. Eight hands were in the air.

Cissie called, "Let's hear it for Kinky!"

O'Reilly did think the roof was going to come off.

Kinky, now also in tears, bowed to the four corners of the hall. And still the cheering continued.

32

Crime and Punishment

O'Reilly half opened two of the Rover's windows and addressed Kenny in the backseat. The dog had immediately stood as soon as the car had stopped. "You'll get your run later, sir. I've business with Donal Donnelly, Dapper Frew, and a certain Mister Finlay, a builders' supplier with a squint in his left eye."

Kenny grunted, shrugged as only a Labrador can shrug, and curled up on his tartan rug with a sigh.

O'Reilly had parked beside the delivery area on the building site, and a quick glance assured him that the weight-supporting cavity walls were growing taller and several teams of men were busy. Since he hated unpunctuality, he was five minutes early for the three o'clock meeting. He looked around. The weather had improved from the drizzle of seven days ago when last he'd been here. He heard cries of *pee-wit, pee-wit,* and looked up to see a large flock of lapwing, their white undersides, green-crested heads, and dark green finger-feathers etched against the blue sky. Probably migrating south, he thought.

A smiling Donal, carrying a trowel and accompanied by a stranger, approached. O'Reilly took a good look at the man. Medium height, close-cut ginger hair, thick spectacles that made it impossible to make out the colour of his eyes, clean-shaven. He wore one-piece khaki dungarees over a blue, open-necked shirt, muddy Wellington boots, and had a slight limp. He carried a clipboard and a trowel.

Donal shook O'Reilly's hand. "Good morning, Doctor O'Reilly. I'd like you to meet Mister Alexander."

"Mister Alexander"—O'Reilly offered a hand, which was shaken—"I'm pleased to meet you."

"The pleasure's all mine."

"Have you come to us recently, Mister Alexander?"

"Aye, hey bye."

Was that a touch of Antrim?

"I see." O'Reilly frowned. "I suppose I must have misunderstood, Donal. I thought Dapper was to be here?"

"He is," said a grinning Donal. "Most of this here gear is hired from Elliot's fancy dress shop in Belfast but shaving off his moustache was an act of true friendship."

"Dapper?"

"The same, Doc. Donal, for you, ould hand, shaving the moustache was a mere nothing."

The voice was indeed Dapper's, and O'Reilly laughed at the sound of it coming from this stranger. Dapper in disguise immediately brought to mind the Sherlock Holmes stories of which O'Reilly had been fond since his boyhood.

"Joan says she prefers me this way, so you may have done me a favour." He pointed to the clipboard. "She's typed what Mister Lars suggested so I can show it to Finlay when he gets here."

O'Reilly was still laughing.

"Well, Doc, we sure fooled you. I just hope you can keep a straight face while we're doing the con job. This here's serious business."

O'Reilly straightened up and wiped his eyes. "You can rely on me, Donal."

"Good. Now Dapper and me, we decided it was too risky passing him off as the local inspector. We've had the fellah out to approve the sewer and water connections and the drive and the foundations and all, so it's just possible Finlay knows him. It was Dapper who had a better idea, based on what your brother told you when you went to see him in Portaferry."

"Lars is a bit of an odd duck," said O'Reilly. "Very proper. Not at all keen to bend the law. I had to lay it on with a trowel, just like one of your brickies, about what a gobshite Finlay is. How you were in trouble,

Donal, and needed help. Eventually he caved in because I'm his brother. All you have to do, Dapper, is exert your authority and scare the living bejasus out of Finlay."

Dapper raised the clipboard. "I'm ready for it."

"Right," said Donal, "when you was here last, Doc, you seen the two useless pallets of bricks. Dusty Miller and me checked all the rest of the pallets in that new load. There was enough good ones so we could keep on building, but there was another two pallets of useless ones. We've kept them four, the first two and the new two, as exhibit A." He pointed to where the half-unloaded pallets and piles of broken bricks stood. Tommy Gillespie sat in the driver's seat of the yellow forklift near the piles.

"We only ordered two for today, so it won't take long til examine 'em." He dropped a slow wink. "If it was me running the scam, I'd make sure a clatter of new consignments was perfect for a while before starting til slip duff ones in again."

O'Reilly smiled and shook his head.

"And you've got your part ready, Dapper?"

"Aye, certainly."

"A bloody good thing. Here comes Finlay. We'll do our bit, Doc. You're just here as a witness. I'll let you know when to speak up. We'll join Tommy by the bricks for now."

The lorry was parked, and Finlay got out. "Two pallets as ordered for three o'clock. Right on time." He puffed out his chest. "You can always rely on Finlay Suppliers." He handed Donal an invoice. "Sign there. I'm in a hurry."

"Then just take your hurry in your hand," Donal said. "I'm signing nothing—nothing, til me and Mister Alexander have examined the load."

Finlay sighed. "I've been in this trade a brave wheen of years"—he gazed at Dapper and there was mistrust in Finlay's eyes—"and I've never met you before."

Dapper thickened his Antrim accent. "Let me introduce myself. I'm Mister Alexander, chief inspector of weights and measures."

"The what? Chief inspector of weights and measures? Never heard of you."

"Well, you have now."

"Nonsense. Sure, them things is only about pounds and ounces and pints and gallons. Nothing to do with building."

"We'll see about that," said Donal. "Right, Tommy. Do your stuff."

It took little time but a lot of diesel exhaust for the forklift driver to unload the two pallets, leaving the bed of the lorry empty.

"Hang on to this, please." Dapper gave O'Reilly the clipboard to hold as he watched and listened to the scraping of bricks being moved and the ringing of tapping trowels.

Finlay hauled out a cigarette, lit up, and cast a nervous glance at Dapper. "So, chief inspector, did you say?"

"That is correct."

Finlay turned to O'Reilly. "And you. I seen you here last week. What do you do for Bertie Bishop?"

"Look after his health. I'm his doctor."

Finlay smiled. "So, what brings you out here two weeks in a row?"

This wasn't quite how the script was meant to unfold, but Donal interrupted. "Right, Finlay. Me and him"—he pointed at Dapper—"me and him's satisfied with them two pallets. I'll sign your invoice. Give me your pen."

Exactly as Donal had predicted.

There was a sneer on Finlay's lips as he accepted the signed piece of paper. "Didn't I say you could always rely on Finlay Suppliers?"

"Aye," said Donal, "but they also said the *Titanic* was unsinkable. Mister Bishop taught me not to believe everything people say."

"What?" There was a hint of anger in the question.

"By the time we'd finished checking last week's fourth load we found two more pallets with a brave wheen of badly fired bricks. You're trying to do me, so you are."

"Rubbish. You think I've time to unstack good bricks and put in bad ones?"

"Yes, I do, because you're getting rid of bad bricks you shouldn't be selling, keeping good bricks to sell a second time, and clearing a bloody good profit."

Finlay laughed and said in a smug tone, "And I'll repeat what else

I said last week. 'You signed for the delivery of them first three loads. Dusty signed for the fourth one, so they're accepted and it's your problem now, not mine.' It still is."

"But it's going to become yours right now."

Finlay laughed. "How?"

Dapper said, "Mister Donnelly came to my office in Belfast last Wednesday and told me of his suspicions. Asked for my help."

"And what can you do, Mister High and Mighty Chief Inspector? The law's very clear. Once you sign, it's your problem. Now, if you've nothing better to do, I'm off." He turned and pointed a finger at Donal. "Donnelly, I'll not forget this insult, but don't you forget that Mister Bertie Bishop and me's got a contract for most of the supplies for this project. I'm going til fulfil it, and by God—your building company's going for til pay it. Every last penny." His voice was rasping, his fists clenched.

"Don't get excited, Mister Finlay, and give me just a minute, please," Dapper said.

"Why the hell should I?"

"Because I suspect, seeing it's my profession, bye, I may know a bit more about the law than you. How much do you know about the Weights and Measures Act?"

"What's all this about weights and measures? Like I said, that's just pounds and ounces and pints and gallons. It's nothing at all to do with putting up a building."

"Is it no'? Mebbe you'd read this. I had it copied from the act."

No, you didn't, O'Reilly thought. It's legal hocus-pocus that Lars cooked up.

Finlay frowned and took the typed page.

"Read it aloud, please."

"Why should I?"

"Because," said Dapper, fixing Finlay with a piercing stare, "I asked you to."

O'Reilly noticed Dapper's accent was slipping a bit, but Finlay didn't seem to notice. He was too busy looking at the sheet of paper, his lips moving slightly as he did. He started to read, "Weights and Measures Act 1963 . . ."

"That's the most recent one."

"'Inspector means a person appointed as an inspector of weights and measures under this Act—'"

"That's me. Chief inspector, by the way."

"'The Bureau shall provide for use by inspectors, and shall maintain or from time to time replace, such standards (in this Act referred to as working standards) set out in the Second Schedule, such testing equipment, as being proper and sufficient for the efficient discharge, by inspectors of their functions under this Act.'" He shook his head. "I can't make head nor tail of this gibberish."

"I can. Read the next section."

"'A standard pallet of bricks shall contain no more than three percent of unusable bricks.'"

"We counted them all long before you got here. In total, thirty-seven percent of the bricks in those four pallets"—he pointed at the offending items—"are unusable, hey bye."

"I told you that's not my fault."

"The act seems to take a different point of view. Read on."

"'Purveyor shall be deemed to describe the person or entity which last provided the said bricks to the using person or entity.'"

"I think that's very clear, Mister Finlay."

"It's not clear to me, so it's not." Finlay frowned, fumbled out another cigarette. His hand trembled as he lit it from the butt of the first. "What the hell's an entity?"

"Let me explain. Who or what received"—he pointed to the offending articles—"those bricks?"

Finlay took a nervous drag on his smoke. "Bishop's Building Company."

"Aye. So, they are the using entity."

Finlay nodded. "I see."

"And who or what delivered the bricks?"

"My company."

"Which, within the meaning of the act, makes your business the person or entity which last provided the said bricks. You are liable and in contravention of the act. The penalties can be quite severe."

Finlay had turned pale. "Honest to God?"

Dapper nodded.

Finlay crushed out his cigarette. "Christ."

O'Reilly, while despising the cheater, felt the same kind of sympathy he might for a rat in a trap. Dislike of the animal but some sadness about its plight.

Dapper said nothing for a while, letting Finlay stew in his own juice.

Finally, Finlay said, and his tone was imploring, "But I didn't load the pallets."

O'Reilly noticed that as he spoke Finlay touched his nose, something people often did when telling a lie.

"That's as may be. Your business was the last entity that provided the bricks. You are responsible. And don't strain your brain wondering who'd be the guilty party if the building collapsed? You, bye."

Finlay said, and his tone was imploring, "Can you do nothing to help me, Mister Alexander?"

"Perhaps, but there are conditions."

"Whatever you say, sir."

"Very well. I do have certain remedies in my power before it becomes incumbent upon me to put your supplier's licence in jeopardy, to say nothing of the fines which will be levied."

O'Reilly heard a glimmer of hope in Finlay's voice. "Remedies? Such as?"

Dapper started counting them off with his right index finger on the digits of his other hand.

"One. You will, at your expense, remove that rubbish. Tommy here will use his forklift to load the pallets in question onto your empty lorry right now, but the loose bricks are your problem."

"All right."

Donal said, "Tommy."

The forklift's engine started.

"Two. You will apply the monies already paid for four bad pallets to four new good ones, which will be supplied at no further charge."

"Four new pallets? But they're not all rubbish. There's good bricks in there." The man's voice was choked.

"The act is very clear," said Dapper sternly. "Very clear." He jabbed at the sheet of paper with a blunt finger. "You must provide a completely new shipment of four new pallets with no more than three percent of useless bricks."

"All right, sir."

"Three. By way of an apology, you will admit in front of witnesses, including the good doctor here, who is most highly regarded as an honest man in this community, that you did try to, ahem, pull a fast one, as it were."

It was a strangled whisper. "Yes, God help me, I did. And I'm sorry, Mister Donnelly. I'm sorry."

"Four. It is within my power to levy a fine. I hereby fine you four free pallets up to the standards defined by the act, to be delivered at Mister Donnelly's convenience, and you will sign this document attesting to all of the above, which will be countersigned by all of us, and by so signing you also promise that you, as you have already stated, will fulfill your contract and personally insure that all deliveries will be absolutely up to standard."

"Yes." He sobbed out the word. "I'll deliver the bricks and make sure them and anything else I supply will be top line." Finlay inhaled deeply. "Where do I sign?"

Dapper said, "Once the signing's done, your licence is safe, and will be—as long as you keep your promises." He handed Finlay the clipboard and the document for signature. It duly made the rounds. O'Reilly received it last. He noticed that Dapper had not signed it. If Finlay demanded a copy now, he'd get one signed Alexander. If he did not, once he'd gone Dapper would sign it John Frew. If Finlay did discover later that Mister Alexander did not exist and tried to make a fuss, there'd be no sign of a false signature on the document and three solid citizens ready to swear that Finlay must have been hallucinating. O'Reilly gave the clipboard to Dapper, who said, "I'll see that this is properly filed," which O'Reilly knew meant "I'll give it to Donal Donnelly for keeping as a backup weapon."

Finlay did not request a copy.

Tommy yelled, "Them pallets is loaded," and turned off the engine.

A chastened Finlay said, "I'll come back tomorrow with a crew to take away the other bricks, and I'll bring four good pallets til start with and four more when you're ready." He nearly choked on the next mumbled words. "And there'll be no charge for either load."

"Good," said Donal.

A red-faced Finlay climbed into his lorry, slammed the door, and drove off so fast that two bricks were dislodged and fell onto the drive.

O'Reilly, who had worked very hard to keep a straight face, burst out laughing. "Dapper, that was Oscar-winning. You put the fear of God into Finlay. Well done."

Dapper resorted to his usual tones. "Thanks, Doc." He pulled off his spectacles and wig. "Good-bye, Mister Alexander. Nice to have known you."

"Dapper, oh boy, but you done good. Thanks, and now me and the crew can get right on with our job," Donal said, and O'Reilly was impressed with his confidence. Bertie Bishop had been right to entrust the project to Donal Donnelly. "Right," said O'Reilly. "Well done, both of you."

"Thanks, Doc, and please thank your brother."

"I will. I've started a letter to Bertie Bishop telling him about the Harvest Festival. Would you like me to tell him about this too? He'll be as proud of you as I am."

"That's right decent, but please don't." That slow wink again. "I'll need to do a wee bit of adjusting of our books. Best only us three know for now. I'll let Bertie in on it when he gets home." Donal's grin was vast.

"Fair enough." O'Reilly jerked his thumb to his parked Rover. "Now, lads, I've a dog in my car waiting for his walk, so I'll be running along." He strode off, hopped in, and drove off singing the Mikado's aria.

> My object all sublime
> I shall achieve in time—
> To let the punishment fit the crime,
> The punishment fit the crime.

He was accompanied by a tuneless yodelling from a happy Kenny.

33

Clearing the World of Its Most Difficult Problems

"Take the next lane on the left please, Harry."

Harry Sloan, now a qualified pathologist at the Royal Victoria Hospital, was a light drinker. "Never really liked the taste of liquor," he'd always say, "but I like the *craic*, so I'll have a jar with you all." He'd given Barry a lift to the Dunadry Inn in Templepatrick, half an hour's drive from Ballybucklebo, to attend the sixth-annual meeting of the Sixty-Four Club. It had been Harry himself, on the night of their houseman's concert in July 1964, who had suggested its formation. "What would you think about us Royal Victoria housemen calling ourselves the Sixty-Four Club, because that marks the end of seven years together since we started medical school? We could meet, formal dress, on the first Friday in December, say, at the Dunadry for dinner?"

The idea had been greeted with unanimous enthusiasm.

Harry turned onto the lane leading to the Lavertys' bungalow, the car bumping over the ruts.

"I think that went off very well," Barry said. "Jack Mills, Curly Maguire, and Norma Fitch were all in great form."

Harry laughed. "The *craic* was ninety, but then, it always is with our lot. Good turnout too."

"It's lucky we're all still near Belfast—odd seeing armoured cars with soldiers pointing rifles out of the backs, though, when we drove through the city."

"Odd, yes; scary, more like."

"I think Mister Chichester-Clark was right, after the riots in October, when he said we're in for a bit of peace. I'm sure having the troops here helps. Not a squeak since October."

"Hope you're right, Barry, but I read in the *Irish Press* on Tuesday about the old Irish Republican Army splitting and a new more radical group, called the Provisional IRA, being formed. Has me worried, I gotta tell you."

"We'll have to wait and see—good Lord. What's Emer McCarthy's car doing here?" In the glare of Harry's headlights, Barry could make out her red Mini. Was Sue all right? He felt his pulse speed up. "Thanks, Harry. Gotta run."

Barry didn't wait for a reply but jumped out of the car, burst through the back gate, let himself into the kitchen, and charged past a barking Max into the well-lit living/dining room.

Sue, now thirty-two weeks and one day, sat in an armchair while a worried-looking Emer perched on the sofa with Tigger curled up on her lap.

"You all right, Sue?"

"I'm fine, Barry. Honestly."

"Thank God for that." Barry felt his pulse rate slacken. "I'm sorry, Emer, I didn't mean to ignore you, but I've been feeling a little guilty going out with my mates and leaving Sue all alone."

"Silly. I told you I didn't mind. It's only once a year, for heaven's sakes." She looked at Max. "Quiet, you."

The dog obeyed.

"When I saw Emer's car outside, I assumed something was wrong, pet, and that you'd called the practice for help."

"Barry, I'm fine. Honestly." She smiled at him. "It's sweet the way you worry about me." Her smile fled. "The one we need to worry about is Emer here."

Barry untied his black bow tie, undid his collar button, and collapsed into the other armchair. "What's up, Emer?"

"For a doctor who should know better, I have been remarkably stupid."

Barry frowned. "How?"

"You know I've been seeing Eamon McCaffrey again."

"Yes, of course. Since July, right? I know how upset you were when you two broke up, just before you started with the practice. We've all been really happy for you."

She nodded but stayed silent.

"Uh-oh. Don't tell me he's dropped you again?"

She shook her head. "Certainly not," she said.

Barry frowned. "I see. Well, we could play Twenty Questions, or you could tell me what's bothering you."

Emer shrugged. "Sorry, Barry."

"Emer, Barry and I are your friends. Would you like me to explain?"

Her "Yes please" was whispered.

"Barry, Emer's pregnant. She's due in early July. She's ten weeks today. It's got her very worried about—"

"I see." Barry was no prude, but what, since the early '60s, was being called "the Sexual Revolution" had not yet hit conservative Ulster with any devastating force. He felt for her. She had few choices. Since the Abortion Act of 1967, termination of pregnancy was legal in the United Kingdom—except in Northern Ireland—and as a Catholic her church forbade it anyway. Adoption? Yes, but she would have to go away. Her shame would be great if she delivered, out of wedlock, locally. Marriage? Perhaps.

Barry stood, took her hands in his, brought her to her feet, dislodging Tigger in the process, and gave her a gentle hug. "Emer, this must be difficult for you." He held her at arms' length and looked her in the eye. "Thank you for coming to us. Sue and I will do anything we can to help."

Emer managed a weak smile through some tears. "Thank you, Barry. Thank you both. I knew you'd want to help. That's why I came here tonight." She sat again and Barry followed suit. "It's been a shock. But it's not that I'm so worried about being pregnant. I've told Eamon. He's asked me to marry him, and in case you're worried about it being a shotgun wedding, he asked me two weeks ago, before I was even certain I was pregnant, and I accepted. Once I was certain, I told him. We hadn't planned to start a family so soon, but he's very happy. He's a good man and he's going to be a wonderful father. He hasn't bought an engagement ring yet, but we'll get married soon after Christmas."

"I'm delighted for you both," Barry said, "and I know Sue is too, but

I can't quite see why you're worried." He smiled. "It'll be just another premature birth."

Sue said, "That's not what's got Emer worried. I didn't explain it very well."

Barry said, "I cut you off. I'm sorry, but the news came as a bit of a shock. Why don't you explain it to me, Emer?"

Tigger had returned to her lap, and she rubbed the cat's head. "You, and Fingal, and Connor, you've all been wonderful to me. Getting the assistantship with a view to partnership was everything I could have wished for, and now this. I'll work as long as I can . . ." Her voice trailed off into uncertainty.

Sue said, "The state pays maternity benefits for eighteen weeks: eleven before your due date and seven after."

Emer shook her head. "I'm not worried about the money. Eamon's a solicitor. He's paid well. What I'm concerned about is putting an extra load on everybody else in the practice, but I'll have to take maternity leave before and after I'm due, and I don't want to work full time again when my leave's over until the wee one's going to school." She inhaled through her nose. "I think the honest thing to do would be to resign, but I love my job here."

Barry beamed. "And that's what you're upset about?"

She nodded.

"Emer. Emer. Don't be. I can tell you exactly what we'll do. Stop worrying. Join Sue and me in a cup of cocoa now. Stay the night. We've everything you need—spare toothbrushes, pajamas, the complete works of Agatha Christie, the lot. If you're very good, Tigger might even sleep on your bed. And tomorrow, you and I will go tell your troubles to Fingal and Kitty. I'll phone him in a minute or two to let him know we're coming."

"You do mean that, don't you? I've been dreading the idea of telling him."

Barry shook his head. "Emer, yes, I do mean it, and I know Doctor Fingal Flahertie O'Reilly better than anyone here. The man has a heart of corn and when it comes to wisdom, beside Fingal, King Solomon would be forced to wear a dunce's cap. Fingal will know exactly what to do, and I'm sure you'll be very pleased."

"Come in. Come in." Fingal opened the front door of Number One to Barry and Emer. "We're just finishing breakfast."

Barry let Emer precede him into the hall and turn right into the dining room.

Kitty smiled from where she sat at the big bog oak dining table. "Morning. Have a pew. Have you two had breakfast?"

Barry, seating himself, said, "Yes, thanks."

"Coffee, then?"

Barry and Emer both said, "Please."

Kitty poured.

Fingal took his place at the head of the table. "Right," he said. "Barry was very cagey last night and didn't tell me much. What seems to be the trouble?"

Typical of the man, Barry thought. No small talk, but a simple nudge to get to the heart of the matter.

Emer put down her coffee cup. "I'm—I'm . . . engaged to be married to Eamon McCaffrey."

Kitty said, "That's wonderful news, Emer. Fingal and I wish you every happiness. If it was teatime instead of breakfast time I'm sure we could find a cold bottle of something bubbly to raise a toast."

"Thank you."

Emer was looking down at her hands. She was taking another circuitous route to the important detail, but Barry could understand that for a Catholic woman like Emer, admitting to being pregnant out of wedlock would be difficult. He was here for support, but he'd let her do this her way. Fingal's initial smile of delight had been replaced by a puzzled expression.

"That is great news, isn't it, Kitty?"

"Indeed, it is."

Fingal inclined his head and asked gently, "But it hardly calls for a meeting on a Saturday morning. Is something wrong?"

Emer looked Fingal in the eye. "Not exactly. I do love Eamon very much."

"Then whatever the problem might be, love will have a solution," Kitty said.

Emer clasped one hand with the other. "I'm—I'm ten weeks pregnant. I'm due in July."

Barry glanced from Fingal to Kitty. Neither showed any sign of disapproval. He'd not have expected them to.

"We hadn't planned to start a family so soon, but a baby brings its own welcome. We're happy about it. Truly we are. Eamon says starting our family young means we'll still be in our forties when they're off to university." She hesitated before saying, "But that's the future. In the here and now, it's going to affect my job at Number One Main. I'm not going to be able to work at all for several weeks before and after I'm due. And I don't want to make more work for everyone else."

"That's understood," Fingal said. "I don't see why it should affect things here. I'm sure we'll be able to get a short-term locum." He looked at Kitty. "You know Kitty's going part time in August, and frankly I'm getting used to less on-call, and more days off, and free weekends."

"Me too," said Barry, noticing the way Kitty looked at Fingal and raised one eyebrow. What did that mean?

"But that's what's making it difficult for me . . ." She sighed and her words tumbled out. "Eamon will go on working, so money won't be a worry, but I want to look after my baby until the little one goes to school."

Fingal said nothing but nodded his shaggy head slowly, as if digesting this information and already formulating a plan.

"I talked it over with Barry and Sue last night. I told them how much I love working here but that I thought I should resign so you could find another assistant."

She glanced at Barry, who recognized the look as a cry for help. He said, "I thought that was very honourable, but suggested before Emer took such a drastic step she should talk it over with you, Fingal."

"And you were right on both counts." He fished out his briar and lit up, a tactic Barry had come to recognize as O'Reilly's way of getting more thinking time. "All right," he said, "let's look at some ideas, but first let me ask you, Emer, how would you feel about working part time when your maternity leave is over?"

Emer's eyes widened. "Part time?"

"For half your salary, of course."

"I think—I think—I think, in fact I know, I'd like that very much."

Fingal nodded and let go a puff of smoke.

"Barry, we've had Sebastian here for four months. Your opinion?"

Fingal already knew Barry's opinion was good. "He and I have become friends. He is well trained, a quick learner, and popular with the patients. And I'm sure he'll ace his Royal College of GPs exams next year."

"I agree. By late May he'll have only three more months of training to go, and George Irwin is happy to let his trainees work unsupervised once their supervisors give him the go-ahead. I think Sebastian could easily fill your spot, Emer, until July the thirty-first, when his training's officially over."

Barry said, "I'll miss him when he goes in August, but that's the time newly qualified GPs will be looking for positions. And because you've been so honest with us, Emer, we'll have lots of time to find one who'd like to work part time. Thank you."

Fingal let go another little cloud. "I have another solution, one that I believe will make the half-unemployed Kitty, with all that spare time on her hands, very happy."

"Go on," Kitty said.

"For me," he said, "'at my back I always hear, Time's wingèd chariot hurrying near . . .'"

"*To His Coy Mistress,* Adrien Marvell," Barry said with a grin.

"Incorrect," said Fingal. "His name was Andrew."

"Blow you, O'Reilly," Barry said, laughing.

"Simple matter of grannies and eggs, young man," Fingal said, "but more seriously, Kitty my dear, I think it would suit me to go part time on August the first."

Kitty gave a shriek of pleasure and clapped her hands, and Barry made a swift deduction. "Two half-time positions vacant makes one full-time position available. Offering it to Sebastian gets my vote."

"And mine," Fingal said, "and for a young, about-to-be-married, expectant mother, Doctor Emer McCarthy, to quote the redoubtable Inspector Clouseau, 'All the problems are solvèd.'"

Emer was in tears. She reached out and touched Fingal's hand. "Thank you, Fingal. Thank you. I think I love you too."

"Sorry," Kitty said with a massive grin, "he's taken, but I couldn't be more pleased. Thank you too, Fingal. I can't wait for August."

"It will be my pleasure, and on a more practical note, please don't mention any of this to Sebastian. I'll have a word with George Irwin, set things up." His grin was wicked. "I think it'll make a wonderful late Christmas present for the young man."

Barry sat chuckling to himself and contemplating the mysterious ways that life worked. Emer McCarthy's pregnancy and abrupt change of plans would now affect the trajectory of someone else's life. Like the ripples that spread over a calm pond when a stone is cast in. It had been a difficult time at the Carson household, but now, with his mother seemingly on the mend and a new job on the horizon, the young man's future looked more secure. Barry looked over at Emer and thought about Sue and their coming baby. What might the fates have in store for their wee one? One thing was for sure, with two sets of grandparents, two parents, and Fingal and Kitty who would be wanting to help, everything humanly possible would be done to protect the wee mite.

He sighed and just wished January might come a little faster.

34

The New Year's Ruin

O'Reilly looked up from where he sat at the rolltop desk in the empty surgery. Now that Christmas and the New Year's festivities ushering in 1970 were over, it was back to porridge. A number of forms had to be filled in and prepared for signatures. The ballpoint he was using left a blue blot where the date was supposed to be, and he threw the pen aside and cursed. The shrill sound of the front doorbell interrupted his frustration. Who would be ringing at six on a Friday evening? Even if it was a patient, they'd be a relief from this bloody paperwork. He whipped off his half-moon spectacles, crossed the room and the hall, and opened the front door. "Bertie. Home from your globetrotting, I see. You're a sight for sore eyes, my friend. And Donal."

"Aye," said Donal, "but a real site for sore eyes is an eye hospital."

O'Reilly chuckled. "Donal Donnelly, you get worse."

A deeply tanned and noticeably rounder Bertie was carrying a parcel. "Flo and me's been desperate busy since we got home two weeks ago, and I've not had a chance til see you, Fingal. Donal and me's just come from the flats, they're going up a treat, and we're going to the Duck for a quick one. I said why don't we pop in and wish Fingal a happy New Year and have a wee natter with him?"

"Why not, indeed, and the same good wishes to you, Bertie. Donal and I have already exchanged the greeting."

"He's right, we did. We was in the Duck and Fingal stood me a pint."

"And if you want to chat, why are we footering around on the doorstep? Come on in. I'll not take you upstairs. Kitty and Kinky are getting things organized. We're having a dinner for the practice doctors this evening but come on into the dining room." He led the way. "Can I get you anything?"

Bertie shook his head. "My doctor has prescribed a ration of one pint a day since I had my heart attack, and we're going on to the Duck."

"And I'm keeping Bertie company," Donal said.

"Fair enough. I'll wait for the party to start, but have a pew."

The three men sat.

"So, how was your cruise, Bertie?"

Bertie beamed. "The greatest thing since sliced pan loaf," he said. "Worth every penny, and the food on board was amazing."

That would account for his increase in waistline. This wasn't the time to suggest a diet. That would come later.

"I took a great clatter of snaps and I kept a wee diary. Give Flo and me another week or two to get organized and we'll have you and Kitty round, and we'll tell you all about it. Once she got used to it, my Flo became the world's greatest tourist."

"Sounds like you had a wonderful time. I'm delighted."

"And I'm pleased too. With how the Harvest Festival went. Thanks for your letter, Fingal. I got it in Honolulu, and by the way, Flo and me took a trip to Pearl Harbour. Thon *Arizona* memorial is something to see. All them poor sailors."

Fingal, ex–Royal Navy, and a battleship sailor at that, nodded in sympathy.

Bertie shook his head. "Anyroad," he leant over and clapped Donal's shoulder, "since I got home and found out how Donal and Dapper had done a great con job on that shyster Finlay, I'm even more proud of him too. Saved the company a bundle of do-re-mi and a lot of men's time now we don't have to check every last nail. We've his signed confession and that promise to supply good materials. We can all rest easy knowing this is a top-of-the-line building we're constructing. Making good homes for a bunch of Ballybucklebo folks."

Donal smiled. "Bertie give me ten percent more shares in the company for my Christmas present, and he was dead generous to Dapper too."

"I'm glad to hear it. The pair of you earned it. Dapper's performance was outstanding. Maybe Mister Greer did clean his brain?"

Bertie chuckled. "The lads did a great job, but they couldn't have pulled it off without your help, Fingal." Bertie held out the parcel. "There's wee somethings in there for you as a wee thank-you, and a souvenir from Bombay for your missus from my Flo."

"Thank you very much, Bertie." Fingal accepted the heavy gift, which was soft but gave an interesting clinking sound.

"You just enjoy them," Bertie said, rising. "Come on, Donal. Time for our pint."

O'Reilly showed them to the door. "Good night to you both."

He couldn't resist taking a peep in the parcel. He peeled off the brown paper to reveal a colourful silk shawl wrapped around four bottles of John Jameson Irish whiskey. Kitty would love the shawl, and the bottles would have pride of place on the O'Reilly sideboard. He glanced into the study and then at the bottles. Bugger it. The paperwork could wait until Monday.

At five minutes past seven, Emer was the first to arrive, accompanied by her fiancée. "Fingal," she said, "may I introduce you to Eamon McCaffrey. Eamon, Doctor O'Reilly."

Both men shook hands and said with formality, "How do you do?"

Eamon was about five foot six, blond like Emer, with blue eyes, and wore an old boys' blazer with the crest of Saint Malachy's college, Belfast, and its motto, *Gloria ab Intus*—glory from within—on his breast pocket.

"Oldest Catholic grammar school in Ireland, I believe. Opened in 1833, four years after the Emancipation, when laws prohibiting the education of Catholics in Ireland were repealed."

"Not many people know that, Doctor."

"I told you. He's an Irish history nut," Emer said with a smile.

"True, and it's Fingal, Eamon. What would you two like?"

"Lemonade for me, please," Emer said. "Alcohol makes me easy."

Fingal coughed. Then smiled. "Ahh, yes." He surely could not have heard what he thought he'd heard. "No, sorry, Emer. I didn't quite catch that." Either he did need to get an audiogram done or he'd just learned more about Emer's personal life than he really should know.

"I said lemonade for me, please, Fingal. Alcohol makes me queasy."

"Right. Yes, queasy. I'm sure it would. And Eamon?"

"If you've a beer, Fingal?"

"Coming up." O'Reilly had to turn quickly to hide his laughter, then headed for the sideboard, where bottles of beer and Bertie's new whiskey rubbed shoulders with open bottles of Jameson and Kitty's favourite dry gin as well as two bottles of Entre-Deux-Mers in ice buckets. As he poured, he overheard Kitty arrive, introductions being made, and her saying, "So this is the lucky man, Emer. And look at the ring. An oval sapphire in white gold. It's stunning. A great pleasure to meet you, Eamon. We're so happy for you both." Kitty had that knack of instantly putting people at their ease. Fingal turned and carried over the drinks. He thought his wife looked entrancing in a long-sleeved, form-fitting, knee-length dress of turquoise wool.

"Here you are," he said, giving Emer and Eamon their drinks. He returned to pour a gin and tonic and a Jameson.

"Barry," Kitty said as the Lavertys came in, "get Sue a seat at once. You poor thing. You must feel like the side wall of a house."

Sue laughed. "I'm thirty-seven weeks and one day, and I feel more like a great white whale." She laughed again and gingerly lowered herself into an armchair.

"You, Barry," O'Reilly said, "are big enough and ugly enough to pour your own. Come and help yourself and get whatever Sue needs." He carried his and Kitty's drinks over just as Kinky and Archie arrived with trays of hors d'oeuvres. And as they distributed them to the sideboard and side tables, Sebastian came in. "Sorry I'm a little late . . ."

O'Reilly saw no reason not to pull the lad's leg. "Barry and I thought it was a Carson tradition, showing up late. It's how the three of us first met at the Crawfordsburn Inn in July last year, and on your first day at work here with me."

"Ouch. Guilty on both counts. This time Mum needed a lift to Ballybucklebo House. She's having dinner there tonight and—well, one hates to be disloyal, but she took rather longer than usual over her toilette. She hasn't worn perfume since Dad died."

"You are forgiven," O'Reilly said. "And your pleasure?"

"Neat Jameson, please. Good medicine's not the only thing you've taught me about, Fingal."

O'Reilly poured and said, "That's everybody. Connor got the short straw because the practice never stops, so he's on call." He handed Sebastian his glass. "But Connor's having dinner with me and Kitty tomorrow night." He turned to Kinky and asked, "All finished?"

"We are, so." Kinky beamed and smoothed down her pinafore.

"You know everyone here except Doctor Emer's fiancée, Mister McCaffrey. Eamon, this is Mister and Mrs. Auchinleck. Mrs. Auchinleck is our part-time housekeeper, and for years the pair of them have been our friends."

All three made little bows.

"So, what would you and Archie like?"

They looked at each other.

"Come on, Kinky, you've been an important part of this practice since 1928. That's eighteen years more than me. It's right and proper you should have a drink with us."

"Thank you, sir." She winked at her husband. "I do think a glass of that white wine would make a pleasant change from dandelion wine, so."

"For those of you who don't know, Mister Auchinleck won the prize for best dandelion wine at the Harvest Festival in October."

There was a small round of applause.

Archie said, "Thank you all, and I do agree with Kinky. It's easy to get used to the dandelion stuff and it's cheap to make, but we opened the marquis's bottle for Christmas. Boys-a-boys. Chalk and cheese. Kinky and I have tried some more French wines since. I'll still make the dandelion wine but tonight, a glass of white, please."

"Good for you, Archie." O'Reilly poured, and handed over the glasses. "Now everyone has a drink, I want to propose a toast and make an announcement." He spoke to Emer and Eamon. "You are being married next Friday, so I ask the company to raise their glasses and wish you every happiness—"

"Every happiness."

"May you be poor in misfortunes, rich in blessings, slow to make enemies, and quick to make friends. And may you know nothing but happiness from that day forward."

"Thank you very much, Fingal—and everybody," Eamon said.

And before anybody could speak, O'Reilly cleared his throat. "In early December I had a visit from Barry and Emer. Emer expressed a wish to take a leave of absence beginning in May"—and there was no need to explain why—"but she was very concerned about what effect that might have on the rest of us doctors." He saw Sebastian nodding. "I have not paid you the courtesy of consulting you, Sebastian, but I have spoken with Professor George Irwin. As of Emer's departure, you will join the rota independently so there will be no gaps in cover."

Sebastian smiled and stuttered, "I-I, golly. I'm very flattered. Thank you, Fingal, Barry, for your confidence. I'll not let you down." He sighed. "I'm just sorry August the first will come so quickly."

"Don't be sorry, Sebastian," Kitty said. "Everybody knows by now that I will start working part time in August. I've been asking Fingal to slow down. And my dear old bear has agreed to it."

Sebastian frowned. "I'm very happy for you both, Mrs. O'Reilly, but I'm not sure what that has to do with me?"

O'Reilly glanced at his junior partner. "Barry?"

"Fingal has asked me to make you the offer, Sebastian, because come August, I'll be senior partner. Fingal will work half time from then on. Emer will come back and do the same. We'd like you to stay on once you are fully qualified, to fill what will become the vacant position as an assistant with a view to partnership."

No one spoke.

Sebastian stared at Barry. Then at O'Reilly. The man paled, clapped his left hand to his chest. Inhaled down to his highly polished brown brogues. Exhaled, and said in a shaky voice, "You're serious, Barry? It's not some kind of a practical joke?"

"We do enjoy a good joke around here, but we've never been more serious. Will you take the job, Doctor Carson?"

"Dear God, of course I will."

O'Reilly offered a hand. "Welcome to Ballybucklebo, Sebastian. You and I will do the legal paperwork next week. I wasn't able to finish it earlier this evening."

A sea of voices called out, "Congratulations. Well done. The village will be lucky to have you."

Sebastian radiated happiness. "Thank you. Thank you. My mother will be so happy."

The noise faded. O'Reilly had a huge smile on his face, but it fled as Sue struggled to her feet, looking frightened. She leant over to Barry and said in a low voice that O'Reilly had to strain to overhear, "Do something, Barry. I've no pain, but my thighs are warm and wet. Either my waters have broken or I'm bleeding."

35

And the Blood Ran Down

Do not panic, Barry told himself. Keep calm. If Sue's going into labour, the baby is premature but it's not a crisis. The little one was only three weeks early, not six like Mildred Anderson's was when she was delivered.

Bleeding was another matter entirely. And either way Sue would be terrified. He stood and took her pulse. "Hold on, pet." He looked over to O'Reilly, who was ignoring the party all around him and watching Sue with concern. Barry said in a low voice, "Fingal. We need your help."

O'Reilly put his drink down abruptly and leaned toward them. "I'm sorry, Barry. I missed that."

"I need your help with Sue. Either her membranes have popped or she's bleeding." He kept looking into her eyes as he spoke. Her pulse was ninety-two per minute. Fast but not surprising given what must be her emotional state, but it was not racing as it would be if she were in shock from loss of blood.

"Right." O'Reilly raised his voice. "Excuse me. Excuse me. Sue's having a little difficulty so I'm going to examine her. So, please, every-body, turn your backs for a minute and give the dear girl a bit of privacy. No, no, Archie, no need to leave. We may need you."

The little crowd hushed immediately, chairs were shifted, and every-one did as they were told.

O'Reilly smiled at Sue. "I'm just going to lift your skirt."

Barry felt his heart shudder. Under her tights, along the insides of her thighs, he could see bright red bloodstains extending from her groin to halfway to her knees. He comforted himself by remembering that a little blood went a long way. This might just be a "show," slight normal bleeding that heralded the onset of labour, but the other possibilities were far from normal. He squeezed her hand and she looked at him with frightened eyes. Until it was proved otherwise, she must be treated as suffering from an antepartum haemorrhage, an all-encompassing term that covered a number of possibilities, some of which were potentially lethal to her and the baby.

"Sorry, Sue, but you are bleeding," O'Reilly said, lowering her skirt.

"Oh God. What'll we do?"

"Everything we can, and I'm afraid we're going to have to get you to hospital. Because you are bleeding, the first thing to do is sedate you, because the sedation can stop labour coming on."

"All right."

"Barry, under any other circumstances we'd get Sue lying down, give her a quarter grain of morphia, and send for the flying squad in case you need a blood transfusion."

Sue clutched Barry's arm. "I'm scared, Fingal."

"I know, but the morphia will help that too." He turned to Barry. "But it'll take the squad at least half an hour to get here. Barry, you can have Sue in the Ulster Hospital in fifteen minutes. They have a blood bank and full obstetrical facilities.

"So." He turned to the others. "Emer, nip down to the surgery and prepare a quarter of morphia for intramuscular use. Sebastian, go and phone the Ulster, tell them there's a woman with an APH on her way. Do you know your blood group, Sue?"

"O Rhesus positive," Barry said.

"Tell them that."

"And ask them to let Doctor Lamki know who the patient is," Barry said.

Emer and Sebastian fled.

Sue looked from O'Reilly to Barry and back. "Will my baby be all right?"

"We'll do everything we can here, and the specialists at the hospital will do more."

"Fingal's right, darling." Barry held her. Let her rest her head on his shoulder.

O'Reilly yelled, "Kinky. A pillow and a blanket to Barry's car."

"Yes, sir." Kinky headed off.

"Right, let's get this young lady into the car." Barry let Sue go and watched open-mouthed as O'Reilly bent his knees and put one arm under Sue's knees and another round her shoulders. With seemingly no effort, he straightened and, carrying Sue, headed for the stairs with Barry in hot pursuit.

Kitty called after them, "Good luck, Sue."

Sebastian was talking into the telephone when they reached the hall and Emer, loaded syringe in one hand and a cotton swab reeking of methylated spirits in the other, came out of the surgery.

O'Reilly stopped. Barry lifted Sue's skirt. Thank God the stains were no bigger. "Wipe the spirits on the nylon, Emer, then inject straight through."

Barry had a sudden flashback to his senior partner giving Vitamin B_{12} as a tonic straight through the antiseptic-dabbed clothes of a bent-over line of patients when he'd first arrived at the practice.

Sue sucked in her breath as the needle bit.

Time passed in a blur and soon a becoming-drowsy Sue was tucked into the backseat of the Imp and Barry was heading for the Ballybucklebo Hills.

"You all right, Sue?"

A drowsy "Muh-huh" reassured him.

As he drove, he found himself mentally going over what he knew about APH.

The blood could be coming from the placental bed. If the placenta was normally sited, the bleeding was called an accidental haemorrhage or *abruptio placentae*. If placed low in the uterus, it was a placenta praevia, which occurred in about one in two hundred deliveries. Sometimes the bleeding wasn't coming from the uterus at all but something related like haemorrhoids, which were common in the later months of pregnancy. He hoped that was the case but was none too hopeful.

He turned right onto the Ballymiscaw Road, then immediately left onto Ballyregan Road. "How are you, pet?"

Another drowsy "Muh-huh" comforted him. The morphine was doing its work.

"Only about five minutes to go."

No reply.

He sighed. At least if Sue had a placenta praevia, she was in the best
place in the world to have it managed. Professor Macafee, who had
taught Barry before retiring in 1963, had altered the treatment used
worldwide—Barry dipped his headlights to accommodate an approaching car. Unless the haemorrhage was torrential, or the patient was actually in labour, Macafee had prescribed keeping the patient in bed with no
interference and gaining as much foetal maturity as possible and then, if
circumstances indicated, no hesitation in carrying out a Caesarean section. In this way, as early as 1945, he had reduced the maternal mortality
rate of 6 or 7 percent to less than 1 percent and had more than halved the
foetal mortality rate, from 50 percent to about 23 percent. Fifteen years
later, Macafee was reporting no maternal deaths and the foetal losses
were less than 10 percent. This wait-and-see practice was now standard.

Barry took a quick look behind him. Sue's eyes were closed, and
she looked comfortable. His dear Sue. The odds were very good that
all would be well, but there was still that 10 percent risk. God damn it,
10 percent of the babies did not make it. After all they—or to be more
precise—Sue had gone through, if they lost this child, he would be heart-
broken, but he shuddered to think what it would do to Sue.

Barry drove up the curving drive of the hospital into the brightly lit area
in front of the admitting area, parked, and got out. "Just be a tick, pet."

He was met inside the door by a white-suited orderly with a wheelchair. "Doctor Laverty?"

"Yes."

"We've been expecting you. I'll get your wife." He headed for the car.

Barry followed and waited as the man roused Sue gently and helped
her out and into the chair. "Mrs. Laverty, I'm going to take you straight
up to maternity to the antenatal ward. Doctor Lamki's waiting for you."

Barry bent and kissed the top of her head. "Darling, I'll be straight up
once I've parked."

He stood for a moment watching the orderly wheel Sue away and jumped into the Imp.

He was short of breath when he arrived on the first-floor antenatal ward to be greeted by a sister midwife. "Doctor Laverty?"

He nodded.

"Please come with me."

She led him along a corridor, past Sister's glassed-in office, and past several beds, each containing a patient, some of whom were chatting, reading, knitting, all under treatment for one of the many ailments that could afflict women and required admission to hospital before delivery. She opened a door to her left. "In here, Doctor."

"Thank you, Sister." Barry went into the single room and closed the door behind him. Harith was sitting on the side of the bed and a student midwife stood on the far side, taking Sue's blood pressure. She was now wearing a blue hospital gown.

"Hello, Harith. Thanks for coming in."

"Barry. It's no trouble. I know how worried you both must be. Sorry this has happened." Harith was holding Sue's antenatal notes. "Once the hiccup at the start settled down, all of your antenatal visits have been very good, Sue."

She nodded drowsily and Barry hoped she was taking in what Harith was saying.

"You've had no excessive weight gain, no high blood pressure, no ankle oedema, no albumin in your urine. So, no pre-eclampsia."

The still ill-understood condition was associated with stillbirth and one of the other kinds of APH—accidental haemorrhage—which also had a high foetal mortality rate and exposed the mother to several risks like uncontrollable bleeding. It was small comfort, but Barry wanted to hear encouraging things. "That's good," he said, and saw Sue's weak smile.

"Blood pressure's one thirty over eighty-five," the student midwife said, straightening up and taking the stethoscope out of her ears.

"So, up a tad from one twenty over eighty so still no sign of pre-eclampsia nor any reading too low indicating shock from blood loss. I'm pretty sure it's only been a small bleed," Harith said. "Now, Sue, I'm going to examine your tummy." Harith very gently palpated her belly. "Did that hurt anywhere?"

Sue shook her head as Barry held his breath.

Accidental haemorrhage was often associated with tenderness.

Harith listened with a Pinard stethoscope. "Foetal heart's at one hundred and forty-four. Perfectly normal." Harith straightened up and smiled at Sue, then at Barry. "Your baby's not been hurt, there's been no more bleeding, and you're not in labour. All in all, I'd say the outlook's good."

Sue gasped and said, "Oh, Barry," and reached out her hand.

He took the two steps to the bed and grasped it in his. "Thank you, Harith," she said, and slumped on her pillow.

Barry could feel the meaning of Harith's words slowly sinking in. The baby was safe. Sue was safe. The anxiety of the last half hour began to seep out of him, leaving him shaken but relieved.

"We've already taken blood samples so we can get a baseline value for your haemoglobin level, Sue, but it was fine last week, and I'll be surprised if it's fallen. I'm cross-matching two pints of compatible blood and have an intravenous kit in here just in case there's more bleeding." He turned to Barry. "Sue's O Rhesus positive, and there's no shortage of that group in the bank."

"And you think it's a placenta praevia?"

"Every APH is until proven otherwise. So, complete bedrest for five days. Sedation. Repeated haemoglobin measurements, twice daily foetal heart rate and blood pressure measurements and urinalysis to detect any albumin." He bent over Sue, then straightened. "She's fast asleep." But nevertheless, he lowered his voice. "Some foetal conditions are associated with praevia. I don't think I've missed twins, but it can happen." He glanced again at the sleeping Sue. "We'll get an X-ray on day five. I'm sorry, Barry, but it will pick up any serious foetal malformation or recent foetal death too . . ."

Barry flinched. Not now. Not after so long.

"The odds are very much against either, but if—if we do, there's no point dragging things out. We'll try for a vaginal delivery there and then."

Barry glanced again at the sleeping Sue.

"If the X-ray's normal, we try to get the baby to thirty-eight weeks, which will be next Saturday. The risks of prematurity are practically negligible by then, so I'll examine her under anaesthesia with everything ready for immediate Caesarean section. Because the only way to establish the location of the placenta is to put my fingers through the cervix and feel for it. That can provoke quite heavy bleeding."

"I know," Barry said, and gritted his teeth.

"Unless there is no or only a tiny encroachment of the placenta into the lower uterus we will deliver by section. It's far safer for mother and child. Occasionally we do return the mother to bed and wait for the spontaneous onset of labour, but I fear Sue's going to have a section next Saturday."

Barry nodded. "Last year we had the flying squad out for a premature breech delivery. The mother had a ten-minute Pentothal knockout. When she woke up, she said, 'I know I had to be put out, but I missed his first cries. I'll never forget his big brother's.' Sue's going to miss that."

Harith stroked his chin. "Maybe not. I'll need to talk to anaesthesia, but we have a gas-passer here who did some residency in the States. Sue had a laparoscopy here last May. It's the same chap who stunned her then. The Americans are ahead of us in using regional blocks, spinal or epidural for sections. And I'd have to talk to Sue too, but if Dennis agrees and it's what Sue wants?"

"I think it will be. Thank you."

"But there'll be a condition."

"What?"

"Sue's going to need all the support she can get. I want you in theatre holding her hand."

36

From Hope and Fear Set Free

"More coffee, Barry?" Kitty asked.

"Please, and then I'll have to be running along." He passed his cup to her.

Fingal, enjoying his after-breakfast pipe, let go a puff of smoke. "I'll bet you thought today would never come."

"You're absolutely right, but it has. At last." He accepted his full cup. "Thanks, Kitty. You two have been wonderful, having me at Number One for breakfast every day and asking Kinky to make enough for your evening meals to share with me, so I'd not have the added chore of cooking." He sipped his coffee. "That's been a very good thing. My skills in the kitchen are, to say the least, limited. Thank you."

Kitty traced a circle in some spilled sugar on the table. "I feel for you and Sue. Thank goodness it'll be all over in a couple of hours. It's the waiting and uncertainty that's horrible."

"I know." Barry nodded. "At least I've had my work to keep my mind off things and looking after Max and Tigger before I've nipped over to Dundonald every day has kept me occupied too." He sipped. "But my dear Sue's had nothing much except reading to keep her mind off things. She said if she'd known how much time she'd be spending in the hospital, she would have taken up knitting." He smiled at the memory. "But she's tried to remain cheerful for my sake." He managed another small smile. "Once she got over the initial shock, each day that passed with no more bleeding, that normal X-ray two days ago, and good old Harith Lamki have all helped."

Fingal puffed. "And today's the big day. Sue may not need one but if she does, Caesarean section has come a long way since I did some extra training in Dublin's Rotunda Maternity Hospital in 1937. It's a safe routine procedure today thanks to much better anaesthesia, and antibiotics and blood transfusion, if they become necessary."

"I know. But if the patient is your wife, it's still a scary prospect." He finished his coffee.

"Of course, it is," Fingal said. "There's a great deal of mythology about it. According to Greek legend, Apollo delivered Aesculapius his son by the operation and Connor McNessa, king of Ulster, did the same for his wife who had drowned."

Kitty shook her head. "Fingal O'Reilly, you should remember the old adage 'Sometimes it's better to keep your mouth shut and let people think you're an idiot than open it and remove all possible doubt.' Poor Barry must be worried sick, and you start prattling about interesting legends?"

Fingal looked contrite. "You're right, Kitty. Sorry, Barry. I didn't know what to say and resorted to history. But you know Kitty and I are praying for you and Sue and the little one."

Barry rose. "Never worry, Fingal. It didn't upset me, and you and Kitty have been wonderful. Thank you. Now, Sue's to be in theatre in an hour and thirty minutes. I want to sit with her for half an hour before she goes in, so I'll be off. Thanks again for breakfast. For all the breakfasts this week. They've been lifesavers."

Kitty said, "Our pleasure. Give our love to Sue, and please give us a ring when it's all over and when, in the words of the classical hospital report, 'mother and child are doing well.'"

Barry chuckled. "I will, after I've phoned Sue's folks in Broughshane and mine in Ballyholme."

Barry sat beside the head of Sue's bed and held her hand.

She smiled up at him. Her pupils were constricted, the results of the premedication she had been given ten minutes previously: Pethidine 100 mg for its sedative and analgesic effects and scopolamine 0.40 mg for its postoperative anti-nausea effects.

"Won't be long now," he said, "and once the anaesthetist has put in the spinal and they've taken you through to theatre, I'll be with you for the whole thing."

"Thank you, darling." Her words were slightly slurred. "I love you."

"And I love you." Barry bent and kissed her forehead. As he straightened, Harith and an orderly, both dressed in surgical whites, entered, pushing a stretcher trolley.

The obstetrician smiled at Barry before saying, "Time to go, Sue." He and the orderly brought the trolley alongside her bed. "Can you wriggle over, please?"

Helped by Harith, Sue moved across and was covered with a blanket.

With her doctor at the front, the orderly at the rear, and Barry by her side holding her hand, they set off along the ward until they stopped in front of double spring doors, which Barry pushed open so the trolley could be brought inside. As the orderly put on a surgical mask, Harith pointed to a single door to the left, then began to don his own. "Changing room."

Barry nodded, squeezed Sue's hand, bent and kissed her forehead. "Don't be scared, pet. I'll see you again very soon."

Sue and her attendants disappeared through a second set of swing doors and Barry let himself into the changing room. He stood for a moment and took a deep breath. He'd read once that taking in one's physical surroundings could help you remain calm. He looked around him. Tall grey steel lockers lined one wall. White theatre trousers and shirts and tube-gauze hats were piled on shelves. White ankle-length rubber boots lined one wall. Four easy chairs surrounded a low table in the middle of the room.

Barry had finished changing and putting his clothes in a locker when Harith came in through a door and sat down. "Won't be long, Barry. Dennis Grant is a slick anaesthetist. He uses a mid-lumbar approach and a fine needle to put in the block so there is never much in the way of post-block headache. Some obstetricians use a local anaesthetic, but it takes quite a while to put in. If there is much bleeding after I've examined Sue vaginally, I want to get the section done as quickly as possible." He squeezed Barry's shoulder. "Your Sue's a very brave woman."

"I'll take your word about Dennis. I do know about Sue." Barry swallowed. "I'm not so sure about me. I did manage to live through her laparoscopy last year, but I'm anxious about how I'll stand up to this. I've seen enough surgery, even done a few sections in the Waveney, but when it's your own wife you're watching being opened up?"

"You won't be. You'll be sitting on Sue's right and Dennis will have set up a screen between you and the operative field. I'll give a running commentary so, unless you want to, you won't actually see anything."

"Very well."

"I'm very glad it's the late twentieth century."

Barry nodded and offered up a huge silent thank-you, knowing that Sue would not be exposed to practices of the past. "You mean how back in the Stone Age, male midwives thought the bleeding was coming from the placenta itself, not the uterine vessels, and tried to get the placenta out."

Harith nodded. "Fatal for the babies."

"And often the mother too," said Barry. "Back then in Europe the mother's life was considered to be more valuable, but the Catholic church taught that if the child wasn't baptized alive, it could not enter heaven."

Harith nodded. "Good thing we're past all that."

The theatre door opened, and a midwife popped her head in. "We're ready, Harith."

"Come on then, Barry. Get a mask and put it on." Harith rose.

Barry did, and followed Harith into the crowded theatre where Sue lay on the table, brightly illuminated by the powerful overhead light. An intravenous line was set up and running saline into a vein in her left arm. Barry knew that at least two pints of compatible blood would be in the blood warmer. His nostrils were assailed by the smell of a powerful antiseptic.

"This is Doctor Laverty, and, Barry, you already know Dennis."

The anaesthetist waved from where he was sitting at the head of the table beside his anaesthetic machine, there in case Sue needed extra oxygen. "The young lady by the incubator over there is Doctor Betty Rea, our paediatrician."

She nodded at Barry.

"Behind that mask and already gowned and gloved is Doctor Fred Spence, my assistant."

Fred paused from painting Sue's upper thighs and abdomen with a brown antiseptic fluid and arranging green sterile drapes over the operative site and nodded at Barry.

Harith whispered in Barry's ear, "Fred will immediately start making the incision if I cause bleeding when I do the pelvic examination, because I'll have to re-scrub and time will be of the essence."

Barry flinched.

Harith spoke in his normal tones, "Sister Barbara Little, on the right of the table, is scrubbed, and as you can see all the packs are open and ready to go on her instrument table. Midwife Denise Wallace is our circulating nurse. Now I'm off to scrub. Go to your wife. I won't be long."

Barry walked round past Dennis to a small circular stool on casters on Sue's right, near her head. He shook Dennis's hand. "Good to see you again. You and Sue must be old friends by now. Thanks for looking after her."

"Any time, my friend."

Barry looked at Sue. "This is all going to be over very soon, pet. I'll be here, and Harith will give us a running commentary because we can't see over where that sterile towel is held up by a barrier. If there's something Harith says that you don't understand, just ask me."

"All right. I think—no, I know I want to understand what's going on. Harith telling us means he's seeing me and the baby as real human beings, not a technical surgical problem." She smiled. "And, besides, it'll give me something to think about instead of just lying here scared stiff."

"Me too. It's the not knowing what's going on, imagining the worst. And Harith has always been a humane man." Barry looked to his right. He could see Barbara and her instrument table.

Harith returned and stood to Sue's left side. "Now, Sue, I'm going to empty your bladder because a full one can get in the way and then examine your tummy and down below. You'll not feel anything."

"All right."

"Usually we put a patient having a pelvic examination up in stirrups, but I just want you to open your legs and flex them."

Barry knew why. As a student he'd seen a woman like Sue in stirrups bleed profusely. In the time it took to get her properly positioned for surgery she must have lost half a pint of blood.

Sue did as she was asked.

Harith slipped a catheter into the bladder and Barry heard the tinkling of urine into a steel basin held by the circulating nurse.

"Now your tummy." His hands moved surely. "We know from the X-ray there's only one baby, lying longitudinally. The foetal heart rate before Fred started prepping you, Sue, was one hundred and forty-four. Now, what I can tell you is that the baby's head is not engaged and seems to be displaced to the left."

"What does that mean, Barry?"

"Perhaps something like the afterbirth is keeping it out of the pelvis."

"I see."

"I'm passing a speculum because since you haven't bled since admission there will be no clot to obscure my view." Harith bent over, peered in, and straightened up. "I can tell you there are no obvious causes for blood loss in here."

This was certainly looking more and more like placenta praevia. Barry reached down and took Sue's right hand.

"Now I'm going to examine you pelvically, and I'm going to try to push the baby's head into the pelvis, but I think I can feel that there's something between my fingers and its head."

Barry took a deep breath. That "something" must be the placenta.

"I'm going to proceed with great caution. I can get one finger through your cervix, Sue and—oh-oh, the inside opening is completely covered."

Harith withdrew his fingers. "Dennis, get a pint started, please."

Barry smelled blood. Sue was going to need a blood transfusion. He closed his eyes. Please, let the bleeding be light. Please.

"Please close your legs and unbend your knees, Sue."

As she did so, Harith spun on his heel, stripping off his gloves. He headed for the scrub sink, saying over his shoulder, "Get going, Fred, and explain as you go along." His voice was calm, but Barry could hear the urgency.

Dennis tilted the table five degrees head-down into the Trendelenberg position, and Fred said, "Mrs. Laverty, the afterbirth is coming first. I'm going to start the section. Scalpel, Barbara, and then assist, please."

Dennis rose, went to the blood warmer, came back, and changed the saline for a pint of blood, sat on his stool, and began to monitor Sue's pulse and blood pressure.

Barbara gave Fred a fifteen-foot strip of nine-inch gauze, specially folded. It would be used for mopping up blood and fluid. As it was used and saturated, it would simply be fed over the edge of the table so it would be easy to find before the wound was finally closed. He said, "I'm making a Pfannenstiel, that's a bikini incision, Mrs. Laverty. Clamp the bleeders, Barbara, but we'll not tie them until we're closing."

Sue screwed up her eyes and clung onto Barry's hand.

That transverse incision was quicker to heal and more cosmetically acceptable than one done vertically in the midline.

"Now the fascia, that's a layer of tough fibrous tissue over the two big up-and-down muscles in the midline of your tummy. Scissors."

By now, clearly aware that she could feel nothing, Sue had opened her eyes and relaxed her crushing grip.

Barry had relaxed too.

A freshly gowned and gloved Harith stood behind Fred until he gave the scissors back to Barbara and said, "Done."

"I'll take over."

Fred went to the other side of the table and Harith moved in.

"Those muscles Fred mentioned, the rectus abdominis? I'm going to part them."

Barry pictured Harith's elbows rising until they were horizontal then moving apart by about eight inches.

"Forceps. Scissors." Pause. "We're in."

Harith had made an incision in the parietal peritoneum, the thin membrane that lines the entire abdominal cavity.

Barry saw Barbara pick up a DeLee universal retractor, a stainless steel handle with a wide and deep blunt curved blade to hand to Fred. He'd use that to hold the lower part of the incision out of the way.

"Pack."

That was the only other swab used. It was a three-foot-long strip of nine-inch gauze that Harith would stuff into the space on the right aside of Sue's uterus, bring across her body, and repeat on the left side. Its tape would be clipped to the sterile towel so no matter how bloody it might become it would be easy to find before closing.

"Uterine peritoneum."

A loose fold of peritoneum in front of the uterus and above the bladder was being incised so the bladder could be pushed down and off the lower uterine segment, the part of the uterus that did not contract during labour, but rather thinned.

"Bladder's off."

Barry tensed. This was the critical moment. Harith would be using a scalpel to make a small incision in the lower segment and puncture the amniotic membrane, the odour of which filled Barry's nostrils. He heard the gurgling of a suction apparatus that Fred would be using to keep the abdominal cavity as dry as possible.

"Curved scissors."

"Harith's going to open your uterus, Sue, and then he'll deliver our baby."

"Please, God. Please." Her grip on his hand increased and he squeezed back.

"Soon, love. Very soon."

"We're in luck," Harith said. "There's no placenta beneath the uterine incision, but clamp that uterine bleeder, Fred. Thanks. Now I'm turning the baby's head so it's facing me."

The pressure on Barry's hand increased. He hauled in a great breath. Held it.

"Obstetric forceps."

Barry knew that the easiest way to deliver the baby's head was to use them. He was aware that Betty Rae, holding a sterile green towel, was standing between him and Barbara. It was the paediatrician's duty to accept and care for the newborn immediately after delivery.

"Head's out. Suck out the naso-pharynx, Fred."

Barry heard a very loud cry. He exhaled and looked at a smiling, tearful Sue.

"Both shoulders are out. Ergometrine."

The drug that provokes powerful uterine contraction and helps control postpartum bleeding.

Fred said, "I'll give point five milligrams directly into the uterine muscle."

Another shrill yell from Baby Laverty.

"Ergometrine given."

Sue asked, "Where's our baby? Why is Harith waiting?"

"It's okay, Sue. Waiting gives the ergometrine, the drug Fred just gave you, time to work. It'll reduce the amount of bleeding once the baby's out. It's an important step."

"I see."

Another yell.

Barry felt Sue squeeze his hand. "Barry, is—is everything okay?"

Barry smiled. "All babies yell when they're born. They've been in a warm, dark, comfy place all their lives. Now it's blinding, cold, and noisy."

"Fine lungs on that one, Mrs. Laverty," Dennis said. "That's a very good sign."

"I'm delivering the rest of the body. You've a little girl."

Sue said nothing, but her grin was vast through her tears.

Barry choked up. It seemed neither of them had words.

"Right, Fred. Clamp and cut the cord and start gentle traction on it once you've given the baby to Betty. I'll control the bleeding from the uterine incision."

"Here you are, Betty."

The paediatrician said, "Hello wee one. Welcome to the world."

Barry could not see the transfer because of the screen.

Barry stood up and got himself and the stool out of Betty's way as she stood over Sue, holding their baby wrapped in a green towel. All that could be seen was its face with its tiny eyebrows, wrinkled shut eyes, button nose, and puckered lips.

"Sue. Barry. You have a beautiful baby girl and I want you to be patient. I need to get her cleaned up, and examine her, and keep her warm. I'll bring her back. I promise."

Sue said, "Don't be long. I want to hold her. Feed her." She smiled up at Barry as she started to slip one side of her gown down off her shoulder.

Barry watched as Sue's gaze never left the back of the paediatrician.

He'd forgotten how many babies he'd delivered since the twenty they'd had to do under supervision as students. He'd always felt joy, but never joy like this.

In moments Betty called, "One-minute Apgar is eight. This one's in very good shape."

"Thanks, Betty," Harith called back.

Barry bent and kissed Sue. "She's beautiful, darling. Takes after her mother."

"Flatterer. But oh, Barry, I can't believe it's true. We waited so long. Then I thought, I really thought, I was going to lose her. Twice. And now she's here. I'm so happy. So happy." Sue tried to raise herself up.

"Just rest, pet. Just rest. You'll be holding her soon."

Sue smiled, nodded, closed her eyes, and heaved a great sigh of satisfaction.

Barry sat looking at his wife, paying little attention to the gurgling of the suction apparatus, and the remarks coming over the screen and from the paediatrician.

"Placenta's out and intact."

"Uterine incision closed in two layers."

"Five-minute Apgar's nine."

"Bladder peritoneum closed."

The suction fell silent.

"Rectus fascia repaired."

"She weighs in at seven and a half pounds."

Betty came back with a blanket-wrapped Baby Laverty wearing a tube-gauze hat to keep her head warm. Betty handed her to Sue, who immediately let the wee one latch onto her left nipple, where the baby began to suck.

Betty said, "I've examined her. She has no difficulty breathing, has all her fingers and toes, and she has passed meconium."

"She's had her first bowel movement, Sue," Barry said. "Green stuff called meconium."

"And if you're going to breastfeed, Sue, and I gather you are, she's well enough to room in with you."

Barry watched Sue holding her daughter in the crook of one arm while supporting her head with a maternal hand. The pair of them, he thought, could have posed for a Renaissance painting of the Madonna and child. He'd always thought seeing a mother feeding her newborn was one of the most moving of moments. Now, the beauty of watching his wife feed their baby had him almost in tears.

"Skin's closed. Dressing please, Barbara."

"Nearly finished, Sue," Dennis said. "We'll have you in recovery and back to your room soon after that. And congratulations and health to your wee one."

"Thank you, Dennis, for everything."

He shrugged and asked, "Have you any names picked out?"

"Yes," she said, "Ella for my favourite aunt."

"And Hope," Barry said. "We've been clinging on to it for so long and now it's been realised." He looked at the perfectly serene look on Sue's face. "Hope fulfilled is a wonderful thing."

AFTERWORD

Hello there. It's me again, Mrs. Maureen "Kinky" Auchinleck, so. You'd've thought that after all the recipes I put in 2017's *Irish Country Cookbook* with help from Dorothy Tinman, Doctor O'Reilly himself would let a body rest. Divil the bit. He's just after saying to me, "Kinky, you did a great job with five recipes for *An Irish Country Cottage* in 2018, and six more for *An Irish Country Family* in 2019. Now your man Patrick Taylor has done it again and written a fifteenth Irish Country story for 2020." That man could charm the birds from the trees, so, and as usual, here I sit, pen in fist to give you six more. Mushroom puffs, fisherman's pie, and roast goose breast with sage and onion stuffing are the savouries. Victoria sandwich cake, meringues with lemon curd and fresh cream topping, and chocolate truffles are the sweets. I hope you'll try them all and enjoy them.

Maureen Auchinleck, lately Kincaid, née O'Hanlon
Number One, Main Street, Ballybucklebo

Mushroom Puffs

Makes about 30 to 40
1 tablespoon of canola oil
2 shallots, chopped
1 clove of garlic, crushed
455 g. / 1 lb. mushrooms (any variety), chopped
Pinch of salt and a little black pepper
455 g. / 1 lb. cream cheese, softened
2 teaspoons of Tabasco or Worcestershire sauce
455 g. / 1 lb. packaged puff pastry
1 egg yolk and a little milk

Preheat the oven 200°C / 400°F.

Heat the oil in a deep skillet and gently sauté the chopped shallots. Add the crushed garlic and fry gently until cooked through but still transparent.

Now add the chopped mushrooms and pepper and when cooked, season with salt to taste.

Drain the liquid from the mushroom mixture. Combine the mushroom, shallots, and garlic with the softened cream cheese and the Tabasco or Worcestershire sauce.

Roll each piece of puff pastry out into 2 rectangles and cut each in half lengthwise.

Place a layer of mushroom and cheese mixture down the middle of each pastry rectangle, then brush each with beaten egg wash on one side edge.

Now fold the unwashed pastry edge over to the other side and press the 2 edges together to seal.

Brush the top with the remaining beaten egg to make a glaze and cut into 8 to 10 bite-size pieces.

Bake for about 15 minutes until puffed up and golden.

FISHERMAN'S PIE

Doctor O'Reilly told me how much he had enjoyed this when he had lunch at the Royal Ulster Yacht Club recently, and asked me to make it for him.
Serves 4

FILLING
590 mL / 20 oz. milk
Salt and freshly ground black pepper
1 or 2 bay leaves
455 g. / 1 lb. mixed fish such as halibut and salmon, snapper, or cod
113 g. / 4 oz. Dublin Bay prawns, peeled
113 g. / 4 oz. scallops without corals
56 g. / 2 oz. butter
2 tablespoons all-purpose flour
2 tablespoons chopped fresh parsley

TOPPING
910 g. / 2 lb. floury potatoes (for example, King Edward, Desirée, or Maris Piper) peeled and quartered
150 mL / 5 oz. light cream
28 g. / 1 oz. butter
2 tablespoons grated cheddar cheese or Parmesan cheese
Salt and freshly ground black pepper

Preheat the oven to 200°C / 400°F. Grease a 25-by-20-cm / 10-by-8-inch pie dish.

For the filling: Bring the milk, seasonings, and bay leaves to the boil in a large saucepan and add the uncooked fish and shellfish, omitting the prawns if they have been precooked. Simmer very gently for about 3 minutes. Remove from heat, cover, and set aside while you prepare the topping.

For the topping: Boil the potatoes until soft, drain, and mash well with the cream and butter. Season with salt and pepper to taste.

Next, drain the fish, reserving the milk, and discard the bay leaf. Remove any skin or bones from the fish, break into bite-size pieces. You can leave the prawns and scallops whole unless they are very big. Spread all the fish and shellfish together in the buttered pie dish.

Melt the butter in a saucepan and carefully stir in the flour. Cook gently for a couple of minutes without letting the roux (a fancy French word for the flour and butter mixture) brown. Now add the milk to the roux very gradually with the parsley and season with salt and pepper. Bring to the boil and simmer gently for 3 or 4 minutes, stirring all the time. Then pour the sauce over the fish.

It's time now to cover with the potato topping. Just spread it across the top of the fish and sauce mixture, pressing down lightly with a fork and covering it from edge to edge. Dot it all over with butter and the grated cheese. Bake for about 30 minutes, or until nicely browned. Serve with fresh garden peas and a crisp salad.

Roast Goose Breast with Sage and Onion Stuffing

1 goose breast
Splash of canola oil
Salt and black pepper

Stuffing
15 g. / ½ oz. butter
1 large onion, chopped finely
½ lemon, zest only
4 or 5 sage leaves, finely chopped, or ½ teaspoon of dried sage
100 g. / 3 ½ oz. bread crumbs
1 egg
Salt and pepper to taste

Preheat the oven to 180°C / 400°F.

Score the goose skin with a sharp knife in a crisscross fashion to release the fat.

Sear the breast in a sauté pan in a little oil for a few minutes. Set aside.

For the stuffing: Melt the butter in a frying pan over a low heat, add the onion, and cook until soft and translucent. Put the onion in a bowl and allow to cool, then mix in the lemon zest, sage, and bread crumbs. Add the egg and season well with salt and pepper, mixing thoroughly.

Stuff the breast with the stuffing.

Put the goose breast top-side down on a rack over a deep baking tin and, depending on size, cook for 45 minutes to 1 hour.

Cover with foil and a dry tea cloth and leave to rest for 30 minutes before carving.

Kinky's Note: Keep the goose fat for roasting potatoes

Victoria Sandwich Cake

Now here is the recipe for one of the cakes that I baked for the Harvest Fair. It's very easy to make and is probably the very first cake that I ever baked for Doctor O'Reilly.

225 g. / 8 oz. flour
2 ½ teaspoons of baking powder
225 g. / 8 oz. butter or good-quality margarine softened to room temperature
225 g. / 8 oz. sugar
4 eggs
A splash of milk
Raspberry or strawberry jam
Heavy cream

Preheat the oven to 180°C / 350F°.

Grease and line 2 circular cake tins, 20 cm. / 8 inches in diameter, and 5 cm. / 2 inches deep, with baking paper.

Sift together the flour and the baking powder until well blended.

Using an electric hand mixer, cream the butter and the sugar together in a separate bowl until pale and fluffy. Beat in the eggs, a little at a time.

To prevent the mixture from curdling, add a spoonful of flour after each egg has been added.

Carefully fold in the flour mixture using a large metal spoon, adding a little extra milk if necessary, to create a batter with a soft dropping consistency.

Divide the mixture between the 2 tins and spread out evenly with a knife or a spatula.

Bake for 20–25 minutes, or until golden-brown on top and a skewer inserted into the middle comes out clean.

Remove from the oven and allow to cool for 5 minutes. Then remove from the tin and peel off the paper. Place onto a wire rack and cover with a dry tea towel.

Whip the cream with an electric mixer until it forms soft peaks when the beater is removed.

Sandwich the cakes together with the whipped cream and jam. Dust the top with confectioner's sugar.

You can make this beautiful sandwich with a variety of flavours: 1) add grated orange or lemon zest and a little juice instead of milk. 2) add a little made-up strong black coffee and fill with a buttercream icing.

RECIPE FOR BUTTERCREAM ICING

After the ingredients add

140 g. / 5 oz. butter, softened

280 g. / 10 oz. confectioner's sugar

1–2 tablespoons milk or other flavouring such as coffee

¼ teaspoon vanilla extract

Beat the ingredients together.

MERINGUES WITH LEMON CURD AND FRESH CREAM TOPPING

8 egg whites

200 g. / 7 oz. of sugar

FILLING

115 mL / 4 oz. lemon curd

285 mL / 10 oz. heavy cream

1 tablespoon of confectioners' sugar

Preheat the oven to 100°C / 200°F.

Line a baking tray with parchment.

Beat the egg whites in a clean bowl with an electric mixer until soft peaks have formed. Gradually add the sugar and continue to beat until the mixture has reached the stiff-peak stage.

Now you can either spoon the mixture into a piping bag or just use a spoon to make circles of meringue on the parchment in the baking tin.

Place in the oven for 20 minutes, then turn off the oven and leave there to dry out and become crisp for about 2 hours.

When cold, spread a little lemon curd on each meringue.

Beat the cream and confectioners' sugar together until thick, and spread on top of the curd on each meringue. Now you can either leave them as halves or sandwich together.

Kinky's note: The secret of successful meringue is to make sure that your bowl and beaters are perfectly clean and completely free of grease by rubbing a splash of vinegar on a paper towel round the bowl and beaters.

CHOCOLATE TRUFFLES

Makes 12 to 18

340 g. / 12 oz. good-quality dark chocolate (at least 70 percent cocoa), chopped

265 mL / 9 oz. heavy cream

113 g. / 4 oz. unsalted butter, softened

1 tablespoon brandy

1 tablespoon unsweetened cocoa powder

Melt the chocolate in a large bowl over a saucepan containing just simmering hot water. Do not let the base of the bowl touch the hot water.

Blend in the cream, butter, and brandy using an electric mixer. Cover and refrigerate overnight.

Sift the cocoa onto a plate. Using a teaspoon or a melon baller, scoop out balls of the mixture and roll between your palms, then in the cocoa. Place each ball in a paper case.

If the mixture is too firm to work with, just warm it up a bit. If it gets too soft, let it chill and start again. Keep the truffles in the fridge until you are ready to serve them.

Kinky's Note: You can, of course, vary the flavour by adding chopped nuts, rum, whiskey, or vanilla essence.

If you are making them for children, you could roll them in hundreds and thousands (called sprinkles in North America) and of course omit the alcohol.

GLOSSARY

I have in all the previous Irish Country novels provided a glossary to help the reader who is unfamiliar with the vagaries of the Queen's English as it may be spoken by the majority of people in Ulster. This is a regional dialect akin to English as spoken in Yorkshire or on Tyneside. It is not Ulster-Scots, which is claimed to be a distinct language in its own right. I confess I am not a speaker.

Today in Ulster (but not 1969 when this book is set) official signs are written in English, Irish, and Ulster-Scots. The washroom sign would read Toilets, *Leithris* (Irish), and *Cludgies* (Ulster-Scots). I hope what follows here will enhance your enjoyment of the work, although, I am afraid, it will not improve your command of Ulster-Scots.

acting the lig: Behaving like an idiot.

almoner: Medical social worker.

anyroad: Anyway.

arse: Ass. Backside.

away off (and feel your head/bumps/and chase yourself): Don't be stupid.

bake: Ulster pronunciation of "beak." Mouth.

baldy-nut: Bald person.

beat Bannagher: Wildly exceed expectations.

bide: Wait patiently.

blethering on: Talking rubbish or inappropriately.

blue: Equivalent of a varsity letter at a North American university.

blurt: A horrid person.

bollix/bollox: Testicles (impolite), or foul-up.

bonkers/stark raving: Mad/completely.

Bonios: A commercial brand of dog food.

bonnaught: Irish mercenary of the fourteenth century.

bore: Of a shotgun, gauge.

borrow: Lend.

bound and determined: Absolutely set upon.

boys-a-dear or boys-a-boys: Expression of amazement.

brave: Large number.

break: At school, recess.

brickie: Bricklayer.

bruit: A murmuring sound. From the French *bruit,* a noise.

bullock: Castrated male bovine. Steer.

burn: Small stream.

can't feel nothing: double negative; can't feel anything.

casualty: ER.

***cèilidh*:** Irish. Pronounced "kaylee." Party with traditional Irish dancing and music.

chancer: A sly and devious person.

chissler/chisler: Dublin slang for "baby."

chuffed: Pleased.

clatter: Indeterminate number. See also **wheen**. The size of the number can be enhanced by adding "brave" or "powerful" as a precedent to either. As an exercise, try to imagine the numerical difference between a "brave clatter" and a "powerful wheen" of spuds.

come on on (on) in: Is not a typographical error. This item of Ulster-speak drives spellcheck mad.

cough up: Give the money.

***craic*:** Pronounced "crack." Practically untranslatable, it can mean great conversation and fun (the *craic* was ninety) or "What has happened since I saw you last?" (What's the *craic*?). Often seen outside pubs in the Republic of Ireland: *"Craic agus ceol"* fun and music.

CS gas: A tear gas used in riot control.

cup of tea/scald in your hand: An informal cup of tea, as opposed to tea that was synonymous with the main evening meal (dinner).

dead/dead on: Very/absolutely right or perfectly.

desperate: Terrible or terribly.

don't try to teach your granny to suck eggs: Do not try to instruct an expert in how to do their job.

do-re-mi: Dough. Money.

drúishin: Irish. Pronounced "drisheen." Dish made of cows' blood, pigs' blood, and oatmeal. A County Cork delicacy.

duff: Useless.

duncher: Flat cloth cap.

eejit/buck eejit: Idiot/complete idiot.

estate agent: Realtor.

fit as a flea: Very well.

ferocious: Extreme.

football pools: A commercial gambling game. Once purchased from a company like Littlewoods, the ticket contained all the top-level soccer teams' games for that Saturday. To win the prize the gambler had to predict from ten, eleven, or twelve matches which would end in a draw. The best prediction won. The stakes were low, the prize high.

footering: Fiddling about uselessly.

gag: Joke or a funny person.

gander: Look-see or male goose.

gargle: Alcoholic drink.

gas-passer: Medical slang for anesthesiologist.

glipe: Idiot.

goat (ould): Stupid person (old), but used as a term of affection.

gobshite: Horrible person. Literally dried nasal mucus.

grand (altogether/so): Good (very good).

gurning: Making inchoate or openly stated noises of complaint.

guttees: Plimsol shoes, or trainers/sneakers. So called because the soles were made of gutta percha.

half cut: Drunk.

hard stuff: Liquor.

heart in my mouth: Scared stiff.

heart of corn: Very good-natured.

hey, bye: Hey, boy. Verbal add-on common in those from County Antrim.

higheejin: Very important person, often only in the subject's own mind.

hobby-horse shite (head is full of): Literally sawdust, and having a head full of it meant you were incredibly stupid.

hooley: Party.

hot press: Cupboard built round the hot-water tank so that clothes stored in there would be warm.

houl' your wheest: Be quiet.

houseman: Medical or surgical intern. In the '60s used regardless of the sex of the young doctor.

how's about ye/you?: How are you?

humdinger: Something exceptional.

ignorant: A most derogatory term suggesting a total lack of education.

I'm your man: "I agree and will go along with what you are proposing."

in soul: Honestly.

jag: Jab or injection.

jammy: Lucky.

keek: Quick look.

kilter (out of): Alignment (out of).

knock your socks off: Beat you soundly.

learning: Teaching. Often the meaning of verbs is reversed as in "learning me to swim."

legless: Drunk.

let the hare sit: Let sleeping dogs lie.

lift: Ride, arrest, and elevator. Context gives meaning.

living bejasus: Literally "living by Jesus." Living daylights.

lummox: Large ungainly creature.

marbles/all her: Wits/completely sane.

MC: Master of ceremonies.

midder: Midwifery, now called obstetrics.

morra, the: Tomorrow.

mind: Remember.

neat: Of a drink of spirits. Straight up.

never: Did not.

no dozer: Very clever or skilled.

no harm til you, but: "I do not mean to cause you any offence," usually followed by, "you are absolutely wrong," or an insult.

no spring chicken: Not young anymore.

not at all: Emphatic no.

och: Exclamation to register whatever emotion you wish. "Och, isn't she lovely?" "Och, he's dead?" "Och, damn it." Pronounced like clearing your throat.

on eggs: Extremely nervous.

operating theatre: OR.

oul'/d: Old.

Oul'/d hand: My friend.

Panadol: Paracetamol, known in North America as Tylenol.

pan loaf: White bread cooked in a pan. Term used most commonly in Scotland and Northern Ireland.

paralytic: Very drunk.

parlour: Lounge.

party piece: Performance to be given at social events.

Peeler: Policeman. (Founded by Sir Robert Peel in 1829. Also, in England known as bobbies.)

peely-wally: Unwell. From lowland Scots.

pethidine: Demerol.

pew: Seat in a church.

potato crisps: Potato chips.

privy: Outside lavatory.

puff (in my): Life. Used in the phrase "never in my puff," meaning "never in my life."

put one over: Cheat.

ranks of junior medical staff and North American equivalents: Houseman: intern. Senior house officer: junior resident. Registrar: more senior resident. Senior registrar (usually attained after passing the speciality examinations): chief resident.

rickets, near taking the: Nothing to do with the vitamin-D-deficiency disease, but an expression of having had a great surprise or shock.

rightly (do): Very well. (Be adequate if not perfect for the task.)

rubbernecker: Someone showing idle curiosity.

run race: Short trip.

sean nos: Traditional hard-shoe Irish dancing.

sharp as a tack: Very quick-witted.

shenanigans: Carryings-on.

shite/shit: "Shite" is the noun ("He's a right shite"); "shit" the verb ("I near shit a brick").

short-changed: Literally, given back less than the correct amount of money when paying a bill with a banknote of larger denomination than the cost. Cheated.

sick line: Physician's certification that a patient has been ill and is entitled to sickness insurance payments.

sicken your happiness: Disappoint you greatly.

sister (nursing): In Ulster hospitals nuns at one time filled important nursing roles. They no longer do so except in some Catholic institutions. Their honorific, "Sister," has been retained to signify a senior nursing rank. Ward sister: charge nurse. Sister tutor: senior nursing teacher. (Now also obsolete because nursing is a university course.) In North America the old rank was charge nurse or head nurse, now nursing team leader unless it has been changed again since I retired.

snaps: Abbreviation of "snapshots." Photographs.

snarky: Bad-tempered. See also **tetchy**.

soft day: Rainy weather.

sojer: Soldier.

so sharp you'll cut yourself: Too clever by half.

so/so it is, etc: Tacked to the end of a sentence for emphasis in Counties Cork/Ulster.

sore: Painful. Sorely. Very badly.

sound (man): Terrific (trustworthy, reliable, admirable man).

spuds: Potatoes.

sticking out/a mile: Good/excellent.

stocious: Drunk.

sweets/sweeties: Candies.

surgery: Doctor's office.

take a grip: Pull yourself together.

take the light from your eyes: Astound you.

take yourself off by the hand: Just go away and stop irritating me.

taste: A small amount and not always edible. "Thon wheel needs a wee taste of oil."

tea: The main evening meal.

tea in your hand: An informal cup of tea.

tetchy: Ill-tempered, perhaps a corruption of "touchy." See also **snarky**.

that there/them there: That/them with emphasis.

the morra: Tomorrow.

thon/thonder: That or there. "Thon eejit shouldn't be standing over thonder."

thran: Bloody-minded.

threw up/off: Vomited.

tick VG: Check mark "Very Good" on a page. Teacher's lauditory assessment of an assignment.

toff: Upper-class person.

toffee-nosed: Stuck-up.

tongue hanging out: Dying for a drink.

took a turn: Suddenly feeling unwell.

townland: A mediaeval administrative region comprising a village and the surrounding countryside.

turn in the eye: Squint.

wee: Small, but in Ulster can be used to modify almost anything without reference to size. A barmaid, an old friend, greeted me by saying, "Come in, Pat. Have a wee seat and I'll get you a wee menu, and would you like a wee drink while you're waiting?"

wee north: Northern Ireland.

well mended: Healed properly.

up the spout: Pregnant.

wheeker: Terrific.

wheen: An indeterminate number. "How many miles is it to the nearest star?" "Dunno, but it must be a brave wheen." See **clatter**.

whiskey/whisky: With the *e* it is Irish whiskey. Without the *e* it is Scotch whisky.

yoke: Whatchamacallit.

you-boy/girl-ye: Words of encouragement.

your man: Someone who is not known. "Your man over there. Who is he?" Or someone known to all. "Your man, Van Morrison."

youse: Plural of "you."